MOLLOY

Shane Weller is Reader in Comparative Literature and Co-Director of the Centre for Modern European Literature at the University of Kent. His publications include *A Taste for the Negative: Beckett and Nihilism* (2005), *Beckett, Literature, and the Ethics of Alterity* (2006), and *Literature, Philosophy, Nihilism: The Uncanniest of Guests* (2008).

SAMUEL BECKETT

Molloy

Edited by Shane Weller

faber and faber

First published in French in 1951
by Les Éditions de Minuit
First published in English in 1955 by the Olympia Press
First published in the United States in 1955 by Grove Press
First published as a *Jupiter Book* in 1966
by Calder and Boyars Publishers

This edition first published in 2009
by Faber and Faber Ltd
Bloomsbury House
74–77 Great Russell Street
London WC1B 3DA

Typeset by RefineCatch Limited, Bungay, Suffolk
Printed in England by CPI Bookmarque, Croydon

The right of Samuel Beckett to be identified as author of this work
has been asserted in accordance with Section 77 of the Copyright,
Designs and Patents Act 1988

The right of Shane Weller to be identified as editor of this work
has been asserted in accordance with Section 77 of the Copyright,
Designs and Patents Act 1988

A CIP record for this book
is available from the British Library

ISBN 978-0-571-24371-6

2 4 6 8 10 9 7 5 3 1

Contents

Preface

In March 1951, Les Éditions de Minuit, a small, financially insecure Paris-based publishing house, released a new novel with the decidedly un-French title *Molloy*. On the verso facing the title page, the publisher listed five other works by the same author: three novels, *Murphy, Malone meurt (Malone Dies)* and *L'Innommable (The Unnamable)*, and two plays, *Eleutheria* and *En attendant Godot (Waiting for Godot)*. With the exception of *Murphy*, however, all of these works were identified as forthcoming. As for the author of so much unpublished material, Samuel Beckett was known at the time only to a small circle of other European writers, painters and intellectuals, his principal publications – a short monograph on Marcel Proust (1931), a collections of short stories, *More Pricks Than Kicks* (1934), and the novel *Murphy* (1938; French translation 1947) – having attracted some favourable reviews but few readers. That reputation was to be transformed irrevocably by the publication of *Molloy*, followed by *Malone meurt* in November of the same year and *L'Innommable* two years later, together with the full stage production of *Godot* in January 1953.[1] Indeed, by 1953 French reviewers were regularly placing Beckett in the company of some of the major writers of the century, including Proust, Joyce, Kafka and Camus.

For a sense of the critical affirmation with which *Molloy* was received in France, one need look no further than the 'press opinions' displayed in an Éditions de Minuit advertisement printed in the Winter 1952–3 issue of *Merlin*, an English-language literary magazine published in Paris, the editors of which were to be instrumental in the publication of the subsequent English translation of *Molloy* by the Olympia Press in 1955. The advertisement includes the following critical judgements on the novel:

'One of the most significant works to appear since the war' (Jean Blanzat, *Le Figaro littéraire*); 'Rarely since Kafka and Joyce have we experienced such ... poetic depth' (Max-Pol Fouchet, *Carrefour*); '*Molloy* is the expression of reality stripped of inessentials' (Georges Bataille); '*Molloy* places Beckett certainly among the greatest writers' (Maurice Nadeau, *Mercure de France*). To these judgements may be added the claim with which the American critic Richard Seaver opened his essay on Beckett in the Autumn 1952 issue of *Merlin*: 'Samuel Beckett, an Irish writer long established in France, has recently published two novels which, although they defy all commentary, merit the attention of anyone interested in this century's literature.'[2]

Begun in Ireland on 2 May 1947 and completed in France only six months later, on 1 November 1947, *Molloy* belongs with a number of other major prose and dramatic works written by Beckett between 1946 and 1951, including not only those listed as forthcoming in the first edition of *Molloy* but also four long stories (all written in 1946) and thirteen short texts (written in 1950–1, after the completion of *L'Innommable*), published together as *Nouvelles et Textes pour rien* in 1955. This remarkable 'frenzy of writing' – as Beckett was to describe it[3] – commenced in February 1946, with the story *La Fin* (*The End*), which was begun in English and completed in French. Beckett himself suggested that 'the siege in the room' (as he also later referred to it[4]) was provoked by what is described in *Krapp's Last Tape* (1958) as the 'vision at last', when Krapp grasps that the 'dark' he has 'always struggled to keep under' is in fact his true material.[5] Whereas Krapp's vision takes place on the pier at Dún Laoghaire, south of Dublin, Beckett later revealed that the event on which it was based occurred in his mother's room at New Place, in Foxrock, probably in the summer of 1945.[6]

If that vision in his mother's room gave Beckett a clearer sense of what he should be writing, it also, and no less importantly, had a major impact on how he would write. As he put it in conversation with Charles Juliet in October 1968: 'When I wrote the first sentence in *Molloy*, I had no idea where I was heading. And when I finished the first part, I didn't know how I was going to go on. It all just came out like that. Without any changes. I hadn't planned it, or thought it out at all.'[7] To John Pilling, Beckett described the writing of *Molloy* as 'like taking a walk'.[8] The manuscript of the original French text appears to support these claims; it has few significant revisions or marginal doodles, and gives the impression of having been written at considerable speed – in striking contrast to the manuscript of *Watt*, the novel Beckett wrote in English in the years immediately preceding the vision.[9]

The early French reception of *Molloy* tended to place it within the then-dominant mode of existentialism, perhaps unsurprisingly. According to Maurice Nadeau, for instance, Beckett 'settles us in the world of the Nothing where some nothings which are men move about for nothing. The absurdity of the world and the meaninglessness of our condition are conveyed in an absurd and deliberately insignificant fashion: never did anybody dare so openly to insult everything which man holds as certain, up to and including this language which he could at least lean upon to scream his doubt and despair.'[10] For Bernard Pingaud, Beckett reveals himself in *Molloy* as 'obsessed by the idea of death and nothingness', and Pingaud goes on to situate the novel in its post-war context, arguing that 'We live in a time of despair, where wrecks are everywhere, and Molloy is a wreck, hardly a man, an absence of a man. He is what would appear in man if all his human, logical, rational, polished and civic attributes were erased at a stroke.'[11] Whereas, in France, this broadly existentialist reading did not necessarily entail criticism, such was not the case across the Channel. Reviewing the English translation for *The Observer* in December 1955, Philip Toynbee concluded that there was no falsity in the novel – except, that is, for the 'gigantic falsity of its whole conception and existence'. For Toynbee, Beckett simply represented the 'end-product' in a long tradition of 'nihilistic writing', emanating from France.[12]

If the early reception of *Molloy* tended to place it in a

philosophical context, subsequent readings often emphasised the novel's engagement with psychoanalysis. As early as March 1954, Thomas Hogan (in *Irish Writing*, no. 26) identified Molloy as a representation of the id, and the narrator of Part II, Jacques Moran, as a representation of the ego. As his 1930s reading notes reveal, when he was in analysis with Wilfred Bion in London, Beckett acquainted himself with a wide range of psychoanalytic writing, including the work of Freud, Jung, Alfred Adler and Otto Rank, of which explicit traces can be found in *Molloy*, with its references to the 'fatal pleasure principle' and to 'the Obidil' (an anagram of 'libido').

Breaking with the existentialist reading, in the late 1980s and 1990s attention was redirected towards the novel's narrative of self-undoing and its rhetoric of paradox and aporia. This concentration on the novel's language included increased reflection upon its status within Beckett's *bilingual* œuvre. In this respect, *Molloy* stands out from the majority of his other works, since it is one of very few French texts the English translation of which he entrusted (in large part) to another. Although completing the original French version of *Molloy* by the beginning of November 1947, it was not until October 1950 that Beckett finally secured a publisher for the novel, and that principally through the efforts of his partner (later to be his wife), Suzanne Deschevaux-Dumesnil. Six months *before* the appearance of the French edition in March 1951, however, part of the text had already been published in Beckett's own English translation in Georges Duthuit's *Transition Fifty*, no. 6.

That the complete English version of *Molloy* came to be published by the Olympia Press is owing to chance. In 1951 Richard Seaver happened to read, and was impressed by, both *Molloy* and *Malone meurt*. Seaver published his introductory essay on Beckett in the Autumn 1952 issue of *Merlin*, the literary magazine run by Alexander Trocchi and a group of other expatriates, including Seaver, Patrick Bowles, Christopher Logue and Austryn Wainhouse (whom Beckett would later refer to collectively as the 'Merlin juveniles').[13] On learning that

Beckett had completed an unpublished novel in English (*Watt*), Seaver requested an extract for *Merlin*. The extract (chosen by Beckett) duly appeared in the Winter 1952–3 issue. Hoping to extend their activities to book publication, the *Merlin* editors next came to an arrangement with Maurice Girodias, who was setting up the English-language Olympia Press in Paris. *Watt* was published by the Olympia Press in its 'Collection Merlin' in August 1953, and, despite his annoyance at the numerous typographical errors, Beckett gave permission for publication in the same collection of an English translation of *Molloy*, which appeared in March 1955.

The title page of the Olympia Press edition of *Molloy* states that the work is 'a novel translated from the French by Patrick Bowles in collaboration with the Author'. According to Bowles, when in July 1953 Beckett chose him as the translator of *Molloy*, he did so because he wanted 'a writer rather than a translator'.[14] That said, Beckett came to be intimately involved in the translation. As Bowles recollects: 'Every day we revised a few pages, pen in hand, but debating virtually every word. Occasionally Beckett would throw the cat among the chickens by saying, "Give it a bit of rhythm." That could mean re-casting an entire paragraph.'[15] It soon became clear to Bowles that the translation of *Molloy* was not a translation 'as that term is usually understood. It was not a mere matter of swapping counters, of substituting one word for another. It was as far apart from machine translation as one could imagine. Time and again Beckett said that what we were trying to do was to write the book again in another language – that is to say, write a new book.'[16] As a result, the translation took fifteen months (nine months longer than it had taken Beckett to write the novel), reaching completion in December 1954. When Bowles asked Beckett why he had not simply translated the work himself, Beckett replied that 'not having spoken or worked in English for seventeen years he felt out of touch with the language and wanted to work with an English writer for a while so as to feel his way back into the language'.[17] While the aim may well have been to write 'a new book in the second language',[18] Beckett remained adamant that his own role was limited to revising Bowles's translation.[19] However, Beckett's comments on the translation process in letters to Pamela Mitchell reveal his strong distaste for such a revising role, and he would translate his subsequent French works on his own.

As mentioned above, in October 1950, six months before the publication of *Molloy* in French, Beckett's own translation of a short passage from Part I was included in *Transition Fifty*, no. 6, as the first of 'Two Fragments', the second being the opening of *Malone Dies* (see Appendix, pp. 187–9).[20] The substantive differences between the text of this 'Fragment' and the corresponding passage in the Olympia Press edition offer insights into Beckett's own translation practice, anticipating, as they do, his role in the revision of Bowles's translation of the novel in 1953–4. Thus, *There is rapture, or there should be, in the motion that crutches give, in the succession of little flights, in the taking off and landing among the thronging sound in wind and limb who have to fasten one foot to the ground before they dare lift the other* (translating 'La démarche du béquillard, cela a, cela devrait avoir, quelque chose d'exaltant. Car c'est une série de petits vols, à fleur de terre. On décolle, on atterrit, parmi la foule des ingambes, qui n'osent soulever un pied de terre avant d'y avoir cloué l'autre') becomes: *There is rapture, or there should be, in the motion crutches give. It is a series of little flights, skimming the ground. You take off, you land, through the thronging sound in wind and limb, who have to fasten one foot to the ground before they dare lift up the other.* Following this passage, the Olympia Press edition adds the sentence: 'And even their most joyous hastening is less aerial than my hobble' (translating 'Et il n'est jusqu'à leur course la plus joyeuse qui ne sois moins aérienne que mon clopinement'). Again, *And while I said to myself that time was running out and that it would be soon too late, if it were not so already, to arrive at the settlement in question, yet at the same time I felt myself carried away towards other cares, other spectres* (translating 'Et tout en me disant que le temps pressait et qu'il serait bientôt trop tard, qu'il l'était peut-être déjà, pour procéder au règlement en question, je me sentais qui dérivais vers d'autres soucis, d'autres spectres') becomes: *And while saying to myself that time was running out, and that soon it would be too late, was perhaps too late already, to settle the matter in question, I felt myself drifting towards other cares, other phantoms.* Or again, *For if my region had come to an end at a reasonable remove, surely a sort of gradation would have marked the fact* (translating 'Car si ma région avait fini à portée de mes pas, il me semble qu'une sorte de dégradement me l'aurait fait pressentir') becomes: *For if my region had ended no further than my feet could carry me, surely I would have felt it changing slowly.*

The reworkings show Beckett striving both for greater clarity and for greater simplicity of expression. Other revisions include the removal of words altogether or the substitution of a simpler, often more concrete, word or phrase. For instance, 'the question of my mother' ('le souci de ma mère') becomes 'my mother'; 'in her vicinity' ('dans son voisinage') becomes 'near her'; 'is it legitimate to speak here' ('est-ce le cas ici de parler') becomes 'can one speak here'; 'going forward' ('allant') becomes 'on'; 'I should necessarily' ('je finirais ... forcément') becomes 'I was bound to'; 'So I applied myself to this, to the best of my ability' ('C'est donc à cela que je m'appliquai, de toute ma science') becomes 'So I set myself to this as best I could'; 'I was obliged to admit that' ('je dus reconnaître que') becomes 'I had to confess'; 'the sun, while its actual disk remained hidden' ('le soleil, sans être exactement visible comme disque') becomes 'the sun, already down'; and 'if I may trust the memory of my observations' ('si je peux me fier au souvenir de mes observations') becomes 'if I remember rightly'. Lastly, there are instances where the substitution of one word for another entails a subtle shift in meaning. Of these, among the most significant is the systematic replacing of 'belief' (translating 'croyance') by 'feeling'.

In the four years separating French (1951) and English publication (1955), three further passages appeared in English, all from Part I, in *Merlin*, *Paris Review* and *New World Writing*.

Like the 'Fragment' published in *Transition Fifty*, these remain important in their own right, since they constitute earlier stages in the translation undertaken by Bowles and revised by Beckett. The first of the three passages, from the opening of the novel, appeared in *Merlin* in September 1953 as an 'Extract from *Molloy*' (see Appendix, pp. 191–212), and is identified as having been 'translated from the french by p. w. bowles'. A comparison of the *Merlin* and Olympia Press texts reveals not only Beckett's close attention to the smallest details of translation, including punctuation, but also some of the key principles governing his approach to his own self-translations: a deliberate impoverishment, an attempt to achieve the greatest possible simplicity, and even a certain stylelessness. Evidence for this is to be found in the recurrent preference for less sophisticated words or phrases. For instance, 'a queer card' in *Merlin* ('un drôle de type') becomes 'a queer one' in the Olympia text; 'folly' ('bête') becomes 'madness'; 'were acquainted' ('se connaissaient') becomes 'knew each other'; 'unmethodical, distracted' ('sans méthode et affolée') becomes 'wildly'; 'disinflame his brain' ('se décongestionner le cerveau') becomes 'cool his brain'; 'leave this place' ('aller ailleurs') becomes 'go'; and 'don't pay any heed to it' ('n'y faites pas attention') becomes 'don't mind it'. There are a few occasions, on the other hand, when Beckett opts for a more expansive translation: 'climbed' ('montait') becomes 'loomed'; 'hold their sabbath' ('tiennent leur sabbat') becomes 'dance their sabbath'; 'what language' ('quelle langue') becomes 'what rigmarole'; and 'bet' ('à bout d'expédients') becomes 'bet to the world'. Beckett also irons out clumsy or too-literal phrasing. Thus, 'describing long girations' ('faisait de longues girations') becomes 'turning in slow circles'; 'caused to come and go in an arc' ('lui fis décrire des arcs') becomes 'moved in an arc, to and fro'; and 'a protector in high places' ('un protecteur en haut lieu') becomes 'a friend at court'. On one occasion, he also increases the obscenity, 'an old fool' ('un vieux con') becoming 'an old ballocks'. And among the most suggestive changes is the inclusion in the Olympia Press edition of a sentence found neither in the original French nor in *Merlin*, describing the boatman (*le nocher* in the original French) – 'He had a long white beard' – anticipating the Boy's confirmation of Godot's beard in Act II: 'I think it's white, Sir.'

The second, similarly titled 'Extract from *Molloy*' was published in George Plimpton's *Paris Review* in March 1954 (see Appendix, pp. 213–24). It recounts Molloy's sojourn by the sea, including the sucking-stones episode, and is identified as having been 'Translated by Patrick Bowles in collaboration with the author'. The variants when compared with the book version reveal changes of both individual words and entire phrases. Again, these include simplifications and reductions; for instance, 'for all my anxiety to be dispelled' ('pour être tout à fait tranquille') becomes 'in order to be quite easy in my mind'; and 'schooled myself to endure' ('encaissé l'altération') becomes 'got used to'. The changes moreover introduce words and habits of phrasing that would recur in Beckett's later works. For instance, 'brooding on endless martingales' ('en ruminant des martingales') becomes 'revolving interminable martingales' – 'revolving' being a key word in the 1976 play *Footfalls*; 'road' ('chemin') becomes 'way', while 'highways' ('routes') becomes 'roads'; 'who cares' ('ça ne fait rien') becomes 'no matter'; and 'I think' ('je crois') becomes 'I fancy'. Some changes also heighten the symmetry of the phrasing, or impart a more pronounced rhythm. These include 'without limit to its stations or hope of crucifixion' ('sans limite de station ni espoir de crucifixion') becoming 'with no limit to its stations and no hope of crucifixion'. Another notable revision is the introduction of possessive pronouns which reflect the original French: 'reducing the number of stones' ('réduire celui [le nombre] de mes pierres') becomes 'reducing the number of my stones'; 'being off balance' ('me sentir en déséquilibre') becomes 'being off my balance'. On the other hand, Beckett's revisions of the *Paris Review* text include instances of what he appears to consider to be a too literal rendering: 'relatively' ('relativement') becomes 'comparatively'; 'on the sensory level at least' ('sur le plan de la sensation tout au moins') becomes 'at least as far as the pain was concerned'.

In April 1954, a third passage was published under the title 'Molloy' in *New World Writing*, vol. 5. Like the 'extract' printed in *Merlin*, this text is a translation of the opening of the novel and, aside from the fact that it is shorter, is almost identical to that in *Merlin*. The most notable difference between the two texts is that, whereas the *Merlin* text renders the two persons seen by Molloy as 'A' and 'C' (translating the 'A' and 'B' of the French original), as in the Olympia Press edition, the *New World Writing* text is inconsistent, rendering them as both 'A' and 'B' and 'A' and 'C'.

In August 1955, six months after its Olympia Press publication, the English *Molloy* was published in the United States by Grove Press. In January 1956, the novel was banned in Ireland on the grounds of obscenity, and later in the same year was also banned in Canada. The first British edition appeared in the 1959 volume *Molloy, Malone Dies, The Unnamable* (published by John Calder), and only in 1966 as a discrete volume. Since its first publication in 1951, the original French version of *Molloy* has been kept in print as an independent volume, Les Éditions de Minuit having thus far resisted calls for its integration with *Malone meurt* and *L'Innommable*. This is in striking contrast to the novel's publication history in English, since both in the United States and in Britain *Molloy* has generally – since 1959 – been published together with *Malone Dies* and *The Unnamable*, often with the subtitle *Three Novels*. In the 'Notes on Contributors' section on Beckett in the Spring 1954 issue of the *Paris Review*, he is identified as the author of a 'trilogy of novels', and later Calder editions of the three works in one volume labelled them *The Beckett Trilogy*, as did the 1979 Picador edition. While Beckett did make clear to Aidan Higgins that he wished to see the novels published together, he was none the less resistant to their being identified as a 'trilogy'.

It is unfortunate that the 'disintegration' both thematised and enacted stylistically in *Molloy* has also been reflected in its textual history. The 1955 Olympia Press edition is marred by typographical errors and orthographical inconsistencies. While the first Calder edition (1959) corrects some (but not all) of these errors, it also introduces new ones, including the omission of words. The first discrete Calder edition (1966) contains further typographical errors, for example rendering Youdi's address as 'Arcadia' (rather than 'Acacia') Square. The American Grove Press edition contains far fewer errors than any of the Calder editions, but some of the obvious errors in the original Olympia Press edition remain uncorrected therein, including inconsistency in the rendering of the name of the Elsner sisters' cook (in the original French text, her name is 'Hanna'; in the English translation this is rendered first as 'Hannah' and then, at the very end of the novel, as 'Hanna').

Given this history of deterioration, the present edition returns for its copy-text to the first English-language edition (Olympia Press, 1955), correcting all obvious typographical errors. For the most part, these errors and inconsistencies take the form of orthographical mistakes ('antechrist' for 'Antichrist', no doubt owing to the fact that the French spelling is *antéchrist*; 'herbacious' for 'herbaceous'; 'langour' for 'languor'), a mixture of English and American spellings, and of '-ise' and '-ize' endings, some irregular hyphenation ('good-bye'/'goodbye'; 'good-will'/'goodwill'; 'handle-bars'/'handlebars'), transposed letters and words, omitted marks of punctuation, and, on a few occasions, omitted words. The text of the Olympia Press edition is also characterised by a number of peculiarities that cannot be described as errors, the most notable being the frequent use of hyphenation for compound nouns (for example, 'police-sergeant'; 'sucking-stones'; 'supply-pocket'; 'lemon-verbena'; and 'garden-gate'). A number of other terms that one might have expected to find as single words are hyphenated in the Olympia Press edition; these include 'arm-chair', 'ash-tray', 'time-table' and 'cork-screw'. All such orthographical peculiarities have been retained in the present edition. A number of the corrections made in the 1959 Calder edition have not been adopted in the present edition, either because these corrections are misguided or because, while arguably justifiable, they interfere with phrasing that is distinctly Beckettian. An example of the former is the 'correction' of 'object of virtu' (translating 'objet de vertu') in the Olympia Press edition to 'object of virtue'; an example of the latter is the changing of the phrase 'And it says that here nothing stirs, has never stirred, will never stir' (translating 'Et il paraît qu'ici rien ne bouge, ni n'a jamais bougé, ni ne bougera jamais') to 'And it says that here nothing stirs, has ever stirred, will ever stir'. Lastly, there are two occasions where the phrasing is strange enough to have led to its being altered in later editions; these are 'bet to the world' (changed to 'beat to the world' in the Calder and Picador editions) and 'let a roar' (changed to 'let out a roar'). In the present edition, the original phrasing has been retained on the grounds that it is characteristic of Beckett's Irish English.

Shane Weller
Canterbury, 2009

Notes

1 The play *Eleutheria*, written in January–February 1947, before *Godot*, remained unpublished until 1995.

2 Richard Seaver, 'Samuel Beckett: An Introduction', *Merlin*, vol. 1, no. 2 (Autumn 1952), p. 73. The two novels to which Seaver is referring here are *Molloy* and *Malone meurt*.

3 Beckett to Lawrence E. Harvey; quoted in James Knowlson, *Damned to Fame: The Life of Samuel Beckett* (London: Bloomsbury, 1996), p. 358.

4 Quoted in Deirdre Bair, *Samuel Beckett: A Biography* (London: Jonathan Cape, 1978), p. 346.

5 Samuel Beckett, *The Complete Dramatic Works* (London: Faber and Faber, 1990), p. 220.

6 See Knowlson, *Damned to Fame*, p. 352. John Pilling observes that while 1945 is the 'most likely date' for this 'vision', it may have occurred in 1946 or 'just possibly' in 1947 (John Pilling, *A Beckett Chronology* (Basingstoke: Palgrave Macmillan, 2006), p. 94).

7 Charles Juliet, *Conversations with Samuel Beckett and Bram van Velde*, trans. Janey Tucker (Leiden: Academic Press, 1995), p. 140.

8 Beckett quoted in John Pilling, *Samuel Beckett* (London: Routledge & Kegan Paul, 1976), p. 11.

9 That, in one respect, Beckett was not being modest when he claimed to have 'no idea' where he was heading when he began *Molloy* is confirmed by an addition to the second paragraph of the English translation of the novel. In the published French text, this paragraph begins: 'Cette fois-ci, puis encore une je pense, puis c'en sera fini je pense, de ce monde-là aussi. C'est le sens de l'avant-dernier.' In the published English translation, these sentences are rendered as: 'This time, then once more I think, *then perhaps a last time*, then I think it'll be over, with that world too. Premonition of the last but one *but one*' (emphasis added). This addition in translation takes account not only of the 'once more' of *Malone meurt* (written between November 1947 and May 1948) but also of the novel he wrote between March 1949 and January 1950, *L'Innommable* – these three novels forming a sequence, though not necessarily (for Beckett) a 'trilogy'.

10 Nadeau in *Combat*, 12 April 1951; reprinted in Lawrence Graver and Raymond Federman (eds.), *Samuel Beckett: The Critical Heritage* (London: Routledge & Kegan Paul, 1979), p. 53 (trans. Françoise Longhurst).

11 Pingaud in *Esprit*, September 1951; reprinted in Graver and Federman (eds.), *Samuel Beckett*, pp. 67–8 (trans. Françoise Longhurst).

12 Reprinted in Graver and Federman (eds.), *Samuel Beckett*, pp. 74–5.

13 See Knowlson, *Damned to Fame*, pp. 393–7.

14 Patrick Bowles, 'How to Fail: Notes on Talks with Samuel Beckett', *PN Review 96*, vol. 20, no. 4 (March–April 1994), p. 24.

15 Bowles, 'How to Fail', p. 24.
16 Bowles, 'How to Fail', p. 27.
17 Bowles, 'How to Fail', p. 27.
18 Bowles, 'How to Fail', p. 33.
19 See Pilling, *A Beckett Chronology*, p. 128.
20 I wish to express my thanks to Mark Nixon for very kindly having supplied me with copies of the 'Fragment' of *Molloy* published in *Transition Fifty*, no. 6, and the passage published under the title 'Molloy' in *New World Writing*, vol. 5.

Table of Dates

Where unspecified, translations from French to English or vice versa are by Beckett.

1906

13 April   Samuel Beckett [Samuel Barclay Beckett] born in 'Cooldrinagh', a house in Foxrock, a village south of Dublin, on Good Friday, the second child of William Beckett and May Beckett, née Roe; he is preceded by a brother, Frank Edward, born 26 July 1902.

1911

Enters kindergarten at Ida and Pauline Elsner's private academy in Leopardstown.

1915

Attends larger Earlsfort House School in Dublin.

1920

Follows Frank to Portora Royal, a distinguished Protestant boarding school in Enniskillen, County Fermanagh (soon to become part of Northern Ireland).

1923

October   Enrols at Trinity College Dublin (TCD) to study for an Arts degree.

1926

August   First visit to France, a month-long cycling tour of the Loire Valley.

1927

April–August   Travels through Florence and Venice, visiting museums, galleries, and churches.

December   Receives B.A. in Modern Languages (French and Italian) and graduates first in the First Class.

1928

Jan.–June   Teaches French and English at Campbell College, Belfast.

September   First trip to Germany to visit seventeen-year-old Peggy Sinclair, a cousin on his father's side, and her family in Kassel.

1 November   Arrives in Paris as an exchange *lecteur* at the École Normale Supérieure. Quickly becomes friends with his predecessor, Thomas McGreevy [after 1943, MacGreevy], who introduces Beckett to James Joyce and other influential anglophone writers and publishers.

December   Spends Christmas in Kassel (as also in 1929, 1930 and 1931).

1929

June   Publishes first critical essay ('Dante . . . Bruno . Vico . . Joyce') and first story ('Assumption') in *transition* magazine.

1930

July   *Whoroscope* (Paris: Hours Press).

October   Returns to TCD to begin a two-year appointment as lecturer in French.

November   Introduced by MacGreevy to the painter and writer Jack B. Yeats in Dublin.

1931

March   *Proust* (London: Chatto and Windus).

September   First Irish publication, the poem 'Alba' in *Dublin Magazine*.

1932

January   Resigns his lectureship via telegram from Kassel and moves to Paris.

Feb.–June   First serious attempt at a novel, the posthumously published *Dream of Fair to Middling Women*.

December   Story 'Dante and the Lobster' appears in *This Quarter* (Paris).

1933

3 May   Death of Peggy Sinclair from tuberculosis.

26 June   Death of William Beckett from a heart attack.

1934

January   Moves to London and begins psychoanalysis with Wilfred Bion at the Tavistock Clinic.

February   *Negro Anthology*, edited by Nancy Cunard and with numerous translations by Beckett from the French (London: Wishart and Company).

May   *More Pricks Than Kicks* (London: Chatto and Windus).

Aug.–Sept.   Contributes several stories and reviews to literary magazines in London and Dublin.

1935

November   *Echo's Bones and Other Precipitates*, a cycle of thirteen poems (Paris: Europa Press).

1936

             Returns to Dublin.

29 September Leaves Ireland for a seven-month stay in Germany.

1937

Apr.–Aug.   First serious attempt at a play, *Human Wishes*, about Samuel Johnson and his household.

October   Settles in Paris.

1938

6/7 January Stabbed by a street pimp in Montparnasse. Among his visitors at Hôpital Broussais is Suzanne Deschevaux-Dumesnil, an acquaintance who is to become Beckett's companion for life.

March   *Murphy* (London: Routledge).

April   Begins writing poetry directly in French.

1939

3 September Great Britain and France declare war on Germany. Beckett abruptly ends a visit to Ireland and returns to Paris the next day.

1940

June   Travels south with Suzanne following the Fall of France, as part of the exodus from the capital.

September   Returns to Paris.

1941

13 January   Death of James Joyce in Zurich.

1 September   Joins the Resistance cell Gloria SMH.

1942

16 August   Goes into hiding with Suzanne after the arrest of close friend Alfred Péron.

6 October   Arrival at Roussillon, a small village in unoccupied southern France.

1944

24 August   Liberation of Paris.

1945

30 March   Awarded the Croix de Guerre.

Aug.–Dec.   Volunteers as a storekeeper and interpreter with the Irish Red Cross in Saint-Lô, Normandy.

1946

July   Publishes first fiction in French – a truncated version of the short story 'Suite' (later to become 'La Fin') in *Les Temps modernes*, owing to a misunderstanding by editors – as well as a critical essay on Dutch painters Geer and Bram van Velde in *Cahiers d'art*.

1947

Jan.–Feb.   Writes first play, in French, *Eleutheria* (published posthumously).

April   *Murphy*, French translation (Paris: Bordas).

1948

Undertakes a number of translations commissioned by UNESCO and by Georges Duthuit.

1950

25 August   Death of May Beckett.

1951

March   *Molloy*, in French (Paris: Les Éditions de Minuit).

November   *Malone meurt* (Paris: Minuit).

1952

       Purchases land at Ussy-sur-Marne, subsequently Beckett's preferred location for writing.

September   *En attendant Godot* (Paris: Minuit).

1953

5 January   Premiere of *Godot* at the Théâtre de Babylone in Montparnasse, directed by Roger Blin.

May   *L'Innommable* (Paris: Minuit).

August   *Watt*, in English (Paris: Olympia Press).

1954

8 September   *Waiting for Godot* (New York: Grove Press).

13 September   Death of Frank Beckett from lung cancer.

1955

March   *Molloy*, translated into English with Patrick Bowles (New York: Grove; Paris: Olympia).

3 August   First English production of *Godot* opens in London at the Arts Theatre.

November   *Nouvelles et Textes pour rien* (Paris: Minuit).

1956

3 January   American *Godot* premiere in Miami.

February   First British publication of *Waiting for Godot* (London: Faber).

October   *Malone Dies* (New York: Grove).

1957

January   First radio broadcast, *All That Fall* on the BBC Third Programme.

       Fin de partie, suivi de Acte sans paroles (Paris: Minuit).

28 March   Death of Jack B. Yeats.

May	Assists with the German production of *Play* (*Spiel*, translated by Elmar and Erika Tophoven) in Ulm.
22 May	Outline of *Film* sent to Grove Press. *Film* would be produced in 1964, starring Buster Keaton, and released at the Venice Film Festival the following year.

1964

March	*Play and Two Short Pieces for Radio* (London: Faber).
April	*How It Is*, translation of *Comment c'est* (London: Calder; New York: Grove).
June	*Comédie*, translation of *Play*, in *Les Lettres nouvelles*.
July–Aug.	First and only trip to the United States, to assist with the production of *Film* in New York.

1965

October	*Imagination morte imaginez* (Paris: Minuit).
November	*Imagination Dead Imagine* (London: *The Sunday Times*; Calder).

1966

January	*Comédie et Actes divers*, including *Dis Joe* and *Va et vient* (Paris: Minuit).
February	*Assez* (Paris: Minuit).
October	*Bing* (Paris: Minuit).

1967

February	*D'un ouvrage abandonné* (Paris: Minuit). *Têtes-mortes* (Paris: Minuit).
16 March	Death of Thomas MacGreevy.
June	*Eh Joe and Other Writings*, including *Act Without Words II* and *Film* (London: Faber).
July	*Come and Go*, English translation of *Va et vient* (London: Calder).
26 September	Directs first solo production, *Endspiel* (translation of *Endgame* by Elmar Tophoven) in Berlin.

November	*No's Knife: Collected Shorter Prose 1945–1966* (London: Calder).
December	*Stories and Texts for Nothing*, illustrated with six ink line drawings by Avigdor Arikha (New York: Grove).

1968

March	*Poèmes* (Paris: Minuit).
December	*Watt*, translated into French with Ludovic and Agnès Janvier (Paris: Minuit).

1969

23 October	Awarded the Nobel Prize for Literature. *Sans* (Paris: Minuit).

1970

April	*Mercier et Camier* (Paris: Minuit). *Premier amour* (Paris: Minuit).
July	*Lessness*, translation of *Sans* (London: Calder).
September	*Le Dépeupleur* (Paris: Minuit).

1972

January	*The Lost Ones*, translation of *Le Dépeupleur* (London: Calder; New York: Grove). *The North*, part of *The Lost Ones*, illustrated with etchings by Arikha (London: Enitharmon Press).

1973

January	*Not I* (London: Faber).
July	*First Love* (London: Calder).

1974

	Mercier and Camier (London: Calder).

1975

Spring	Directs *Godot* in Berlin and *Pas moi* (translation of *Not I*) in Paris.

1976

February	*Pour finir encore et autres foirades* (Paris: Minuit).
20 May	Directs Billie Whitelaw in *Footfalls*, which is performed with *That Time* at London's Royal

	Court Theatre in honour of Beckett's seventieth birthday.
Autumn	*All Strange Away*, illustrated with etchings by Edward Gorey (New York: Gotham Book Mart).
	Foirades/Fizzles, in French and English, illustrated with etchings by Jasper Johns (New York: Petersburg Press).
December	*Footfalls* (London: Faber).
1977	
March	*Collected Poems in English and French* (London: Calder; New York: Grove).
1978	
May	*Pas*, translation of *Footfalls* (Paris: Minuit).
August	*Poèmes, suivi de mirlitonnades* (Paris: Minuit).
1980	
January	*Compagnie* (Paris: Minuit).
	Company (London: Calder).
May	Directs *Endgame* in London with Rick Cluchey and the San Quentin Drama Workshop.
1981	
March	*Mal vu mal dit* (Paris: Minuit).
April	*Rockaby and Other Short Pieces* (New York: Grove).
October	*Ill Seen Ill Said*, translation of *Mal vu mal dit* (New York: *New Yorker*; Grove).
1983	
April	*Worstward Ho* (London: Calder).
September	*Disjecta: Miscellaneous Writings and a Dramatic Fragment*, containing critical essays on art and literature as well as the unfinished play *Human Wishes* (London: Calder).
1984	
February	Oversees San Quentin Drama Workshop

	production of *Godot*, directed by Walter Asmus, in London.
	Collected Shorter Plays (London: Faber; New York: Grove).
May	*Collected Poems 1930–1978* (London: Calder).
July	*Collected Shorter Prose 1945–1980* (London: Calder).

1989

April	*Stirrings Still*, with illustrations by Louis le Brocquy (New York: Blue Moon Books).
June	*Nohow On: Company, Ill Seen Ill Said, Worstward Ho*, illustrated with etchings by Robert Ryman (New York: Limited Editions Club).
17 July	Death of Suzanne Beckett.
22 December	Death of Samuel Beckett. Burial in Cimetière de Montparnasse.

★

1990

As the Story Was Told: Uncollected and Late Prose (London: Calder; New York: Riverrun Press).

1992

Dream of Fair to Middling Women (Dublin: Black Cat Press).

1995

Eleutheria (Paris: Minuit).

1996

Eleutheria, translated into English by Barbara Wright (London: Faber).

1998

No Author Better Served: The Correspondence of Samuel Beckett and Alan Schneider, edited by Maurice Harmon (Cambridge MA: Harvard University Press).

2000

Beckett on Film: nineteen films, by different directors, of Beckett's works for the stage (RTÉ, Channel 4, and Irish Film Board; DVD, London: Clarence Pictures).

2006

Samuel Beckett: Works for Radio: The Original Broadcasts: five works spanning the period 1957–1976 (CD, London: British Library Board).

2009

The Letters of Samuel Beckett 1929–1940, edited by Martha Dow Fehsenfeld and Lois More Overbeck (Cambridge: Cambridge University Press).

Compiled by Cassandra Nelson

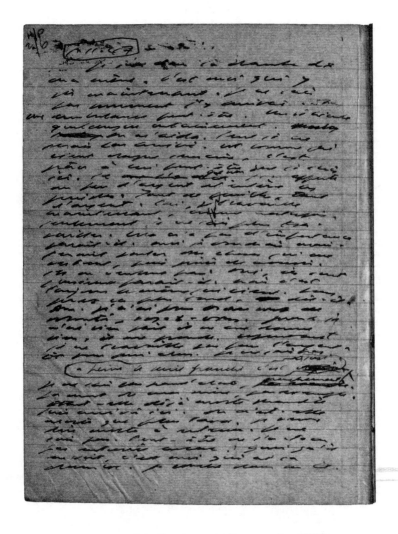

Opening page of the French autograph manuscript of *Molloy*
Courtesy of Harry Ransom Humanities Research Centre,
The University of Texas at Austin.
© The Estate of Samuel Beckett.

Molloy

Translated from the French by Patrick Bowles in collaboration with the author

I

I am in my mother's room. It's I who live there now. I don't know how I got there. Perhaps in an ambulance, certainly a vehicle of some kind. I was helped. I'd never have got there alone. There's this man who comes every week. Perhaps I got here thanks to him. He says not. He gives me money and takes away the pages. So many pages, so much money. Yes, I work now, a little like I used to, except that I don't know how to work any more. That doesn't matter apparently. What I'd like now is to speak of the things that are left, say my goodbyes, finish dying. They don't want that. Yes, there is more than one, apparently. But it's always the same one that comes. You'll do that later, he says. Good. The truth is I haven't much will left. When he comes for the fresh pages he brings back the previous week's. They are marked with signs I don't understand. Anyway I don't read them. When I've done nothing he gives me nothing, he scolds me. Yet I don't work for money. For what then? I don't know. The truth is I don't know much. For example my mother's death. Was she already dead when I came? Or did she only die later? I mean enough to bury. I don't know. Perhaps they haven't buried her yet. In any case I have her room. I sleep in her bed. I piss and shit in her pot. I have taken her place. I must resemble her more and more. All I need now is a son. Perhaps I have one somewhere. But I think not. He would be old now, nearly as old as myself. It was a little chambermaid. It wasn't true love. The true love was in another. We'll come to that. Her name? I've forgotten it again. It seems to me sometimes that I even knew my son, that I helped him. Then I tell myself it's impossible. It's impossible I could ever have helped anyone. I've forgotten how to spell too, and half the words. That doesn't matter apparently. Good. He's a queer one the one who comes to see me. He comes every Sunday apparently. The other days he isn't free. He's always thirsty. It was he told me I'd begun all wrong, that I should have begun differently. He must be right. I began at the beginning, like an old ballocks, can you imagine that? Here's my beginning. Because they're keeping it apparently. I took a lot of trouble with it. Here it is. It gave me a lot of trouble. It was the beginning, do you understand? Whereas now it's nearly the end. Is what I do now any better? I don't know. That's beside the point. Here's my beginning. It must mean something, or they wouldn't keep it. Here it is.

This time, then once more I think, then perhaps a last time, then I think it'll be over, with that world too. Premonition of the last but one but one. All grows dim. A little more and you'll go blind. It's in the head. It doesn't work any more, it says, I don't work any more. You go dumb as well and sounds fade. The threshold scarcely crossed that's how it is. It's the head. It must have had enough. So that you say, I'll manage this time, then perhaps once more, then perhaps a last time, then nothing more. You are hard set to formulate this thought, for it is one, in a sense. Then you try to pay attention, to consider with attention all those dim things, saying to yourself, laboriously, It's my fault. Fault? That was the word. But what fault? It's not goodbye, and what magic in those dim things to which it will be time enough, when next they pass, to say goodbye. For you must say goodbye, it would be madness not to say goodbye, when the time comes. If you think of the forms and light of other days it is without regret. But you seldom think of them, with what would you think of them? I don't know. People pass too, hard to distinguish from yourself. That is discouraging. So I saw A and C going slowly towards each other, unconscious of what they were doing. It was on a road remarkably bare, I mean without hedges or ditches or any kind of edge, in the country, for cows were chewing in enormous fields, lying and standing, in the evening silence. Perhaps I'm inventing a little, perhaps embellishing, but on the whole that's the way it was. They chew, swallow, then after a short pause effortlessly bring up the next mouthful. A neck muscle stirs and the jaws begin to grind again.

But perhaps I'm remembering things. The road, hard and white, seared the tender pastures, rose and fell at the whim of hills and hollows. The town was not far. It was two men, unmistakably, one small and one tall. They had left the town, first one, then the other, and then the first, weary or remembering a duty, had retraced his steps. The air was sharp, for they wore greatcoats. They looked alike, but no more than others do. At first a wide space lay between them. They couldn't have seen each other, even had they raised their heads and looked about, because of this wide space, and then because of the undulating land, which caused the road to be in waves, not high, but high enough, high enough. But the moment came when together they went down into the same trough and in this trough finally met. To say they knew each other, no, nothing warrants it. But perhaps at the sound of their steps, or warned by some obscure instinct, they raised their heads and observed each other, for a good fifteen paces, before they stopped, breast to breast. Yes, they did not pass each other by, but halted, face to face, as in the country, of an evening, on a deserted road, two wayfaring strangers will, without there being anything extraordinary about it. But they knew each other perhaps. Now in any case they do, now I think they will know each other, greet each other, even in the depths of the town. They turned towards the sea which, far in the east, beyond the fields, loomed high in the waning sky, and exchanged a few words. Then each went on his way. Each went on his way, A back towards the town, C on by ways he seemed hardly to know, or not at all, for he went with uncertain step and often stopped to look about him, like someone trying to fix landmarks in his mind, for one day perhaps he may have to retrace his steps, you never know. The treacherous hills where fearfully he ventured were no doubt only known to him from afar, seen perhaps from his bedroom window or from the summit of a monument which, one black day, having nothing in particular to do and turning to height for solace, he had paid his few coppers to climb, slower and slower, up the winding stones. From there he must have seen it all, the plain, the sea, and then these selfsame hills that some call mountains, indigo in places in the evening light, their serried ranges crowding to the skyline, cloven with hidden valleys that the eye divines from sudden shifts of colour and then from other signs for which there are no words, nor even thoughts. But all are not divined, even from that height, and often where only one escarpment is discerned, and one crest, in reality there are two, two escarpments, two crests, riven by a valley. But now he knows these hills, that is to say he knows them better, and if ever again he sees them from afar it will be I think with other eyes, and not only that but the within, all that inner space one never sees, the brain and heart and other caverns where thought and feeling dance their sabbath, all that too quite differently disposed. He looks old and it is a sorry sight to see him solitary after so many years, so many days and nights unthinkingly given to that rumour rising at birth and even earlier, What shall I do? What shall I do? now low, a murmur, now precise as the headwaiter's And to follow? and often rising to a scream. And in the end, or almost, to be abroad alone, by unknown ways, in the gathering night, with a stick. It was a stout stick, he used it to thrust himself onward, or as a defence, when the time came, against dogs and marauders. Yes, night was gathering, but the man was innocent, greatly innocent, he had nothing to fear, though he went in fear, he had nothing to fear, there was nothing they could do to him, or very little. But he can't have known it. I wouldn't know it myself, if I thought about it. Yes, he saw himself threatened, his body threatened, his reason threatened, and perhaps he was, perhaps they were, in spite of his innocence. What business has innocence here? What relation to the innumerable spirits of darkness? It's not clear. It seemed to me he wore a cocked hat. I remember being struck by it, as I wouldn't have been for example by a cap or by a bowler. I watched him recede, overtaken (myself) by his anxiety, at least by an anxiety which was not necessarily his, but of which as it were he partook. Who knows if it wasn't my own anxiety overtaking him. He hadn't seen me. I was perched higher than the road's highest point and

6

flattened what is more against a rock the same colour as myself, that is grey. The rock he probably saw. He gazed around as if to engrave the landmarks on his memory and must have seen the rock in the shadow of which I crouched like Belacqua, or Sordello, I forget. But a man, a fortiori myself, isn't exactly a landmark, because. I mean if by some strange chance he were to pass that way again, after a long lapse of time, vanquished, or to look for some lost thing, or to destroy something, his eyes would search out the rock, not the haphazard in its shadow of that unstable fugitive thing, still living flesh. No, he certainly didn't see me, for the reasons I've given and then because he was in no humour for that, that evening, no humour for the living, but rather for all that doesn't stir, or stirs so slowly that a child would scorn it, let alone an old man. However that may be, I mean whether he saw me or whether he didn't, I repeat I watched him recede, at grips (myself) with the temptation to get up and follow him, perhaps even to catch up with him one day, so as to know him better, be myself less lonely. But in spite of my soul's leap out to him, at the end of its elastic, I saw him only darkly, because of the dark and then because of the terrain, in the folds of which he disappeared from time to time, to re-emerge further on, but most of all I think because of other things calling me and towards which too one after the other my soul was straining, wildly. I mean of course the fields, whitening under the dew, and the animals, ceasing from wandering and settling for the night, and the sea, of which nothing, and the sharpening line of crests, and the sky where without seeing them I felt the first stars tremble, and my hand on my knee and above all the other wayfarer, A or C, I don't remember, going resignedly home. Yes, towards my hand also, which my knee felt tremble and of which my eyes saw the wrist only, the heavily veined back, the pallid rows of knuckles. But that is not, I mean my hand, what I wish to speak of now, everything in due course, but A or C returning to the town he had just left. But after all what was there particularly urban in his aspect? He was bare-headed, wore sand-shoes, smoked a cigar. He moved with a

7

kind of loitering indolence which rightly or wrongly seemed to me expressive. But all that proved nothing, refuted nothing. Perhaps he had come from afar, from the other end of the island even, and was approaching the town for the first time or returning to it after a long absence. A little dog followed him, a pomeranian I think, but I don't think so. I wasn't sure at the time and I'm still not sure, though I've hardly thought about it. The little dog followed wretchedly, after the fashion of pomeranians, stopping, turning in slow circles, giving up and then, a little further on, beginning all over again. Constipation is a sign of good health in pomeranians. At a given moment, pre-established if you like, I don't much mind, the gentleman turned back, took the little creature in his arms, drew the cigar from his lips and buried his face in the orange fleece, for it was a gentleman, that was obvious. Yes, it was an orange pomeranian, the less I think of it the more certain I am. And yet. But would he have come from afar, bare-headed, in sand-shoes, smoking a cigar, followed by a pomeranian? Did he not seem rather to have issued from the ramparts, after a good dinner, to take his dog and himself for a walk, like so many citizens, dreaming and farting, when the weather is fine? But was not perhaps in reality the cigar a cutty, and were not the sand-shoes boots, hobnailed, dust-whitened, and what prevented the dog from being one of those stray dogs that you pick up and take in your arms, from compassion or because you have long been straying with no other company than the endless roads, sands, shingle, bogs and heather, than this nature answerable to another court, than at long intervals the fellow-convict you long to stop, embrace, suck, suckle and whom you pass by, with hostile eyes, for fear of his familiarities? Until the day when, your endurance gone, in this world for you without arms, you catch up in yours the first mangy cur you meet, carry it the time needed for it to love you and you it, then throw it away. Perhaps he had come to that, in spite of appearances. He disappeared, his head on his chest, the smoking object in his hand. Let me try and explain. From things about to disappear I turn away in

8

time. To watch them out of sight, no, I can't do it. It was in this sense he disappeared. Looking away I thought of him, saying, He is dwindling, dwindling. I knew what I meant. I knew I could catch him, lame as I was. I had only to want to. And yet no, for I did want to. To get up, to get down on the road, to set off hobbling in pursuit of him, to hail him, what could be easier? He hears my cries, turns, waits for me. I am up against him, up against the dog, gasping, between my crutches. He is a little frightened of me, a little sorry for me, I disgust him not a little. I am not a pretty sight, I don't smell good. What is it I want? Ah that tone I know, compounded of pity, of fear, of disgust. I want to see the dog, see the man, at close quarters, know what smokes, inspect the shoes, find out other things. He is kind, tells me of this and that and other things, whence he comes, whither he goes. I believe him, I know it's my only chance to—my only chance, I believe all I'm told, I've disbelieved only too much in my long life, now I swallow everything, greedily. What I need now is stories, it took me a long time to know that, and I'm not sure of it. There I am then, informed as to certain things, knowing certain things about him, things I didn't know, things I had craved to know, things I had never thought of. What rigmarole. I am even capable of having learnt what his profession is, I who am so interested in professions. And to think I try my best not to talk about myself. In a moment I shall talk about the cows, about the sky, if I can. There I am then, he leaves me, he's in a hurry. He didn't seem to be in a hurry, he was loitering, I've already said so, but after three minutes of me he is in a hurry, he has to hurry. I believe him. And once again I am I will not say alone, no, that's not like me, but, how shall I say, I don't know, restored to myself, no, I never left myself, free, yes, I don't know what that means but it's the word I mean to use, free to do what, to do nothing, to know, but what, the laws of the mind perhaps, of my mind, that for example water rises in proportion as it drowns you and that you would do better, at least no worse, to obliterate texts than to blacken margins, to fill in the holes of words till all is blank and flat and the whole ghastly business looks like what it is, senseless, speechless, issueless misery. So I doubtless did better, at least no worse, not to stir from my observation post. But instead of observing I had the weakness to return in spirit to the other, the man with the stick. Then the murmurs began again. To restore silence is the role of objects. I said, Who knows if he hasn't simply come out to take the air, relax, stretch his legs, cool his brain by stamping the blood down to his feet, so as to make sure of a good night, a joyous awakening, an enchanted morrow. Was he carrying so much as a scrip? But the way of walking, the anxious looks, the club, could these be reconciled with one's conception of what is called a little turn? But the hat, a town hat, an old-fashioned town hat, which the least gust would carry far away. Unless it was attached under the chin, by means of a string or an elastic. I took off my hat and looked at it. It is fastened, it has always been fastened, to my buttonhole, always the same buttonhole, at all seasons, by a long lace. I am still alive then. That may come in useful. The hand that held the hat I thrust as far as possible from me and moved in an arc, to and fro. As I did so, I watched the lapel of my greatcoat and saw it open and close. I understand now why I never wore a flower in my buttonhole, though it was large enough to hold a whole nosegay. My buttonhole was set aside for my hat. It was my hat that I beflowered. But it is neither of my hat nor of my greatcoat that I hope to speak at present, it would be premature. Doubtless I shall speak of them later, when the time comes to draw up the inventory of my goods and possessions. Unless I lose them between now and then. But even lost they will have their place, in the inventory of my possessions. But I am easy in my mind, I shall not lose them. Nor my crutches, I shall not lose my crutches either. But I shall perhaps one day throw them away. I must have been on the top, or on the slopes, of some considerable eminence, for otherwise how could I have seen, so far away, so near at hand, so far beneath, so many things, fixed and moving. But what was an eminence doing in this land with hardly a ripple? And I, what was I doing there, and why come? These are things that we shall try and discover. But these are things we must not take seriously. There is a little of everything, apparently, in nature, and freaks are common. And I am perhaps confusing several different occasions, and different times, deep down, and deep down is my dwelling, oh not deepest down, somewhere between the mud and the scum. And perhaps it was A one day at one place, then C another at another, then a third the rock and I, and so on for the other components, the cows, the sky, the sea, the mountains. I can't believe it. No, I will not lie, I can easily conceive it. No matter, no matter, let us go on, as if all arose from one and the same weariness, on and on heaping up and up, until there is no room, no light, for any more. What is certain is that the man with the stick did not pass by again that night, because I would have heard him, if he had. I don't say I would have seen him, I say I would have heard him. I sleep little and that little by day. Oh not systematically, in my life without end I have dabbled with every kind of sleep, but at the time now coming back to me I took my doze in the daytime and, what is more, in the morning. Let me hear nothing of the moon, in my night there is no moon, and if it happens that I speak of the stars it is by mistake. Now of all the noises that night not one was of those heavy uncertain steps, or of that club with which he sometimes smote the earth until it quaked. How agreeable it is to be confirmed, after a more or less long period of vacillation, in one's first impressions. Perhaps that is what tempers the pangs of death. Not that I was so conclusively, I mean confirmed, in my first impressions with regard to—wait—C. For the wagons and carts which a little before dawn went thundering by, on their way to market with fruit, eggs, butter and perhaps cheese, in one of these perhaps he would have been found, overcome by fatigue or discouragement, perhaps even dead. Or he might have gone back to the town by another way too far away for me to hear its sounds, or by little paths through the fields, crushing the silent grass, pounding the silent ground. And so at last I came out of that distant night, divided between the murmurs of my little world, its dutiful confusions, and those so different (so different?) of all that between two suns abides and passes away. Never once a human voice. But the cows, when the peasants passed, crying in vain to be milked. A and C I never saw again. But perhaps I shall see them again. But shall I be able to recognize them? And am I sure I never saw them again? And what do I mean by seeing and seeing again? An instant of silence, as when the conductor taps on his stand, raises his arms, before the unanswerable clamour. Smoke, sticks, flesh, hair, at evening, afar, flung about the craving for a fellow. I know how to summon these rags to cover my shame. I wonder what that means. But I shall not always be in need. But talking of the craving for a fellow let me observe that having waked between eleven o'clock and midday (I heard the angelus, recalling the incarnation, shortly after) I resolved to go and see my mother. I needed, before I could resolve to go and see that woman, reasons of an urgent nature, and with such reasons, since I did not know what to do, or where to go, it was child's play for me, the play of an only child, to fill my mind until it was rid of all other preoccupation and I seized with a trembling at the mere idea of being hindered from going there, I mean to my mother, there and then. So I got up, adjusted my crutches and went down to the road, where I found my bicycle (I didn't know I had one) in the same place I must have left it. Which enables me to remark that, crippled though I was, I was no mean cyclist, at that period. This is how I went about it. I fastened my crutches to the crossbar, one on either side, I propped the foot of my stiff leg (I forget which, now they're both stiff) on the projecting front axle, and I pedalled with the other. It was a chainless bicycle, with a free-wheel, if such a bicycle exists. Dear bicycle, I shall not call you bike, you were green, like so many of your generation, I don't know why. It is a pleasure to meet it again. To describe it at length would be a pleasure. It had a little red horn instead of the bell fashionable in your days. To blow this horn was for me a real pleasure, almost a vice. I will go further and declare that if I were obliged to record, in a roll of honour, those activities which in the course of my interminable existence have given me only a mild pain in the balls, the blowing of a rubber horn—toot!—would figure among the first. And when I had to part from my bicycle I took off the horn and kept it about me. I believe I have it still, somewhere, and if I blow it no more it is because it has gone dumb. Even motor-cars have no horns nowadays, as I understand the thing, or rarely. When I see one, through the lowered window of a stationary car, I often stop and blow it. This should all be rewritten in the pluperfect. What a rest to speak of bicycles and horns. Unfortunately it is not of them I have to speak, but of her who brought me into the world, through the hole in her arse if my memory is correct. First taste of the shit. So I shall only add that every hundred yards or so I stopped to rest my legs, the good one as well as the bad, and not only my legs, not only my legs. I didn't properly speaking get down off the machine, I remained astride it, my feet on the ground, my arms on the handlebars, my head on my arms, and I waited until I felt better. But before I leave this earthly paradise, suspended between the mountains and the sea, sheltered from certain winds and exposed to all that Auster vents, in the way of scents and languors, on this accursed country, it would ill become me not to mention the awful cries of the corncrakes that run in the corn, in the meadows, all the short summer night long, dinning their rattles. And this enables me, what is more, to know when that unreal journey began, the second last but one of a form fading among fading forms, and which I here declare without further ado to have begun in the second or third week of June, at the moment that is to say most painful of all when over what is called our hemisphere the sun is at its pitilessmost and the arctic radiance comes pissing on our midnights. It is then the corncrakes are heard. My mother never refused to see me, that is she never refused to receive me, for it was many a long day since she had seen anything at all. I shall try and speak calmly. We were so old, she and I, she had had me so young, that we were like a couple of old cronies, sexless, unrelated, with the same memories, the same rancours, the same expectations. She never called me son, fortunately, I couldn't have borne it, but Dan, I don't know why, my name is not Dan. Dan was my father's name perhaps, yes, perhaps she took me for my father. I took her for my mother and she took me for my father. Dan, you remember the day I saved the swallow. Dan, you remember the day you buried the ring. I remembered, I remembered, I mean I knew more or less what she was talking about, and if I hadn't always taken part personally in the scenes she evoked, it was just as if I had. I called her Mag, when I had to call her something. And I called her Mag because for me, without my knowing why, the letter g abolished the syllable Ma, and as it were spat on it, better than any other letter would have done. And at the same time I satisfied a deep and doubtless unacknowledged need, the need to have a Ma, that is a mother, and to proclaim it, audibly. For before you say mag you say ma, inevitably. And da, in my part of the world, means father. Besides for me the question did not arise, at the period I'm worming into now, I mean the question of whether to call her Ma, Mag or the Countess Caca, she having for countless years been as deaf as a post. I think she was quite incontinent, both of faeces and water, but a kind of prudishness made us avoid the subject when we met, and I could never be certain of it. In any case it can't have amounted to much, a few niggardly wetted goat-droppings every two or three days. The room smelt of ammonia, oh not merely of ammonia, but of ammonia, ammonia. She knew it was me, by my smell. Her shrunken hairy old face lit up, she was happy to smell me. She jabbered away with a rattle of dentures and most of the time didn't realize what she was saying. Anyone but myself would have been lost in this clattering gabble, which can only have stopped during her brief instants of unconsciousness. In any case I didn't come to listen to her. I got into communication with her by knocking on her skull. One knock meant yes, two no, three I don't know, four money, five goodbye. I was hard put to ram this code into her ruined and frantic understanding, but I did it, in the end. That she should confuse yes, no, I don't know and goodbye, was all the same to me, I confused them myself. But that she should associate the four knocks with anything but money was something to be avoided at all costs. During the period of training therefore, at the same time as I administered the four knocks on her skull, I stuck a bank-note under her nose or in her mouth. In the innocence of my heart! For she seemed to have lost, if not absolutely all notion of mensuration, at least the faculty of counting beyond two. It was too far for her, yes, the distance was too great, from one to four. By the time she came to the fourth knock she imagined she was only at the second, the first two having been erased from her memory as completely as if they had never been felt, though I don't quite see how something never felt can be erased from the memory, and yet it is a common occurrence. She must have thought I was saying no to her all the time, whereas nothing was further from my purpose. Enlightened by these considerations I looked for and finally found a more effective means of putting the idea of money into her head. This consisted in replacing the four knocks of my index-knuckle by one or more (according to my needs) thumps of the fist, on her skull. That she understood. In any case I didn't come for money. I took her money, but I didn't come for that. My mother. I don't think too harshly of her. I know she did all she could not to have me, except of course the one thing, and if she never succeeded in getting me unstuck, it was that fate had earmarked me for less compassionate sewers. But it was well-meant and that's enough for me. No, it is not enough for me, but I give her credit, though she is my mother, for what she tried to do for me. And I forgive her for having jostled me a little in the first months and spoiled the only endurable, just endurable, period of my enormous history. And I also give her credit for not having done it again, thanks to me, or for having stopped in time, when she did. And if ever I'm reduced to looking for a meaning to my life, you never can tell, it's in that old mess I'll stick my nose to begin with, the mess of that poor old uniparous whore and myself the last of my foul brood, neither man nor beast. I should add, before I get down to the facts, you'd swear they were facts, of that distant summer afternoon, that with this deaf blind impotent mad old woman, who called me Dan and whom I called Mag, and with her alone, I—no, I can't say it. That is to say I could say it but I won't say it, yes, I could say it easily, because it wouldn't be true. What did I see of her? A head always, the hands sometimes, the arms rarely. A head always. Veiled with hair, wrinkles, filth, slobber. A head that darkened the air. Not that seeing matters, but it's something to go on with. It was I who took the key from under the pillow, who took the money out of the drawer, who put the key back under the pillow. But I didn't come for money. I think there was a woman who came each week. Once I touched with my lips, vaguely, hastily, that little grey wizened pear. Pah. Did that please her? I don't know. Her babble stopped for a second, then began again. Perhaps she said to herself, Pah. I smelt a terrible smell. It must have come from the bowels. Odour of antiquity. Oh I'm not criticizing her, I don't diffuse the perfumes of Araby myself. Shall I describe the room? No. I shall have occasion to do so later perhaps. When I seek refuge there, bet to the world, all shame drunk, my prick in my rectum, who knows. Good. Now that we know where we're going, let's go there. It's so nice to know where you're going, in the early stages. It almost rids you of the wish to go there. I was distraught, who am so seldom distraught, from what should I be distraught, and as to my motions even more uncertain than usual. The night must have tired me, at least weakened me, and the sun, hoisting itself higher and higher in the east, had poisoned me, while I slept. I ought to have put the bulk of the rock between it and me before closing my eyes. I confuse east and west, the poles too, I invert them readily. I was out of sorts. They are deep, my sorts, a deep ditch, and I am not often out of them. That's why I mention it. Nevertheless I covered several miles and found myself under the ramparts. There I dismounted in compliance with the regulations. Yes, cyclists entering and leaving town are required by the police to dismount, cars to go into bottom gear and horse-drawn vehicles to slow down to a walk. The reason for this regulation is I think this, that the ways into and of course out of this town are narrow and darkened by enormous vaults, without exception. It is a good rule and I observe it religiously, in spite of the difficulty I have in advancing on my crutches pushing my bicycle at the same time. I managed somehow. Being ingenious. Thus we cleared these difficult straits, my bicycle and I, together. But a little further on I heard myself hailed. I raised my head and saw a policeman. Elliptically speaking, for it was only later, by way of induction, or deduction, I forget which, that I knew what it was. What are you doing there? he said. I'm used to that question, I understood it immediately. Resting, I said. Resting, he said. Resting, I said. Will you answer my question? he cried. So it always is when I'm reduced to confabulation, I honestly believe I have answered the question I am asked and in reality I do nothing of the kind. I won't reconstruct the conversation in all its meanderings. It ended in my understanding that my way of resting, my attitude when at rest, astride my bicycle, my arms on the handlebars, my head on my arms, was a violation of I don't know what, public order, public decency. Modestly I pointed to my crutches and ventured one or two noises regarding my infirmity, which obliged me to rest as I could, rather than as I should. But there are not two laws, that was the next thing I thought I understood, not two laws, one for the healthy, another for the sick, but one only to which all must bow, rich and poor, young and old, happy and sad. He was eloquent. I pointed out that I was not sad. That was a mistake. Your papers, he said, I knew it a moment later. Not at all, I said, not at all. Your papers! he cried. Ah my papers. Now the only papers I carry with me are bits of newspaper, to wipe myself, you understand, when I have a stool. Oh I don't say I wipe myself every time I have a stool, no, but I like to be in a position to do so, if I have to. Nothing strange about that, it seems to me. In a panic I took this paper from my pocket and thrust it under his nose. The weather was fine. We took the little side streets, quiet, sunlit, I springing along between my crutches, he pushing my bicycle, with the tips of his white-gloved fingers. I wasn't—I didn't feel

unhappy. I stopped a moment, I made so bold, to lift my hand
and touch the crown of my hat. It was scorching. I felt the faces
turning to look after us, calm faces and joyful faces, faces of
men, of women and of children. I seemed to hear, at a certain
moment, a distant music. I stopped, the better to listen. Go on,
he said. Listen, I said. Get on, he said. I wasn't allowed to listen
to the music. It might have drawn a crowd. He gave me a shove.
I had been touched, oh not my skin, but none the less my skin
had felt it, it had felt a man's hard fist, through its coverings.
While still putting my best foot foremost I gave myself up to that
golden moment, as if I had been someone else. It was the hour
of rest, the forenoon's toil ended, the afternoon's to come. The
wisest perhaps, lying in the squares or sitting on their doorsteps,
were savouring its languid ending, forgetful of recent cares,
indifferent to those at hand. Others on the contrary were using
it to hatch their plans, their heads in their hands. Was there one
among them to put himself in my place, to feel how removed I
was then from him I seemed to be, and in that remove what
strain, as of hawsers about to snap? It's possible. Yes, I was
straining towards those spurious deeps, their lying promise of
gravity and peace, from all my old poisons I struggled towards
them, safely bound. Under the blue sky, under the watchful
gaze. Forgetful of my mother, set free from the act, merged in
this alien hour, saying, Respite, respite. At the police-station I
was haled before a very strange official. Dressed in plain-
clothes, in his shirt-sleeves, he was sprawling in an arm-chair,
his feet on his desk, a straw hat on his head and protruding from
his mouth a thin flexible object I could not identify. I had time
to become aware of these details before he dismissed me. He
listened to his subordinate's report and then began to interrogate me in a tone which, from the point of view of civility, left
increasingly to be desired, in my opinion. Between his questions
and my answers, I mean those deserving of consideration, the
intervals were more or less long and turbulent. I am so little
used to being asked anything that when I am asked something
I take some time to know what. And the mistake I make then is

this, that instead of quietly reflecting on what I have just heard, and heard distinctly, not being hard of hearing, in spite of all I have heard, I hasten to answer blindly, fearing perhaps lest my silence fan their anger to fury. I am full of fear, I have gone in fear all my life, in fear of blows. Insults, abuse, these I can easily bear, but I could never get used to blows. It's strange. Even spits still pain me. But they have only to be a little gentle, I mean refrain from hitting me, and I seldom fail to give satisfaction, in the long run. Now the sergeant, content to threaten me with a cylindrical ruler, was little by little rewarded for his pains by the discovery that I had no papers in the sense this word had a sense for him, nor any occupation, nor any domicile, that my surname escaped me for the moment and that I was on my way to my mother, whose charity kept me dying. As to her address, I was in the dark, but knew how to get there, even in the dark. The district? By the shambles, your honour, for from my mother's room, through the closed windows, I had heard, stilling her chatter, the bellowing of the cattle, that violent raucous tremulous bellowing not of the pastures but of the towns, their shambles and cattle-markets. Yes, after all, I had perhaps gone too far in saying that my mother lived near the shambles, it could equally well have been the cattle-market, near which she lived. Never mind, said the sergeant, it's the same district. I took advantage of the silence which followed these kind words to turn towards the window, blindly or nearly, for I had closed my eyes, proffering to that blandness of blue and gold my face and neck alone, and my mind empty too, or nearly, for I must have been wondering if I did not feel like sitting down, after such a long time standing, and remembering what I had learnt in that connection, namely that the sitting posture was not for me any more, because of my short stiff leg, and that there were only two postures for me any more, the vertical, drooping between my crutches, sleeping on my feet, and the horizontal, down on the ground. And yet the desire to sit down came upon me from time to time, back upon me from a vanished world. And I did not always resist it, forewarned though I was. Yes, my mind felt it surely, this tiny sediment, incomprehensibly stirring like grit at the bottom of a puddle, while on my face and great big Adam's apple the air of summer weighed and the splendid summer sky. And suddenly I remembered my name, Molloy. My name is Molloy, I cried, all of a sudden, now I remember. Nothing compelled me to give this information, but I gave it, hoping to please I suppose. They let me keep my hat on, I don't know why. Is it your mother's name? said the sergeant, it must have been a sergeant. Molloy, I cried, my name is Molloy. Is that your mother's name? said the sergeant. What? I said. Your name is Molloy, said the sergeant. Yes, I said, now I remember. And your mother? said the sergeant. I didn't follow. Is your mother's name Molloy too? said the sergeant. I thought it over. Your mother, said the sergeant, is your mother's—. Let me think! I cried. At least I imagine that's how it was. Take your time, said the sergeant. Was mother's name Molloy? Very likely. Her name must be Molloy too, I said. They took me away, to the guard-room I suppose, and there I was told to sit down. I must have tried to explain. I won't go into it. I obtained permission, if not to lie down on a bench, at least to remain standing, propped against the wall. The room was dark and full of people hastening to and fro, malefactors, policemen, lawyers, priests and journalists I suppose. All that made a dark, dark forms crowding in a dark place. They paid no attention to me and I repaid the compliment. Then how could I know they were paying no attention to me, and how could I repay the compliment, since they were paying no attention to me? I don't know. I knew it and I did it, that's all I know. But suddenly a woman rose up before me, a big fat woman dressed in black, or rather in mauve. I still wonder today if it wasn't the social worker. She was holding out to me, on an odd saucer, a mug full of a greyish concoction which must have been green tea with saccharine and powdered milk. Nor was that all, for between mug and saucer a thick slab of dry bread was precariously lodged, so that I began to say, in a kind of anguish, It's going to fall, it's going to fall, as if it mattered whether it fell or not. A moment later I myself was holding, in my trembling hands, this little pile of tottering disparates, in which the hard, the liquid and the soft were joined, without understanding how the transfer had been effected. Let me tell you this, when social workers offer you, free, gratis and for nothing, something to hinder you from swooning, which with them is an obsession, it is useless to recoil, they will pursue you to the ends of the earth, the vomitory in their hands. The Salvation Army is no better. Against the charitable gesture there is no defence, that I know of. You sink your head, you put out your hands all trembling and twined together and you say, Thank you, thank you lady, thank you kind lady. To him who has nothing it is forbidden not to relish filth. The liquid overflowed, the mug rocked with a noise of chattering teeth, not mine, I had none, and the sodden bread sagged more and more. Until, panic-striken, I flung it all far from me. I did not let it fall, no, but with a convulsive thrust of both my hands I threw it to the ground, where it smashed to smithereens, or against the wall, far from me, with all my strength. I will not tell what followed, for I am weary of this place, I want to go. It was late afternoon when they told me I could go. I was advised to behave better in future. Conscious of my wrongs, knowing now the reasons for my arrest, alive to my irregular situation as revealed by the enquiry, I was surprised to find myself so soon at freedom once again, if that is what it was, unpenalized. Had I, without my knowledge, a friend at court? Had I, without knowing it, favourably impressed the sergeant? Had they succeeded in finding my mother and obtaining from her, or from the neighbours, partial confirmation of my statements? Were they of the opinion that it was useless to prosecute me? To apply the letter of the law to a creature like me is not an easy matter. It can be done, but reason is against it. It is better to leave things to the police. I don't know. If it is unlawful to be without papers, why did they not insist on my getting them. Because that costs money and I had none? But in that case could they not have appropriated my bicycle? Probably not, without a court order. All that is incomprehensible. What is certain is this, that I never rested in that way again, my feet obscenely resting on the earth, my arms on the handlebars and on my arms my head, rocking and abandoned. It is indeed a deplorable sight, a deplorable example, for the people, who so need to be encouraged, in their bitter toil, and to have before their eyes manifestations of strength only, of courage and of joy, without which they might collapse, at the end of the day, and roll on the ground. I have only to be told what good behaviour is and I am well-behaved, within the limits of my physical possibilities. And so I have never ceased to improve, from this point of view, for I—I used to be intelligent and quick. And as far as goodwill is concerned, I had it to overflowing, the exasperated goodwill of the over-anxious. So that my repertory of permitted attitudes has never ceased to grow, from my first steps until my last, executed last year. And if I have always behaved like a pig, the fault lies not with me but with my superiors, who corrected me only on points of detail instead of showing me the essence of the system, after the manner of the great English schools, and the guiding principles of good manners, and how to proceed, without going wrong, from the former to the latter, and how to trace back to its ultimate source a given comportment. For that would have allowed me, before parading in public certain habits such as the finger in the nose, the scratching of the balls, digital emunction and the peripatetic piss, to refer them to the first rules of a reasoned theory. On this subject I had only negative and empirical notions, which means that I was in the dark, most of the time, and all the more completely as a lifetime of observations had left me doubting the possibility of systematic decorum, even within a limited area. But it is only since I have ceased to live that I think of these things and the other things. It is in the tranquillity of decomposition that I remember the long confused emotion which was my life, and that I judge it, as it is said that God will judge me, and with no less impertinence. To decompose is to live too, I know, I know, don't torment me, but one sometimes forgets. And of that life too I shall tell you perhaps one day, the day I know that when I thought I knew I was merely existing and that passion without form or stations will have devoured me down to the rotting flesh itself and that when I know that I know nothing, am only crying out as I have always cried out, more or less piercingly, more or less openly. Let me cry out then, it's said to be good for you. Yes, let me cry out, this time, then another time perhaps, then perhaps a last time. Cry out that the declining sun fell full on the white wall of the barracks. It was like being in China. A confused shadow was cast. It was I and my bicycle. I began to play, gesticulating, waving my hat, moving my bicycle to and fro before me, blowing the horn, watching the wall. They were watching me through the bars, I felt their eyes upon me. The policeman on guard at the door told me to go away. He needn't have, I was calm again. The shadow in the end is no better than the substance. I asked the man to help me, to have pity on me. He didn't understand. I thought of the food I had refused. I took a pebble from my pocket and sucked it. It was smooth, from having been sucked so long, by me, and beaten by the storm. A little pebble in your mouth, round and smooth, appeases, soothes, makes you forget your hunger, forget your thirst. The man came towards me, angered by my slowness. Him too they were watching, through the windows. Somewhere someone laughed. Inside me too someone was laughing. I took my sick leg in my hands and passed it over the frame. I went. I had forgotten where I was going. I stopped to think. It is difficult to think riding, for me. When I try and think riding I lose my balance and fall. I speak in the present tense, it is so easy to speak in the present tense, when speaking of the past. It is the mythological present, don't mind it. I was already settling in my raglimp stasis when I remembered it wasn't done. I went on my way, that way of which I knew nothing, qua way, which was nothing more than a surface, bright or dark, smooth or rough, and always dear to me, in spite of all, and the dear sound of that which goes and is gone, with a brief dust, when the weather is dry. There I am then, before I knew I had left the town, on the canal-bank. The canal goes through the town, I know, I know,

there are even two. But then these hedges, these fields? Don't
torment yourself, Molloy. Suddenly I see, it was my right leg the
stiff one, then. Toiling towards me along the tow-path I saw a
team of little grey donkeys, on the far bank, and I heard angry
cries and dull blows. I got down. I put my foot to the ground the
better to see the approaching barge, so gently approaching that
the water was unruffled. It was a cargo of nails and timber, on
its way to some carpenter I suppose. My eyes caught a donkey's
eyes, they fell to his little feet, their brave fastidious tread. The
boatman rested his elbow on his knee, his head on his hand. He
had a long white beard. Every three or four puffs, without taking
his pipe from his mouth, he spat into the water. I could not see
his eyes. The horizon was burning with sulphur and phospho-
rus, it was there I was bound. At last I got right down, hobbled
down to the ditch and lay down, beside my bicycle. I lay at full
stretch, with outspread arms. The white hawthorn stooped
towards me, unfortunately I don't like the smell of hawthorn. In
the ditch the grass was thick and high, I took off my hat and
pressed about my face the long leafy stalks. Then I could smell
the earth, the smell of the earth was in the grass that my hands
wove round my face till I was blinded. I ate a little too, a little
grass. It came back to my mind, from nowhere, as a moment
before my name, that I had set out to see my mother, at the
beginning of this ending day. My reasons? I had forgotten them.
But I knew them, I must have known them, I had only to find
them again and I would sweep, with the clipped wings of necessity, to my mother. Yes, it's all easy when you know why, a mere
matter of magic. Yes, the whole thing is to know what saint to
implore, any fool can implore him. For the particulars, if you are
interested in particulars, there is no need to despair, you may
scrabble on the right door, in the right way, in the end. It's for
the whole there seems to be no spell. Perhaps there is no whole,
before you're dead. An opiate for the life of the dead, that
should be easy. What am I waiting for then, to exorcize mine?
It's coming, it's coming. I hear from here the howl resolving all,
even if it is not mine. Meanwhile there's no use knowing you are

gone, you are not, you are writhing yet, the hair is growing, the nails are growing, the entrails emptying, all the morticians are dead. Someone has drawn the blinds, you perhaps. Not the faintest sound. Where are the famous flies? Yes, there is no denying it, any longer, it is not you who are dead, but all the others. So you get up and go to your mother, who thinks she is alive. That's my impression. But now I shall have to get myself out of this ditch. How joyfully I would vanish there, sinking deeper and deeper under the rains. No doubt I'll come back some day, here, or to a similar slough, I can trust my feet for that, as no doubt some day I'll meet again the sergeant and his merry men. And if, too changed to know it is they, I do not say it is they, make no mistake, it will be they, though changed. For to contrive a being, a place, I nearly said an hour, but I would not hurt anyone's feelings, and then to use them no more, that would be, how shall I say, I don't know. Not to want to say, not to know what you want to say, not to be able to say what you think you want to say, and never to stop saying, or hardly ever, that is the thing to keep in mind, even in the heat of composition. That night was not like the other night, if it had been I would have known. For when I try and think of that night, on the canal-bank, I find nothing, no night properly speaking, nothing but Molloy in the ditch, and perfect silence, and behind my closed lids the little night and its little lights, faint at first, then flaming and extinguished, now ravening, now fed, as fire by filth and martyrs. I say that night, but there was more than one perhaps. The lie, the lie, to lying thought. But I find the morning, a morning, and the sun already high, and the little sleep I had then, according to my custom, and space with its sounds again, and the shepherd watching me sleep and under whose eyes I opened my eyes. Beside him a panting dog, watching me too, but less closely than his master, for from time to time he stopped watching me to gnaw at his flesh, furiously, where the ticks were in him I suppose. Did he take me for a black sheep entangled in the brambles and was he waiting for an order from his master to drag me out? I don't think so. I don't smell like a sheep, I wish I smelt like a sheep, or a buck-goat. When I wake I see the first things quite clearly, the first things that offer, and I understand them, when they are not too difficult. Then in my eyes and in my head a fine rain begins to fall, as from a rose, highly important. So I knew at once it was a shepherd and his dog I had before me, above me rather, for they had not left the path. And I identified the bleating too, without any trouble, the anxious bleating of the sheep, missing the dog at their heels. It is then too that the meaning of words is least obscure to me, so that I said, with tranquil assurance, Where are you taking them, to the fields or to the shambles? I must have completely lost my sense of direction, as if direction had anything to do with the matter. For even if he was going towards the town, what prevented him from skirting it, or from leaving it again by another gate, on his way to new pastures, and if he was going away from it that meant nothing either, for slaughter-houses are not confined to towns, no, they are everywhere, the country is full of them, every butcher has his slaughter-house and the right to slaughter, according to his lights. But whether it was he didn't understand, or didn't want to reply, he didn't reply, but went on his way without a word, without a word for me I mean, for he spoke to his dog who listened attentively, cocking his ears. I got to my knees, no, that doesn't work, I got up and watched the little procession recede. I heard the shepherd whistle, and I saw him flourishing his crook, and the dog bustling about the flock, which but for him would no doubt have fallen into the canal. All that through a glittering dust, and soon through that mist too which rises in me every day and veils the world from me and veils me from myself. The bleating grew faint, because the sheep were less anxious, or because they were further away, or because my hearing was worse than a moment before, which would surprise me, for my hearing is still very good, scarcely blunted coming up to dawn, and if I sometimes hear nothing for hours on end it is for reasons of which I know nothing, or because about me all goes really silent, from time to time, whereas for the righteous the tumult of the world never stops. That then is how that second day began, unless it was the third, or the fourth, and it was a bad beginning, because it left me with persisting doubts, as to the destination of those sheep, among which there were lambs, and often wondering if they had safely reached some commonage or fallen, their skulls shattered, their thin legs crumpling, first to their knees, then over on their fleecy sides, under the pole-axe, though that is not the way they slaughter sheep, but with a knife, so that they bleed to death. But there is much to be said too for these little doubts. Good God, what a land of breeders, you see quadrupeds everywhere. And it's not over yet, there are still horses and goats, to mention only them, I feel them watching out for me, to get in my path. I have no need of that. But I did not lose sight of my immediate goal, which was to get to my mother as quickly as possible, and standing in the ditch I summoned to my aid the good reasons I had for going there, without a moment's delay. And though there were many things I could do without thinking, not knowing what I was going to do until it was done, and not even then, going to my mother was not one of them. My feet, you see, never took me to my mother unless they received a definite order to do so. The glorious, the truly glorious weather would have gladdened any other heart than mine. But I have no reason to be gladdened by the sun and I take good care not to be. The Aegean, thirsting for heat and light, him I killed, he killed himself, early on, in me. The pale gloom of rainy days was better fitted to my taste, no, that's not it, to my humour, no, that's not it either, I had neither taste nor humour, I lost them early on. Perhaps what I mean is that the pale gloom, etc., hid me better, without its being on that account particularly pleasing to me. Chameleon in spite of himself, there you have Molloy, viewed from a certain angle. And in winter, under my greatcoat, I wrapped myself in swathes of newspaper, and did not shed them until the earth awoke, for good, in April. The Times Literary Supplement was admirably adapted to this purpose, of a never-failing toughness and impermeability. Even farts made no impression on it. I can't help it, gas escapes from my fundament on the least pretext, it's hard not to mention it now and then, however great my distaste. One day I counted them. Three hundred and fifteen farts in nineteen hours, or an average of over sixteen farts an hour. After all it's not excessive. Four farts every fifteen minutes. It's nothing. Not even one fart every four minutes. It's unbelievable. Damn it, I hardly fart at all, I should never have mentioned it. Extraordinary how mathematics help you to know yourself. In any case this whole question of climate left me cold, I could stomach any mess. So I will only add that the mornings were often sunny, in that part of the world, until ten o'clock or coming up to eleven, and that then the sky darkened and the rain fell, fell till evening. Then the sun came out and went down, the drenched earth sparkled an instant, then went out, bereft of light. There I am then back in the saddle, in my numbed heart a prick of misgiving, like one dying of cancer obliged to consult his dentist. For I did not know if it was the right road. All roads were right for me, a wrong road was an event, for me. But when I was on my way to my mother only one road was right, the one that led to her, or one of those that led to her, for all did not lead to her. I did not know if I was on one of those right roads and that disturbed me, like all recall to life. Judge then of my relief when I saw, ahead of me, the familiar ramparts loom. I passed beyond them, into a district I did not know. And yet I knew the town well, for I was born there and had never succeeded in putting between it and me more than ten or fifteen miles, such was its grasp on me, I don't know why. So that I came near to wondering if I was in the right town, where I first saw the murk of day and which still harboured my mother, somewhere or other, or if I had not stumbled, as a result of a wrong turn, on a town whose very name I did not know. For my native town was the only one I knew, having never set foot in any other. But I had read with care, while I still could read, accounts of travellers more fortunate than myself, telling of other towns as beautiful as mine, and even more beautiful, though with a different beauty. And now it was a name I sought, in my memory, the name of the only town it had been given me to know, with the intention, as soon as I had found it, of stopping, and saying to a passer-by, doffing my hat, I beg your pardon, Sir, this *is* X, is it not?, X being the name of my town. And this name that I sought, I felt sure that it began with a B or with a P, but in spite of this clue, or perhaps because of its falsity, the other letters continued to escape me. I had been living so far from words so long, you understand, that it was enough for me to see my town, since we're talking of my town, to be unable, you understand. It's too difficult to say, for me. And even my sense of identity was wrapped in a namelessness often hard to penetrate, as we have just seen I think. And so on for all the other things which made merry with my senses. Yes, even then, when already all was fading, waves and particles, there could be no things but nameless things, no names but thingless names. I say that now, but after all what do I know now about then, now when the icy words hail down upon me, the icy meanings, and the world dies too, foully named. All I know is what the words know, and the dead things, and that makes a handsome little sum, with a beginning, a middle and an end as in the well-built phrase and the long sonata of the dead. And truly it little matters what I say, this or that or any other thing. Saying is inventing. Wrong, very rightly wrong. You invent nothing, you think you are inventing, you think you are escaping, and all you do is stammer out your lesson, the remnants of a pensum one day got by heart and long forgotten, life without tears, as it is wept. To hell with it anyway. Where was I. Unable to remember the name of my town I resolved to stop by the kerb, to wait for a passer-by with a friendly and intelligent air and then to whip off my hat and say, with my smile, I beg your pardon, Sir, excuse me, Sir, what is the name of this town, if you please? For the word once let fall I would know if it was the right word, the one I was seeking, in my memory, or another, and so where I stood. This resolution, actually formed as I rode along, was never to be carried out, an absurd mishap prevented it. Yes, my resolutions were remarkable in this, that they were no sooner formed than something always happened to prevent their execution. That must be why I am even less resolute now than then, just as then I was even less so than I once had been. But to tell the truth (to tell the truth!) I have never been particularly resolute, I mean given to resolutions, but rather inclined to plunge headlong into the shit, without knowing who was shitting against whom or on which side I had the better chance of skulking with success. But from this leaning too I derived scant satisfaction and if I have never quite got rid of it it is not for want of trying. The fact is, it seems, that the most you can hope is to be a little less, in the end, the creature you were in the beginning, and the middle. For I had hardly perfected my plan, in my head, when my bicycle ran over a dog, as subsequently appeared, and fell to the ground, an ineptness all the more unpardonable as the dog, duly leashed, was not out on the road, but in on the pavement, docile at its mistress's heels. Precautions are like resolutions, to be taken with precaution. The lady must have thought she had left nothing to chance, so far as the safety of her dog was concerned, whereas in reality she was setting the whole system of nature at naught, no less surely than I myself with my insane demands for more light. But instead of grovelling in my turn, invoking my great age and infirmities, I made things worse by trying to run away. I was soon overtaken, by a bloodthirsty mob of both sexes and all ages, for I caught a glimpse of white beards and little, almost angel faces, and they were preparing to tear me to pieces when the lady intervened. She said in effect, she told me so later on and I believed her, Leave this poor old man alone. He has killed Teddy, I grant you that, Teddy whom I loved like my own child, but it is not so serious as it seems, for as it happens I was taking him to the veterinary surgeon, to have him put out of his misery. For Teddy was old, blind, deaf, crippled with rheumatism and perpetually incontinent, night and day, indoors and out of doors. Thanks then to this poor old man I have been spared a painful task, not to mention the expense which I am ill able to afford, having no other means of support than the pension of my dear departed, fallen in defence of a country that

called itself his and from which in his lifetime he never derived
the smallest benefit, but only insults and vexations. The crowd
was beginning to disperse, the danger was past, but the lady was
in her stride. You may say, she said, that he did wrong to run
away, that he should have explained, asked to be forgiven.
Granted. But it is clear he has not all his wits about him, that he
is beside himself, for reasons of which we know nothing and
which might put us all to shame, if we did know them. I even
wonder if he knows what he has done. There emanated such
tedium from this droning voice that I was making ready to move
on when the unavoidable police constable rose up before me.
He brought down heavily on my handlebars his big red hairy
paw, I noticed it myself, and had it appears with the lady the
following conversation. Is this the man who ran over your dog,
Madam? He is, sergeant, and what of it? No, I can't record this
fatuous colloquy. So I will merely observe that finally in his turn
the constable too dispersed, the word is not too strong, grumbling and growling, followed by the last idlers who had given up
all hope of my coming to a bad end. But he turned back and
said, Remove that dog. Free at last to go I began to do so. But
the lady, a Mrs Loy, I might as well say it now and be done with
it, or Lousse, I forget, Christian name something like Sophie,
held me back, by the tail of my coat, and said, assuming the
words were the same when I heard them as when first spoken,
Sir, I need you. And seeing I suppose from my expression,
which frequently betrays me, that she had made herself understood, she must have said, If he understands that he can understand anything. And she was not mistaken, for after some time
I found myself in possession of certain ideas or points of view
which could only have come to me from her, namely that having
killed her dog I was morally obliged to help her carry it home
and bury it, that she did not wish to prosecute me for what I had
done, but that it was not always possible to do as one did not
wish, that she found me likeable enough in spite of my hideous
appearance and would be happy to hold out to me a helping
hand, and so on, I've forgotten the half of it. Ah yes, I too

needed her, it seemed. She needed me to help her get rid of her dog, and I needed her, I've forgotten for what. She must have told me, for that was an insinuation I could not decently pass over in silence as I had the rest, and I made no bones about telling her I needed neither her nor anyone else, which was perhaps a slight exaggeration, for I must have needed my mother, otherwise why this frenzy of wanting to get to her? That is one of the many reasons why I avoid speaking as much as possible. For I always say either too much or too little, which is a terrible thing for a man with a passion for truth like mine. And I shall not abandon this subject, to which I shall probably never have occasion to return, with such a storm blowing up, without making this curious observation, that it often happened to me, before I gave up speaking for good, to think I had said too little when in fact I had said too much and in fact to have said too little when I thought I had said too much. I mean that on reflection, in the long run rather, my verbal profusion turned out to be penury, and inversely. So time sometimes turns the tables. In other words, or perhaps another thing, whatever I said it was never enough and always too much. Yes, I was never silent, whatever I said I was never silent. Divine analysis that conduces thus to knowledge of yourself, and of your fellow-men, if you happen to have any. For to say I needed no one was not to say too much, but an infinitesimal part of what I should have said, could not have said, should never have said. Need of my mother! No, there were no words for the want of need in which I was perishing. So that she, I mean Sophie, must have told me the reasons why I needed her, since I had dared to disagree. And perhaps if I took the trouble I might find them again, but trouble, many thanks, some other time. And now enough of this boulevard, it must have been a boulevard, of all these righteous ones, these guardians of the peace, all these feet and hands, stamping, clutching, clenched in vain, these bawling mouths that never bawl out of season, this sky beginning to drip, enough of being abroad, trapped, visible. Someone was poking the dog, with a malacca. The dog was uniformly yellow, a mongrel I suppose, or a pedigree, I can never tell the difference. His death must have hurt him less than my fall me. And he at least was dead. We slung him across the saddle and set off like an army in retreat, helping each other I suppose, to keep the corpse from falling, to keep the bicycle moving, to keep ourselves moving, through the jeering crowd. The house where Sophie—no, I can't call her that any more, I'll try calling her Lousse, without the Mrs—the house where Lousse lived was not far away. Oh it was not nearby either, I had my bellyful by the time I got there. That is to say I didn't have it really. You think you have your bellyful but you seldom have it really. It was because I knew I was there that I had my bellyful, a mile more to go and I would only have had my bellyful an hour later. Human nature. Marvellous thing. The house where Lousse lived. Must I describe it? I don't think so. I won't, that's all I know, for the moment. Perhaps later on, if I get to know it. And Lousse? Must I describe her? I suppose so. Let's first bury the dog. It was she dug the hole, under a tree. You always bury your dog under a tree, I don't know why. But I have my suspicions. It was she dug the hole because I couldn't, though I was the gentleman, because of my leg. That is to say I could have dug with a trowel, but not with a spade. For when you dig a grave one leg supports the weight of the body while the other, flexing and unflexing, drives the spade into the earth. Now my sick leg, I forget which, it's immaterial here, was in a condition neither to dig, because it was rigid, nor alone to support me, because it would have collapsed. I had so to speak only one leg at my disposal, I was virtually one-legged, and I would have been happier, livelier, amputated at the groin. And if they had removed a few testicles into the bargain I wouldn't have objected. For from such testicles as mine, dangling at mid-thigh at the end of a meagre cord, there was nothing more to be squeezed, not a drop. So that non che la speme il desiderio, and I longed to see them gone, from the old stand where they bore false witness, for and against, in the lifelong charge against me. For if they accused me of having made a balls of it, of me, of them, they thanked me for it too, from the depths of their rotten bag, the right lower than the left, or inversely, I forget, decaying circus clowns. And, worse still, they got in my way when I tried to walk, when I tried to sit down, as if my sick leg was not enough, and when I rode my bicycle they bounced up and down. So the best thing for me would have been for them to go, and I would have seen to it myself, with a knife or secateurs, but for my terror of physical pain and festered wounds, so that I shook. Yes, all my life I have gone in terror of festered wounds, I who never festered, I was so acid. My life, my life, now I speak of it as of something over, now as of a joke which still goes on, and it is neither, for at the same time it is over and it goes on, and is there any tense for that? Watch wound and buried by the watchmaker, before he died, whose ruined works will one day speak of God, to the worms. But those cullions, I must be attached to them after all, cherish them as others do their scars, or the family album. In any case it wasn't their fault I couldn't dig, but my leg's. It was Lousse dug the hole while I held the dog in my arms. He was heavy already and cold, but he had not yet begun to stink. He smelt bad, if you like, but bad like an old dog, not like a dead dog. He too had dug holes, perhaps at this very spot. We buried him as he was, no box or wrapping of any kind, like a Carthusian monk, but with his collar and lead. It was she put him in the hole, though I was the gentleman. For I cannot stoop, neither can I kneel, because of my infirmity, and if ever I stoop, forgetting who I am, or kneel, make no mistake, it will not be me, but another. To throw him in the hole was all I could have done, and I would have done it gladly. And yet I did not do it. All the things you would do gladly, oh without enthusiasm, but gladly, all the things there seems no reason for your not doing, and that you do not do! Can it be we are not free? It might be worth looking into. But what was my contribution to this burial? It was she dug the hole, put in the dog, filled up the hole. On the whole I was a mere spectator, I contributed my presence. As if it had been my own burial. And it was. It was a larch. It is the only tree I can identify, with certainty. Funny she should have chosen, to bury her dog beneath, the only tree I can identify, with certainty. The sea-green needles are like silk and speckled, it always seemed to me, with little red, how shall I say, with little red specks. The dog had ticks in his ears, I have an eye for such things, they were buried with him. When she had finished her grave she handed me the spade and began to muse, or brood. I thought she was going to cry, it was the thing to do, but on the contrary she laughed. It was perhaps her way of crying. Or perhaps I was mistaken and she was really crying, with the noise of laughter. Tears and laughter, they are so much Gaelic to me. She would see him no more, her Teddy she had loved like an only child. I wonder why, since she had obviously made up her mind to bury the dog at home, she had not asked the vet to call and destroy the brute on the premises. Was she really on her way to the vet at the moment her path crossed mine? Or had she said so solely in order to attenuate my guilt? Private calls are naturally more expensive. She ushered me into the drawing-room and gave me food and drink, good things without a doubt. Unfortunately I didn't much care for good things to eat. But I quite liked getting drunk. If she lived in embarrassed circumstances there was no sign of it. That kind of embarrassment I feel at once. Seeing how painful the sitting posture was for me she fetched a chair for my stiff leg. Without ceasing to ply me with delicacies she kept up a chatter of which I did not understand the hundredth part. With her own hand she took off my hat, and carried it away, to hang it up somewhere, on a hat-rack I suppose, and seemed surprised when the lace pulled her up in her stride. She had a parrot, very pretty, all the most approved colours. I understood him better than his mistress. I don't mean I understood him better than she understood him, I mean I understood him better than I understood her. He exclaimed from time to time, Fuck the son of a bitch, fuck the son of a bitch. He must have belonged to an American sailor, before he belonged to Lousse. Pets often change masters. He didn't say much else. No, I'm wrong, he also said, Putain de merde! He must have belonged to a French sailor before he

belonged to the American sailor. Putain de merde! Unless he
had hit on it alone, it wouldn't surprise me. Lousse tried to
make him say, Pretty Polly! I think it was too late. He listened,
his head on one side, pondered, then said, Fuck the son of a
bitch. It was clear he was doing his best. Him too one day she
would bury. In his cage probably. Me too, if I had stayed, she
would have buried. If I had her address I'd write to her, to come
and bury me. I fell asleep. I woke up in a bed, in my skin. They
had carried their impertinence to the point of washing me, to
judge by the smell I gave off, no longer gave off. I went to the
door. Locked. To the window. Barred. It was not yet quite dark.
What is there left to try when you have tried the door and the
window? The chimney perhaps. I looked for my clothes. I found
a light switch and switched it on. No result. What a story! All
that left me cold, or nearly. I found my crutches, against an easy
chair. It may seem strange that I was able to go through the
motions I have described without their help. I find it strange.
You don't remember immediately who you are, when you wake.
On a chair I found a white chamber-pot with a roll of toilet-
paper in it. Nothing was being left to chance. I recount these
moments with a certain minuteness, it is a relief from what I feel
coming. I set a pouffe against the easy chair, sat down in the
latter and on the former laid my stiff leg. The room was chock-
full of pouffes and easy chairs, they thronged all about me, in
the gloom. There were also occasional tables, footstools, tall-
boys, etc., in abundance. Strange feeling of congestion that the
night dispersed, though it lit the chandelier, which I had left
turned on. My beard was missing, when I felt for it with
anguished hand. They had shaved me, they had shorn me of my
scant beard. How had my sleep withstood such liberties? My
sleep as a rule so uneasy. To this question I found a number of
replies. But I did not know which of them was right. Perhaps
they were all wrong. My beard grows properly only on my chin
and dewlap. Where the pretty bristles grow on other faces, on
mine there are none. But such as it was they had docked my
beard. Perhaps they had dyed it too, I had no proof they had

not. I thought I was naked, in the easy chair, but I finally realized I was wearing a nightdress, very flimsy. If they had come
and told me I was to be sacrificed at sunrise I would not have
been taken aback. How foolish one can be. It seemed to me too
that I had been perfumed, lavender perhaps. I said, If only your
poor mother could see you now. I am no enemy of the common-
place. She seemed far away, my mother, far away from me, and
yet I was a little closer to her than the night before, if my reck-
oning was accurate. But was it? If I was in the right town, I had
made progress. But was I? If on the other hand I was in the
wrong town, from which my mother would necessarily be
absent, then I had lost ground. I must have fallen asleep, for all
of a sudden there was the moon, a huge moon framed in the
window. Two bars divided it in three segments, of which the
middle remained constant, while little by little the right gained
what the left lost. For the moon was moving from left to right,
or the room was moving from right to left, or both together
perhaps, or both were moving from left to right, but the room
not so fast as the moon, or from right to left, but the moon not
so fast as the room. But can one speak of right and left in such
circumstances? That movements of an extreme complexity were
taking place seemed certain, and yet what a simple thing it
seemed, that vast yellow light sailing slowly behind my bars
and which little by little the dense wall devoured, and finally
eclipsed. And now its tranquil course was written on the walls,
a radiance scored with shadow, then a brief quivering of leaves,
if they were leaves, then that too went out, leaving me in the
dark. How difficult it is to speak of the moon and not lose one's
head, the witless moon. It must be her arse she shows us always.
Yes, I once took an interest in astronomy, I don't deny it. Then
it was geology that killed a few years for me. The next pain in
the balls was anthropology and the other disciplines, such as
psychiatry, that are connected with it, disconnected, then
connected again, according to the latest discoveries. What I
liked in anthropology was its inexhaustible faculty of negation,
its relentless definition of man, as though he were no better than

God, in terms of what he is not. But my ideas on this subject were always horribly confused, for my knowledge of men was scant and the meaning of being beyond me. Oh I've tried everything. In the end it was magic that had the honour of my ruins, and still today, when I walk there, I find its vestiges. But mostly they are a place with neither plan nor bounds and of which I understand nothing, not even of what it is made, still less into what. And the thing in ruins, I don't know what it is, what it was, nor whether it is not less a question of ruins than the indestructible chaos of timeless things, if that is the right expression. It is in any case a place devoid of mystery, deserted by magic, because devoid of mystery. And if I do not go there gladly, I go perhaps more gladly there than anywhere else, astonished and at peace, I nearly said as in a dream, but no, no. But it is not the kind of place where you go, but where you find yourself, sometimes, not knowing how, and which you cannot leave at will, and where you find yourself without any pleasure, but with more perhaps than in those places you can escape from, by making an effort, places full of mystery, full of the familiar mysteries. I listen and the voice is of a world collapsing endlessly, a frozen world, under a faint untroubled sky, enough to see by, yes, and frozen too. And I hear it murmur that all wilts and yields, as if loaded down, but here there are no loads, and the ground too, unfit for loads, and the light too, down towards an end it seems can never come. For what possible end to these wastes where true light never was, nor any upright thing, nor any true foundation, but only these leaning things, forever lapsing and crumbling away, beneath a sky without memory of morning or hope of night. These things, what things, come from where, made of what? And it says that here nothing stirs, has never stirred, will never stir, except myself, who do not stir either, when I am there, but see and am seen. Yes, a world at an end, in spite of appearances, its end brought it forth, ending it began, is it clear enough? And I too am at an end, when I am there, my eyes close, my sufferings cease and I end, I wither as the living cannot. And if I went on listening to that far whisper, silent long since and which I still hear, I would learn still more, about this. But I will listen no longer, for the time being, to that far whisper, for I do not like it, I fear it. But it is not a sound like the other sounds, that you listen to, when you choose, and can sometimes silence, by going away or stopping your ears, no, but it is a sound which begins to rustle in your head, without your knowing how, or why. It's with your head you hear it, not your ears, you can't stop it, but it stops itself, when it chooses. It makes no difference therefore whether I listen to it or not, I shall hear it always, no thunder can deliver me, until it stops. But nothing compels me to speak of it, when it doesn't suit me. And it doesn't suit me, at the moment. No, what suits me, at the moment, is to be done with this business of the moon which was left unfinished, by me, for me. And if I get done with it less successfully than if I had all my wits about me, I shall none the less get done with it, as best I can, at least I think so. That moon then, all things considered, filled me suddenly with amaze, with surprise, perhaps better. Yes, I was considering it, after my fashion, with indifference, seeing it again, in a way, in my head, when a great fright came suddenly upon me. And deeming this deserved to be looked into I looked into it and quickly made the following discovery, among others, but I confine myself to the following, that this moon which had just sailed gallant and full past my window had appeared to me the night before, or the night before that, yes, more likely, all young and slender, on her back, a shaving. And then I had said, Now I see, he has waited for the new moon before launching forth on unknown ways, leading south. And then a little later, Perhaps I should go to mother tomorrow. For all things hang together, by the operation of the Holy Ghost, as the saying is. And if I failed to mention this detail in its proper place, it is because you cannot mention everything in its proper place, you must choose, between the things not worth mentioning and those even less so. For if you set out to mention everything you would never be done, and that's what counts, to be done, to have done. Oh I know, even when you mention only a few of the things there are, you do not get done either, I know, I know. But it's a change of muck. And if all muck is the same muck that doesn't matter, it's good to have a change of muck, to move from one heap to another a little further on, from time to time, fluttering you might say, like a butterfly, as if you were ephemeral. And if you are wrong, and you are wrong, I mean when you record circumstances better left unspoken, and leave unspoken others, rightly, if you like, but how shall I say, for no good reason, yes, rightly, but for no good reason, as for example that new moon, it is often in good faith, excellent faith. Had there then elapsed, between that night on the mountain, that night when I saw A and C and then made up my mind to go and see my mother, and this other night, more time than I had thought, namely fourteen full days, or nearly? And if so, what had happened to those fourteen days, or nearly, and where had they flown? And what possible chance was there of finding a place for them, no matter what their burden, in the so rigorous chain of events I had just undergone? Was it not wiser to suppose either that the moon seen two nights before, far from being new as I had thought, was on the eve of being full, or else that the moon seen from Lousse's house, far from being full, as it had appeared to me, was in fact merely entering on its first quarter, or else finally that here I had to do with two moons, as far from the new as from the full and so alike in outline that the naked eye could hardly tell between them, and that whatever was at variance with these hypotheses was so much smoke and delusion. It was at all events with the aid of these considerations that I grew calm again and was restored, in the face of nature's pranks, to my old ataraxy, for what it was worth. And it came back also to my mind, as sleep stole over it again, that my nights were moonless and the moon foreign, to my nights, so that I had never seen, drifting past the window, carrying me back to other nights, other moons, this moon I had just seen, I had forgotten who I was (excusably) and spoken of myself as I would have of another, if I had been compelled to speak of another. Yes, it sometimes happens and will sometimes happen again that I forget who I am and strut before my eyes, like a stranger. Then I see the sky different from what it is and the earth too takes on false colours. It looks like rest, it is not, I vanish happy in that alien light, which must have once been mine, I am willing to believe it, then the anguish of return, I won't say where, I can't, to absence perhaps, you must return, that's all I know, it's misery to stay, misery to go. The next day I demanded my clothes. The valet went to find out. He came back with the news they had been burnt. I continued my inspection of the room. It was at first sight a perfect cube. Through the lofty window I saw boughs. They rocked gently, but not all the time, shaken now and then by sudden spasms. I noticed the chandelier was burning. My clothes, I said, my crutches, forgetting my crutches were there, against the chair. He left me alone again, leaving the door open. Through the door I saw a big window, bigger than the door which it overlapped entirely, and opaque. The valet came back with the news my clothes had been sent to the dyers, to have the shine taken off. He held my crutches, which should have seemed strange to me, but seemed natural to me, on the contrary. I took hold of one and began to strike the pieces of furniture with it, not very hard, just hard enough to overturn them, without breaking them. They were fewer than in the night. To tell the truth I pushed them rather than struck them, I thrust at them, I lunged, and that is not pushing either, but it's more like pushing than striking. But recalling who I was I soon threw away my crutch and came to a standstill in the middle of the room, determined to stop asking for things, to stop pretending to be angry. For to want my clothes, and I thought I wanted them, was no reason for pretending to be angry, when they were refused. And alone once more I resumed my inspection of the room and was on the point of endowing it with other properties when the valet came back with the news my clothes had been sent for and I would have them soon. Then he began to straighten the tables and chairs I had overturned and to put them back into place, dusting them as he did so with a feather duster which suddenly appeared in his hand. And so I began to help him as best I could, by way of proving that I bore no grudge against anyone. And though I could not do much, because of my stiff leg, yet I did what I could, that is to say I took each object as he straightened it and proceeded with excruciating meticulousness to restore it to its proper place, stepping back with raised arms the better to assess the result and then springing forward to effect minute improvements. And with the tail of my nightdress as with a duster I petulantly flicked them one by one. But of this little game too I soon wearied and suddenly stood stock still in the middle of the room. But seeing him ready to go I took a step forward and said, My bicycle. And I said it again, and again, the same words, until he appeared to understand. I don't know to what race he belonged, he was so tiny and ageless, assuredly not to mine. He was an oriental perhaps, a vague oriental, a child of the Rising Sun. He wore white trousers, a white shirt and a yellow waistcoat, like a chamois he was, with brass buttons and sandals. It is not often that I take cognizance so clearly of the clothes that people wear and I am happy to give you the benefit of it. The reason for that was perhaps this, that all morning the talk had been of clothes, of mine. And perhaps I had been saying, to myself, words to this effect, Look at him, peaceful in his own clothes, and look at me, floating about inside another man's nightdress, another woman's probably, for it was pink and transparent and adorned with ribands and frills and lace. Whereas the room, I saw the room but darkly, at each fresh inspection it seemed changed, and that is known as seeing darkly, in the present state of our knowledge. The boughs themselves seemed to shift, as though endowed with an orbital velocity of their own, and in the big frosted window the door was no longer inscribed, but had slightly shifted to the right, or to the left, I forget, so that there now appeared within its frame a panel of white wall, on which I succeeded in casting faint shadows when I moved. But that there were natural causes to all these things I am willing to concede, for the resources of nature are infinite apparently. It was I who was not natural enough to enter into that order of things, and appreciate its niceties. But I was used to seeing the sun rise in the south, used to not knowing where I was going, what I was leaving, what was going with me, all things turning and twisting confusedly about me. It is difficult, is it not, to go to one's mother with things in such a state, more difficult than to the Lousses of this world, or to its police-stations, or to the other places that are waiting for me, I know. But the valet having brought my clothes, in a paper which he unwrapped in front of me, I saw that my hat was not among them, so that I said, My hat. And when he finally understood what I wanted he went away and came back a little later with my hat. Nothing was missing then except the lace to fasten my hat to my buttonhole, but that was something I could not hope to make him understand, and so I did not mention it. An old lace, you can always find an old lace, no lace lasts for ever, the way clothes do, real clothes. As for the bicycle, I had hopes that it was waiting for me somewhere below stairs, perhaps even before the front door, ready to carry me away from these horrible scenes. And I did not see what good it would do to ask for it again, to submit him and myself to this fresh ordeal, when it could be avoided. These considerations crossed my mind with a certain rapidity. Now with regard to the pockets, four in all, of my clothes, I verified their contents in front of the valet and discovered that certain things were missing. My sucking-stone in particular was no longer there. But sucking-stones abound on our beaches, when you know where to look for them, and I deemed it wiser to say nothing about it, all the more so as he would have been capable, after an hour's argument, of going and fetching me from the garden a completely unsuckable stone. This was a decision too which I took almost instantaneously. But of the other objects which had disappeared why speak, since I did not know exactly what they were. And perhaps they had been taken from me at the police-station, without my knowing it, or scattered and lost, when I fell, or at some other time, or thrown away, for I would sometimes throw away all I had about me, in a burst of irritation. So why speak of them? I resolved nevertheless to declare loudly that a knife was missing,

a noble knife, and I did so to such effect that I soon received a
very fine vegetable knife, so-called stainless, but it didn't take
me long to stain it, and which opened and shut into the bargain,
unlike all the vegetable knives I had ever known, and which had
a safety catch, highly dangerous as soon appeared and the cause
of innumerable cuts, all over my fingers caught between the
handle of so-called genuine Irish horn and the blade red with
rust and so blunted that it was less a matter of cuts than of
contusions. And if I deal at such length with this knife it is
because I have it somewhere still I think, among my possessions, and because having dealt with it here at such length I
shall not have to deal with it again, when the moment comes, if
it ever comes, to draw up the list of my possessions, and that will
be a relief, a welcome relief, when that moment comes, I know.
For it is natural I should dilate at lesser length on what I lost
than on what I could not lose, that goes without saying. And if
I do not always appear to observe this principle it is because it
escapes me, from time to time, and vanishes, as utterly as if I
had never educed it. Mad words, no matter. For I no longer
know what I am doing, nor why, those are things I understand
less and less, I don't deny it, for why deny it, and to whom, to
you, to whom nothing is denied? And then doing fills me with
such a, I don't know, impossible to express, for me, now, after
so long, yes, that I don't stop to enquire in virtue of what principle. And all the less so as whatever I do, that is to say whatever
I say, it will always as it were be the same thing, yes, as it were.
And if I speak of principles, when there are none, I can't help it,
there must be some somewhere. And if always doing the same
thing as it were is not the same as observing the same principle,
I can't help it either. And then how can you know whether you
are observing it or not? And how can you want to know? No, all
that is not worth while, not worth while bothering about, and
yet you do bother about it, your sense of values gone. And the
things that are worth while you do not bother about, you let
them be, for the same reason, or wisely, knowing that all these
questions of worth and value have nothing to do with you, who

don't know what you're doing, nor why, and must go on not knowing it, on pain of, I wonder what, yes, I wonder. For anything worse than what I do, without knowing what, or why, I have never been able to conceive, and that doesn't surprise me, for I never tried. For had I been able to conceive something worse than what I had I would have known no peace until I got it, if I know anything about myself. And what I have, what I am, is enough, was always enough for me, and as far as my dear little sweet little future is concerned I have no qualms, I have a good time coming. So I put on my clothes, having first made sure they had not been tampered with, that is to say I put on my trousers, my greatcoat, my hat and my boots. My boots. They came up to where my calves would have been if I had had calves, and partly they buttoned, or would have buttoned, if they had had buttons, and partly they laced, and I have them still, I think, somewhere. Then I took my crutches and left the room. The whole day had gone in this tomfoolery and it was dusk again. Going down the stairs I inspected the window I had seen through the door. It lit the staircase with its wild tawny light. Lousse was in the garden, fussing around the grave. She was sowing grass on it, as if grass wouldn't have sown itself on it. She was taking advantage of the cool of evening. Seeing me, she came warmly towards me and gave me food and drink. I ate and drank standing, casting about me in search of my bicycle. She talked and talked. Soon sated, I began the search for my bicycle. She followed me. In the end I found it, half buried in a soft bush. I threw aside my crutches and took it in my hands, by the saddle and the handlebars, intending to wheel it a little, back and forth, before getting on and leaving for ever this accursed place. But I pushed and pulled in vain, the wheels would not turn. It was as though the brakes were jammed, and heaven knows they were not, for my bicycle had no brakes. And suddenly overcome by a great weariness, in spite of the dying day when I always felt most alive, I threw the bicycle back in the bush and lay down on the ground, on the grass, careless of the dew, I never feared the dew. It was then that Lousse, taking

45

advantage of my weakness, squatted down beside me and began to make me propositions, to which I must confess I listened, absent-mindedly, I had nothing else to do, I could do nothing else, and doubtless she had poisoned my beer with something intended to mollify me, to mollify Molloy, with the result that I was nothing more than a lump of melting wax, so to speak. And from these propositions, which she enunciated slowly and distinctly, repeating each clause several times, I finally elicited the following, or gist. I could not prevent her having a weakness for me, neither could she. I would live in her home, as though it were my own. I would have plenty to eat and drink, to smoke too if I smoked, for nothing, and my remaining days would glide away without a care. I would as it were take the place of the dog I had killed, as it for her had taken the place of a child. I would help in the garden, in the house, when I wished, if I wished. I would not go out on the street, for once out I would never find my way in again. I would adopt the rhythm of life which best suited me, getting up, going to bed and taking my meals at whatsoever hours I pleased. If I did not choose to be clean, to wear nice clothes, to wash and so on, I need not. She would be grieved, but what was her grief, compared to my grief? All she asked was to feel me near her, with her, and the right to contemplate from time to time this extraordinary body both at rest and in motion. Every now and then I interrupted her, to ask what town I was in. But either because she did not understand me, or because she preferred to leave me in ignorance, she did not reply to my question, but went on with her soliloquy, reiterating tirelessly each new proposition, then expounding further, slowly, gently, the benefits for both of us if I would make my home with her. Till nothing was left but this monotonous voice, in the deepening night and the smell of the damp earth and of a strongly scented flower which at the time I could not identify, but which later I identified as spike-lavender. There were beds of it everywhere, in this garden, for Lousse loved spike, she must have told me herself, otherwise I would not have known, she loved it above all other herbs and flowers, because of its smell, and then also because of its spikes, and its colour. And if I had not lost my sense of smell the smell of lavender would always make me think of Lousse, in accordance with the well-known mechanism of association. And she gathered this lavender when it bloomed I presume, left it to dry and then made it up into lavender-bags that she put in her cupboards to perfume her handkerchiefs, her underclothing and house-linen. But none the less from time to time I heard the chiming of the hours, from the clocks and belfries, chiming out longer and longer, then suddenly briefly, then longer and longer again. This will give some idea of the time she took to cozen me, of her patience and physical endurance, for all the time she was squatting or kneeling beside me, whereas I was stretched out at my ease on the grass, now on my back, now on my stomach, now on one side, now on the other. And all the time she never stopped talking, whereas I only opened my mouth to ask, at long intervals, more and more feebly, what town we were in. And sure of her victory at last, or simply feeling she had done all she could and that further insistence was useless, she got up and went away, I don't know where, for I stayed where I was, with regret, mild regret. For in me there have always been two fools, among others, one asking nothing better than to stay where he is and the other imagining that life might be slightly less horrible a little further on. So that I was never disappointed, so to speak, whatever I did, in this domain. And these inseparable fools I indulged turn about, that they might understand their foolishness. And that night there was no question of moon, nor any other light, but it was a night of listening, a night given to the faint soughing and sighing stirring at night in little pleasure gardens, the shy sabbath of leaves and petals and the air that eddies there as it does not in other places, where there is less constraint, and as it does not during the day, when there is more vigilance, and then something else that is not clear, being neither the air nor what it moves, perhaps the far unchanging noise the earth makes and which other noises cover, but not for long. For they do not account for that noise you hear when you really listen, when all seems hushed. And there was another noise, that of my life become the life of this garden as it rode the earth of deeps and wildernesses. Yes, there were times when I forgot not only who I was, but that I was, forgot to be. Then I was no longer that sealed jar to which I owed my being so well preserved, but a wall gave way and I filled with roots and tame stems for example, stakes long since dead and ready for burning, the recess of night and the imminence of dawn, and then the labour of the planet rolling eager into winter, winter would rid it of these contemptible scabs. Or of that winter I was the precarious calm, the thaw of the snows which make no difference and all the horrors of it all all over again. But that did not happen to me often, mostly I stayed in my jar which knew neither seasons nor gardens. And a good thing too. But in there you have to be careful, ask yourself questions, as for example whether you still are, and if no when it stopped, and if yes how long it will still go on, anything at all to keep you from losing the thread of the dream. For my part I willingly asked myself questions, one after the other, just for the sake of looking at them. No, not willingly, wisely, so that I might believe I was still there. And yet it meant nothing to me to be still there. I called that thinking. I thought almost without stopping, I did not dare stop. Perhaps that was the cause of my innocence. It was a little the worse for wear, a little threadbare perhaps, but I was glad to have it, yes, I suppose. Thanks I suppose, as the urchin said when I picked up his marble, I don't know why, I didn't have to, and I suppose he would have preferred to pick it up himself. Or perhaps it wasn't to be picked up. And the effort it cost me, with my stiff leg. The words engraved themselves for ever on my memory, perhaps because I understood them at once, a thing I didn't often do. Not that I was hard of hearing, for I had quite a sensitive ear, and sounds unencumbered with precise meaning were registered perhaps better by me than by most. What was it then? A defect of the understanding perhaps, which only began to vibrate on repeated solicitations, or which did vibrate, if you like, but at a lower frequency, or a higher, than that of ratiocination, if such a thing is conceivable, and such a thing is conceivable, since I conceive it. Yes, the words I heard, and heard distinctly, having quite a sensitive ear, were heard a first time, then a second, and often even a third, as pure sounds, free of all meaning, and this is probably one of the reasons why conversation was unspeakably painful to me. And the words I uttered myself, and which must nearly always have gone with an effort of the intelligence, were often to me as the buzzing of an insect. And this is perhaps one of the reasons I was so untalkative, I mean this trouble I had in understanding not only what others said to me, but also what I said to them. It is true that in the end, by dint of patience, we made ourselves understood, but understood with regard to what, I ask of you, and to what purpose? And to the noises of nature too, and of the works of men, I reacted I think in my own way and without desire of enlightenment. And my eye too, the seeing one, must have been ill-connected with the spider, for I found it hard to name what was mirrored there, often quite distinctly. And without going so far as to say that I saw the world upside down (that would have been too easy) it is certain I saw it in a way inordinately formal, though I was far from being an aesthete, or an artist. And of my two eyes only one functioning more or less correctly, I misjudged the distance separating me from the other world, and often I stretched out my hand for what was far beyond my reach, and often I knocked against obstacles scarcely visible on the horizon. But I was like that even when I had my two eyes, it seems to me, but perhaps not, for it is long since that era of my life, and my recollection of it is more than imperfect. And now I come to think of it, my attempts at taste and smell were scarcely more fortunate, I smelt and tasted without knowing exactly what, nor whether it was good, nor whether it was bad, and seldom twice running the same thing. I would have been I think an excellent husband, incapable of wearying of my wife and committing adultery only from absent-mindedness. Now as to telling you why I stayed a good while with Lousse, no, I cannot. That is to say I could I suppose, if I took the trouble.

But why should I? In order to establish beyond all question that I could not do otherwise? For that is the conclusion I would come to, fatally. I who had loved the image of old Geulincx, dead young, who left me free, on the black boat of Ulysses, to crawl towards the East, along the deck. That is a great measure of freedom, for him who has not the pioneering spirit. And from the poop, poring upon the wave, a sadly rejoicing slave, I follow with my eyes the proud and futile wake. Which, as it bears me from no fatherland away, bears me onward to no shipwreck. A good while then with Lousse. It's vague, a good while, a few months perhaps, a year perhaps. I know it was warm again the day I left, but that meant nothing, in my part of the world, where it seemed to be warm or cold or merely mild at any moment of the year and where the days did not run gently up and down, no, not gently. Perhaps things have changed since. So all I know is that it was much the same weather when I left as when I came, so far as I was capable of knowing what the weather was. And I had been under the weather so long, under all weathers, that I could tell quite well between them, my body could tell between them and seemed even to have its likes, its dislikes. I think I stayed in several rooms one after the other, or alternately, I don't know. In my head there are several windows, that I do know, but perhaps it is always the same one, open variously on the parading universe. The house was fixed, that is perhaps what I mean by these different rooms. House and garden were fixed, thanks to some unknown mechanism of compensation, and I, when I stayed still, as I did most of the time, was fixed too, and when I moved, from place to place, it was very slowly, as in a cage out of time, as the saying is, in the jargon of the schools, and out of space too to be sure. For to be out of one and not out of the other was for cleverer than me, who was not clever, but foolish. But I may be quite wrong. And these different windows that open in my head, when I grope again among those days, really existed perhaps and perhaps do still, in spite of my being no longer there, I mean there looking at them, opening them and shutting them, or crouched in a corner of the room marvelling at the things they framed. But I will not dwell on this episode, so ludicrously brief when you think of it and so poor in substance. For I helped neither in the house nor the garden and knew nothing of what work was going forward, day and night, nothing save the sounds that came to me, dull sounds and sharp ones too, and then often the roar of air being vigorously churned, it seemed to me, and which perhaps was nothing more than the sound of burning. I preferred the garden to the house, to judge by the long hours I spent there, for I spent there the greater part of the day and of the night, whether it was wet or whether it was fine. Men were always busy there, working at I know not what. For the garden seemed hardly to change, from day to day, apart from the tiny changes due to the customary cycle of birth, life and death. And in the midst of those men I drifted like a dead leaf on springs, or else I lay down on the ground, and then they stepped gingerly over me as though I had been a bed of rare flowers. Yes, it was doubtless in order to preserve the garden from apparent change that they laboured at it thus. My bicycle had disappeared again. Sometimes I felt the wish to look for it again, to find it again and find out what was wrong with it or even go for a little ride on the walks and paths connecting the different parts of the garden. But instead of trying to satisfy this wish I stayed where I was looking at it, if I may say so, looking at it as it shrivelled up and finally disappeared, like the famous fatal skin, only much quicker. For there seem to be two ways of behaving in the presence of wishes, the active and the contemplative, and though they both give the same result it was the latter I preferred, matter of temperament I presume. The garden was surrounded with a high wall, its top bristling with broken glass like fins. But what must have been absolutely unexpected was this, that this wall was broken by a wicket-gate giving free access to the road, for it was never locked, of that I was all but convinced, having opened and closed it without the least trouble on more than one occasion, both by day and by night, and seen it used by others than myself, for the purpose as well of entrance as of exit. I would stick out my nose, then hastily call it in again. A few further remarks. Never did I see a woman within these precincts, and by precincts I do not merely mean the garden, as I probably should, but the house too, but only men, with the obvious exception of Lousse. What I saw and did not see did not matter much admittedly, but I mention it all the same. Lousse herself I saw but little, she seldom showed herself, to me, out of tact perhaps, fearing to alarm me. But I think she spied on me a great deal, hiding behind the bushes, or the curtains, or skulking in the shadows of a first-floor room, with a spy-glass perhaps. For had she not said she desired above all to see me, both coming and going and rooted to the spot. And to get a good view you need the keyhole, the little chink among the leaves, and so on, whatever prevents you from being seen and from seeing more than a little at a time. No? I don't know. Yes, she inspected me, little by little, and even in my very going to bed, my sleeping and my getting up, the mornings that I went to bed. For in this matter I remained faithful to my custom, which was to sleep in the morning, when I slept at all. For it sometimes happened that I did not sleep at all, for several days, without feeling at all the worse for it. For my waking was a kind of sleeping. And I did not always sleep in the same place, but now I slept in the garden, which was large, and now I slept in the house, which was large too, really extremely spacious. And this uncertainty as to the hour and place of my sleeping must have entranced her, I imagine, and made the time pass pleasantly. But it is useless to dwell on this period of my life. If I go on long enough calling that my life I'll end up by believing it. It's the principle of advertising. This period of my life. It reminds me, when I think of it, of air in a water-pipe. So I will only add that this woman went on giving me slow poison, slipping I know not what poisons into the drink she gave me, or into the food she gave me, or both, or one day one, the next the other. That is a grave charge to bring and I do not bring it lightly. And I bring it without ill-feeling, yes, I accuse her without ill-feeling of having drugged my food and drink with noxious and insipid powders and potions. But even sipid they would have made no difference, I would have swallowed it all down with the same whole-heartedness. That celebrated whiff of almonds for example would never have taken away my appetite. My appetite! What a subject. For conversation. I had hardly any. I ate like a thrush. But the little I did eat I devoured with a voracity usually attributed to heavy eaters, and wrongly, for heavy eaters as a rule eat ponderously and with method, that follows from the very notion of heavy eating. Whereas I flung myself at the mess, gulped down the half or the quarter of it in two mouthfuls without chewing (with what would I have chewed?), then pushed it from me with loathing. One would have thought I ate to live! Similarly I would engulf five or six mugs of beer with one swig, then drink nothing for a week. What do you expect, one is what one is, partly at least. Nothing or little to be done. Now as to the substances she insinuated thus into my various systems, I could not say whether they were stimulants or whether they were not rather depressants. The truth is, coenaesthetically speaking of course, I felt more or less the same as usual, that is to say, if I may give myself away, so terror-stricken that I was virtually bereft of feeling, not to say of consciousness, and drowned in a deep and merciful torpor shot with brief abominable gleams, I give you my word. Against such harmony of what avail the miserable molys of Lousse, administered in infinitesimal doses probably, to draw the pleasure out. Not that they remained entirely without effect, no, that would be an exaggeration. For from time to time I caught myself making a little bound in the air, two or three feet off the ground at least, at least, I who never bounded. It looked like levitation. And it happened too, less surprisingly, when I was walking, or even propped up against something, that I suddenly collapsed, like a puppet when its strings are dropped, and lay long where I fell, literally boneless. Yes, that struck me as less strange, for I was used to collapsing thus, but with this difference, that I felt it coming, and prepared myself accordingly, as an epileptic does when he feels the fit coming. I mean that knowing I was going to fall I lay down, or I wedged myself where I stood so firmly that nothing short of an earthquake could have dislodged me, and I waited. But these were precautions I did not always take, preferring the fall to the trouble of having to lie down or stand fast. Whereas the falls I suffered when with Lousse did not give me a chance to circumvent them. But all the same they surprised me less, they were more in keeping with me, than the little bounds. For even as a child I do not remember ever having bounded, neither rage nor pain ever made me bound, even as a child, however ill-qualified I am to speak of that time. Now with regard to my food, it seems to me I ate it as, when and where it best suited me. I never had to call for it. It was brought to me, wherever I happened to be, on a tray. I can still see the tray, almost at will, it was round, with a low rim, to keep the things from falling off, and coated with red lacquer, cracking here and there. It was small too, as became a tray having to hold a single dish and one slab of bread. For the little I ate I crammed into my mouth with my hands, and the bottles I drank from the bottle were brought to me separately, in a basket. But this basket made no impression on me, good or bad, and I could not tell you what it was like. And many a time, having strayed for one reason or another from the place where the meal had been brought to me, I couldn't find it again, when I felt the desire to eat. Then I searched high and low, often with success, being fairly familiar with the places where it was likely to have been, but often too in vain. Or I did not search at all, preferring hunger and thirst to the trouble of having to search without being sure of finding, or of having to ask for another tray to be brought, and another basket, or the same, to the place where I was. It was then I regretted my sucking-stone. And when I talk of preferring, for example, or regretting, it must not be supposed that I opted for the least evil, and adopted it, for that would be wrong. But not knowing exactly what I was doing or avoiding, I did it and avoided it all unsuspecting that one day, much later, I would have to go back over all these acts and omissions, dimmed and mellowed by age, and drag them into the eudemonistic slop. But I must say that with Lousse my health got no worse, or scarcely. By which I mean that what was already wrong with me got worse and worse, little by little, as was only to be expected. But there was kindled no new seat of suffering or infection, except of course those arising from the spread of existing plethoras and deficiencies. But I may very well be wrong. For of the disorders to come, as for example the loss of the toes of my left foot, no, I am wrong, my right foot, who can say exactly when on my helpless clay the fatal seeds were sown. So all I can say, and I do my best to say no more, is that during my stay with Lousse no more new symptoms appeared, of a pathological nature, I mean nothing new or strange, nothing I could not have foreseen if I could have, nothing at all comparable to the sudden loss of half my toes. For that is something I could never have foreseen and the meaning of which I have never fathomed, I mean its connection with my other discomforts, from my ignorance of medical matters, I suppose. For all things run together, in the body's long madness, I feel it. But it is useless to drag out this chapter of my, how shall I say, my existence, for it has no sense, to my mind. It is a dug at which I tug in vain, it yields nothing but wind and spatter. So I will confine myself to the following brief additional remarks, and the first of which is this, that Lousse was a woman of an extraordinary flatness, physically speaking of course, to such a point that I am still wondering this evening, in the comparative silence of my last abode, if she was not a man rather or at least an androgyne. She had a somewhat hairy face, or am I imagining it, in the interests of the narrative? The poor woman, I saw her so little, so little looked at her. And was not her voice suspiciously deep? So she appears to me today. Don't be tormenting yourself, Molloy, man or woman, what does it matter? But I cannot help asking myself the following question. Could a woman have stopped me as I swept towards mother? Probably. Better still, was such an encounter possible, I mean between me and a woman? Now men, I have rubbed up against a few men in my time, but women? Oh well, I may as well confess it now, yes, I once rubbed up against one. I don't mean my mother, I did more than rub up against her. And if you don't mind we'll leave my mother out of all this. But another who might have been my mother, and even I think my grandmother, if chance had not willed otherwise. Listen to him now talking about chance. It was she made me acquainted with love. She went by the peaceful name of Ruth I think, but I can't say for certain. Perhaps the name was Edith. She had a hole between her legs, oh not the bunghole I had always imagined, but a slit, and in this I put, or rather she put, my so-called virile member, not without difficulty, and I toiled and moiled until I discharged or gave up trying or was begged by her to stop. A mug's game in my opinion and tiring on top of that, in the long run. But I lent myself to it with a good enough grace, knowing it was love, for she had told me so. She bent over the couch, because of her rheumatism, and in I went from behind. It was the only position she could bear, because of her lumbago. It seemed all right to me, for I had seen dogs, and I was astonished when she confided that you could go about it differently. I wonder what she meant exactly. Perhaps after all she put me in her rectum. A matter of complete indifference to me, I needn't tell you. But is it true love, in the rectum? That's what bothers me sometimes. Have I never known true love, after all? She too was an eminently flat woman and she moved with short stiff steps, leaning on an ebony stick. Perhaps she too was a man, yet another of them. But in that case surely our testicles would have collided, while we writhed. Perhaps she held hers tight in her hand, on purpose to avoid it. She favoured voluminous tempestuous shifts and petticoats and other undergarments whose names I forget. They welled up all frothing and swishing and then, congress achieved, broke over us in slow cascades. And all I could see was her taut yellow nape which every now and then I set my teeth in, forgetting I had none, such is the power of instinct. We met in a rubbish dump, unlike any other, and yet they are all alike, rubbish dumps. I don't know what she was doing there. I was limply poking about in the garbage saying probably, for at that age I must still have been capable of general ideas, This is life. She had no time to lose, I had nothing to lose, I would have made love with a goat, to know what love was. She had a dainty flat, no, not dainty, it made you want to lie down in a corner and never get up again. I liked it. It was full of dainty furniture, under our desperate strokes the couch moved forward on its castors, the whole place fell about our ears, it was pandemonium. Our commerce was not without tenderness, with trembling hands she cut my toe-nails and I rubbed her rump with winter cream. This idyll was of short duration. Poor Edith, I hastened her end perhaps. Anyway it was she who started it, in the rubbish dump, when she laid her hand upon my fly. More precisely, I was bent double over a heap of muck, in the hope of finding something to disgust me for ever with eating, when she, undertaking me from behind, thrust her stick between my legs and began to titillate my privates. She gave me money after each session, to me who would have consented to know love, and probe it to the bottom, without charge. But she was an idealist. I would have preferred it seems to me an orifice less arid and roomy, that would have given me a higher opinion of love it seems to me. However. Twixt finger and thumb 'tis heaven in comparison. But love is no doubt above such base contingencies. And not when you are comfortable, but when your frantic member casts about for a rubbing-place, and the unction of a little mucous membrane, and meeting with none does not beat a retreat, but retains its tumefaction, it is then no doubt that true love comes to pass, and wings away, high above the tight fit and the loose. And when you add a little pedicure and massage, having nothing to do with the instant of bliss strictly speaking, then I feel no further doubt is justified, in this connection. The other thing that bothers me, in this connection, is the indifference with which I learnt of her death, one black night I was crawling towards her, an indifference softened indeed by the pain of losing a source of revenue. She died taking a warm tub, as her custom was before receiving me. It limbered her up. When I think she might have expired in my arms! The tub overturned and the dirty water split all over the floor and down on top of the lodger below, who gave the alarm. Well, well, I didn't think I knew this story so well. She must have been a woman after all, if she hadn't been it would have got around, in the neighbourhood. It is true they were extraordinarily reserved, in my part of the world, about everything connected with sexual matters. But things have perhaps changed since my time. And it is quite possible that the fact of having found a man when they should have found a woman was immediately repressed and forgotten, by the few unfortunate enough to know about it. As it is quite possible that everybody knew about it, and spoke about it, with the sole exception of myself. But there is one thing that torments me, when I delve into all this, and that is to know whether all my life has been devoid of love or whether I really met with it, in Ruth. What I do know for certain is that I never sought to repeat the experience, having I suppose the intuition that it had been unique and perfect, of its kind, achieved and inimitable, and that it behoved me to preserve its memory, pure of all pastiche, in my heart, even if it meant my resorting from time to time to the alleged joys of so-called self-abuse. Don't talk to me about the chambermaid, I should never have mentioned her, she was long before, I was sick, perhaps there was no chambermaid, ever, in my life. Molloy, or life without a chambermaid. All of which goes to demonstrate that the fact of having met Lousse and even frequented her, in a way, proved nothing as to her sex. And I am quite willing to go on thinking of her as an old woman, widowed and withered, and of Ruth as another, for she too used to speak of her defunct husband and of his inability to satisfy her legitimate cravings. And there are days, like this evening, when my memory confuses them and I am tempted to think of them as one and the same old hag, flattened and crazed by life. And God forgive me, to tell you the horrible truth, my mother's image sometimes mingles with theirs, which is literally unendurable, like being crucified, I don't know why and I don't want to. But I left Lousse at last, one warm airless night, without saying goodbye,

as I might at least have done, and without her trying to hold me
back, except perhaps by spells. But she must have seen me go,
get up, take my crutches and go away, springing on them
through the air. And she must have seen the wicket close behind
me, for it closed by itself, with the help of a spring, and known
me gone, for ever. For she knew the way I had of going to the
wicket and peeping out, then quickly drawing back. And she did
not try and hold me back but she went and sat down on her
dog's grave, perhaps, which was mine too in a way, and which
by the way she had not sown with grass, as I had thought, but
with all kinds of little many-coloured flowers and herbaceous
plants, selected I imagine in such a way that when some went
out others lit up. I left her my bicycle which I had taken a dislike
to, suspecting it to be the vehicle of some malignant agency and
perhaps the cause of my recent misfortunes. But all the same I
would have taken it with me if I had known where it was and
that it was in running order. But I did not. And I was afraid, if
I tried to find out, of wearing out the small voice saying, Get out
of here, Molloy, take your crutches and get out of here, and
which I had taken so long to understand, for I had been hearing
it for a long time. And perhaps I understood it all wrong, but I
understood it and that was the novelty. And it seemed to me I
was not necessarily going for good and that I might come back
one day, by devious winding ways, to the place I was leaving.
And perhaps my course is not yet fully run. Outside in the road
the wind was blowing, it was another world. Not knowing where
I was nor consequently what way I ought to go I went with the
wind. And when, well slung between my crutches, I took off,
then I felt it helping me, that little wind blowing from what
quarter I could not tell. And don't come talking at me of the
stars, they look all the same to me, yes, I cannot read the stars,
in spite of my astronomical studies. But I entered the first
shelter I came to and stayed there till dawn, for I knew I was
bound to be stopped by the first policeman and asked what I
was doing, a question to which I have never been able to find
the correct reply. But it cannot have been a real shelter and I did

not stay till dawn, for a man came in soon after me and drove
me out. And yet there was room for two. I think he was a kind
of nightwatchman, a man of some kind certainly, he must have
been employed to watch over some kind of public works,
digging I suppose. I see a brazier. There must have been a touch
of autumn in the air, as the saying is. I therefore moved on and
ensconced myself on a flight of stairs, in a mean lodging-house,
because there was no door or it didn't shut, I don't know. Long
before dawn this lodging-house began to empty. People came
down the stairs, men and women. I glued myself against the
wall. They paid no heed to me, nobody interfered with me. In
the end I too went away, when I deemed it prudent, and
wandered about the town in search of a familiar monument, so
that I might say, I am in my town, after all, I have been there all
the time. The town was waking, doors opening and shutting,
soon the noise would be deafening. But espying a narrow alley
between two high buildings I looked about me, then slipped
into it. Little windows overlooked it, on either side, on every
floor, facing one another. Lavatory lights I suppose. There are
things from time to time, in spite of everything, that impose
themselves on the understanding with the force of axioms, for
unknown reasons. There was no way out of the alley, it was not
so much an alley as a blind alley. At the end there were two
recesses, no, that's not the word, opposite each other, littered
with miscellaneous rubbish and with excrements, of dogs and
masters, some dry and odourless, others still moist. Ah those
papers never to be read again, perhaps never read. Here lovers
must have lain at night and exchanged their vows. I entered one
of the alcoves, wrong again, and leaned against the wall. I would
have preferred to lie down and there was no proof that I would
not. But for the moment I was content to lean against the wall,
my feet far from the wall, on the verge of slipping, but I had
other props, the tips of my crutches. But a few minutes later I
crossed the alley into the other chapel, that's the word, where I
felt I might feel better, and settled myself in the same
hypotenusal posture. And at first I did actually seem to feel a

little better, but little by little I acquired the conviction that such was not the case. A fine rain was falling and I took off my hat to give my skull the benefit of it, my skull all cracked and furrowed and on fire, on fire. But I also took it off because it was digging into my neck, because of the thrust of the wall. So I had two good reasons for taking it off and they were none too many, neither alone would ever have prevailed I feel. I threw it from me with a careless lavish gesture and back it came, at the end of its string or lace, and after a few throes came to rest against my side. At last I began to think, that is to say to listen harder. Little chance of my being found there, I was in peace for as long as I could endure peace. For the space of an instant I considered settling down there, making it my lair and sanctuary, for the space of an instant. I took the vegetable knife from my pocket and set about opening my wrist. But pain soon got the better of me. First I cried out, then I gave up, closed the knife and put it back in my pocket. I wasn't particularly disappointed, in my heart of hearts I had not hoped for anything better. So much for that. And backsliding has always depressed me, but life seems made up of backsliding, and death itself must be a kind of back-sliding, I wouldn't be surprised. Did I say the wind had fallen? A fine rain falling, somehow that seems to exclude all idea of wind. My knees are enormous, I have just caught a glimpse of them, when I got up for a second. My two legs are as stiff as a life-sentence and yet I sometimes get up. What can you expect? Thus from time to time I shall recall my present existence compared to which this is a nursery tale. But only from time to time, so that it may be said, if necessary, whenever necessary, Is it possible that thing is still alive? Or again, Oh it's only a diary, it'll soon be over. That my knees are enormous, that I still get up from time to time, these are things that do not seem at first sight to signify anything in particular. I record them all the more willingly. In the end I left the impasse, where half-standing half-lying I may have had a little sleep, my little morning sleep, and I set off, believe it or not, towards the sun, why not, the wind having fallen. Or rather towards the least gloomy quarter of the heavens which a vast cloud was shrouding from the zenith to the skylines. It was from this cloud the above rain was falling. See how all things hang together. And as to making up my mind which quarter of the heavens was the least gloomy, it was no easy matter. For at first sight the heavens seemed uniformly gloomy. But by taking a little pains, for there were moments in my life when I took a little pains, I obtained a result, that is to say I came to a decision, in this matter. So I was able to continue on my way, saying, I am going towards the sun, that is to say in theory towards the East, or perhaps the South-East, for I am no longer with Lousse, but out in the heart again of the pre-established harmony, which makes so sweet a music, which is so sweet a music, for one who has an ear for music. People were hastening angrily to and fro, most of them, some in the shelter of the umbrella, others in that perhaps a little less effective of the rainproof coat. A few had taken refuge under trees and archways. And among those who, more courageous or less delicate, came and went, and among those who had stopped, to avoid getting wet, many a one must have said, They are right, I am wrong, meaning by they the category to which he did not belong, or so I imagine. As many a one too must have said, I am right, they are wrong, while continuing to storm against the foul weather that was the occasion of his superiority. But at the sight of a young old man of wretched aspect, shivering all alone in a narrow doorway, I suddenly remembered the project conceived the day of my encounter with Lousse and her dog and which this encounter had prevented me from carrying out. So I went and stood beside him, with the air, I hoped, of one who says, Here's a clever fellow, let me follow his example. But before I should make my little speech, which I wished to seem spontaneous and so did not make at once, he went out into the rain and away. For this speech was one liable, in virtue of its content, if not to offend at least to astonish. And that was why it was important to deliver it at the right moment and in the right tone. I apologize for these details, in a moment we'll go faster, much faster. And then perhaps relapse again into a wealth of filthy circumstance. But which in its turn again will give way to vast frescoes, dashed off with loathing. Homo mensura can't do without staffage. There I am then in my turn alone, in the doorway. I could not hope for anyone to come and stand beside me, and yet it was a possibility I did not exclude. That's a fairly good caricature of my state of mind at that instant. Net result, I stayed where I was. I had stolen from Lousse a little silver, oh nothing much, massive teaspoons for the most part, and other small objects whose utility I did not grasp but which seemed as if they might have some value. Among these latter there was one which haunts me still, from time to time. It consisted of two crosses joined, at their points of intersection, by a bar, and resembled a tiny sawing-horse, with this difference however, that the crosses of the true sawing-horse are not perfect crosses, but truncated at the top, whereas the crosses of the little object I am referring to were perfect, that is to say composed each of two identical V's, one upper with its opening above, like all V's for that matter, and the other lower with its opening below, or more precisely of four rigorously identical V's, the two I have just named and then two more, one on the right hand, the other on the left, having their openings on the right and the left respectively. But perhaps it is out of place to speak here of right and left, of upper and lower. For this little object did not seem to have any base properly so-called, but stood with equal stability on any one of its four bases, and without any change of appearance, which is not true of the sawing-horse. This strange instrument I think I still have some-where, for I could never bring myself to sell it, even in my worst need, for I could never understand what possible purpose it could serve, nor even contrive the faintest hypothesis on the subject. And from time to time I took it from my pocket and gazed upon it, with an astonished and affectionate gaze, if I had not been incapable of affection. But for a certain time I think it inspired me with a kind of veneration, for there was no doubt in my mind that it was not an object of virtu, but that it had a most specific function always to be hidden from me. I could therefore puzzle over it endlessly without the least risk. For to know nothing is nothing, not to want to know anything likewise, but to be beyond knowing anything, to know you are beyond knowing anything, that is when peace enters in, to the soul of the incurious seeker. It is then the true division begins, of twenty-two by seven for example, and the pages fill with the true ciphers at last. But I would rather not affirm anything on this subject. What does seem undeniable to me on the contrary is this, that giving in to the evidence, to a very strong probability rather, I left the shelter of the doorway and began levering myself forward, swinging slowly through the sullen air. There is rapture, or there should be, in the motion crutches give. It is a series of little flights, skimming the ground. You take off, you land, through the thronging sound in wind and limb, who have to fasten one foot to the ground before they dare lift up the other. And even their most joyous hastening is less aerial than my hobble. But these are reasonings, based on analysis. And though my mind was still taken up with my mother, and with the desire to know if I was near her, it was gradually less so, perhaps because of the silver in my pockets, but I think not, and then too because these were ancient cares and the mind cannot always brood on the same cares, but needs fresh cares from time to time, so as to revert with renewed vigour, when the time comes, to ancient cares. But can one speak here of fresh and ancient cares? I think not. But it would be hard for me to prove it. What I can assert, without fear of—without fear, is that I gradually lost interest in knowing, among other things, what town I was in and if I should soon find my mother and settle the matter between us. And even the nature of that matter grew dim, for me, without however vanishing completely. For it was no small matter and I was bent on it. All my life, I think, I had been bent on it. Yes, so far as I was capable of being bent on anything all a lifetime long, and what a lifetime, I had been bent on settling this matter between my mother and me, but had never succeeded. And while saying to myself that time was running out, and that soon it would be too late, was perhaps too

late already, to settle the matter in question, I felt myself drifting towards other cares, other phantoms. And far more than to
know what town I was in, my haste was now to leave it, even
were it the right one, where my mother had waited so long and
perhaps was waiting still. And it seemed to me that if I kept on
in a straight line I was bound to leave it, sooner or later. So I set
myself to this as best I could, making allowance for the drift to
the right of the feeble light that was my guide. And my pertinacity was such that I did indeed come to the ramparts as night
was falling, having described a good quarter of a circle, through
bad navigation. It is true I stopped many times, to rest, but not
for long, for I felt harried, wrongly perhaps. But in the country
there is another justice, other judges, at first. And having cleared
the ramparts I had to confess the sky was clearing, prior to its
winding in the other shroud, night. Yes, the great cloud was
ravelling, discovering here and there a pale and dying sky, and
the sun, already down, was manifest in the livid tongues of fire
darting towards the zenith, falling and darting again, ever more
pale and languid, and doomed no sooner lit to be extinguished.
This phenomenon, if I remember rightly, was characteristic of
my region. Things are perhaps different today. Though I fail to
see, never having left my region, what right I have to speak of its
characteristics. No, I never escaped, and even the limits of my
region were unknown to me. But I felt they were far away. But
this feeling was based on nothing serious, it was a simple
feeling. For if my region had ended no further than my feet
could carry me, surely I would have felt it changing slowly. For
regions do not suddenly end, as far as I know, but gradually
merge into one another. And I never noticed anything of the
kind, but however far I went, and in no matter what direction,
it was always the same sky, always the same earth, precisely, day
after day and night after night. On the other hand, if it is true
that regions gradually merge into one another, and this remains
to be proved, then I may well have left mine many times, thinking I was still within it. But I preferred to abide by my simple
feeling and its voice that said, Molloy, your region is vast, you

have never left it and you never shall. And wheresoever you wander, within its distant limits, things will always be the same, precisely. It would thus appear, if this is so, that my movements owed nothing to the places they caused to vanish, but were due to something else, to the buckled wheel that carried me, in unforeseeable jerks, from fatigue to rest, and inversely, for example. But now I do not wander any more, anywhere any more, and indeed I scarcely stir at all, and yet nothing is changed. And the confines of my room, of my bed, of my body, are as remote from me as were those of my region, in the days of my splendour. And the cycle continues, joltingly, of flight and bivouac, in an Egypt without bounds, without infant, without mother. And when I see my hands, on the sheet, which they love to floccillate already, they are not mine, less than ever mine, I have no arms, they are a couple, they play with the sheet, love-play perhaps, trying to get up perhaps, one on top of the other. But it doesn't last, I bring them back, little by little, towards me, it's resting time. And with my feet it's the same, sometimes, when I see them at the foot of the bed, one with toes, the other without. And that is more deserving of mention. For my legs, corresponding here to my arms of a moment ago, are both stiff now and very sore, and I shouldn't be able to forget them as I can my arms, which are more or less sound and well. And yet I do forget them and I watch the couple as they watch each other, a great way off. But my feet are not like my hands, I do not bring them back to me, when they become my feet again, for I cannot, but they stay there, far from me, but not so far as before. End of the recall. But you'd think that once well clear of the town, and having turned round to look at it, what there was to see of it, you'd think that then I should have realized whether it was really my town or not. But no, I looked at it in vain, and perhaps unquestioningly, and simply to give the gods a chance, by turning round. Perhaps I only made a show of looking at it. I didn't feel I missed my bicycle, no, not really, I didn't mind going on my way the way I said, swinging low in the dark over the earth, along the little empty country roads. And I said there was little likelihood of my being molested and that it was more likely I should molest them, if they saw me. Morning is the time to hide. They wake up, hale and hearty, their tongues hanging out for order, beauty and justice, baying for their due. Yes, from eight or nine till noon is the dangerous time. But towards noon things quiet down, the most implacable are sated, they go home, it might have been better but they've done a good job, there have been a few survivors but they'll give no more trouble, each man counts his rats. It may begin again in the early afternoon, after the banquet, the celebrations, the congratulations, the orations, but it's nothing compared to the morning, mere fun. Coming up to four or five of course there is the night-shift, the watchmen, beginning to bestir themselves. But already the day is over, the shadows lengthen, the walls multiply, you hug the walls, bowed down like a good boy, oozing with obsequiousness, having nothing to hide, hiding from mere terror, looking neither right nor left, hiding but not provocatively, ready to come out, to smile, to listen, to crawl, nauseating but not pestilent, less rat than toad. Then the true night, perilous too but sweet to him who knows it, who can open to it like the flower to the sun, who himself is night, day and night. No, there is not much to be said for the night either, but compared to the day there is much to be said for it, and notably compared to the morning there is everything to be said for it. For the night purge is in the hands of technicians, for the most part. They do nothing else, the bulk of the population have no part in it, preferring their warm beds, all things considered. Day is the time for lynching, for sleep is sacred, and especially the morning, between breakfast and lunch. My first care then, after a few miles in the desert dawn, was to look for a place to sleep, for sleep too is a kind of protection, strange as it may seem. For sleep, if it excites the lust to capture, seems to appease the lust to kill, there and then and bloodily, any hunter will tell you that. For the monster on the move, or on the watch, lurking in his lair, there is no mercy, whereas he taken unawares, in his sleep, may sometimes get the benefit of milder feelings, which deflect the barrel, sheathe

the kris. For the hunter is weak at heart and sentimental, overflowing with repressed treasures of gentleness and compassion. And it is thanks to this sweet sleep of terror or exhaustion that many a foul beast, and worthy of extermination, can live on till he dies in the peace and quiet of our zoological gardens, broken only by the innocent laughter, the knowing laughter, of children and their elders, on Sundays and Bank Holidays. And I for my part have always preferred slavery to death, I mean being put to death. For death is a condition I have never been able to conceive to my satisfaction and which therefore cannot go down in the ledger of weal and woe. Whereas my notions on being put to death inspired me with confidence, rightly or wrongly, and I felt I was entitled to act on them, in certain emergencies. Oh they weren't notions like yours, they were notions like mine, all spasm, sweat and trembling, without an atom of common sense or lucidity. But they were the best I had. Yes, the confusion of my ideas on the subject of death was such that I sometimes wondered, believe me or not, if it wasn't a state of being even worse than life. So I found it natural not to rush into it and, when I forgot myself to the point of trying, to stop in time. It's my only excuse. So I crawled into some hole somewhere I suppose and waited, half sleeping, half sighing, groaning and laughing, or feeling my body, to see if anything had changed, for the morning frenzy to abate. Then I resumed my spirals. And as to saying what became of me, and where I went, in the months and perhaps the years that followed, no. For I weary of these inventions and others beckon to me. But in order to blacken a few more pages may I say I spent some time at the seaside, without incident. There are people the sea doesn't suit, who prefer the mountains or the plain. Personally I feel no worse there than anywhere else. Much of my life has ebbed away before this shivering expanse, to the sound of the waves in storm and calm, and the claws of the surf. Before, no, more than before, one with, spread on the sand, or in a cave. In the sand I was in my element, letting it trickle between my fingers, scooping holes that I filled in a moment later or that filled themselves in, flinging it in the air by handfuls, rolling in it. And in the cave, lit by the beacons at night, I knew what to do in order to be no worse off than elsewhere. And that my land went no further, in one direction at least, did not displease me. And to feel there was one direction at least in which I could go no further, without first getting wet, then drowned, was a blessing. For I have always said, First learn to walk, then you can take swimming lessons. But don't imagine my region ended at the coast, that would be a grave mistake. For it was this sea too, its reefs and distant islands, and its hidden depths. And I too once went forth on it, in a sort of oarless skiff, but I paddled with an old bit of driftwood. And I sometimes wonder if I ever came back, from that voyage. For if I see myself putting to sea, and the long hours without landfall, I do not see the return, the tossing on the breakers, and I do not hear the frail keel grating on the shore. I took advantage of being at the seaside to lay in a store of sucking-stones. They were pebbles but I call them stones. Yes, on this occasion I laid in a considerable store. I distributed them equally between my four pockets, and sucked them turn and turn about. This raised a problem which I first solved in the following way. I had say sixteen stones, four in each of my four pockets, these being the two pockets of my trousers and the two pockets of my greatcoat. Taking a stone from the right pocket of my greatcoat, and putting it in my mouth, I replaced it in the right pocket of my greatcoat by a stone from the right pocket of my trousers, which I replaced by a stone from the left pocket of my trousers, which I replaced by a stone from the left pocket of my greatcoat, which I replaced by the stone which was in my mouth, as soon as I had finished sucking it. Thus there were still four stones in each of my four pockets, but not quite the same stones. And when the desire to suck took hold of me again, I drew again on the right pocket of my greatcoat, certain of not taking the same stone as the last time. And while I sucked it I rearranged the other stones in the way I have just described. And so on. But this solution did not satisfy me fully. For it did not escape me that, by an extraordinary hazard, the four stones circulating thus might always be the same four. In which case, far from sucking the sixteen stones turn and turn about, I was really only sucking four, always the same, turn and turn about. But I shuffled them well in my pockets, before I began to suck, and again, while I sucked, before transferring them, in the hope of obtaining a more general circulation of the stones from pocket to pocket. But this was only a makeshift that could not long content a man like me. So I began to look for something else. And the first thing I hit upon was that I might do better to transfer the stones four by four, instead of one by one, that is to say, during the sucking, to take the three stones remaining in the right pocket of my greatcoat and replace them by the four in the right pocket of my trousers, and these by the four in the left pocket of my trousers, and these by the four in the left pocket of my greatcoat, and finally these by the three from the right pocket of my greatcoat, plus the one, as soon as I had finished sucking it, which was in my mouth. Yes, it seemed to me at first that by so doing I would arrive at a better result. But on further reflection I had to change my mind and confess that the circulation of the stones four by four came to exactly the same thing as their circulation one by one. For if I was certain of finding each time, in the right pocket of my greatcoat, four stones totally different from their immediate predecessors, the possibility nevertheless remained of my always chancing on the same stone, within each group of four, and consequently of my sucking, not the sixteen turn and turn about as I wished, but in fact four only, always the same, turn and turn about. So I had to seek elsewhere than in the mode of circulation. For no matter how I caused the stones to circulate, I always ran the same risk. It was obvious that by increasing the number of my pockets I was bound to increase my chances of enjoying my stones in the way I planned, that is to say one after the other until their number was exhausted. Had I had eight pockets, for example, instead of the four I did have, then even the most diabolical hazard could not have prevented me from sucking at least eight of my sixteen stones, turn and turn about. The truth is I should have needed sixteen pockets in order to be quite easy in my mind. And for a long time I could see no other conclusion than this, that short of having sixteen pockets, each with its stone, I could never reach the goal I had set myself, short of an extraordinary hazard. And if at a pinch I could double the number of my pockets, were it only by dividing each pocket in two, with the help of a few safety-pins let us say, to quadruple them seemed to be more than I could manage. And I did not feel inclined to take all that trouble for a half-measure. For I was beginning to lose all sense of measure, after all this wrestling and wrangling, and to say, All or nothing. And if I was tempted for an instant to establish a more equitable proportion between my stones and my pockets, by reducing the former to the number of the latter, it was only for an instant. For it would have been an admission of defeat. And sitting on the shore, before the sea, the sixteen stones spread out before my eyes, I gazed at them in anger and perplexity. For just as I had difficulty in sitting on a chair, or in an arm-chair, because of my stiff leg you understand, so I had none in sitting on the ground, because of my stiff leg and my stiffening leg, for it was about this time that my good leg, good in the sense that it was not stiff, began to stiffen. I needed a prop under the ham you understand, and even under the whole length of the leg, the prop of the earth. And while I gazed thus at my stones, revolving interminable martingales all equally defective, and crushing handfuls of sand, so that the sand ran through my fingers and fell back on the strand, yes, while thus I lulled my mind and part of my body, one day suddenly it dawned on the former, dimly, that I might perhaps achieve my purpose without increasing the number of my pockets, or reducing the number of my stones, but simply by sacrificing the principle of trim. The meaning of this illumination, which suddenly began to sing within me, like a verse of Isaiah, or of Jeremiah, I did not penetrate at once, and notably the word trim, which I had never met with, in this sense, long remained obscure. Finally I seemed to grasp that this word trim could not here mean anything else, anything better, than the distribution of the sixteen stones in four groups of four, one group in each pocket, and that it was my refusal to consider any distribution other than this that had vitiated my calculations until then and rendered the problem literally insoluble. And it was on the basis of this interpretation, whether right or wrong, that I finally reached a solution, inelegant assuredly, but sound, sound. Now I am willing to believe, indeed I firmly believe, that other solutions to this problem might have been found, and indeed may still be found, no less sound, but much more elegant, than the one I shall now describe, if I can. And I believe too that had I been a little more insistent, a little more resistant, I could have found them myself. But I was tired, but I was tired, and I contented myself ingloriously with the first solution that was a solution, to this problem. But not to go over the heart-breaking stages through which I passed before I came to it, here it is, in all its hideousness. All (all!) that was necessary was to put for example, to begin with, six stones in the right pocket of my greatcoat, or supply-pocket, five in the right pocket of my trousers, and five in the left pocket of my trousers, that makes the lot, twice five ten plus six sixteen, and none, for none remained, in the left pocket of my greatcoat, which for the time being remained empty, empty of stones that is, for its usual contents remained, as well as occasional objects. For where do you think I hid my vegetable knife, my silver, my horn and the other things that I have not yet named, perhaps shall never name. Good. Now I can begin to suck. Watch me closely. I take a stone from the right pocket of my greatcoat, suck it, stop sucking it, put it in the left pocket of my greatcoat, the one empty (of stones). I take a second stone from the right pocket of my greatcoat, suck it, put it in the left pocket of my greatcoat. And so on until the right pocket of my greatcoat is empty (apart from its usual and casual contents) and the six stones I have just sucked, one after the other, are all in the left pocket of my greatcoat. Pausing then, and concentrating, so as not to make a balls of it, I transfer to the right pocket of my greatcoat, in which there are no stones left, the five stones in the right pocket of my trousers, which I replace by the five stones in the left pocket of my trousers, which I replace by the six stones in the left pocket of my greatcoat. At this stage then the left pocket of my great-coat is again empty of stones, while the right pocket of my great-coat is again supplied, and in the right way, that is to say with other stones than those I have just sucked. These other stones I then begin to suck, one after the other, and to transfer as I go along to the left pocket of my greatcoat, being absolutely certain, as far as one can be in an affair of this kind, that I am not sucking the same stones as a moment before, but others. And when the right pocket of my greatcoat is again empty (of stones), and the five I have just sucked are all without exception in the left pocket of my greatcoat, then I proceed to the same redistribution as a moment before, or a similar redistribution, that is to say I transfer to the right pocket of my greatcoat, now again available, the five stones in the right pocket of my trousers, which I replace by the six stones in the left pocket of my trousers, which I replace by the five stones in the left pocket of my greatcoat. And there I am ready to begin again. Do I have to go on? No, for it is clear that after the next series, of sucks and transfers, I shall be back where I started, that is to say with the first six stones back in the supply-pocket, the next five in the right pocket of my stinking old trousers and finally the last five in left pocket of same, and my sixteen stones will have been sucked once at least in impeccable succession, not one sucked twice, not one left unsucked. It is true that the next time I could scarcely hope to suck my stones in the same order as the first time and that the first, seventh and twelfth for example of the first cycle might very well be the sixth, eleventh and sixteenth respectively of the second, if the worst came to the worst. But that was a drawback I could not avoid. And if in the cycles taken together utter confusion was bound to reign, at least within each cycle taken separately I could be easy in my mind, at least as easy as one can be, in a proceeding of this kind. For in order for each cycle to be identical, as to the succession of stones in my mouth, and God knows I had set my heart on it, the only means were numbered stones or sixteen pockets. And rather than make twelve more pockets or number my stones, I preferred to make the best of the comparative peace of mind I enjoyed within each cycle taken separately. For it was not enough to number the stones, but I would have had to remember, every time I put a stone in my mouth, the number I needed and look for it in my pocket. Which would have put me off stone for ever, in a very short time. For I would never have been sure of not making a mistake, unless of course I had kept a kind of register, in which to tick off the stones one by one, as I sucked them. And of this I believed myself incapable. No, the only perfect solution would have been the sixteen pockets, symmetrically disposed, each one with its stone. Then I would have needed neither to number nor to think, but merely, as I sucked a given stone, to move on the fifteen others, each to the next pocket, a delicate business admittedly, but within my power, and to call always on the same pocket when I felt like a suck. This would have freed me from all anxiety, not only within each cycle taken separately, but also for the sum of all cycles, though they went on forever. But however imperfect my own solution was, I was pleased at having found it all alone, yes, quite pleased. And if it was perhaps less sound than I had thought in the first flush of discovery, its inelegance never diminished. And it was above all inelegant in this, to my mind, that the uneven distribution was painful to me, bodily. It is true that a kind of equilibrium was reached, at a given moment, in the early stages of each cycle, namely after the third suck and before the fourth, but it did not last long, and the rest of the time I felt the weight of the stones dragging me now to one side, now to the other. So it was something more than a principle I abandoned, when I abandoned the equal distribution, it was a bodily need. But to suck the stones in the way I have described, not haphazard, but with method, was also I think a bodily need. Here then were two incompatible bodily needs, at loggerheads. Such things happen. But deep down I didn't give a tinker's curse about being off my balance, dragged to the right hand and the left, backwards and forwards. And deep down it was all the same to me whether I sucked a different stone each time or always the same stone, until the end of time. For they all tasted exactly the same. And if I had collected sixteen, it was not in order to ballast myself in such and such a way, or to suck them turn about, but simply to have a little store, so as never to be without. But deep down I didn't give a fiddler's curse about being without, when they were all gone they would be all gone, I wouldn't be any the worse off, or hardly any. And the solution to which I rallied in the end was to throw away all the stones but one, which I kept now in one pocket, now in another, and which of course I soon lost, or threw away, or gave away, or swallowed. It was a wild part of the coast. I don't remember having been seriously molested. The black speck I was, in the great pale stretch of sand, who could wish it harm? Some came near, to see what it was, whether it wasn't something of value from a wreck, washed up by the storm. But when they saw the jetsam was alive, decently if wretchedly clothed, they turned away. Old women and young ones, yes, too, come to gather wood, came and stared, in the early days. But they were always the same and it was in vain I moved from one place to another, in the end they all knew what I was and kept their distance. I think one of them one day, detaching herself from her companions, came and offered me something to eat and that I looked at her in silence, until she went away. Yes, it seems to me some such incident occurred about this time. But perhaps I am thinking of another stay, at an earlier time, for this will be my last, my last but one, or two, there is never a last, by the sea. However that may be I see a young woman coming towards me and stopping from time to time to look back at her companions. Huddled together like sheep they watch her recede, urging her on, and laughing no doubt, I seem to hear laughter, far away. Then it is her back I see, as she goes away, now it is towards me she looks back, but without stopping. But perhaps I am merging two times in one, and two women, one coming towards me, shyly, urged on by the cries and laughter of her companions, and the other going away from me, unhesitatingly. For those who came towards me I saw coming from afar, most of the time, that is one of the advantages of the seaside. Black specks in the distance I saw them coming, I could follow all their manœuvres, saying, It's getting smaller, or, It's getting bigger. Yes, to be taken unawares was so to speak impossible, for I turned often towards the land too. Let me tell you something, my sight was better at the seaside! Yes, ranging far and wide over these vast flats, where nothing lay, nothing stood, my good eye saw more clearly and there were even days when the bad one too had to look away. And not only did I see more clearly, but I had less difficulty in saddling with a name the rare things I saw. These are some of the advantages and disadvantages of the seaside. Or perhaps it was I who was changing, why not? And in the morning, in my cave, and even sometimes at night, when the storm raged, I felt reasonably secure from the elements and mankind. But there too there is a price to pay. In your box, in your caves, there too there is a price to pay. And which you pay willingly, for a time, but which you cannot go on paying forever. For you cannot go on buying the same thing forever, with your little pittance. And unfortunately there are other needs than that of rotting in peace, it's not the word, I mean of course my mother whose image, blunted for some time past, was beginning now to harrow me again. So I went back inland, for my town was not strictly speaking on the sea, whatever may have been said to the contrary. And to get to it you had to go inland, I at least knew of no other way. For between my town and the sea there was a kind of swamp which, as far back as I can remember, and some of my memories have their roots deep in the immediate past, there was always talk of draining, by means of canals I suppose, or of transforming into a vast port and docks, or into a city on piles for the workers, in a word of redeeming somehow or other. And with the same stone they would have killed the scandal, at the gates of their metropolis, of a stinking steaming swamp in which an incalculable number of human lives were yearly engulfed, the statistics escape me for the moment and doubtless always will, so

complete is my indifference to this aspect of the question. It is
true they actually began to work and that work is still going on
in certain areas in the teeth of adversity, setbacks, epidemics
and the apathy of the Public Works Department, far from me to
deny it. But from this to proclaiming that the sea came lapping
at the ramparts of my town, there was a far cry. And I for my
part will never lend myself to such a perversion (of the truth),
until such time as I am compelled or find it convenient to do so.
And I knew this swamp a little, having risked my life in it,
cautiously, on several occasions, at a period of my life richer in
illusions than the one I am trying to patch together here, I mean
richer in certain illusions, in others poorer. So there was no way
of coming at my town directly, by sea, but you had to disembark
well to the north or the south and take to the roads, just imagine
that, for they had never heard of Watt, just imagine that too.
And now my progress, slow and painful at all times, was more
so than ever, because of my short stiff leg, the same which I
thought had long been as stiff as a leg could be, but damn the
bit of it, for it was growing stiffer than ever, a thing I would not
have thought possible, and at the same time shorter every day,
but above all because of the other leg, supple hitherto and now
growing rapidly stiff in its turn but not yet shortening, unhappily. For when the two legs shorten at the same time, and at the
same speed, then all is not lost, no. But when one shortens, and
the other not, then you begin to be worried. Oh not that I was
exactly worried, but it was a nuisance, yes, a nuisance. For I
didn't know which foot to land on, when I came down. Let us
try and get this dilemma clear. Follow me carefully. The stiff leg
hurt me, admittedly, I mean the old stiff leg, and it was the other
which I normally used as a pivot, or prop. But now this latter,
as a result of its stiffening I suppose, and the ensuing commo-
tion among nerves and sinews, was beginning to hurt me even
more than the other. What a story, God send I don't make a
balls of it. For the old pain, do you follow me, I had got used to
it, in a way, yes, in a kind of way. Whereas to the new pain,
though of the same family exactly, I had not yet had time to

adjust myself. Nor should it be forgotten that having one bad leg plus another more or less good, I was able to nurse the former, and reduce its sufferings to the minimum, to the maximum, by using the former exclusively, with the help of my crutches. But I no longer had this resource! For I no longer had one bad leg plus another more or less good, but now both were equally bad. And the worse, to my mind, was that which till now had been good, at least comparatively good, and whose change for the worse I had not yet got used to. So in a way, if you like, I still had one bad leg and one good, or rather less bad, with this difference however, that the less bad now was the less good of heretofore. It was therefore on the old bad leg that I often longed to lean, between one crutchstroke and the next. For while still extremely sensitive, it was less so than the other, or it was equally so, if you like, but it did not seem so, to me, because of its seniority. But I couldn't! What? Lean on it. For it was shortening, don't forget, whereas the other, though stiffening, was not yet shortening, or so far behind its fellow that to all intents and purposes, intents and purposes, I'm lost, no matter. If I could even have bent it, at the knee, or even at the hip, I could have made it seem as short as the other, long enough to land on the true short one, before taking off again. But I couldn't. What? Bend it. For how could I bend it, when it was stiff? I was therefore compelled to work the same old leg as heretofore, in spite of its having become, at least as far as the pain was concerned, the worse of the two and the more in need of nursing. Sometimes to be sure, when I was lucky enough to chance on a road conveniently cambered, or by taking advantage of a not too deep ditch or any other breach of surface, I managed to lengthen my short leg, for a short time. But it had done no work for so long that it did not know how to go about it. And I think a pile of dishes would have better supported me than it, which had so well supported me, when I was a tiny tot. And another factor of disequilibrium was here involved, I mean when I thus made the best of the lie of the land, I mean my crutches, which would have needed to be unequal, one short and one long, if I was to remain vertical. No? I don't know. In any case the ways I went were for the most part little forest paths, that's understandable, where differences of level, though abounding, were too confused and too erratic to be of any help to me. But did it make such a difference after all, as far as the pain was concerned, whether my leg was free to rest or whether it had to work? I think not. For the suffering of the leg at rest was constant and monotonous. Whereas the leg condemned to the increase of pain inflicted by work knew the decrease of pain dispensed by work suspended, the space of an instant. But I am human, I fancy, and my progress suffered, from this state of affairs, and from the slow and painful progress it had always been, whatever may have been said to the contrary, was changed, saving your presence, to a veritable calvary, with no limit to its stations and no hope of crucifixion, though I say it myself, and no Simon, and reduced me to frequent halts. Yes, my progress reduced me to stopping more and more often, it was the only way to progress, to stop. And though it is no part of my tottering intentions to treat here in full, as they deserve, these brief moments of the immemorial expiation, I shall never-theless deal with them briefly, out of the goodness of my heart, so that my story, so clear till now, may not end in darkness, the darkness of these towering forests, these giant fronds, where I hobble, listen, fall, rise, listen and hobble on, wondering some-times, need I say, if I shall ever see again the hated light, at least unloved, stretched palely between the last boles, and my mother, to settle with her, and if I would not do better, at least just as well, to hang myself from a bough, with a liane. For frankly light meant nothing to me now, and my mother could scarcely be waiting for me still, after so long. And my leg, my legs. But the thought of suicide had little hold on me, I don't know why, I thought I did, but I see I don't. The idea of stran-gulation in particular, however tempting, I always overcame, after a short struggle. And between you and me there was never anything wrong with my respiratory tracts, apart of course from the agonies intrinsic to that system. Yes, I could count the days when I could neither breathe in the blessed air with its life-giving oxygen nor, when I had breathed it in, breathe out the bloody stuff, I could have counted them. Ah yes, my asthma, how often I was tempted to put an end to it, by cutting my throat. But I never succumbed. The noise betrayed me, I turned purple. It came on mostly at night, fortunately, or unfortunately, I could never make up my mind. For if sudden changes of colour matter less at night, the least unusual noise is then more noticeable, because of the silence of the night. But these were mere crises, and what are crises compared to all that never stops, knows neither ebb nor flow, its surface leaden above infernal depths. Not a word, not a word against the crises that seized me, wrung me, and finally threw me away, mercifully, safe from help. And I wrapped my head in my coat, to stifle the obscene noise of choking, or I disguised it as a fit of coughing, universally accepted and approved and whose only disadvantage is this, that it is liable to let you in for pity. And this is perhaps the moment to observe, better late than never, that when I speak of my progress being slowed down, consequent on the defection of my good leg, I express only an infinitesimal part of the truth. For the truth is I had other weak points, here and there, and they too were growing weaker and weaker, as was only to be expected. But what was not to be expected was the speed at which their weakness had increased, since my departure from the seaside. For as long as I had remained at the seaside my weak points, while admittedly increasing in weakness, as was only to be expected, only increased imperceptibly, in weakness I mean. So that I would have hesitated to exclaim, with my finger up my arse-hole for example, Jesus Christ, it's much worse than yesterday, I can hardly believe it is the same hole. I apologize for having to revert to this lewd orifice, 'tis my muse will have it so. Perhaps it is less to be thought of as the eyesore here called by its name than as the symbol of those passed over in silence, a distinction due perhaps to its centrality and its air of being a link between me and the other excrement. We underestimate this little hole, it seems to me, we call it the arse-hole and affect to despise it. But is it not rather the true portal of our being and the celebrated mouth no more than the kitchen door. Nothing goes in, or so little, that is not rejected on the spot, or very nearly. Almost everything revolts it that comes from without and what comes from within does not seem to receive a very warm welcome either. Are not these significant facts? Time will tell. But I shall do my utmost none the less to keep it in the background, in the future. And that will be easy, for the future is by no means uncertain, the unspeakable future. And when it comes to neglecting fundamentals, I think I have nothing to learn, and indeed I confuse them with accidentals. But to return to my weak points, let me say again that at the seaside they had developed normally, yes, I had noticed nothing abnormal. Either because I did not pay enough attention to them, absorbed as I was in the metamorphosis of my excellent leg, or because there was in fact nothing special to report, in this connection. But I had hardly left the shore, harried by the dread of waking one fine day, far from my mother, with my two legs as stiff as my crutches, when they suddenly began to gallop, my weak points did, and their weakness became literally the weakness of death, with all the disadvantages that this entails, when they are not vital points. I fix at this period the dastardly desertion of my toes, so to speak in the thick of the fray. You may object that this is covered by the business of my legs, that it has no importance, since in any case I could not put to the ground the foot in question. Quite, quite. But do you as much as know what foot we're talking about? No. Nor I. Wait till I think. But you are right, that wasn't a weak point properly speaking, I mean my toes, I thought they were in excellent fettle, apart from a few corns, bunions, ingrowing nails and a tendency to cramp. No, my true weak points were elsewhere. And if I do not draw up here and now the impressive list of them it is because I shall never draw it up. No, I shall never draw it up, yes, perhaps I shall. And then I should be sorry to give a wrong idea of my health which, if it was not exactly rude, to the extent of my bursting with it, was at bottom of an incredible robustness. For otherwise how could I have reached the enormous age I have reached. Thanks to moral qualities? Hygienic habits? Fresh air? Starvation? Lack of sleep? Solitude? Persecution? The long silent screams (dangerous to scream)? The daily longing for the earth to swallow me up? Come come. Fate is rancorous, but not to that extent. Look at Mammy. What rid me of her, in the end? I sometimes wonder. Perhaps they buried her alive, it wouldn't surprise me. Ah the old bitch, a nice dose she gave me, she and her lousy unconquerable genes. Bristling with boils ever since I was a brat, a fat lot of good that ever did me. The heart beats, and what a beat. That my ureters—no, not a word on that subject. And the capsules. And the bladder. And the urethra. And the glans. Santa Maria. I give you my word, I cannot piss, my word of honour, as a gentleman. But my prepuce, sat verbum, oozes urine, day and night, at least I think it's urine, it smells of kidney. What's all this, I thought I had lost the sense of smell. Can one speak of pissing, under these conditions? Rubbish! My sweat too, and God knows I sweat, has a queer smell. I think it's in my dribble as well, and heaven knows I dribble. How I eliminate, to be sure, uremia will never be the death of me. Me too they would bury alive, in despair, if there was any justice in the world. And this list of my weak points I shall never draw up, for fear of its finishing me, I shall perhaps, one day, when the time comes for the inventory of my goods and chattels. For that day, if it ever dawns, I shall be less afraid, of being finished, than I am today. For today, if I do not feel precisely at the beginning of my career, I have not the presumption either to think I am near the end. So I husband my strength, for the spurt. For to be unable to spurt, when the hour strikes, no, you might as well give up. But it is forbidden to give up and even to stop an instant. So I wait, jogging along, for the bell to say, Molloy, one last effort, it's the end. That's how I reason, with the help of images little suited to my situation. And I can't shake off the feeling, I don't know why, that the day will come for me to say what is left of all I had. But I must first wait, to be sure there is nothing more I can acquire, or lose, or throw away, or give away. Then I can say, without fear of error, what is left, in the end, of my possessions. For it will be the end. And between now and then I may get poorer, or richer, oh not to the extent of being any better off, or any worse off, but sufficiently to preclude me from announcing, here and now, what is left of all I had, for I have not yet had all. But I can make no sense of this presentiment, and that I understand is very often the case with the best presentiments, that you can make no sense of them. So perhaps it is a true presentiment, apt to be borne out. But can any more sense be made of false presentiments? I think so, yes, I think that all that is false may more readily be reduced, to notions clear and distinct, distinct from all other notions. But I may be wrong. But I was not given to presentiments, but to sentiments sweet and simple, to episentiments rather, if I may venture to say so. For I knew in advance, which made all presentiment superfluous. I will even go further (what can I lose?), I knew only in advance, for when the time came I knew no longer, you may have noticed it, or only when I made a superhuman effort, and when the time was past I no longer knew either, I regained my ignorance. And all that taken together, if that is possible, should serve to explain many things, and notably my astonishing old age, still green in places, assuming the state of my health, in spite of all I have said about it, is insufficient to account for it. Simple supposition, committing me to nothing. But I was saying that if my progress, at this stage, was becoming more and more slow and painful, this was not due solely to my legs, but also to innumerable so-called weak points, having nothing to do with my legs. Unless one is to suppose, gratuitously, that they and my legs were part of the same syndrome, which in that case would have been of a diabolical complexity. The fact is, and I deplore it, but it is too late now to do anything about it, that I have laid too much stress on my legs, throughout these wanderings, to the detriment of the rest. For I was no ordinary cripple, far from it, and there were days when my legs were the best part of me, with the exception of the brain capable of forming such a judgement. I was therefore obliged to stop more and more often, I shall never weary of repeating it, and to lie down, in defiance of the rules, now prone, now supine, now on one side, now on the other, and as much as possible with the feet higher than the head, to dislodge the clots. And to lie with the feet higher than the head, when your legs are stiff, is no easy matter. But don't worry, I did it. When my comfort was at stake there was no trouble I would not go to. The forest was all about me and the boughs, twining together at a prodigious height, compared to mine, sheltered me from the light and the elements. Some days I advanced no more than thirty or forty paces, I give you my oath. To say I stumbled in impenetrable darkness, no, I cannot. I stumbled, but the darkness was not impenetrable. For there reigned a kind of blue gloom, more than sufficient for my visual needs. I was aston- ished this gloom was not green, rather than blue, but I saw it blue and perhaps it was. The red of the sun, mingling with the green of the leaves, gave a blue result, that is how I reasoned. But from time to time. From time to time. What tenderness in these little words, what savagery. But from time to time I came on a kind of crossroads, you know, a star, or circus, of the kind to be found in even the most unexplored of forests. And turning then methodically to face the radiating paths in turn, hoping for I know not what, I described a complete circle, or less than a circle, or more than a circle, so great was the resemblance between them. Here the gloom was not so thick and I made haste to leave it. I don't like gloom to lighten, there's something shady about it. I had a certain number of encounters in this forest, naturally, where does one not, but nothing to signify. I notably encountered a charcoal-burner. I might have loved him, I think, if I had been seventy years younger. But it's not certain. For then he too would have been younger by as much, oh not quite as much, but much younger. I never really had much love to spare, but all the same I had my little quota, when I was small, and it went to the old men, when it could. And I even think I had time to love one or two, oh not with true love, no, nothing like the old woman, I've lost her name again, Rose, no, anyway you see who I mean, but all the same, how shall I say, tenderly, as those on the brink of a better earth. Ah I was a precocious child, and then I was a precocious man. Now they all give me the shits, the ripe, the unripe and the rotting from the bough. He was all over me, begging me to share his hut, believe it or not. A total stranger. Sick with solitude probably. I say charcoal-burner, but I really don't know. I see smoke somewhere. That's something that never escapes me, smoke. A long dialogue ensued, interspersed with groans. I could not ask him the way to my town, the name of which escaped me still. I asked him the way to the nearest town, I found the necessary words, and accents. He did not know. He was born in the forest probably and had spent his whole life there. I asked him to show me the nearest way out of the forest. I grew eloquent. His reply was exceedingly confused. Either I didn't understand a word he said, or he didn't understand a word I said, or he knew nothing, or he wanted to keep me near him. It was towards this fourth hypothesis that in all modesty I leaned, for when I made to go, he held me back by the sleeve. So I smartly freed a crutch and dealt him a good dint on the skull. That calmed him. The dirty old brute. I got up and went on. But I hadn't gone more than a few paces, and for me at this time a few paces meant something, when I turned and went back to where he lay, to examine him. Seeing he had not ceased to breathe I contented myself with giving him a few warm kicks in the ribs, with my heels. This is how I went about it. I carefully chose the most favourable position, a few paces from the body, with my back of course turned to it. Then, nicely balanced on my crutches, I began to swing, backwards, forwards, feet pressed together, or rather legs pressed together, for how could I press my feet together, with my legs in the state they were? But how could I press my legs together, in the state they were? I pressed them together, that's all I can tell you. Take it or leave it. Or I didn't press them together. What can that possibly matter? I swung, that's all that matters, in an ever-widening arc, until I decided the moment had come and launched myself forward with all my strength and consequently, a moment later, backward, which gave the desired result. Where did I get this access of vigour? From my weakness perhaps. The shock knocked me down. Naturally. I came a cropper. You can't have everything, I've often noticed it. I rested a moment, then got up, picked up my crutches, took up my position on the other side of the body and applied myself with method to the same exercise. I always had a mania for symmetry. But I must have aimed a little low and one of my heels sank in something soft. However. For if I had missed the ribs, with that heel, I had no doubt landed in the kidney, oh not hard enough to burst it, no, I fancy not. People imagine, because you are old, poor, crippled, terrified, that you can't stand up for yourself, and generally speaking that is so. But given favourable conditions, a feeble and awkward assailant, in your own class what, and a lonely place, and you have a good chance of showing what stuff you are made of. And it is doubtless in order to revive interest in this possibility, too often forgotten, that I have delayed over an incident of no interest in itself, like all that has a moral. But did I at least eat, from time to time? Perforce, perforce, roots, berries, sometimes a little mulberry, a mushroom from time to time, trembling, knowing nothing about mushrooms. What else, ah yes, carobs, so dear to goats. In a word whatever I could find, forests abound in good things. And having heard, or more probably read somewhere, in the days when I thought I would be well advised to educate myself, or amuse myself, or stupefy myself, or kill time, that when a man in a forest thinks he is going forward in a straight line, in reality he is going in a circle, I did my best to go in a circle, hoping in this way to go in a straight line. For I stopped being half-witted and became sly, whenever I took the trouble. And my head was a storehouse of useful knowledge. And if I did not go in a rigorously straight line, with my system of going in a circle, at least I did not go in a circle, and that was something. And by going on doing this, day after day, and night after night, I looked forward to getting out of the forest, some day. For my region was not all forest, far from it. But there were plains too, mountains and sea, and some towns and villages, connected by highways and byways. And I was all the more convinced that I would get out of the forest some day as I had already got out of it, more than once, and I knew how difficult it was not to do again what you have done before. But things had been rather different then. And yet I did not despair of seeing the light tremble, some day, through the still boughs, the strange light of the plain, its pale wild eddies, through the bronze-still boughs, which no breath ever stirred. But it was a day I dreaded too. So that I was sure it would come sooner or later. For it was not so bad being in the forest, I could imagine worse, and I could have stayed there till I died, unrepining, yes, without pining for the light and the plain and the other amenities of my region. For I knew them well, the amenities of my region, and I considered that the forest was no worse. And it was not only no worse, to my mind, but it was better, in this sense, that I was there. That is a strange way, is it not, of looking at things. Perhaps less strange than it seems. For being in the forest, a place neither worse nor better than the others, and being free to stay there, was it not natural I should think highly of it, not because of what it was, but because I was there. For I was there. And being there I did not have to go there, and that was not to be despised, seeing the state of my legs and my body in general. That is all I wished to say, and if I did not say it at the outset it is simply that something was against it. But I could not, stay in the forest I mean, I was not free to. That is to say I could have, physically nothing could have been easier, but I was not purely physical, I lacked something, and I would have had the feeling, if I had stayed in the forest, of going against an imperative, at least I had that impression. But perhaps I was mistaken, perhaps I would have been better advised to stay in the forest, perhaps I could have stayed there, without remorse, without the painful impression of committing a fault, almost a sin. For I have greatly sinned, at all times, greatly sinned against my prompters. And if I cannot decently be proud of this I see no reason either to be sorry. But imperatives are a little different, and I have always been inclined to submit to them, I don't know why. For they never led me anywhere, but tore me from places where, if all was not well, all was no worse than anywhere else, and then went silent, leaving me stranded. So I knew my imperatives well, and yet I submitted to them. It had become a habit. It is true they nearly all bore on the same question, that of my relations with my mother, and on the importance of bringing as soon as possible some light to bear on these and even on the kind of light that should be brought to bear and the most effective means of doing so. Yes, these imperatives were quite explicit and even detailed until, having set me in motion at last, they began to falter, then went silent, leaving me there like a fool who neither knows where he is going nor why he is going there. And they nearly all bore, as I may have said already, on the same painful and thorny question. And I do not think I could mention even one having a different purport. And the one enjoining me then to leave the forest without delay was in no way different from those I was used to, as to its meaning. For in its framing I thought I noticed something new. For after the usual blarney there followed this solemn warning, Perhaps it is already too late. It was in Latin, nimis sero, I think that's Latin. Charming things, hypothetical imperatives. But if I had never succeeded in liquidating this matter of my mother, the fault must not be imputed solely to that voice which deserted me, prematurely. It was partly to blame, that's all it can be reproached with. For the outer world opposed my succeeding too, with its wiles, I have given some examples. And even if the voice could have harried me to the very scene of action, even then I might well have succeeded no better, because of the other obstacles barring my way. And in this command which faltered, then died, it was hard not to hear the unspoken entreaty, Don't do it, Molloy. In forever reminding me thus of my duty was its purpose to show me the folly of it? Perhaps. Fortunately it did no more than stress, the better to mock if you like, an innate velleity. And of myself, all my life, I think I had been going to my mother, with the purpose of establishing our relations on a less precarious footing. And when I was with her, and I often succeeded, I left her without having done anything. And when I was no longer with her I was again on my way to her, hoping to do better the next time. And when I appeared to give up and to busy myself with something else, or with nothing at all any more, in reality I was hatching my plans and seeking the way to her house. This is taking a queer turn. So even without this so-called imperative I impugn, it would have been difficult for me to stay in the forest, since I was forced to assume my mother was not there. And yet it might have been better for me to try and stay. But I also said, Yet a little while, at the rate things are going, and I won't be able to move, but will have to stay, where I happen to be, unless someone comes and carries me. Oh I did not say it in such limpid language. And when I say I said, etc., all I mean is that I knew confusedly things were so, without knowing exactly what it was all about. And every time I say, I said this, or, I said that, or speak of a voice saying, far away inside me, Molloy, and then a fine phrase more or less clear and simple, or find myself compelled to attribute to others intelligible words, or hear my own voice uttering to others more or less articulate sounds, I am merely complying with the convention that demands you either lie or hold your peace. For what really happened was quite different. And I did not say, Yet a little while, at the rate things are going, etc., but that resembled perhaps what I would have said, if I had been able. In reality I said nothing at all, but I heard a murmur, something gone wrong with the silence, and I pricked up my ears, like an animal I imagine, which gives a start and pretends to be dead. And then sometimes there arose within me, confusedly, a kind of consciousness, which I express by saying, I said, etc., or, Don't do it, Molloy, or, Is that your mother's name? said the sergeant, I quote from memory. Or which I express without sinking to the level of oratio recta, but by means of other figures quite as deceitful, as for example, It seemed to me that, etc., or, I had the impression that, etc., for it seemed to me nothing at all, and I had no impression of any kind, but simply somewhere something had changed, so that I too had to change, or the world too had to change, in order for nothing to be changed. And it was these little adjustments, as between Galileo's vessels, that I can only express by saying, I feared that, or, I hoped that, or, Is that your mother's name? said the sergeant, for example, and that I might doubtless have expressed otherwise and better, if I had gone to the trouble. And so I shall perhaps some day when I have less horror of trouble than today. But I think not. So I said, Yet a little while, at the rate things are going, and I won't be able to move, but will have to stay, where I happen to be, unless some kind person comes and carries me. For my marches got shorter and shorter and my halts in consequence more and more frequent and I may add prolonged. For the notion of the long halt does not necessarily follow from that of the short march, nor that of the frequent halt either, when you come to think of it, unless you give frequent a meaning it does not possess, and I could never bring myself to do a thing like that. And it seemed to me all the more important to get out of this forest with all possible speed as I would very soon be powerless to get out of anything whatsoever, were it but a bower. It was winter, it must have been winter, and not only many trees had lost their leaves, but these lost leaves had gone all black and spongy and my crutches sank into them, in places right up to the fork. Strange to say I felt no colder than usual. Perhaps it was only autumn. But I was never very sensitive to changes of temperature. And the gloom, if it seemed less blue than before, was as thick as ever. Which made me say in the end, It is less blue because there is less green, but it is no less thick thanks to the leaden winter sky. Then something about the black dripping from the black boughs, something in that line. The black slush of leaves slowed me down even more. But leaves or no leaves I would have abandoned erect motion, that of man. And I still remember the day when, flat on my face by way of rest, in defiance of the rules, I suddenly cried, striking my brow, Christ, there's crawling, I never thought of that. But could I crawl, with my legs in such a state, and my trunk? And my head. But before I go on, a word about the forest murmurs. It was in vain I listened, I could hear nothing of the kind. But rather, with much goodwill and a little imagination, at long intervals a distant gong. A horn goes well with the forest, you expect it. It is the huntsman. But a gong! Even a tom-tom, at a pinch, would not have shocked me. But a gong! It was mortifying, to have been looking forward to the celebrated murmurs if to nothing else, and to succeed only in hearing, at long intervals, in the far distance, a gong. For a moment I dared hope it was only my heart, still beating. But only for a moment. For it does not beat, not my heart, I'd have to refer you to hydraulics for the squelch that old pump makes. To the leaves too I listened, before their fall, attentively in vain. They made no sound, motionless and rigid, like brass, have I said that before? So much for the forest murmurs. From time to time I blew my horn, through the cloth of my pocket. Its hoot was fainter every time. I had taken it off my bicycle. When? I don't know. And now, let us have done. Flat on my belly, using my crutches like grapnels, I plunged them ahead of me into the undergrowth, and when I felt they had a hold, I pulled myself forward, with an effort of the wrists. For my wrists were still quite strong, fortunately, in spite of my decrepitude, though all swollen and racked by a kind of chronic arthritis probably. That then briefly is how I went about it. The advantage of this mode of locomotion compared to others, I mean those I have tried, is this, that when you want to rest you stop and rest, without further ado. For standing there is no rest, nor sitting either. And there are men who move about sitting, and even kneeling, hauling themselves to right and left, forward and backward, with the help of hooks. But he who moves in this way, crawling on his belly, like a reptile, no sooner comes to rest than he begins to rest, and even the very movement is a kind of rest, compared to other movements, I mean those that have worn me out. And in this way I moved onward in the forest, slowly, but with a certain regularity, and I covered my fifteen paces, day in, day out, without killing myself. And I even crawled on my back, plunging my crutches blindly behind me into the thickets, and with the black boughs for sky to my closing eyes. I was on my way to mother. And from time to time I said, Mother, to encourage me I suppose. I kept losing my hat, the lace had broken long ago, until in a fit of temper I banged it down on my skull with such violence that I couldn't get it off again. And if I had met any lady friends, if I had had any lady friends, I would have been powerless to salute them correctly. But there was always present to my mind, which was still working, if laboriously, the need to turn, to keep on turning, and every three or four jerks I altered course, which permitted me to describe, if not a circle, at least a great polygon, perfection is not of this world, and to hope that I was going forward in a straight line, in spite of everything, day and night, towards my mother. And true enough the day came when the forest ended and I saw the light, the light of the plain, exactly as I had foreseen. But I did not see it from afar, trembling beyond the harsh trunks, as I had foreseen, but suddenly I was in it, I opened my eyes and saw I had arrived. And the reason for that was probably this, that for some time past I had not opened my eyes, or seldom. And even my little changes of course were made blindly, in the dark. The forest ended in a ditch, I don't know why, and it was in this ditch that I became aware of what had happened to me. I suppose it was the fall into the ditch that opened my eyes, for why would they have opened otherwise? I looked at the plain rolling away as far as the eye could see. No, not quite so far as that. For my eyes having got used to the light I fancied I saw, faintly outlined against the horizon, the towers and steeples of a town, which of course I could not assume was mine, on such slight evidence. It is true the plain seemed familiar, but in my region all the plains looked alike, when you knew one you knew them all. In any case, whether it was my town or not, whether somewhere under that faint haze my mother panted on or whether she poisoned the air a hundred miles away, were ludicrously idle questions for a man in my position, though of undeniable interest on the plane of pure knowledge. For how could I drag myself over that vast moor, where my crutches would fumble in vain. Rolling perhaps. And then?

Would they let me roll on to my mother's door? Fortunately for me at this painful juncture, which I had vaguely foreseen, but not in all its bitterness, I heard a voice telling me not to fret, that help was coming. Literally. These words struck it is not too much to say as clearly on my ear, and on my understanding, as the urchin's thanks I suppose when I stooped and picked up his marble. Don't fret, Molloy, we're coming. Well, I suppose you have to try everything once, succour included, to get a complete picture of the resources of their planet. I lapsed down to the bottom of the ditch. It must have been spring, a morning in spring. I thought I heard birds, skylarks perhaps. I had not heard a bird for a long time. How was it I had not heard any in the forest? Nor seen any. It had not seemed strange to me. Had I heard any at the seaside? Mews? I could not remember. I remembered the corncrakes. The two travellers came back to my memory. One had a club. I had forgotten them. I saw the sheep again. Or so I say now. I did not fret, other scenes of my life came back to me. There seemed to be rain, then sunshine, turn about. Real spring weather. I longed to go back into the forest. Oh not a real longing. Molloy could stay, where he happened to be.

II

It is midnight. The rain is beating on the windows. I am calm. All is sleeping. Nevertheless I get up and go to my desk. I can't sleep. My lamp sheds a soft and steady light. I have trimmed it. It will last till morning. I hear the eagle-owl. What a terrible battle-cry! Once I listened to it unmoved. My son is sleeping. Let him sleep. The night will come when he too, unable to sleep, will get up and go to his desk. I shall be forgotten.

My report will be long. Perhaps I shall not finish it. My name is Moran, Jacques. That is the name I am known by. I am done for. My son too. All unsuspecting. He must think he's on the threshold of life, of real life. He's right there. His name is Jacques, like mine. This cannot lead to confusion.

I remember the day I received the order to see about Molloy. It was a Sunday in summer. I was sitting in my little garden, in a wicker chair, a black book closed on my knees. It must have been about eleven o'clock, still too early to go to church. I was savouring the day of rest, while deploring the importance attached to it, in certain parishes. To work, even to play on Sunday, was not of necessity reprehensible, in my opinion. It all depended on the state of mind of him who worked, or played, and on the nature of his work, of his play, in my opinion. I was reflecting with satisfaction on this, that this slightly libertarian view was gaining ground, even among the clergy, more and more disposed to admit that the sabbath, so long as you go to mass and contribute to the collection, may be considered a day like any other, in certain respects. This did not affect me personally, I've always loved doing nothing. And I would gladly have rested on weekdays too, if I could have afforded it. Not that I was positively lazy. It was something else. Seeing something done which I could have done better myself, if I had wished, and which I did do better whenever I put my mind to it, I had the impression of discharging a function to which no form of activity could have exalted me. But this was a joy in which, during the week, I could seldom indulge.

The weather was fine. I watched absently the coming and going of my bees. I heard on the gravel the scampering steps of my son, caught up in I know not what fantasy of flight and pursuit. I called to him not to dirty himself. He did not answer.

All was still. Not a breath. From my neighbours' chimneys the smoke rose straight and blue. None but tranquil sounds, the clicking of mallet and ball, a rake on pebbles, a distant lawn-mower, the bell of my beloved church. And birds of course, blackbird and thrush, their song sadly dying, vanquished by the heat, and leaving dawn's high boughs for the bushes' gloom. Contentedly I inhaled the scent of my lemon-verbena.

In such surroundings slipped away my last moments of peace and happiness.

A man came into the garden and walked swiftly towards me. I knew him well. Now I have no insuperable objection to a neighbour's dropping in, on a Sunday, to pay his respects, if he feels the need, though I much prefer to see nobody. But this man was not a neighbour. Our dealings were strictly of a business nature and he had journeyed from afar, on purpose to disturb me. So I was disposed to receive him frostily enough, all the more so as he had the impertinence to come straight to where I was sitting, under my Beauty of Bath. With people who took this liberty I had no patience. If they wished to speak to me they had only to ring at the door of my house. Martha had her instructions. I thought I was hidden from anybody coming into my grounds and following the short path which led from the garden-gate to the front door, and in fact I must have been. But at the noise of the gate being slammed I turned angrily and saw, blurred by the leaves, this high mass bearing down on me, across the lawn. I neither got up nor invited him to sit down. He stopped in front of me and we stared at each other in silence. He was dressed in his heavy, sombre Sunday best, and at this my displeasure knew no bounds. This gross external observance, while the soul exults in its rags, has always appeared to me an abomination. I watched the enormous feet crushing my daisies. I would gladly have driven him away, with a knout. Unfortunately it was not he who mattered. Sit down, I said, mollified by the reflection that after all he was only acting his part of go-between. Yes, suddenly I had pity on him, pity on myself. He sat down and mopped his forehead. I caught a glimpse of my son spying on us from behind a bush. My son was thirteen or fourteen at the time. He was big and strong for his age. His intelligence seemed at times little short of average. My son, in fact. I called him and ordered him to go and fetch some beer. Peeping and prying were part of my profession. My son imitated me instinctively. He returned after a remarkably short interval with two glasses and a quart bottle of beer. He uncorked the bottle and served us. He was very fond of uncorking bottles. I told him to go and wash himself, to straighten his clothes, in a word to get ready to appear in public, for it would soon be time for mass. He can stay, said Gaber. I don't wish him to stay, I said. And turning to my son I told him again to go and get ready. If there was one thing displeased me, at that time, it was being late for the last mass. Please yourself, said Gaber. Jacques went away grumbling with his finger in his mouth, a detestable and unhygienic habit, but preferable, all things considered, to that of the finger in the nose, in my opinion. If putting his finger in his mouth prevented my son from putting it in his nose, or elsewhere, he was right to do it, in a sense.

Here are your instructions, said Gaber. He took a notebook from his pocket and began to read. Every now and then he closed the notebook, taking care to leave his finger in it as a marker, and indulged in comments and observations of which I had no need, for I knew my business. When at last he had finished I told him the job did not interest me and that the chief would do better to call on another agent. He wants it to be you, God knows why, said Gaber. I presume he told you why, I said, scenting flattery, for which I had a weakness. He said, replied Gaber, that no one could do it but you. This was more or less what I wanted to hear. And yet, I said, the affair seems childishly simple. Gaber began bitterly to inveigh against our employer, who had made him get up in the middle of the night, just as he was getting into position to make love to his wife. For this kind of nonsense, he added. And he said he had confidence in no one but me? I said. He doesn't know what he says, said Gaber. He added, Nor what he does. He wiped the lining of his bowler, peering inside as if in search of something. In that case it's hard for me to refuse, I said, knowing perfectly well that in any case it was impossible for me to refuse. Refuse! But we agents often amused ourselves with grumbling among ourselves and giving ourselves the airs of free men. You leave today, said Gaber. Today! I cried, but he's out of his mind! Your son goes with you, said Gaber. I said no more. When it came to the point we said no more. Gaber buttoned his notebook and put it back in his pocket, which he also buttoned. He stood up, rubbing his hands over his chest. I could do with another beer, he said. Go to the kitchen, I said, the maid will serve you. Goodbye, Moran, he said.

It was too late for mass. I did not need to consult my watch to know, I could feel mass had begun without me. I who never missed mass, to have missed it on that Sunday of all Sundays! When I so needed it! To buck me up! I decided to ask for a private communion, in the course of the afternoon. I would go without lunch. Father Ambrose was always very kind and accommodating.

I called Jacques. Without result. I said, Seeing me still in conference he has gone to mass alone. This explanation turned out subsequently to be the correct one. But I added, He might have come and seen me, before leaving. I liked thinking in monologue and then my lips moved visibly. But no doubt he was afraid of disturbing me and of being reprimanded. For I was sometimes inclined to go too far when I reprimanded my son, who was consequently a little afraid of me. I myself had never been sufficiently chastened. Oh I had not been spoiled either, merely neglected. Whence bad habits ingrained beyond remedy and of which even the most meticulous piety has never been able to break me. I hoped to spare my son this misfortune, by giving him a good clout from time to time, together with my reasons for doing so. Then I said, Is he barefaced enough to tell me, on his return, that he has been to mass if he has not, if for example he has merely run off to join his little friends, behind the slaughterhouse? And I determined to get the truth out of Father Ambrose, on this subject. For it was imperative my son should not imagine he was capable of lying to me with impunity. And if Father Ambrose could not enlighten me, I would apply to the verger, whose vigilance it was inconceivable that the presence of my son at twelve o'clock mass had escaped. For I knew for a fact that the verger had a list of the faithful and that, from his place beside the font, he ticked us off when it came to the absolution. It is only fair to say that Father Ambrose knew nothing of these manœuvres, yes, anything in the nature of surveillance was hateful to the good Father Ambrose. And he would have sent the verger flying about his business if he had suspected him of such a work of supererogation. It must have been for his own edification that the verger kept this register, with such assiduity. Admittedly I knew only what went on at the last mass, having no experience personally of the other offices, for the good reason that I never went within a mile of them. But I had heard it said that they were the occasion of exactly the same supervision, at the hands either of the verger himself or, when his duties called him elsewhere, of one of his sons. A strange parish whose flock knew more than its pastor of a circumstance which seemed rather in his province than in theirs.

Such were my thoughts as I waited for my son to come back and Gaber, whom I had not yet heard leave, to go. And tonight I find it strange I could have thought of such things, I mean my son, my lack of breeding, Father Ambrose, Verger Joly with his register, at such a time. Had I not something better to do, after what I had just heard? The fact is I had not yet begun to take the matter seriously. And I am all the more surprised as such light-mindedness was not like me. Or was it in order to win a few more moments of peace that I instinctively avoided giving my mind to it? Even if, as set forth in Gaber's report, the affair had seemed unworthy of me, the chief's insistence on having me, me Moran, rather than anybody else, ought to have warned me that it was no ordinary one. And instead of bringing to bear upon it without delay all the resources of my mind and of my experience, I sat dreaming of my breed's infirmities and the singularities of those about me. And yet the poison was already acting on me, the poison I had just been given. I stirred restlessly in my arm-chair, ran my hands over my face, crossed and uncrossed my legs, and so on. The colour and weight of the world were changing already, soon I would have to admit I was anxious.

I remembered with annoyance the lager I had just absorbed. Would I be granted the body of Christ after a pint of Wallenstein? And if I said nothing? Have you come fasting, my son? He would not ask. But God would know, sooner or later. Perhaps he would pardon me. But would the eucharist produce the same effect, taken on top of beer, however light? I could always try. What was the teaching of the Church on the matter? What if I were about to commit sacrilege? I decided to suck a few peppermints on the way to the presbytery.

I got up and went to the kitchen. I asked if Jacques was back. I haven't seen him, said Martha. She seemed in bad humour. And the man? I said. What man? she said. The man who came for a glass of beer, I said. No one came for anything, said Martha. By the way, I said, unperturbed apparently, I shall not eat lunch today. She asked if I were ill. For I was naturally a rather heavy eater. And my Sunday midday meal especially I always liked extremely copious. It smelt good in the kitchen. I shall lunch a little later today, that's all, I said. Martha looked at me furiously. Say four o'clock, I said. In that wizened grey skull what raging and rampaging then, I knew. You will not go out today, I said coldly, I regret. She flung herself at her pots and pans, dumb with anger. You will keep all that hot for me, I said, as best you can. And knowing her capable of poisoning me I added, You can have the whole day off tomorrow, if that is any good to you.

I left her and went out on the road. So Gaber had gone without his beer. And yet he had wanted it badly. It was a good brand, Wallenstein. I stood there on the watch for Jacques. Coming from church he would appear on my right, on my left if he came from the slaughter-house. A neighbour passed. A free-thinker. Well well, he said, no worship today? He knew my habits, my Sunday habits I mean. Everyone knew them and the chief perhaps better than any, in spite of his remoteness. You look as if you had seen a ghost, said the neighbour. Worse than that, I said, you. I went in, at my back the dutifully hideous smile. I could see him running to his concubine with the news, You know that poor bastard Moran, you should have heard me, I had him lepping! Couldn't speak! Took to his heels!

Jacques came back soon afterwards. No trace of frolic. He said he had been to church alone. I asked him a few pertinent questions concerning the march of the ceremony. His answers were plausible. I told him to wash his hands and sit down to his lunch. I went back to the kitchen. I did nothing but go to and fro. You may dish up, I said. She had wept. I peered into the pots. Irish stew. A nourishing and economical dish, if a little indigestible. All honour to the land it has brought before the world. I shall sit down at four o'clock, I said. I did not need to add sharp. I liked punctuality, all those whom my roof sheltered had to like it too. I went up to my room. And there, stretched on my bed, the curtains drawn, I made a first attempt to grasp the Molloy affair.

My concern at first was only with its immediate vexations and the preparations they demanded of me. The kernel of the affair I continued to shirk. I felt a great confusion coming over me.

Should I set out on my autocycle? This was the question with which I began. I had a methodical mind and never set out on a mission without prolonged reflection as to the best way of setting out. It was the first problem to solve, at the outset of each enquiry, and I never moved until I had solved it, to my satisfaction. Sometimes I took my autocycle, sometimes the train, sometimes the motor-coach, just as sometimes too I left on foot, or on my bicycle, silently, in the night. For when you are beset with enemies, as I am, you cannot leave on your autocycle, even in the night, without being noticed, unless you employ it as an ordinary bicycle, which is absurd. But if I was in the habit of first settling this delicate question of transport, it was never without having, if not fully sifted, at least taken into account the factors on which it depended. For how can you decide on the way of setting out if you do not first know where you are going, or at least with what purpose you are going there? But in the present case I was tackling the problem of transport with no other preparation than the languid cognizance I had taken of Gaber's report. I would be able to recover the minutest details of this report when I wished. But I had not yet troubled to do so, I had avoided doing so, saying, The affair is banal. To try and solve the problem of transport under such conditions was madness. Yet that was what I was doing. I was losing my head already.

I liked leaving on my autocycle, I was partial to this way of getting about. And in my ignorance of the reasons against it I decided to leave on my autocycle. Thus was inscribed, on the threshold of the Molloy affair, the fatal pleasure principle.

The sun's beams shone through the rift in the curtains and made visible the sabbath of the motes. I concluded from this that the weather was still fine and rejoiced. When you leave on your autocycle fine weather is to be preferred. I was wrong, the weather was fine no longer, the sky was clouding over, soon it would rain. But for the moment the sun was still shining. It was on this that I went, with inconceivable levity, having nothing else to go on.

Next I attacked, according to my custom, the capital question of the effects to take with me. And on this subject too I should have come to a quite otiose decision but for my son, who burst in wanting to know if he might go out. I controlled myself. He was wiping his mouth with the back of his hand, a thing

I do not like to see. But there are nastier gestures, I speak from experience.

Out? I said. Where? Out! Vagueness I abhor. I was beginning to feel hungry. To the Elms, he replied. So we call our little public park. And yet there is not an elm to be seen in it, I have been told. What for? I said. To go over my botany, he replied. There were times I suspected my son of deceit. This was one. I would almost have preferred him to say, For a walk, or, To look at the tarts. The trouble was he knew far more than I, about botany. Otherwise I could have set him a few teasers, on his return. Personally I just liked plants, in all innocence and simplicity. I even saw in them at times a superfetatory proof of the existence of God. Go, I said, but be back at half-past four, I want to talk to you. Yes papa, he said. Yes papa! Ah!

I slept a little. Faster, faster. Passing the church, something made me stop. I looked at the door, baroque, very fine. I found it hideous. I hastened on to the presbytery. The Father is sleeping, said the servant. I can wait, I said. Is it urgent? she said. Yes and no, I said. She showed me into the sitting-room, bare and bleak, dreadful. Father Ambrose came in, rubbing his eyes. I disturb you, Father, I said. He clicked his tongue against the roof of his mouth, protestingly. I shall not describe our attitudes, characteristic his of him, mine of me. He offered me a cigar which I accepted with good grace and put in my pocket, between my fountain-pen and my propelling-pencil. He flattered himself, Father Ambrose, with being a man of the world and knowing its ways, he who never smoked. And everyone said he was most broad. I asked him if he had noticed my son at the last mass. Certainly, he said, we even spoke together. I must have looked surprised. Yes, he said, not seeing you at your place, in the front row, I feared you were ill. So I called for the dear child, who reassured me. A most untimely visitor, I said, whom I could not shake off in time. So your son explained to me, he said. He added, But let us sit down, we have no train to catch. He laughed and sat down, hitching up his heavy cassock. May I offer you a little glass of something? he said. I was in a quandary. Had

Jacques let slip an allusion to the lager. He was quite capable of it. I came to ask you a favour, I said. Granted, he said. We observed each other. It's this, I said, Sunday for me without the Body and Blood is like—. He raised his hand. Above all no profane comparisons, he said. Perhaps he was thinking of the kiss without a moustache or beef without mustard. I dislike being interrupted. I sulked. Say no more, he said, a wink is as good as a nod, you want communion. I bowed my head. It's a little unusual, he said. I wondered if he had fed. I knew he was given to prolonged fasts, by way of mortification certainly, and then because his doctor advised it. Thus he killed two birds with one stone. Not a word to a soul, he said, let it remain between us and—. He broke off, raising a finger, and his eyes, to the ceiling. Heavens, he said, what is that stain? I looked in turn at the ceiling. Damp, I said. Tut tut, he said, how annoying. The words tut tut seemed to me the maddest I had heard. There are times, he said, when one feels like weeping. He got up. I'll go and get my kit, he said. He called that his kit. Alone, my hands clasped until it seemed my knuckles would crack, I asked the Lord for guidance. Without result. That was some consolation. As for Father Ambrose, in view of his alacrity to fetch his kit, it seemed evident to me he suspected nothing. Or did it amuse him to see how far I would go? Or did it tickle him to have me commit a sin? I summarized the situation briefly as follows. If knowing I have beer taken he gives me the sacrament, his sin, if sin there be, is as great as mine. I was therefore risking little. He came back with a kind of portable pyx, opened it and dispatched me without an instant's hesitation. I rose and thanked him warmly. Pah! he said, it's nothing. Now we can talk.

I had nothing else to say to him. All I wanted was to return home as quickly as possible and stuff myself with stew. My soul appeased, I was ravenous. But being slightly in advance of my schedule I resigned myself to allowing him eight minutes. They seemed endless. He informed me that Mrs Clement, the chemist's wife and herself a highly qualified chemist, had fallen, in her laboratory, from the top of a ladder, and broken the neck—. The neck! I cried. Of her femur, he said, can't you let me finish. He added that it was bound to happen. And I, not to be outdone, told him how worried I was about my hens, particularly my grey hen, which would neither brood nor lay and for the past month and more had done nothing but sit with her arse in the dust, from morning to night. Like Job, haha, he said. I too said haha. What a joy it is to laugh, from time to time, he said. Is it not? I said. It is peculiar to man, he said. So I have noticed, I said. A brief silence ensued. What do you feed her on? he said. Corn chiefly, I said. Cooked or raw? he said. Both, I said. I added that she ate nothing any more. Nothing! he cried. Next to nothing, I said. Animals never laugh, he said. It takes us to find that funny, I said. What? he said. It takes us to find that funny, I said loudly. He mused. Christ never laughed either, he said, so far as we know. He looked at me. Can you wonder? I said. There it is, he said. He smiled sadly. She has not the pip, I hope, he said. I said she had not, certainly not, anything he liked, but not the pip. He meditated. Have you tried bicarbonate? he said. I beg your pardon? I said. Bicarbonate of soda, he said, have you tried it? Why no, I said. Try it! he cried, flushing with pleasure, have her swallow a few dessertspoonfuls, several times a day, for a few months. You'll see, you won't know her. A powder? I said. Bless my heart to be sure, he said. Many thanks, I said, I'll begin today. Such a fine hen, he said, such a good layer. Or rather tomorrow, I said. I had forgotten the chemist was closed. Except in case of emergency. And now that little cordial, he said. I declined.

This interview with Father Ambrose left me with a painful impression. He was still the same dear man, and yet not. I seemed to have surprised, on his face, a lack, how shall I say, a lack of nobility. The host, it is only fair to say, was lying heavy on my stomach. And as I made my way home I felt like one who, having swallowed a pain-killer, is first astonished, then indignant, on obtaining no relief. And I was almost ready to suspect Father Ambrose, alive to my excesses of the forenoon, of having fobbed me off with unconsecrated bread. Or of mental reservation as he pronounced the magic words. And it was in vile humour that I arrived home, in the pelting rain.

The stew was a great disappointment. Where are the onions? I cried. Gone to nothing, replied Martha. I rushed into the kitchen, to look for the onions I suspected her of having removed from the pot, because she knew how much I liked them. I even rummaged in the bin. Nothing. She watched me mockingly.

I went up to my room again, drew back the curtains on a calamitous sky and lay down. I could not understand what was happening to me. I found it painful at that period not to understand. I tried to pull myself together. In vain. I might have known. My life was running out, I knew not through what breach. I succeeded however in dozing off, which is not so easy, when pain is speculative. And I was marvelling, in that half-sleep, at my half sleeping, when my son came in, without knocking. Now if there is one thing I abhor, it is someone coming into my room, without knocking. I might just happen to be masturbating, before my cheval-glass. Father with yawning fly and starting eyes, toiling to scatter on the ground his joyless seed, that was no sight for a small boy. Harshly I recalled him to the proprieties. He protested he had knocked twice. If you had knocked a hundred times, I replied, it would not give you the right to come in without being invited. But, he said. But what? I said. You told me to be here at half-past four, he said. There is something, I said, more important in life than punctuality, and that is decorum. Repeat. In that disdainful mouth my phrase put me to shame. He was soaked. What have you been looking at? I said. The liliaceae, papa, he answered. The liliaceae papa! My son had a way of saying papa, when he wanted to hurt me, that was very special. Now listen to me, I said. His face took on an expression of anguished attention. We leave this evening, I said in substance, on a journey. Put on your school suit, the green—. But it's blue, papa, he said. Blue or green, put it on, I said violently. I went on. Put in your little knapsack, the one I gave you for your birthday, your toilet things, one shirt, one pair of socks and seven pairs of drawers. Do you understand? Which shirt, papa? he said. It doesn't matter which shirt, I cried, any shirt! Which shoes am I to wear? he said. You have two pairs of shoes, I said, one for Sundays and one for weekdays, and you ask me which you are to wear. I sat up. I want none of your lip, I said.

Thus to my son I gave precise instructions. But were they the right ones? Would they stand the test of second thoughts? Would I not be impelled, in a very short time, to cancel them? I who never changed my mind before my son. The worst was to be feared.

Where are we going, papa? he said. How often had I told him not to ask me questions. And where were we going, in point of fact. Do as you're told, I said. I have an appointment with Mr Py tomorrow, he said. You'll see him another day, I said. But I have an ache, he said. There exist other dentists, I said, Mr Py is not the unique dentist of the northern hemisphere. I added rashly, We are not going into the wilderness. But he's a very good dentist, he said. All dentists are alike, I said. I could have told him to get to hell out of that with his dentist, but no, I reasoned gently with him, I spoke with him as with an equal. I could furthermore have pointed out to him that he was lying when he said he had an ache. He did have an ache, in a bicuspid I believe, but it was over. Py himself had told me so. I have dressed the tooth, he said, your son cannot possibly feel any more pain. I remembered this conversation well. He has naturally very bad teeth, said Py. Naturally, I said, what do you mean, naturally? What are you insinuating? He was born with bad teeth, said Py, and all his life he will have bad teeth. Naturally I shall do what I can. Meaning, I was born with the disposition to do all I can, all my life I shall do all I can, necessarily. Born with bad teeth! As for me, I was down to my incisors, the nippers.

Is it still raining? I said. My son had drawn a small glass from his pocket and was examining the inside of his mouth, prising away his upper lip with his finger. Aaw, he said, without interrupting his inspection. Stop messing about with your mouth! I

MOLLOY

cried. Go to the window and tell me if it's still raining. He went
to the window and told me it was still raining. Is the sky
completely overcast? I said. Yes, he said. Not the least rift? I said.
No, he said. Draw the curtains, I said. Delicious instants, before
one's eyes get used to the dark. Are you still there? I said. He
was still there. I asked him what he was waiting for to do as I
had told him. If I had been my son I would have left me long
ago. He was not worthy of me, not in the same class at all. I
could not escape this conclusion. Cold comfort that is, to feel
superior to one's son, and hardly sufficient to calm the remorse
of having begotten him. May I bring my stamps? he said. My
son had two albums, a big one for his collection properly speaking and a small one for the duplicates. I authorized him to bring
the latter. When I can give pleasure, without doing violence to
my principles, I do so gladly. He withdrew.

I got up and went to the window. I could not keep still. I
passed my head between the curtains. Fine rain, lowering sky.
He had not lied to me. Likely to lift round about eight. Fine
sunset, twilight, night. Waning moon, rising towards midnight. I
rang for Martha and lay down again. We shall dine at home, I
said. She looked at me in astonishment. Did we not always dine
at home? I had not yet told her we were leaving. I would not tell
her till the last moment, one foot in the stirrup as the saying is.
I did not wholly trust her. I would call her at the last moment
and say, Martha, we're leaving, for one day, two days, three
days, a week, two weeks, God knows, goodbye. It was important
to leave her in the dark. Then why had I called her? She would
have served us dinner in any case, as she did every day. I had
made the mistake of putting myself in her place. That was
understandable. But to tell her we would dine at home, what a
blunder. For she knew it already, thought she knew, did know.
And as a result of this useless reminder she would sense that
something was afoot and spy on us, in the hope of learning what
it was. First mistake. The second, first in time, was my not
having enjoined my son to keep what I had told him to himself.
Not that this would have served any purpose. Nevertheless I

108

should have insisted on it, as due to myself. I was floundering.
I so sly as a rule. I tried to mend matters, saying, A little later
than usual, not before nine. She turned to go, her simple mind
already in a turmoil. I am at home to no one, I said. I knew what
she would do, she would throw a sack over her shoulders and
slip off to the bottom of the garden. There she would call
Hannah, the old cook of the Elsner sisters, and they would
whisper together for a long time, through the railings. Hannah
never went out, she did not like going out. The Elsner sisters
were not bad neighbours, as neighbours go. They made a little
too much music, that was the only fault I could find with them.
If there is one thing gets on my nerves it is music. What I assert,
deny, question, in the present, I still can. But mostly I shall use
the various tenses of the past. For mostly I do not know, it is
perhaps no longer so, it is too soon to know, I simply do not
know, perhaps shall never know. I thought a little of the Elsner
sisters. Everything remained to be planned and there I was
thinking of the Elsner sisters. They had an aberdeen called
Zulu. People called it Zulu. Sometimes, when I was in a good
humour, I called, Zulu! Little Zulu! and he would come and
talk to me, through the railings. But I had to be feeling gay. I
don't like animals. It's a strange thing, I don't like men and I
don't like animals. As for God, he is beginning to disgust me.
Crouching down I would stroke his ears, through the railings,
and utter wheedling words. He did not realize he disgusted me.
He reared up on his hind legs and pressed his chest against the
bars. Then I could see his little black penis ending in a thin wisp
of wetted hair. He felt insecure, his hams trembled, his little
paws fumbled for purchase, one after the other. I too wobbled,
squatting on my heels. With my free hand I held on to the railings. Perhaps I disgusted him too. I found it hard to tear myself
away from these vain thoughts.

I wondered, suddenly rebellious, what compelled me to
accept this commission. But I had already accepted it, I had
given my word. Too late. Honour. It did not take me long to gild
my impotence.

But could I not postpone our departure to the following day? Or leave alone? Ah shilly-shally. But we would wait till the very last moment, a little before midnight. This decision is irrevocable, I said. It was justified moreover by the state of the moon.

I did as when I could not sleep. I wandered in my mind, slowly, noting every detail of the labyrinth, its paths as familiar as those of my garden and yet ever new, as empty as the heart could wish or alive with strange encounters. And I heard the distant cymbals, There is still time, still time. But there was not, for I ceased, all vanished and I tried once more to turn my thoughts to the Molloy affair. Unfathomable mind, now beacon, now sea.

The agent and the messenger. We agents never took anything in writing. Gaber was not an agent in the sense I was. Gaber was a messenger. He was therefore entitled to a notebook. A messenger had to be possessed of singular qualities, good messengers were even more rare than good agents. I who was an excellent agent would have made but a sorry messenger. I often regretted it. Gaber was protected in numerous ways. He used a code incomprehensible to all but himself. Each messenger, before being appointed, had to submit his code to the directorate. Gaber understood nothing about the messages he carried. Reflecting on them he arrived at the most extravagantly false conclusions. Yes, it was not enough for him to understand nothing about them, he had also to believe he understood everything about them. This was not all. His memory was so bad that his messages had no existence in his head, but only in his notebook. He had only to close his notebook to become, a moment later, perfectly innocent as to its contents. And when I say that he reflected on his messages and drew conclusions from them, it was not as we would have reflected on them, you and I, the book closed and probably the eyes too, but little by little as he read. And when he raised his head and indulged in his commentaries, it was without losing a second, for if he had lost a second he would have forgotten everything, both text and gloss. I have often wondered if the messengers were not compelled to undergo a surgical operation, to induce in them such a degree of amnesia. But I think not. For otherwise their memory was good enough. And I have heard Gaber speak of his childhood, and of his family, in extremely plausible terms. To be undecipherable to all but oneself, dead without knowing it to the meaning of one's instructions and incapable of remembering them for more than a few seconds, these are capacities rarely united in the same individual. No less however was demanded of our messengers. And that they were more highly esteemed than the agents, whose qualities were sound rather than brilliant, is shown by the fact that they received a weekly wage of eight pounds as against ours of six pounds ten only, these figures being exclusive of bonuses and travelling expenses. And when I speak of agents and of messengers in the plural, it is with no guarantee of truth. For I had never seen any other messenger than Gaber nor any other agent than myself. But I supposed we were not the only ones and Gaber must have supposed the same. For the feeling that we were the only ones of our kind would, I believe, have been more than we could have borne. And it must have appeared natural, to me that each agent had his own particular messenger, and to Gaber that each messenger had his own particular agent. Thus I was able to say to Gaber, Let him give this job to someone else, I don't want it, and Gaber was able to reply, He wants it to be you. And these last words, assuming Gaber had not invented them especially to annoy me, had perhaps been uttered by the chief with the sole purpose of fostering our illusion, if it was one. All this is not very clear.

That we thought of ourselves as members of a vast organization was doubtless also due to the all too human feeling that trouble shared, or is it sorrow, is trouble something, I forget the word. But to me at least, who knew how to listen to the falsetto of reason, it was obvious that we were perhaps alone in doing what we did. Yes, in my moments of lucidity I thought it possible. And, to keep nothing from you, this lucidity was so acute at times that I came even to doubt the existence of Gaber himself. And if I had not hastily sunk back into my darkness I might have gone to the extreme of conjuring away the chief too and regarding myself as solely responsible for my wretched existence. For I knew I was wretched, at six pounds ten a week plus bonuses and expenses. And having made away with Gaber and the chief (one Youdi), could I have denied myself the pleasure of—you know. But I was not made for the great light that devours, a dim lamp was all I had been given, and patience without end, to shine it on the empty shadows. I was a solid in the midst of other solids.

I went down to the kitchen. I did not expect to find Martha there, but I found her there. She was sitting in her rocking-chair, in the chimney-corner, rocking herself moodily. This rocking-chair, she would have you believe, was the only possession to which she clung and she would not have parted with it for an empire. It is interesting to note that she had installed it not in her room, but in the kitchen, in the chimney-corner. Late to bed and early to rise, it was in the kitchen that she benefited by it most. The wage-payers are numerous, and I was one of them, who do not like to see, in the place set aside for toil, the furniture of reclining and repose. The servant wishes to rest? Let her retire to her room. In the kitchen all must be of wood, white and rigid. I should mention that Martha had insisted, before entering my service, that I permit her to keep her rocking-chair in the kitchen. I had refused, indignantly. Then, seeing she was inflexible, I had yielded. I was too kind-hearted.

My weekly supply of lager, half-a-dozen quart bottles, was delivered every Saturday. I never touched them until the next day, for lager must be left to settle after the least disturbance. Of these six bottles Gaber and I, together, had emptied one. There should therefore be five left, plus the remains of a bottle from the previous week. I went into the pantry. The five bottles were there, corked and sealed, and one open bottle three-quarters empty. Martha followed me with her eyes. I left without a word to her and went upstairs. I did nothing but go to and fro. I went into my son's room. Sitting at his little desk he was admiring his stamps, the two albums, large and small, open before him. On my approach he shut them hastily. I saw at once what he was up to. But first I said, Have you got your things ready? He stood up, got his pack and gave it to me. I looked inside. I put my hand inside and felt through the contents, staring vacantly before me. Everything was in. I gave it back to him. What are you doing? I said. Looking at my stamps, he said. You call that looking at your stamps? I said. Yes papa, he said, with unimaginable effrontery. Silence, you little liar! I cried. Do you know what he was doing? Transferring to the album of duplicates, from his good collection properly so-called, certain rare and valuable stamps which he was in the habit of gloating over daily and could not bring himself to leave, even for a few days. Show me your new Timor, the five reis orange, I said. He hesitated. Show it to me! I cried. I had given it to him myself, it had cost me a florin. A bargain, at the time. I've put it in here, he said piteously, picking up the album of duplicates. That was all I wanted to know, to hear him say rather, for I knew it already. Very good, I said. I went to the door. You leave both your albums at home, I said, the small one as well as the large one. Not a word of reproach, a simple prophetic present, on the model of those employed by Youdi. Your son goes with you. I went out. But as with delicate steps, almost mincing, congratulating myself as usual on the resilience of my Wilton, I followed the corridor towards my room, I was struck by a thought which made me go back to my son's room. He was sitting in the same place, but in a slightly different attitude, his arms on the table and his head on his arms. This sight went straight to my heart, but nevertheless I did my duty. He did not move. To make assurance doubly sure, I said, we shall put the albums in the safe, until our return. He still did not move. Do you hear me? I said. He rose with a bound that knocked over his chair and uttered the furious words, Do what you like with them! I never want to see them again! Anger should be left to cool, in my opinion, crisis to pass, before one operates. I took the albums and withdrew, without a word. He had been lacking in respect, but this was not the moment to have him admit it. Motionless in the corridor I heard sounds of falling and collision. Another, less master of himself than I of myself, would have intervened. But it did not positively displease me that my son should give free vent to his grief. It purges. Sorrow does more harm when dumb, to my mind.

The albums under my arm, I returned to my room. I had spared my son a grave temptation, that of putting in his pocket his most cherished stamps, in order to gloat on them, during our journey. Not that his having one or two stamps about him was reprehensible in itself. But it would have been an act of disobedience. To look at them he would have had to hide from his father. And when he had lost them, as he inevitably would, he would have been driven to lie, to account for their disappearance. No, if he could not really bear to be parted from the gems of his collection, it would have been better for him to take the entire album. For an album is less readily lost than a stamp. But I was a better judge than he of what he could and could not. For I knew what he did not yet know, among other things that this ordeal would be of profit to him. *Sollst entbehren*, that was the lesson I desired to impress upon him, while he was still young and tender. Magic words which I had never dreamt, until my fifteenth year, could be coupled together. And should this undertaking make me odious in his eyes and not only me, but the very idea of fatherhood, I would pursue it none the less, with everything in my power. The thought that between my death and his own, ceasing for an instant from heaping curses on my memory, he might wonder, in a flash, whether I had not been right, that was enough for me, that repaid me for all the trouble I had taken and was still to take. He would answer in the negative, the first time, and resume his execrations. But the doubt would be sown. He would go back to it. That was how I reasoned.

I still had a few hours left before dinner. I decided to make the most of them. Because after dinner I drowse. I took off my coat and shoes, opened my trousers and got in between the sheets. It is lying down, in the warmth, in the gloom, that I best

pierce the outer turmoil's veil, discern my quarry, sense what
course to follow, find peace in another's ludicrous distress. Far
from the world, its clamours, frenzies, bitterness and dingy
light, I pass judgement on it and on those, like me, who are
plunged in it beyond recall, and on him who has need of me to
be delivered, who cannot deliver myself. All is dark, but with
that simple darkness that follows like a balm upon the great
dismemberings. From their places masses move, stark as laws.
Masses of what? One does not ask. There somewhere man is
too, vast conglomerate of all of nature's kingdoms, as lonely
and as bound. And in that block the prey is lodged and thinks
himself a being apart. Anyone would serve. But I am paid to
seek. I arrive, he comes away. His life has been nothing but a
waiting for this, to see himself preferred, to fancy himself
damned, blessed, to fancy himself everyman, above all others.
Warmth, gloom, smells of my bed, such is the effect they sometimes have on me. I get up, go out, and everything is changed.
The blood drains from my head, the noise of things bursting,
merging, avoiding one another, assails me on all sides, my eyes
search in vain for two things alike, each pinpoint of skin screams
a different message, I drown in the spray of phenomena. It
is at the mercy of these sensations, which happily I know to
be illusory, that I have to live and work. It is thanks to them I
find myself a meaning. So he whom a sudden pain awakes. He
stiffens, ceases to breathe, waits, says, It's bad dream, or, It's a
touch of neuralgia, breathes again, sleeps again, still trembling.
And yet it is not unpleasant, before setting to work, to steep
oneself again in this slow and massive world, where all things
move with the ponderous sullenness of oxen, patiently through
the immemorial ways, and where of course no investigation
would be possible. But on this occasion, I repeat, on this occasion, my reasons for doing so were I trust more serious and
imputable less to pleasure than to business. For it was only by
transferring it to this atmosphere, how shall I say, of finality
without end, why not, that I could venture to consider the work
I had on hand. For where Molloy could not be, nor Moran

either for that matter, there Moran could bend over Molloy. And though this examination prove unprofitable and of no utility for the execution of my orders, I should nevertheless have established a kind of connection, and one not necessarily false. For the falsity of the terms does not necessarily imply that of the relation, so far as I know. And not only this, but I should have invested my man, from the outset, with the air of a fabulous being, which something told me could not fail to help me later on. So I took off my coat and my shoes, I opened my trousers and I slipped in between the sheets, with an easy conscience, knowing only too well what I was doing.

Molloy, or Mollose, was no stranger to me. If I had had colleagues, I might have suspected I had spoken of him to them, as of one destined to occupy us, sooner or later. But I had no colleagues and knew nothing of the circumstances in which I had learnt of his existence. Perhaps I had invented him, I mean found him ready-made in my head. There is no doubt one sometimes meets with strangers who are not entire strangers, through their having played a part in certain cerebral reels. This had never happened to me, I considered myself immune from such experiences, and even the simple *déjà vu* seemed infinitely beyond my reach. But it was happening to me then, or I was greatly mistaken. For who could have spoken to me of Molloy if not myself and to whom if not to myself could I have spoken of him? I racked my mind in vain. For in my rare conversations with men I avoided such subjects. If anyone else had spoken to me of Molloy I would have requested him to stop and I myself would not have confided his existence to a living soul for anything in the world. If I had had colleagues things would naturally have been different. Among colleagues one says things which in any other company one keeps to oneself. But I had no colleagues. And perhaps this accounts for the immense uneasiness I had been feeling ever since the beginning of this affair. For it is no small matter, for a grown man thinking he is done with surprises, to see himself the theatre of such ignominy. I had really good cause to be alarmed.

Mother Molloy, or Mollose, was not completely foreign to me either, it seemed. But she was much less alive than her son, who God knows was far from being so. After all perhaps I knew nothing of mother Molloy, or Mollose, save in so far as such a son might bear, like a scurf of placenta, her stamp.

Of these two names, Molloy and Mollose, the second seemed to me perhaps the more correct. But barely. What I heard, in my soul I suppose, where the acoustics are so bad, was a first syllable, Mol, very clear, followed almost at once by a second, very thick, as though gobbled by the first, and which might have been oy as it might have been ose, or one, or even oc. And if I inclined towards ose, it was doubtless that my mind had a weakness for this ending, whereas the others left it cold. But since Gaber had said Molloy, not once but several times, and each time with equal incisiveness, I was compelled to admit that I too should have said Molloy and that in saying Mollose I was at fault. And henceforward, unmindful of my preferences, I shall force myself to say Molloy, like Gaber. That there may have been two different persons involved, one my own Mollose, the other the Molloy of the enquiry, was a thought which did not so much as cross my mind, and if it had I should have driven it away, as one drives away a fly, or a hornet. How little one is at one with oneself, good God. I who prided myself on being a sensible man, cold as crystal and as free from spurious depth.

I knew then about Molloy, without however knowing much about him. I shall say briefly what little I did know about him. I shall also draw attention, in my knowledge of Molloy, to the most striking lacunae.

He had very little room. His time too was limited. He hastened incessantly on, as if in despair, towards extremely close objectives. Now, a prisoner, he hurled himself at I know not what narrow confines, and now, hunted, he sought refuge near the centre.

He panted. He had only to rise up within me for me to be filled with panting.

Even in open country he seemed to be crashing through jungle. He did not so much walk as charge. In spite of this he advanced but slowly. He swayed, to and fro, like a bear.

He rolled his head, uttering incomprehensible words.

He was massive and hulking, to the point of misshapenness. And, without being black, of a dark colour.

He was forever on the move. I had never seen him rest. Occasionally he stopped and glared furiously about him.

This was how he came to me, at long intervals. Then I was nothing but uproar, bulk, rage, suffocation, effort unceasing, frenzied and vain. Just the opposite of myself, in fact. It was a change. And when I saw him disappear, his whole body a vociferation, I was almost sorry.

What it was all about I had not the slightest idea.

I had no clue to his age. As he appeared to me, so I felt he must have always appeared and would continue to appear until the end, an end indeed which I was hard put to imagine. For being unable to conceive what had brought him to such a pass, I was no better able to conceive how, left to his own resources, he could put an end to it. A natural end seemed unlikely to me, I don't know why. But then my own natural end, and I was resolved to have no other, would it not at the same time be his? Modest, I had my doubts. And then again, what end is not natural, are they not all by the grace of nature, the undeniably good and the so-called bad? Idle conjectures.

I had no information as to his face. I assumed it was hirsute, craggy and grimacing. Nothing justified my doing so.

That a man like me, so meticulous and calm in the main, so patiently turned towards the outer world as towards the lesser evil, creature of his house, of his garden, of his few poor possessions, discharging faithfully and ably a revolting function, reining back his thoughts within the limits of the calculable so great is his horror of fancy, that a man so contrived, for I was a contrivance, should let himself be haunted and possessed by chimeras, this ought to have seemed strange to me and been a warning to me to have a care, in my own interest. Nothing of the kind. I saw it only as the weakness of a solitary, a weakness admittedly to be deplored, but which had to be indulged in if I wished to remain a solitary, and I did, I clung to that, with as little enthusiasm as to my hens or to my faith, but no less lucidly. Besides this took up very little room in the inenarrable contraption I called my life, jeopardized it as little as my dreams and was as soon forgotten. Don't wait to be hunted to hide, that was always my motto. And if I had to tell the story of my life I should not so much as allude to these apparitions, and least of all to that of the unfortunate Molloy. For his was a poor thing, compared to others.

But images of this kind the will cannot revive without doing them violence. Much of what they had it takes away, much they never had it foists upon them. And the Molloy I brought to light, that memorable August Sunday, was certainly not the true denizen of my dark places, for it was not his hour. But so far as the essential features were concerned, I was easy in my mind, the likeness was there. And the discrepancy could have been still greater for all I cared. For what I was doing I was doing neither for Molloy, who mattered nothing to me, nor for myself, of whom I despaired, but on behalf of a cause which, while having need of us to be accomplished, was in its essence anonymous, and would subsist, haunting the minds of men, when its miserable artisans should be no more. It will not be said, I think, that I did not take my work to heart. But rather, tenderly, Ah those old craftsmen, their race is extinct and the mould broken.

Two remarks.

Between the Molloy I stalked within me thus and the true Molloy, after whom I was so soon to be in full cry, over hill and dale, the resemblance cannot have been great.

I was annexing perhaps already, without my knowing it, to my private Molloy, elements of the Molloy described by Gaber.

The fact was there were three, no, four Molloys. He that inhabited me, my caricature of same, Gaber's and the man of flesh and blood somewhere awaiting me. To these I would add Youdi's were it not for Gaber's corpse fidelity to the letter of his messages. Bad reasoning. For could it seriously be supposed that Youdi had confided to Gaber all he knew, or thought he knew (all one to Youdi) about his protégé? Assuredly not. He had only revealed what he deemed of relevance for the prompt and proper execution of his orders. I will therefore add a fifth Molloy, that of Youdi. But would not this fifth Molloy necessarily coincide with the fourth, the real one as the saying is, him dogged by his shadow? I would have given a lot to know. There were others too, of course. But let us leave it at that, if you don't mind, the party is big enough. And let us not meddle either with the question as to how far these five Molloys were constant and how far subject to variation. For there was this about Youdi, that he changed his mind with great facility.

That makes three remarks. I had only anticipated two.

The ice thus broken, I felt equal to facing Gaber's report and getting down to the official facts. It seemed as if the enquiry were about to start at last.

It was then that the sound of a gong, struck with violence, filled the house. True enough, it was nine o'clock. I got up, adjusted my clothes and hurried down. To give notice that the soup was in, nay, that it had begun to coagulate, was always for Martha a little triumph and a great satisfaction. For as a rule I was at table, my napkin tucked into my collar, crumbling the bread, fiddling with the cover, playing with the knife-rest, waiting to be served, a few minutes before the appointed hour. I attacked the soup. Where is Jacques? I said. She shrugged her shoulders. Detestable slavish gesture. Tell him to come down at once, I said. The soup before me had stopped steaming. Had it ever steamed? She came back. He won't come down, she said. I laid down my spoon. Tell me, Martha, I said, what is this preparation? She named it. Have I had it before? I said. She assured me I had. I then made a joke which pleased me enormously, I laughed so much I began to hiccup. It was lost on Martha who stared at me dazedly. Tell him to come down, I said at last. What? said Martha. I repeated my phrase. She still looked genuinely perplexed. There are three of us in this charming home, I said, you, my son and finally myself. What I said was, Tell him to come down. But he's sick, said Martha. Were he dying, I said, down he must come. Anger led me sometimes to slight excesses of language. I could not regret them. It seemed to me that all language was an excess of language. Naturally I confessed them. I was short of sins.

Jacques was scarlet in the face. Eat your soup, I said, and tell me what you think of it. I'm not hungry, he said. Eat your soup, I said. I saw he would not eat it. What ails you? I said. I don't feel well, he said. What an abominable thing is youth. Try and be more explicit, I said. I was at pains to use this term, a little difficult for juveniles, having explained its meaning and application to him a few days before. So I had high hopes of his telling me he didn't understand. But he was a cunning little fellow, in his way. Martha! I bellowed. She appeared. The sequel, I said. I looked more attentively out of the window. Not only had the rain stopped, that I knew already, but in the west scarves of fine red sheen were mounting in the sky. I felt them rather than saw them, through my little wood. A great joy, it is hardly too much to say, surged over me at the sight of so much beauty, so much promise. I turned away with a sigh, for the joy inspired by beauty is often not unmixed, and saw in front of me what with good reason I had called the sequel. Now what have we here? I said. Usually on Sunday evening we had the cold remains of a fowl, chicken, duck, goose, turkey, I can think of no other fowl, from Saturday evening. I have always had great success with my turkeys, they are a better proposition than ducks, in my opinion, for rearing purposes. More delicate, possibly, but more remunerative, for one who knows and caters for their little ways, who likes them in a word and is liked by them in return. Shepherd's pie, said Martha. I tasted it, from the dish. And what have you done with yesterday's bird? I said. Martha's face took on an expression of triumph. She was waiting for this question, that was obvious, she was counting on it. I thought, she said, you ought to eat something hot, before you left. And who told you I was leaving? I said. She went to the door, a sure sign she was about to launch a shaft. She could only be insulting when in flight. I'm not blind, she said. She opened the door. More's the pity, she said. She closed the door behind her.

I looked at my son. He had his mouth open and his eyes closed. Was it you blabbed on us? I said. He pretended not to know what I was talking about. Did you tell Martha we were leaving? I said. He said he had not. And why not? I said. I didn't see her, he said brazenly. But she has just been up to your room, I said. The pie was already made, he said. At times he was almost worthy of me. But he was wrong to invoke the pie. But he was still young and inexperienced and I refrained from humbling him. Try and tell me, I said, a little more precisely, what it is you feel. I've a stomach-ache, he said. A stomach-ache! Have you a temperature? I said. I don't know, he said. Find out, I said. He was looking more and more stupefied. Fortunately I rather enjoyed dotting my i's. Go and get the minute-thermometer, I said, out of the second right-hand drawer of my desk, counting from the top, take your temperature and bring me the thermometer. I let a few minutes go by and then, without being asked, repeated slowly, word for word, this rather long and difficult sentence, which contained no fewer than three or four imperatives. As he went out, having presumably understood the gist of it, I added jocosely, You know which mouth to put it in? I was not averse, in conversation with my son, to jests of doubtful taste, in the interests of his education. Those whose pungency he could not fully savour at the time, and they must have been many, he could reflect on at his leisure or seek in company with his little friends to interpret as best he might. Which was in itself an excellent exercise. And at the same time I inclined his young mind towards that most fruitful of dispositions, horror of the body and its functions. But I had turned my phrase badly, mouth was not the word I should have used. It was while examining the shepherd's pie more narrowly that I had this afterthought. I lifted the crust with my spoon and looked inside. I probed it with my fork. I called Martha and said, His dog wouldn't touch it. I thought with a smile of my desk which had only six drawers in all and for all, three on each side of the space where I put my legs. Since your dinner is uneatable, I said, be good enough to prepare a packet of sandwiches, with the chicken you couldn't finish. My son came back at last. That's all the thanks you get for having a minute-thermometer. He handed it to me. Did you have time to wipe it? I said. Seeing me squint at the mercury he went to the door and switched on the light. How remote Youdi was at that instant. Sometimes in the winter, coming home harassed and weary after a day of fruitless errands, I would find my slippers warming in front of the fire, the uppers turned to the flame. He had a temperature. There's nothing wrong with you, I said. May I go up? he said. What for? I said. To lie down, he said. Was not this the providential hindrance for which I could not be held responsible? Doubtless, but I would never dare invoke it. I was not going to expose myself to thunderbolts which might be fatal, simply because my son had the gripes. If he fell seriously ill on the way, it would be another matter. It was not for nothing I had studied the old testament. Have you shat, my child? I said gently. I've tried, he said. Do you want to? I said. Yes, he said. But nothing comes, I said. No, he said. A little wind, I said. Yes, he said. Suddenly I remembered Father Ambrose's cigar. I lit it. We'll see what we can do, I said, getting up. We went upstairs. I gave him an enema, with salt water. He struggled, but not for long. I withdrew the nozzle. Try and hold it, I said, don't stay sitting on the pot, lie flat on your stomach. We were in the bath-room. He lay down on the tiles, his big fat bottom sticking up. Let it soak well in, I said. What a day. I looked at the ash on my cigar. It was firm and blue. I sat down on the edge of the bath. The porcelain, the mirrors, the chromium, instilled a great peace within me. At least I suppose it was they. It wasn't a great peace in any case. I got up, laid down my cigar and brushed my incisors. I also brushed the back gums. I looked at myself, puffing out my lips which normally recede into my mouth. What do I look like? I said. The sight of my moustache, as always, annoyed me. It wasn't quite right. It suited me, without a moustache I was inconceivable. But it ought to have suited me better. A slight change in the cut would have sufficed. But what change? Was there too much of it, not enough? Now, I said, without ceasing to inspect myself, get back on the pot and strain. Was it not rather the colour? A noise as of a waste recalled me to less elevated preoccupations. He stood up trembling all over. We bent together over the pot which at length I took by the handle and tilted from side to side. A few fibrous shreds floated in the yellow liquid. How can you hope to shit, I said, when you've nothing in your stomach? He protested he had had his lunch. You ate nothing, I said. He said no more. I had scored a hit. You forget we are leaving in an hour or so, I said. I can't, he said. So that, I pursued, you will have to eat something. An acute pain shot through my knee. What's the matter, papa? he said. I let myself fall on the stool, pulled up the leg of my trousers and examined my knee, flexing and unflexing it. Quick the iodex, I said. You're sitting on it, he said. I stood up and the leg of my trousers fell down over my ankle. This inertia of things is enough to drive one literally insane. I let out a bellow which must have been heard by the Elsner sisters. They stop reading, raise their heads, look at each other, listen. Nothing more. Just another cry in the night. Two old hands, veined, ringed, seek each other, clasp. I pulled up the leg of my trousers again, rolled it in a fury round my thigh, raised the lid of the stool, took out the iodex and rubbed it into my knee. The knee is full of little loose bones. Let it soak well in, said my son. He would pay for that later on. When I had finished I put everything back in place, rolled down the leg of my trousers, sat down on the stool again and listened. Nothing more. Unless you'd like to try a real emetic, I said, as if nothing had happened. I'm tired, he said. You go and lie down, I said, I'll bring you something nice and light in bed, you'll have a little sleep and then we'll leave together. I drew him to me. What do you say to that? I said. He said to it, Yes papa. Did he love me then as much as I loved him? You could never be sure with that little hypocrite. Be off with you now, I said, cover yourself up well, I won't be long. I went down to the kitchen, prepared and set out on my handsome lacquer tray a bowl of hot milk and a slice of bread and jam. He asked for a report, he'll get his report. Martha watched me in silence, lolling in her rocking-chair. Like a Fate who had run out of thread. I cleaned up everything after me and turned to the door. May I go to bed? she said. She had waited till I was standing up, the laden tray in my hands, to ask me this question. I went out, set down the tray on the chair at the foot of the stairs and went back to the kitchen. Have you made the sandwiches? I said. Meanwhile the milk was getting cold and forming a revolting skin. She had made them. I'm going to bed, she said. Everyone was going to bed. You will have to get up in an hour or so, I said, to lock up. It was for her to decide if it was worth while going to bed, under these conditions. She asked me how long I expected to be away. Did she realize I was not setting out alone? I suppose so. When she went up to tell my son to come down, even if he had told her nothing, she must have noticed the knapsack. I have no idea, I said. Then almost in the same breath, seeing her so old, worse than old, ageing, so sad and solitary in her everlasting corner, There, there, it won't be long. And I advised her, in terms for me warm, to have a good rest while I was away and a good time visiting her friends and receiving them. Stint neither tea nor sugar, I said, and if by any chance you should happen to need money, apply to Mr Savory. I carried this sudden cordiality so far as to shake her by the hand, which she hastily wiped, as soon as she grasped my intention, on her apron. When I had finished shaking it, that flabby red hand, I did not let it go. But I took one finger between the tips of mine, drew it towards me and gazed at it. And had I had any tears to shed I should have shed them then, in torrents, for hours. She must have wondered if I was not on the point of making an attempt on her virtue. I gave her back her hand, took the sand-wiches and left her.

Martha had been a long time in my service. I was often away from home. I had never taken leave of her in this way, but always off-handedly, even when a prolonged absence was to be feared, which was not the case on this occasion. Sometimes I departed without a word to her.

Before going into my son's room I went into my own. I still had the cigar in my mouth, but the pretty ash had fallen off. I reproached myself with this negligence. I dissolved a sleeping-powder in the milk. He asked for a report, he'll get his report. I was going out with the tray when my eyes fell on the two albums lying on my desk. I wondered if I might not relent, at any rate so far as the album of duplicates was concerned. A little while ago he had come here to fetch the thermometer. He had been a long time. Had he taken advantage of the opportunity to secure some of his favourite stamps? I had not time to check them all. I put down the tray and looked for a few stamps at random, the Togo one mark carmine with the pretty boat, the Nyassa 1901 ten reis, and several others. I was very fond of the Nyassa. It was green and showed a giraffe grazing off the top of a palm-tree. They were all there. That proved nothing. It only proved that those particular stamps were there. I finally decided that to go back on my decision, freely taken and clearly stated, would deal a blow to my authority which it was in no condition to sustain. I did so with sorrow. My son was already sleeping. I woke him. He ate and drank, grimacing in disgust. That was all the thanks I got. I waited until the last drop, the last crumb, had disappeared. He turned to the wall and I tucked him in. I was within a hair's breadth of kissing him. Neither he nor I had uttered a word. We had no further need of words, for the time being. Besides my son rarely spoke to me unless I spoke to him. And when I did so he answered but lamely and as it were with reluctance. And yet with his little friends, when he thought I was out of the way, he was incredibly voluble. That my presence had the effect of dampening this disposition was far from displeasing me. Not one person in a hundred knows how to be silent and listen, no, nor even to conceive what such a thing means. Yet only then can you detect, beyond the fatuous clamour, the silence of which the universe is made. I desired this advantage for my son. And that he should hold aloof from those who pride themselves on their eagle gaze. I had not struggled, toiled, suffered, made good, lived like a Hottentot, so that my son should do the same. I tiptoed out. I quite enjoyed playing my parts through to the bitter end.

Since in this way I shirked the issue, have I to apologize for saying so? I let fall this suggestion for what it is worth. And perfunctorily. For in describing this day I am once more he who suffered it, who crammed it full of futile anxious life, with no other purpose than his own stultification and the means of not doing what he had to do. And as then my thoughts would have none of Molloy, so tonight my pen. This confession has been preying on my mind for some time past. To have made it gives me no relief.

I reflected with bitter satisfaction that if my son lay down and died by the wayside, it would be none of my doing. To every man his own responsibilities. I know of some they do not keep awake.

I said, There is something in this house tying my hands. A man like me cannot forget, in his evasions, what it is he evades. I went down to the garden and moved about in the almost total darkness. If I had not known my garden so well I would have blundered into my shrubberies, or my bee-hives. My cigar had gone out unnoticed. I shook it and put it in my pocket, intending to discard it in the ash-tray, or in the waste-paper basket, later on. But the next day, far from Turdy, I found it in my pocket and indeed not without satisfaction. For I was able to get a few more puffs out of it. To discover the cold cigar between my teeth, to spit it out, to search for it in the dark, to pick it up, to wonder what I should do with it, to shake it needlessly and put it in my pocket, to conjure up the ash-tray and the waste-paper basket, these were merely the principal stages of a sequence which I spun out for a quarter of an hour at least. Others concerned the dog Zulu, the perfumes sharpened tenfold by the rain and whose sources I amused myself exploring, in my head and with my hands, a neighbour's light, another's noise, and so on. My son's window was faintly lit. He liked sleeping with a night-light beside him. I sometimes felt it was wrong of me to let him humour this weakness. Until quite recently he could not sleep unless he had his woolly bear to hug. When he had forgotten the bear (Baby Jack) I would forbid the night-light. What would I have done that day without my son to distract me? My duty perhaps.

Finding my spirits as low in the garden as in the house, I turned to go in, saying to myself it was one of two things, either my house had nothing to do with the kind of nothingness in the midst of which I stumbled or else the whole of my little property was to blame. To adopt this latter hypothesis was to condone what I had done and, in advance, what I was to do, pending my departure. It brought me a semblance of pardon and a brief moment of factitious freedom. I therefore adopted it.

From a distance the kitchen had seemed to be in darkness. And in a sense it was. But in another sense it was not. For gluing my eyes to the window-pane I discerned a faint reddish glow which could not have come from the oven, for I had no oven, but a simple gas-stove. An oven if you like, but a gas-oven. That is to say there was a real oven too in the kitchen, but out of service. I'm sorry, but there it is, in a house without a gas-oven I would not have felt easy. In the night, interrupting my prowl, I like to go up to a window, lit or unlit, and look into the room, to see what is going on. I cover my face with my hands and peer through my fingers. I have terrified more than one neighbour in this way. He rushes outside, finds no one. For me then from their darkness the darkest rooms emerge, as if still instant with the vanished day or with the light turned out a moment before, for reasons perhaps of which less said the better. But the gloaming in the kitchen was of another kind and came from the night-light with the red chimney which, in Martha's room, adjoining the kitchen, burned eternally at the feet of a little Virgin carved in wood, hanging on the wall. Weary of rocking herself she had gone in and lain down on her bed, leaving the door of her room open so as to miss none of the sounds in the house. But perhaps she had gone to sleep.

I went upstairs again. I stopped at my son's door. I stooped and applied my ear to the keyhole. Some apply the eye, I the ear, to keyholes. I heard nothing, to my great surprise. For my son slept noisily, with open mouth. I took good care not to open the door. For this silence was of a nature to occupy my mind, for some little time. I went to my room.

It was then the unheard of sight was to be seen of Moran making ready to go without knowing where he was going, having consulted neither map nor time-table, considered neither itinerary nor halts, heedless of the weather outlook, with only the vaguest notion of the outfit he would need, the time the expedition was likely to take, the money he would require and even the very nature of the work to be done and consequently the means to be employed. And yet there I was whistling away while I stuffed into my haversack a minimum of effects, similar to those I had recommended to my son. I put on my old pepper-and-salt shooting-suit with the knee-breeches, stockings to match and a pair of stout black boots. I bent down, my hands on my buttocks, and looked at my legs. Knock-kneed and skeleton thin they made a poor show in this accoutrement, unknown locally I may add. But when I left at night, for a distant place, I wore it with pleasure, for the sake of comfort, though I looked a sight. All I needed was a butterfly-net to have vaguely the air of a country schoolmaster on convalescent leave. The heavy glittering black boots, which seemed to implore a pair of navy-blue serge trousers, gave the finishing blow to this get-up which otherwise might have appeared, to the uninformed, an example of well-bred bad taste. On my head, after mature hesitation, I decided to wear my straw boater, yellowed by the rain. It had lost its band, which gave it an appearance of inordinate height. I was tempted to take my black cloak, but finally rejected it in favour of a heavy massive-handled winter umbrella. The cloak is a serviceable garment and I had more than one. It leaves great freedom of movement to the arms and at the same time conceals them. And there are times when a cloak is so to speak indispensable. But the umbrella too has great merits. And if it had been winter, or even autumn, instead of summer, I might have taken both. I had already done so, with most gratifying results.

Dressed thus I could hardly hope to pass unseen. I did not wish to. Conspicuousness is the A B C of my profession. To call forth feelings of pity and indulgence, to be the butt of jeers and hilarity, is indispensable. So many vent-holes in the cask of secrets. On condition you cannot feel, nor denigrate, nor laugh. This state was mine at will. And then there was night.

My son could only embarrass me. He was like a thousand other boys of his age and condition. There is something about a father that discourages derision. Even grotesque he commands a certain respect. And when he is seen out with his young hopeful, whose face grows longer and longer and longer with every step, then no further work is possible. He is taken for a widower, the gaudiest colours are of no avail, rather make things worse, he finds himself saddled with a wife long since deceased, in child-bed as likely as not. And my antics would be viewed as the harmless effect of my widowhood, presumed to have unhinged my mind. I boiled with anger at the thought of him who had shackled me thus. If he had desired my failure he could not have devised a better means to it. If I could have reflected with my usual calm on the work I was required to do, it would perhaps have seemed of a nature more likely to benefit than to suffer by the presence of my son. But let us not go back on that. Perhaps I could pass him off as my assistant, or a mere nephew. I would forbid him to call me papa, or show me any sign of affection, in public, if he did not want to get one of those clouts he so dreaded.

And if I whistled fitfully while revolving these lugubrious thoughts, I suppose it was because I was happy at heart to leave my house, my garden, my village, I who usually left them with regret. Some people whistle for no reason at all. Not I. And while I came and went in my room, tidying up, putting back my clothes in the wardrobe and my hats in the boxes from which I had taken them the better to make my choice, locking the various drawers, while thus employed I had the joyful vision of myself far from home, from the familiar faces, from all my sheet-anchors, sitting on a milestone in the dark, my legs crossed, one hand on my thigh, my elbow in that hand, my chin cupped in the other, my eyes fixed on the earth as on a chess-board, coldly hatching my plans, for the next day, for the day after, creating time to come. And then I forgot that my son would be at my side, restless, plaintive, whinging for food, whinging for sleep, dirtying his drawers. I opened the drawer of my night-table and took out a full tube of morphine tablets, my favourite sedative.

I have a huge bunch of keys, it weighs over a pound. Not a door, not a drawer in my house but the key to it goes with me, wherever I go. I carry them in the right-hand pocket of my trousers, of my breeches in this case. A massive chain, attached to my braces, prevents me from losing them. This chain, four or five times longer than necessary, lies, coiled, on the bunch, in my pocket. Its weight gives me a list to the right, when I am tired, or when I forget to counteract it, by a muscular effort.

I looked round for the last time, saw that I had neglected certain precautions, rectified this, took up my haversack, I nearly wrote my bagpipes, my boater, my umbrella, I hope I'm not forgetting anything, switched off the light, went out into the passage and locked my door. That at least is clear. Immediately I heard a strangling noise. It was my son, sleeping. I woke him. We haven't a moment to lose, I said. Desperately he clung to his sleep. That was natural. A few hours' sleep however deep are not enough for an organism in the first stages of puberty suffering from stomach trouble. And when I began to shake him and help him out of bed, pulling him first by the arms, then by the hair, he turned away from me in fury, to the wall, and dug his nails into the mattress. I had to muster all my strength to overcome his resistance. But I had hardly freed him from the bed when he broke from my hold, threw himself down on the floor and rolled about, screaming with anger and defiance. The fun was begin-ning already. This disgusting exhibition left me no choice but to use my umbrella, holding it by the end with both hands. But a word on the subject of my boater, before I forget. Two holes were bored in the brim, one on either side of course, I had bored them myself, with my little gimlet. And in these holes I had secured the ends of an elastic long enough to pass under my chin, under my jaws rather, but not too long, for it had to hold fast, under my jaws rather. In this way, however great my exertions, my boater stayed in its place, which was on my head. Shame on you, I cried, you ill-bred little pig! I would get angry if I were not careful. And anger is a luxury I cannot afford. For then I go blind, blood veils my eyes and I hear what the great Gustave heard, the benches creaking in the court of assizes. Oh it is not without scathe that one is gentle, courteous, reasonable, patient, day after day, year after year. I threw down my umbrella and ran from the room. On the stairs I met Martha coming up, capless, dishevelled, her clothes in disorder. What's going on? she cried. I looked at her. She went back to her kitchen. Trembling I hastened to the shed, seized my axe, went into the yard and began hacking madly at an old chopping-block that lay there and on which in winter, tranquilly, I split my logs. Finally the blade sank into it so deeply that I could not get it out. The efforts I made to do so brought me, with exhaustion, calm. I went upstairs again. My son was dressing. He was crying. Everybody was crying. I helped him put on his knapsack. I told him not to forget his raincoat. He began to put it in his knapsack. I told him to carry it over his arm, for the moment. It was nearly midnight. I picked up my umbrella. Intact. Get on, I said. He went out of the room which I paused for a moment to survey, before I followed him. It was a shambles. The night was fine, in my humble opinion. Scents filled the air. The gravel crunched under our feet. No, I said, this way. I entered the little wood. My son floundered behind me, bumping into the trees. He did not know how to find his way in the dark. He was still young, the words of reproach died on my lips. I stopped. Take my hand, I said. I might have said, Give me your hand. I said, Take my hand. Strange. But the path was too narrow for us to walk abreast. So I put my hand behind me and my son grasped it, gratefully I fancied. So we came to the little wicket-gate. It was locked. I unlocked it and stood aside, to let my son precede me. I turned back to look at my house. It was partly hidden by the little wood. The roof's serrated ridge, the single chimney-stack with its four flues, stood out faintly against the sky spattered with a few dim stars. I offered my face to the black mass of fragrant vegetation that was mine and with which I could do as I pleased and never be gainsaid. It was full of song-birds, their heads under their wings, fearing nothing, for they knew me. My trees, my bushes, my flower-beds, my tiny lawns, I used to think I loved them. If I sometimes cut a branch, a flower, it was solely for their good, that they might increase in strength and happiness. And I never did it without a pang. Indeed if the truth were known, I did not do it at all, I got Christy to do it. I grew no vegetables. Not far off was the hen-house. When I said I had turkeys, and so on, I lied. All I had was a few hens. My grey hen was there, not on the perch with the others, but on the ground, in a corner, in the dust, at the mercy of the rats. The cock no longer sought her out to tread her angrily. The day was at hand, if she did not take a turn for the better, when the other hens would join forces and tear her to pieces, with their beaks and claws. All was silent. I have an extremely sensitive ear. Yet I have no ear for music. I could just hear that adorable murmur of tiny feet, of quivering feathers and feeble, smothered clucking that hen-houses make at night and that dies down long before dawn. How often I had listened to it, entranced, in the evening, saying, Tomorrow I am free. And so I turned again a last time towards my little all, before I left it, in the hope of keeping it.

In the lane, having locked the wicket-gate, I said to my son, Left. I had long since given up going for walks with my son, though I sometimes longed to do so. The least outing with him was torture, he lost his way so easily. Yet when alone he seemed to know all the short cuts. When I sent him to the grocer's, or to Mrs Clement's, or even further afield, on the road to V for grain, he was back in half the time I would have taken for the journey myself, and without having run. For I did not want my son to be seen capering in the streets like the little hooligans he frequented on the sly. No, I wanted him to walk like his father, with little rapid steps, his head up, his breathing even and economical, his arms swinging, looking neither to left nor right, apparently oblivious to everything and in reality missing nothing. But with me he invariably took the wrong turn, a crossing or a simple corner was all he needed to stray from the right road, it of my election. I do not think he did this on purpose. But leaving everything to me he did not heed what he was doing, or look where he was going, and went on mechanically plunged in a kind of dream. It was as though he let himself be sucked in out of sight by every opening that offered. So that we had got into the habit of taking our walks separately. And the only walk we regularly took together was that which led us, every Sunday, from home to church and, mass over, from church to home. Caught up then in the slow tide of the faithful my son was not alone with me. But he was part of that docile herd going yet again to thank God for his goodness and to implore his mercy and forgiveness, and then returning, their souls made easy, to other gratifications.

I waited for him to come back, then spoke the words calculated to settle this matter once and for all. Get behind me, I said, and keep behind me. This solution had its points, from several points of view. But was he capable of keeping behind me? Would not the time be bound to come when he would raise his head and find himself alone, in a strange place, and when I, waking from my reverie, would turn and find him gone? I toyed briefly with the idea of attaching him to me by means of a long rope, its two ends tied about our waists. There are various ways of attracting attention and I was not sure that this was one of the good ones. And he might have undone his knots in silence and escaped, leaving me to go on my way alone, followed by a long rope trailing in the dust, like a burgess of Calais. Until such time as the rope, catching on some fixed or heavy object, should stop me dead in my stride. We should have needed, not the soft and silent rope, but a chain, which was not to be dreamt of. And yet I did dream of it, for an instant I amused myself dreaming of it, imagining myself in a world less ill contrived and wondering how, having nothing more than a simple chain, without collar or band or gyves or fetters of any kind, I could chain my son to me in such a way as to prevent him from ever shaking me off again. It was a simple problem of toils and knots and I could have solved it at a pinch. But already I was called elsewhere by the image of my son no longer behind me, but before me. Thus in the rear I could keep my eye on him and intervene, at the least false movement he might make. But apart from having other parts to play, during this expedition, than those of keeper and sick-nurse, the prospect was more than I could bear of being unable to move a step without having before my eyes my son's little sullen plump body. Come here! I cried. For on hearing me say we were to go to the left he had gone to the left, as if his dearest wish was to infuriate me. Slumped over my umbrella, my head sunk as beneath a malediction, the fingers of my free hand between two slats of the wicket, I no more stirred than if I had been of stone. So he came back a second time. I tell you to keep behind me and you go before me, I said.

It was the summer holidays. His school cap was green with initials and a boar's head, or a deer's, in gold braid on the front. It lay plumb on his big blond skull as precise as a lid on a pot. There is something about this strict sit of hats and caps that never fails to exasperate me. As for his raincoat, instead of carrying it folded over his arm, or flung across his shoulder, as I had told him, he had rolled it in a ball and was holding it with both hands, on his belly. There he was before me, his big feet splayed, his knees sagging, his stomach sticking out, his chest sunk, his chin in the air, his mouth open, in the attitude of a veritable half-wit. I myself must have looked as if only the support of my umbrella and the wicket were keeping me from falling. I managed finally to articulate, Are you capable of following me? He did not answer. But I seized his thoughts as clearly as if he had spoken them, namely, And you, are you capable of leading me? Midnight struck, from the steeple of my beloved church. It did not matter. I was gone from home. I sought in my mind, where all I need is to be found, what treasured possession he was likely to have about him. I hope, I said, you have not forgotten your scout-knife, we might need it. This knife comprised, apart from the five or six indispensable blades, a cork-screw, a tin-opener, a punch, a screw-driver, a claw, a gouge for removing stones from hooves and I know not what other futilities besides. I had given it to him myself, on the occasion of his first first prize for history and geography, subjects which, at the school he attended, were for obscure reasons regarded as inseparable. The veriest dunce when it came to literature and the so-called exact sciences, he had no equal for the dates of battles, revolutions, restorations and other exploits of the human race, in its slow ascension towards the light, and for the configuration of frontiers and the heights of mountain peaks. He deserved his scout-knife. Don't tell me you've left it behind, I said. Not likely, he said, with pride and satisfaction, tapping his pocket. Then give it to me, I said. Naturally he did not answer. Prompt obedience was contrary to his habits. Give me that knife! I cried. He gave it to me. What could he do, alone with me in the night that tells no tales? It was for his own good, to save him from getting lost. For where a scout's knife is, there will his heart be also, unless he can afford to buy another, which was not the case with my son. For he never had any money in his pocket, not needing it. But every penny he received, and he did not receive many, he deposited first in his savings-box, then in the savings-bank, where they were entered in a book that remained in my possession. He would doubtless at that moment with pleasure have cut my throat, with that selfsame knife I was putting so placidly in my pocket. But he was still a little on the young side, my son, a little on the soft side, for the great deeds of vengeance. But time was on his side and he consoled himself perhaps with that thought, foolish though he was. Be that as it may, he kept back his tears, for which I was obliged to him. I straightened myself and laid my hand on his shoulder, saying, Patience, my child, patience. The awful thing in affairs of this kind is that when you have the will you do not have the way, and vice versa. But of that my unfortunate son could as yet have no suspicion, he must have thought that the rage which distorted his features and made him tremble would never leave him till the day he could vent it as it deserved. And not even then. Yes, he must have felt his soul the soul of a pocket Monte Cristo, with whose antics as adumbrated in the Schoolboys' Classics he was needless to say familiar. Then with a good clap on that impotent back I said, Off we go. And off indeed I did go, what is more, and my son drew out behind me. I had left, accompanied by my son, in accordance with instructions received.

I have no intention of relating the various adventures which befell us, me and my son, together and singly, before we came to the Molloy country. It would be tedious. But that is not what stops me. All is tedious, in this relation that is forced upon me. But I shall conduct it in my own way, up to a point. And if it has not the good fortune to give satisfaction, to my employer, if there are passages that give offence to him and to his colleagues, then so much the worse for us all, for them all, for there is no worse for me. That is to say, I have not enough imagination to imagine it. And yet I have more than before. And if I submit to this paltry scrivening which is not of my province, it is for reasons very different from those that might be supposed. I am still obeying orders, if you like, but no longer out of fear. No, I am still afraid, but simply from force of habit. And the voice I listen to needs no Gaber to make it heard. For it is within me and exhorts me to continue to the end the faithful servant I have always been, of a cause that is not mine, and patiently fulfil in all its bitterness my calamitous part, as it was my will, when I had a will, that others should. And this with hatred in my heart, and scorn, of my master and his designs. Yes, it is rather an ambiguous voice and not always easy to follow, in its reasonings and decrees. But I follow it none the less, more or less, I follow it in this sense, that I know what it means, and in this sense, that I do what it tells me. And I do not think there are many voices of which as much may be said. And I feel I shall follow it from this day forth, no matter what it commands. And when it ceases, leaving me in doubt and darkness, I shall wait for it to come back, and do nothing, even though the whole world, through the channel of its innumerable authorities speaking with one accord, should enjoin upon me this and that, under pain of unspeakable punishments. But this evening, this morning, I have drunk a little more than usual and tomorrow I may be of a different mind. It also tells me, this voice I am only just beginning to know, that the memory of this work brought scrupulously to a close will help me to endure the long anguish of vagrancy and freedom. Does this mean I shall one day be banished from my house, from my garden, lose my trees, my lawns, my birds of which the least is known to me and the way all its own it has of singing, of flying, of coming up to me or fleeing at my coming, lose and be banished from the absurd comforts of my home where all is snug and neat and all those things at hand without which I could not bear being a man, where my enemies cannot reach me, which it was my life's work to build, to adorn, to perfect, to keep? I am too old to lose all this, and begin again, I am too old! Quiet, Moran, quiet. No emotion, please.

I was saying I would not relate all the vicissitudes of the journey from my country to Molloy's, for the simple reason that I do not intend to. And in writing these lines I know in what danger I am of offending him whose favour I know I should court, now more than ever. But I write them all the same, and with a firm hand weaving inexorably back and forth and devouring my page with the indifference of a shuttle. But some I shall relate briefly, because that seems to me desirable, and in order to give some idea of the methods of my full maturity. But before coming to that I shall say what little I knew, on leaving my home, about the Molloy country, so different from my own. For it is one of the features of this penance that I may not pass over what is over and straightway come to the heart of the matter. But that must again be unknown to me which is no longer so and that again fondly believed which then I fondly believed, at my setting out. And if I occasionally break this rule, it is only over details of little importance. And in the main I observe it. And with such zeal that I am far more he who finds than he who tells what he has found, now as then, most of the time, I do not exaggerate. And in the silence of my room, and all over as far as I am concerned, I know scarcely any better where I am going and what awaits me than the night I clung to the wicket, beside my idiot of a son, in the lane. And it would not surprise me if I deviated, in the pages to follow, from the true and exact succession of events. But I do not think even Sisyphus is required to scratch himself, or to groan, or to rejoice, as the fashion is now, always at the same appointed places. And it may even be they are not too particular about the route he takes provided it gets him to his destination safely and on time. And perhaps he thinks each journey is the first. This would keep hope alive, would it not, hellish hope. Whereas to see yourself doing the same thing endlessly over and over again fills you with satisfaction.

By the Molloy country I mean that narrow region whose administrative limits he had never crossed and presumably never would, either because he was forbidden to, or because he had no wish to, or of course because of some extraordinary fortuitous conjunction of circumstances. This region was situated in the north, I mean in relation to mine, less bleak, and comprised a settlement, dignified by some with the name of market-town, by others regarded as no more than a village, and the surrounding country. This market-town, or village, was, I hasten to say, called Bally, and represented, with its dependent lands, a surface area of five or six square miles at the most. In modern countries this is what I think is called a commune, or a canton, I forget, but there exists with us no abstract and generic term for such territorial subdivisions. And to express them we have another system, of singular beauty and simplicity, which consists in saying Bally (since we are talking of Bally) when you mean Bally and Ballyba when you mean Bally plus its domains and Ballybaba when you mean the domains exclusive of Bally itself. I myself for example lived, and come to think of it still live, in Turdy, hub of Turdyba. And in the evening, when I went for a stroll, in the country outside Turdy, to get a breath of fresh air, it was the fresh air of Turdybaba that I got, and no other.

Ballybaba, in spite of its limited range, could boast of a certain diversity. Pastures so-called, a little bogland, a few copses and, as you neared its confines, undulating and almost smiling aspects, as if Ballybaba was glad to go no further.

But the principal beauty of this region was a kind of strangled creek which the slow grey tides emptied and filled, emptied and filled. And the people came flocking from the town, unromantic people, to admire this spectacle. Some said, There is nothing more beautiful than these wet sands. Others, High tide is the best time to see the creek of Ballyba. How lovely then that leaden water, you would swear it was stagnant, if you did not know it was not. And yet others held it was like an underground lake. But all were agreed, like the inhabitants of Blackpool, that their town was on the sea. And they had Bally-on-Sea printed on their notepaper.

The population of Ballyba was small. I confess this thought gave me great satisfaction. The land did not lend itself to cultivation. No sooner did a tilth, or a meadow, begin to be sizeable than it fell foul of a sacred grove or a stretch of marsh from which nothing could be obtained beyond a little inferior turf or scraps of bogoak used for making amulets, paper-knives, napkinrings, rosaries and other knick-knacks. Martha's madonna, for example, came from Ballyba. The pastures, in spite of the torrential rains, were exceedingly meagre and strewn with boulders. Here only quitchweed grew in abundance, and a curious bitter blue grass fatal to cows and horses, though tolerated apparently by the ass, the goat and the black sheep. What then was the source of Ballyba's prosperity? I'll tell you. No, I'll tell you nothing. Nothing.

That then is a part of what I thought I knew about Ballyba when I left home. I wonder if I was not confusing it with some other place.

Some twenty paces from my wicket-gate the lane skirts the graveyard wall. The lane descends, the wall rises, higher and higher. Soon you are faring below the dead. It is there I have my plot in perpetuity. As long as the earth endures that spot is mine, in theory. Sometimes I went and looked at my grave. The stone was up already. It was a simple Latin cross, white. I wanted to have my name put on it, with the here lies and the date of my birth. Then all it would have wanted was the date of my death. They would not let me. Sometimes I smiled, as if I were dead already.

We walked for several days, by sequestered ways. I did not want to be seen on the highways.

The first day I found the butt of Father Ambrose's cigar. Not only had I not thrown it away, in the ash-tray, in the waste-paper basket, but I had put it in my pocket, when changing my suit. That had happened unbeknown to me. I looked at it in astonishment, lit it, took a few puffs, threw it away. This was the outstanding event of the first day.

I showed my son how to use his pocket-compass. This gave him great pleasure. He was behaving well, better than I had hoped. On the third day I gave him back his knife.

The weather was kind. We easily managed our ten miles a day. We slept in the open. Safety first.

I showed my son how to make a shelter out of branches. He was in the scouts, but knew nothing. Yes, he knew how to make a camp-fire. At every halt he implored me to let him exercise this talent. I saw no point in doing so.

We lived on tinned food which I sent him to get in the villages. He was that much use to me. We drank the water of the streams.

All these precautions were assuredly useless. One day in a field I saw a farmer I knew. He was coming towards us. I turned immediately, took my son by the arm and led him away in the direction we were coming from. The farmer overtook us, as I had foreseen. Having greeted me, he asked where we were going. It must have been his field. I replied that we were going home. Fortunately we had not yet left it far behind. Then he asked me where we had been. Perhaps one of his cows had been stolen, or one of his pigs. Out walking, I said. I'd give you a lift and welcome, he said, but I won't be leaving till night. Oh how very unfortunate, I said. If you care to wait, he said, you're very welcome. I declined with thanks. Fortunately it was not yet midday. There was nothing strange in not wanting to wait till night. Well, safe home, he said. We made a wide detour and turned our faces to the north again.

These precautions were doubtless exaggerated. The right thing would have been to travel by night and hide during the day, at least in the early stages. But the weather was so fine I could not bring myself to do it. My pleasure was not my sole consideration, but it was a consideration! Such a thing had never happened to me before, in the course of my work. And our snail's pace! I cannot have been in a hurry to arrive.

I gave fitful thought, while basking in the balm of the warm summer days, to Gaber's instructions. I could not reconstruct them to my entire satisfaction. In the night, under the boughs, screened from the charms of nature, I devoted myself to this problem. The sounds my son made during his sleep hindered me considerably. Sometimes I went out of the shelter and walked up and down, in the dark. Or I sat down with my back against a trunk, drew my feet up under me, took my legs in my arms and rested my chin on my knee. Even in this posture I could throw no light on the matter. What was I looking for exactly? It is hard to say. I was looking for what was wanting to make Gaber's statement complete. I felt he must have told me what to do with Molloy once he was found. My particular duties never terminated with the running to earth. That would have been too easy. But I had always to deal with the client in one way or another, according to instructions. Such operations took on a multitude of forms, from the most vigorous to the most discreet. The Yerk affair, which took me nearly three months to conclude successfully, was over on the day I succeeded in possessing myself of his tiepin and destroying it. Establishing contact was the least important part of my work. I found Yerk on the third day. I was never required to prove I had succeeded,

my word was enough. Youdi must have had some way of verify-
ing. Sometimes I was asked for a report.

On another occasion my mission consisted in bringing the
person to a certain place at a certain time. A most delicate
affair, for the person concerned was not a woman. I have never
had to deal with a woman. I regret it. I don't think Youdi had
much interest in them. That reminds me of the old joke about
the female soul. Question, Have women a soul? Answer, Yes.
Question, Why? Answer, In order that they may be damned.
Very witty. Fortunately I had been allowed considerable licence
as to the day. The hour was the important thing, not the date.
He came to the appointed place and there I left him, on some
pretext or other. He was a nice youth, rather sad and silent. I
vaguely remember having invented some story about a woman.
Wait, it's coming back. Yes, I told him she had been in love with
him for six months and greatly desired to meet him in some
secluded place. I even gave her name. Quite a well-known
actress. Having brought him to the place appointed by her, it
was only natural I should withdraw, out of delicacy. I can see
him still, looking after me. I fancy he would have liked me for a
friend. I don't know what became of him. I lost interest in my
patients, once I had finished with them. I may even truthfully
say I never saw one of them again, subsequently, not a single
one. No conclusions need be drawn from this. Oh the stories I
could tell you, if I were easy. What a rabble in my head, what a
gallery of moribunds. Murphy, Watt, Yerk, Mercier and all the
others. I would never have believed that—yes, I believe it willingly. Stories, stories. I have not been able to tell them. I shall
not be able to tell this one.

I could not determine therefore how I was to deal with
Molloy, once I had found him. The directions which Gaber must
certainly have given me with reference to this had gone clean out
of my head. That is what came of wasting the whole of that
Sunday on stupidities. There was no good my saying, Let me see
now, what is the usual thing? There were no usual things, in my
instructions. Admittedly there was one particular operation that

recurred from time to time, but not often enough to be, with any degree of probability, the one I was looking for. But even if it had always figured in my instructions, except on one single occasion, then that single occasion would have been enough to tie my hands, I was so scrupulous.

I told myself I had better give it no more thought, that the first thing to do was to find Molloy, that then I would devise something, that there was no hurry, that the thing would come back to me when I least expected it and that if, having found Molloy, I still did not know what to do with him, I could always manage to get in touch with Gaber without Youdi's knowing. I had his address just as he had mine. I would send him a telegram, How deal with M? To give me an explicit reply, though in terms if necessary veiled, was not beyond his powers. But was there a telegraph in Ballyba? But I also told myself, being only human, that the longer I took to find Molloy the greater my chances of remembering what I was to do with him. And we would have peaceably pursued our way on foot, but for the following incident.

One night, having finally succeeded in falling asleep beside my son as usual, I woke with a start, feeling as if I had just been dealt a violent blow. It's all right, I am not going to tell you a dream properly so called. It was pitch dark in the shelter. I listened attentively without moving. I heard nothing save the snoring and gasping of my son. I was about to conclude as usual that it was just another bad dream when a fulgurating pain went through my knee. This then was the explanation of my sudden awakening. The sensation could indeed well be compared to that of a blow, such as I fancy a horse's hoof might give. I waited anxiously for it to recur, motionless and hardly breathing, and of course sweating. I acted in a word precisely as one does, if my information was correct, at such a juncture. And sure enough the pain did recur a few minutes later, but not so bad as the first time, as the second rather. Or did it only seem less bad to me because I was expecting it? Or because I was getting used to it already? I think not. For it recurred again, several times, and each time less bad than the time before, and finally subsided altogether so that I was able to get to sleep again more or less reassured. But before getting to sleep again I had time to remember that the pain in question was not altogether new to me. For I had felt it before, in my bathroom, when giving my son his enema. But then it had only attacked me once and never recurred, till now. And I went to sleep again wondering, by way of lullaby, whether it had been the same knee then as the one which had just excruciated me, or the other. And that is a thing I have never been able to determine. And my son too, when asked, was incapable of telling me which of my two knees I had rubbed in front of him, with iodex, the night we left. And I went to sleep again a little reassured, saying, It's a touch of neuralgia brought on by all the tramping and trudging and the chill damp nights, and promising myself to procure a packet of thermogene wool, with the pretty demon on the outside, at the first opportunity. Such is the rapidity of thought. But there was more to come. For waking again towards dawn, this time in consequence of a natural need, and with a mild erection, to make things more lifelike, I was unable to get up. That is to say I did get up finally to be sure, I simply had to, but by dint of what exertions! Unable, unable, it's easy to talk about being unable, whereas in reality nothing is more difficult. Because of the will I suppose, which the least opposition seems to lash into a fury. And this explains no doubt how it was I despaired at first of ever bending my leg again and then, a little later, through sheer determination, did succeed in bending it, slightly. The anchylosis was not total! I am still talking about my knee. But was it the same one that had waked me early in the night? I could not have sworn it was. It was not painful. It simply refused to bend. The pain, having warned me several times in vain, had no more to say. That is how I saw it. It would have been impossible for me to kneel, for example, for no matter how you kneel you must always bend both knees, unless you adopt an attitude frankly grotesque and impossible to maintain for more than a few seconds, I mean with the bad leg stretched out before you, like a Caucasian dancer. I examined the bad knee in the light of my torch. It was neither red nor swollen. I fiddled with the knee-cap. It felt like a clitoris. All this time my son was puffing like a grampus. He had no suspicion of what life could do to you. I too was innocent. But I knew it.

The sky was that horrible colour which heralds dawn. Things steal back into position for the day, take their stand, sham dead. I sat down cautiously, and I must say with a certain curiosity, on the ground. Anyone else would have tried to sit down as usual, off-handedly. Not I. New as this new cross was I at once found the most comfortable way of being crushed. But when you sit down on the ground you must sit down tailor-wise, or like a foetus, these are so to speak the only possible positions, for a beginner. So that I was not long in letting myself fall back flat on my back. And I was not long either in making the following addition to the sum of my knowledge, that when of the innumer-able attitudes adopted unthinkingly by the normal man all are precluded but two or three, then these are enhanced. I would have sworn just the opposite, but for this experience. Yes, when you can neither stand nor sit with comfort, you take refuge in the horizontal, like a child in its mother's lap. You explore it as never before and find it possessed of unsuspected delights. In short it becomes infinite. And if in spite of all you come to tire of it in the end, you have only to stand up, or indeed sit up, for a few seconds. Such are the advantages of a local and painless paralysis. And it would not surprise me if the great classical paralyses were to offer analogous and perhaps even still more unspeakable satisfactions. To be literally incapable of motion at last, that must be something! My mind swoons when I think of it. And mute into the bargain! And perhaps as deaf as a post! And who knows as blind as a bat! And as likely as not your memory a blank! And just enough brain intact to allow you to exult! And to dread death like a regeneration.

I considered the problem of what I should do if my leg did not get better or got worse. I watched, through the branches, the sky sinking. The sky sinks in the morning, this fact has been

insufficiently observed. It stoops, as if to get a better look.
Unless it is the earth that lifts itself up, to be approved, before
it sets out.

I shall not expound my reasoning. I could do so easily, so
easily. Its conclusion made possible the composition of the
following passage.

Did you have a good night? I said, as soon as my son opened
his eyes. I could have waked him, but no, I let him wake naturally. Finally he told me he did not feel well. My son's replies
were often beside the point. Where are we, I said, and what is
the nearest village? He named it. I knew it, I had been there, it
was a small town, luck was on our side. I even had a few
acquaintances, among its inhabitants. What day is it? I said. He
specified the day without a moment's hesitation. And he had
only just regained consciousness! I told you he had a genius for
history and geography. It was from him I learned that Condom
is on the Baise. Good, I said, off you go now to Hole, it'll take
you—I worked it out—at the most three hours. He stared at me
in astonishment. There, I said, buy a bicycle to fit you, second-
hand for preference. You can go up to five pounds. I gave him
five pounds, in ten-shilling notes. It must have a very strong
carrier, I said, if it isn't very strong get it changed, for a very
strong one. I was trying to be clear. I asked him if he was
pleased. He did not look pleased. I repeated these instructions
and asked him again if he was pleased. He looked if anything
stupefied. A consequence perhaps of the great joy he felt.
Perhaps he could not believe his ears. Do you understand if
nothing else? I said. What a boon it is from time to time, a little
real conversation. Tell me what you are to do, I said. It was the
only way of knowing if he understood. Go to Hole, he said,
fifteen miles away. Fifteen miles! I cried. Yes, he said. All right,
I said, go on. And buy a bicycle, he said. I waited. Silence. A
bicycle! I cried. But there are millions of bicycles in Hole! What
kind of bicycle? He reflected. Second-hand, he said, at a
venture. And if you can't find one second-hand? I said. You told
me second-hand, he said. I remained silent for some time. And

if you can't find one second-hand, I said at last, what will you do? You didn't tell me, he said. What a restful change it is from time to time, a little dialogue. How much money did I give you? I said. He counted the notes. Four pounds ten, he said. Count them again, I said. He counted them again. Four pounds ten, he said. Give it to me, I said. He gave me the notes and I counted them. Four pounds ten. I gave you five, I said. He did not answer, he let the figures speak for themselves. Had he stolen ten shillings and hidden them on his person? Empty your pockets, I said. He began to empty them. It must not be forgotten that all this time I was lying down. He did not know I was ill. Besides I was not ill. I looked vaguely at the objects he was spreading out before me. He took them out of his pockets one by one, held them up delicately between finger and thumb, turned them this way and that before my eyes and laid them finally on the ground beside me. When a pocket was emptied he pulled out its lining and shook it. Then a little cloud of dust arose. I was very soon overcome by the absurdity of this verification. I told him to stop. Perhaps he was hiding the ten shillings up his sleeve, or in his mouth. I should have had to get up and search him myself, inch by inch. But then he would have seen I was ill. Not that I was exactly ill. And why did I not want him to know I was ill? I don't know. I could have counted the money I had left. But what use would that have been? Did I even know the amount I had brought with me? No. To me too I cheerfully applied the maieutic method. Did I know how much I had spent? No. Usually I kept the most rigorous accounts when away on business and was in a position to justify my expenditure down to the last penny. This time no. For I was throwing my money away with as little concern as if I had been travelling for my pleasure. Let us suppose I am wrong, I said, and that I only gave you four pounds ten. He was calmly picking up the objects littered on the ground and putting them back in his pockets. How could he be made to understand? Stop that and listen, I said. I gave him the notes. Count them, I said. He counted them. How much? I said. Four pounds ten, he said. Ten what? I said. Ten shillings, he said. You have four pounds ten shillings? I said. Yes, he said. It was not true, I had given him five. You agree, I said. Yes, he said. And why do you think I have given you all that money? I said. His face brightened. To buy a bicycle, he said, without hesitation. Do you imagine a second-hand bicycle costs four pounds ten shillings? I said. I don't know, he said. I did not know either. But that was not the point. What did I tell you exactly? I said. We racked our brains together. Second-hand for preference, I said finally, that's what I told you. Ah, he said. I am not giving this duet in full. Just the main themes. I didn't tell you second-hand, I said, I told you second-hand for preference. He had started picking up his things again. Will you stop that, I cried, and pay attention to what I am saying. He ostentatiously let fall a big ball of tangled string. The ten shillings were perhaps inside it. You see no difference between second-hand and second-hand for preference, I said, do you? I looked at my watch. It was ten o'clock. I was only making our ideas more confused. Stop trying to understand, I said, just listen to what I am going to say, because I shall not say it twice. He came over to me and knelt down. You would have thought I was about to breathe my last. Do you know what a new bicycle is? I said. Yes papa, he said. Very well, I said, if you can't find a second-hand bicycle buy a new bicycle. I repeat. I repeated. I who had said I would not repeat. Now tell me what you are to do, I said. I added, Take your face away, your breath stinks. I almost added, You don't brush your teeth and you complain of having abscesses, but I stopped myself in time. It was not the moment to introduce another theme. I repeated, Tell me what you are to do. He pondered. Go to Hole, he said, fifteen miles away—. Don't worry about the miles, I said. You're in Hole. What for? No, I can't. Finally he understood. Who is this bicycle for, I said, Goering? He had not yet grasped that the bicycle was for him. Admittedly he was nearly my size already. As for the carrier, I might just as well not have mentioned it. But in the end he had the whole thing off pat. So much so that he actually asked me what he was to do if he had not enough

money. Come back here and ask me, I said. I had naturally foreseen, while reflecting on all these matters before my son woke,
that he might have trouble with people asking him how he came
by so much money and he so young. And I knew what he was
to do in that event, namely go and see, or send for, the police-
sergeant, give his name and say it was I, Jacques Moran, osten-
sibly at home in Turdy, who had sent him to buy a bicycle in
Hole. Here obviously two distinct operations were involved, the
first consisting in foreseeing the difficulty (before my son woke),
the second in overcoming it (at the news that Hole was the
nearest locality). But there was no question of my conveying
instructions of such complexity. But don't worry, I said, you've
enough and to spare to buy yourself a good bicycle. I added,
And bring it back here as fast as you can. You had to allow for
everything with my son. He could never have guessed what to
do with the bicycle once he had it. He was capable of hanging
about Hole, under God knows what conditions, waiting for
further instructions. He asked me what was wrong. I must have
winced. I'm sick of the sight of you, I said, that's what's wrong.
And I asked him what he was waiting for. I don't feel well, he
said. When he asked me how I was I said nothing, and when no
one asked him anything he announced he was not feeling well.
Are you not pleased, I said, to have a nice brand-new bicycle,
all your own? I was decidedly set on hearing him say he was
pleased. But I regretted my phrase, it could only add to his
confusion. But perhaps this family chat has lasted long enough.
He left the shelter and when I judged he was at a safe distance
I left it too, painfully. He had gone about twenty paces. Leaning
nonchalantly against a tree-trunk, my good leg boldly folded
across the other, I tried to look light-hearted. I hailed him. He
turned. I waved my hand. He stared at me an instant, then
turned away and went on. I shouted his name. He turned again.
A lamp! I cried. A good lamp! He did not understand. How
could he have understood, at twenty paces, he who could not
understand at one. He came back towards me. I waved him
away, crying, Go on! Go on! He stopped and stared at me, his

head on one side like a parrot, utterly bewildered apparently. Foolishly I made to stoop, to pick up a stone or a piece of wood or a clod, anything in the way of a projectile, and nearly fell. I reached up above my head, broke off a live bough and hurled it violently in his direction. He spun round and took to his heels. Really there were times I could not understand my son. He must have known he was out of range, even of a good stone, and yet he took to his heels. Perhaps he was afraid I would run after him. And indeed, I think there is something terrifying about the way I run, with my head flung back, my teeth clenched, my elbows bent to the full and my knees nearly hitting me in the face. And I have often caught faster runners than myself thanks to this way of running. They stop and wait for me, rather than prolong such a horrible outburst at their heels. As for the lamp, we did not need a lamp. Later, when the bicycle had taken its place in my son's life, in the round of his duties and his innocent games, then a lamp would be indispensable, to light his way in the night. And no doubt it was in anticipation of those happy days that I had thought of the lamp and cried out to my son to buy a good one, that later on his comings and his goings should not be hemmed about with darkness and with dangers. And similarly I might have told him to be careful about the bell, to unscrew the little cap and examine it well inside, so as to make sure it was a good bell and in good working order, before concluding the transaction, and to ring it to hear the ring it made. But we would have time enough, later on, to see to all these things. And it would be my joy to help my son, when the time came, to fit his bicycle with the best lamps, both front and rear, and the best bell and the best brakes that money could buy.

The day seemed very long. I missed my son! I busied myself as best I could. I ate several times. I took advantage of being alone at last, with no other witness than God, to masturbate. My son must have had the same idea, he must have stopped on the way to masturbate. I hope he enjoyed it more than I did. I circled the shelter several times, thinking the exercise would benefit my knee. I moved at quite a good speed and without much pain, but I soon tired. After ten or eleven steps a great weariness seized hold of my leg, a heaviness rather, and I had to stop. It went away at once and I was able to go on. I took a little morphine. I asked myself certain questions. Why had I not told my son to bring me back something for my leg? Why had I hidden my condition from him? Was I secretly glad that this had happened to me, perhaps even to the point of not wanting to get well? I surrendered myself to the beauties of the scene, I gazed at the trees, the fields, the sky, the birds, and I listened attentively to the sounds, faint and clear, borne to me on the air. For an instant I fancied I heard the silence mentioned, if I am not mistaken, above. Stretched out in the shelter, I brooded on the undertaking in which I was embarked. I tried again to remember what I was to do with Molloy, when I found him. I dragged myself down to the stream. I lay down and looked at my reflection, then I washed my face and hands. I waited for my image to come back, I watched it as it trembled towards an ever increasing likeness. Now and then a drop, falling from my face, shattered it again. I did not see a soul all day. But towards evening I heard a prowling about the shelter. I did not move, and the footsteps died away. But a little later, having left the shelter for some reason or other, I saw a man a few paces off, standing motionless. He had his back to me. He wore a coat much too heavy for the time of the year and was leaning on a stick so massive, and so much thicker at the bottom than at the top, that it seemed more like a club. He turned and we looked at each other for some time in silence. That is to say I looked him full in the face, as I always do, to make people think I am not afraid, whereas he merely threw me a rapid glance from time to time, then lowered his eyes, less from timidity apparently than in order quietly to think over what he had just seen, before adding to it. There was a coldness in his stare, and a thrust, the like of which I never saw. His face was pale and noble, I could have done with it. I was thinking he could not be much over fifty-five when he took off his hat, held it for a moment in his hand, then put it back on his head. No resemblance to what is called raising one's hat. But I thought it advisable to nod. The hat was quite extraordinary, in shape and colour. I shall not attempt to describe it, it was like none I had ever seen. He had a huge shock of dirty snow-white hair. I had time, before he squeezed it in back under his hat, to see the way it swelled up on his skull. His face was dirty and hairy, yes, pale, noble, dirty and hairy. He made a curious movement, like a hen that puffs up its feathers and slowly dwindles till it is smaller than before. I thought he was going to depart without a word to me. But suddenly he asked me to give him a piece of bread. He accompanied this humiliating request with a fiery look. His accent was that of a foreigner or of one who had lost the habit of speech. But had I not said already, with relief, at the mere sight of his back, He's a foreigner. Would you like a tin of sardines? I said. He asked for bread and I offered him fish. That is me all over. Bread, he said. I went into the shelter and took the piece of bread I was keeping for my son, who would proba-bly be hungry when he came back. I gave it to him. I expected him to devour it there and then. But he broke it in two and put the pieces in his coat-pockets. Do you mind if I look at your stick? I said. I stretched out my hand. He did not move. I put my hand on the stick, just under his. I could feel his fingers gradually letting go. Now it was I who held the stick. Its light-ness astounded me. I put it back in his hand. He threw me a last look and went. It was almost dark. He walked with swift uncer-tain step, often changing his course, dragging the stick like a hindrance. I wished I could have stood there looking after him, and time at a standstill. I wished I could have been in the middle of a desert, under the midday sun, to look after him till he was only a dot, on the edge of the horizon. I stayed out in the air for a long time. Every now and then I listened. But my son did not come. Beginning to feel cold I went back into the shelter and lay down, under my son's raincoat. But beginning to feel sleepy I went out again and lit a big wood-fire, to guide my son towards me. When the fire had kindled I said, Why of course, now I can warm myself! I warmed myself, rubbing my hands together after having held them to the flame and before holding them to it again, and turning my back to the flame and lifting the tail of my coat, and turning as on a spit. And in the end, overcome with heat and weariness, I lay down on the ground near the fire and fell asleep, saying, Perhaps a spark will set fire to my clothes and I wake a living torch. And saying many other things besides, belonging to separate and apparently unconnected trains of thought. But when I woke it was day again and the fire was out. But the embers were still warm. My leg was no better, but it was no worse either. That is to say it was perhaps a little worse, without my being in a condition to realize it, for the simple reason that this leg was becoming a habit, mercifully. But I think not. For at the same time as I listened to my knee, and then submitted it to various tests, I was on my guard against the effects of this habit and tried to discount them. And it was not so much Moran as another, in the secret of Moran's sensations exclusively, who said, No change, Moran, no change. This may seem impossible. I went into the copse to cut myself a stick. But having finally found a suitable branch, I remembered I had no knife. I went back to the shelter, hoping to find my son's knife among the things he had laid on the ground and neglected to pick up. It was not among them. To make up for this I came across my umbrella and said, Why cut myself a stick when I have my umbrella? And I practised walking with the help of my umbrella. And though in this way I moved no faster and no less painfully, at least I did not tire so quickly. And instead of having to stop every ten steps, to rest, I easily managed fifteen, before having to stop. And even while I rested my umbrella was a help. For I found that when I leaned upon it the heaviness in my leg, due probably to a defect in the bloodstream, disappeared even more quickly than when I stood supported only by my muscles and the tree of life. And thus equipped I no longer confined myself to circling about the shelter, as I had done the previous day, but I radiated from it in every direction. And I even gained a little knoll from which I had a better view of the expanse where my son might suddenly rise into view, at any moment.

And in my mind's eye from time to time I saw him, bent over the handlebars or standing on the pedals, drawing near, and I heard him panting and I saw written on the chubby face his joy at being back at last. But at the same time I kept my eye on the shelter, which drew me with an extraordinary pull, so that to cut across from the terminus of one sally to the terminus of the next, and so on, which would have been convenient, was out of the question. But each time I had to retrace my steps, the way I had come, to the shelter, and make sure all was in order, before I sallied forth again. And I consumed the greater part of this second day in these vain comings and goings, these vigils and imaginings, but not all of it. For I also lay down from time to time in the shelter, which I was beginning to think of as my little house, to ruminate in peace on certain things, and notably on my provisions of food which were rapidly running out, so that after a meal devoured at five o'clock I was left with only two tins of sardines, a handful of biscuits and a few apples. But I also tried to remember what I was to do with Molloy, once I had found him. And on myself too I pored, on me so changed from what I was. And I seemed to see myself ageing as swiftly as a day-fly. But the idea of ageing was not exactly the one which offered itself to me. And what I saw was more like a crumbling, a frenzied collapsing of all that had always protected me from all I was always condemned to be. Or it was like a kind of clawing towards a light and countenance I could not name, that I had once known and long denied. But what words can describe this sensation at first all darkness and bulk, with a noise like the grinding of stones, then suddenly as soft as water flowing. And then I saw a little globe swaying up slowly from the depths, through the quiet water, smooth at first, and scarcely paler than its escorting ripples, then little by little a face, with holes for the eyes and mouth and other wounds, and nothing to show if it was a man's face or a woman's face, a young face or an old face, or if its calm too was not an effect of the water trembling between it and the light. But I confess I attended but absently to these poor figures, in which I suppose my sense of

MOLLOY

disaster sought to contain itself. And that I did not labour at them more diligently was a further index of the great changes I had suffered and of my growing resignation to being dispossessed of self. And doubtless I should have gone from discovery to discovery, concerning myself, if I had persisted. But at the first faint light, I mean in these wild shadows gathering about me, dispensed by a vision or by an effort of thought, at the first light I fled to other cares. And all had been for nothing. And he who acted thus was a stranger to me too. For it was not my nature, I mean it was not my custom, to conduct my calculations simultaneously, but separately and turn about, pushing each one as far as it would go before turning in desperation to another. Similarly the missing instructions concerning Molloy, when I felt them stirring in the depths of my memory, I turned from them in haste towards other unknowns. And I who a fortnight before would joyfully have reckoned how long I could survive on the provisions that remained, probably with reference to the question of calories and vitamins, and established in my head a series of menus asymptotically approaching nutritional zero, was now content to note feebly that I should soon be dead of inanition, if I did not succeed in renewing my provisions. So much for the second day. But one incident remains to be noted, before I go on to the third.

It was evening. I had lit my fire and was watching it take when I heard myself hailed. The voice, already so near that I started violently, was that of a man. But after this one violent start I collected myself and continued to busy myself with my fire as if nothing had happened, poking it with a branch I had torn from its tree for the purpose a little earlier and stripped of its twigs and leaves and even part of its bark, with my bare nails. I have always loved skinning branches and laying bare the pretty white glossy shaft of sapwood. But obscure feelings of love and pity for the tree held me back most of the time. And I numbered among my familiars the dragon-tree of Teneriffe that perished at the age of five thousand years, struck by lightning. It was an example of longevity. The branch was thick and full of sap and did not burn when I stuck it in the fire. I held it by the thin end. The crackling of the fire, of the writhing brands rather, for fire triumphant does not crackle, but makes an altogether different noise, had permitted the man to come right up to me, without my knowledge. If there is one thing infuriates me it is being taken myself by surprise. I continued then, in spite of my spasm of fright, hoping it had passed unnoticed, to poke the fire as if I were alone. But at the thump of his hand on my shoulder I had no choice but to do what anyone else would have done in my place, and this I achieved by suddenly spinning round in what I trust was a good imitation of fear and anger. There I was face to face with a dim man, dim of face and dim of body, because of the dark. Put it there, he said. But little by little I formed an idea of the type of individual it was. And indeed there reigned between his various parts great harmony and concord, and it could be truly said that his face was worthy of his body, and vice versa. And if I could have seen his arse, I do not doubt I should have found it on a par with the whole. What are you doing in this God-forsaken place, he said, you unexpected pleasure. And moving aside from the fire which was now burning merrily, so that its light fell full on the intruder, I could see he was precisely the kind of pest I had thought he was, without being sure, because of the dark. Can you tell me, he said. I shall have to describe him briefly, though such a thing is contrary to my principles. He was on the small side, but thick-set. He wore a thick navy-blue suit (double-breasted) of hideous cut and a pair of outrageously wide black shoes, with the toe-caps higher than the uppers. This dreadful shape seems only to occur in black shoes. Do you happen to know, he said. The fringed extremities of a dark muffler, seven feet long at least, wound several times round his neck, hung down his back. He had a narrow-brimmed dark blue felt hat on his head, with a fish-hook and an artificial fly stuck in the band, which produced a highly sporting effect. Do you hear me? he said. But all this was nothing compared to the face which I regret to say vaguely resembled my own, less the refinement of course, same little abortive moustache, same little ferrety eyes, same paraphimosis of the nose, and a thin red mouth that looked as if it was raw from trying to shit its tongue. Hey you! He said. I turned back to my fire. It was doing nicely. I threw more wood on it. Do you hear me talking to you? he said. I went towards the shelter, he barred my way, emboldened by my limp. Have you a tongue in your head? he said. I don't know you, I said. I laughed. I had not intended to be witty. Would you care to see my card? he said. It would mean nothing to me, I said. He came closer to me. Get out of my way, I said. It was his turn to laugh. You refuse to answer? he said. I made a great effort. What do you want to know? I said. He must have thought I was weakening. That's more like it, he said. I called to my aid the image of my son who might arrive at any moment. I've already told you, he said. I was trembling all over. Have the goodness to tell me again, I said. To cut a long story short he wanted to know if I had seen an old man with a stick pass by. He described him. Badly. The voice seemed to come to me from afar. No, I said. What do you mean no? he said. I have seen no one, I said. And yet he passed this way, he said. I said nothing. How long have you been here? he said. His body too grew dim, as if coming asunder. What is your business here? he said. Are you on night patrol? I said. He thrust his hand at me. I have an idea I told him once again to get out of my way. I can still see the hand coming towards me, pallid, opening and closing. As if self-propelled. I do not know what happened then. But a little later, perhaps a long time later, I found him stretched on the ground, his head in a pulp. I am sorry I cannot indicate more clearly how this result was obtained, it would have been something worth reading. But it is not at this late stage of my relation that I intend to give way to literature. I myself was unscathed, except for a few scratches I did not discover till the following day. I bent over him. As I did so I realized my leg was bending normally. He no longer resembled me. I took him by the ankles and dragged him backwards into the shelter. His shoes shone with highly polished blacking. He wore fancy socks. The trousers slid back, disclosing the white hairless legs. His ankles were bony, like my own. My fingers encircled them nearly. He was wearing suspenders, one of which had come undone and was hanging loose. This detail went to my heart. Already my knee was stiffening again. It no longer required to be supple. I went back to the shelter and took my son's raincoat. I went back to the fire and lay down, with the coat over me. I did not get much sleep, but I got some. I listened to the owls. They were not eagle-owls, it was a cry like the whistle of a locomotive. I listened to a nightingale. And to distant corncrakes. If I had heard of other birds that cry and sing at night, I should have listened to them too. I watched the fire dying, my cheek pillowed on my hands. I watched out for the dawn. It was hardly breaking when I got up and went to the shelter. His legs too were on the stiff side, but there was still some play in the hip joints, fortunately. I dragged him into the copse, with frequent rests on the way, but without letting go his legs, so as not to have to stoop again to pick them up. Then I dismantled the shelter and threw the branches over the body. I packed and shouldered the two bags, took the raincoat and the umbrella. In a word I struck camp. But before leaving I consulted with myself to make sure I was forgetting nothing, and without relying on my intelligence alone, for I felt my pockets and looked around me. And it was while feeling my pockets that I discovered something of which my mind had been powerless to inform me, namely that my keys were no longer there. I was not long in finding them, scattered on the ground, the ring having broken. And to tell the truth first I found the chain, then the keys and last the ring, in two pieces. And since it was out of the question, even with the help of my umbrella, to stoop each time to pick up a key, I put down my bags, my umbrella and the coat and lay down flat on my stomach among the keys which in this way I was able to recover without much difficulty. And when a key was beyond my reach I took hold of the grass and dragged myself over to it. And I wiped each key on the grass, before putting it in my pocket, whether it needed wiping or not. And from time to time I raised myself on my hands, to get a better view. And in this way

I located a number of keys at some distance from me, and these I reached by rolling over and over, like a great cylinder. And finding no more keys, I said, There is no use my counting them, for I do not know how many there were. And my eyes resumed their search. But finally I said, Hell to it, I'll do with those I have. And while looking in this way for my keys I found an ear which I threw into the copse. And, to my even greater surprise, I found my straw hat which I thought was on my head! One of the holes for the elastic had expanded to the edge of the rim and consequently was no longer a hole, but a slit. But the other had been spared and the elastic was still in it. And finally I said, I shall rise now and, from my full height, run my eyes over this area for the last time. Which I did. It was then I found the ring, first one piece, then the other. Then, finding nothing more belonging either to me or to my son, I shouldered my bags again, jammed the straw hat hard down on my skull, folded my son's raincoat over my arm, caught up the umbrella and went.

But I did not go far. For I soon stopped on the crest of a rise from where I could survey, without fatigue, the camp-site and the surrounding country. And I made this curious observation, that the land from where I was, and even the clouds in the sky, were so disposed as to lead the eyes gently to the camp, as in a painting by an old master. I made myself as comfortable as possible. I got rid of my various burdens and I ate a whole tin of sardines and one apple. I lay down flat on my stomach on my son's coat. And now I propped my elbows on the ground and my jaws between my hands, which carried my eyes towards the horizon, and now I made a little cushion of my two hands on the ground and laid my cheek upon it, five minutes one, five minutes the other, all the while flat on my stomach. I could have made myself a pillow of the bags, but I did not, it did not occur to me. The day passed tranquilly, without incident. And the only thing that relieved the monotony of this third day was a dog. When I first saw him he was sniffing about the remains of my fire, then he went into the copse. But I did not see him come out again, either because my attention was elsewhere, or because he went out the other side, having simply as it were gone straight through it. I mended my hat, that is to say with the tin-opener I pierced a new hole beside the old one and made fast the elastic again. And I also mended the ring, twisting the two pieces together, and I slipped on the keys and made fast the long chain again. And to kill time I asked myself a certain number of questions and tried to answer them. For example.

Question. What had happened to the blue felt hat?
Answer.

Question. Would they not suspect the old man with the stick?
Answer. Very probably.

Question. What were his chances of exonerating himself?
Answer. Slight.

Question. Should I tell my son what had happened?
Answer. No, for then it would be his duty to denounce me.

Question. Would he denounce me?
Answer.

Question. How did I feel?
Answer. Much as usual.

Question. And yet I had changed and was still changing?
Answer. Yes.

Question. And in spite of this I felt much as usual?
Answer. Yes.

Question. How was this to be explained?
Answer.

These questions and others too were separated by more or less prolonged intervals of time not only from one another, but also from the answers appertaining to them. And the answers did not always follow in the order of the questions. But while looking for the answer, or the answers, to a given question, I found the answer, or the answers, to a question I had already asked myself in vain, in the sense that I had not been able to answer it, or I found another question, or other questions, demanding in their turn an immediate answer.

Translating myself now in imagination to the present moment, I declare the foregoing to have been written with a firm and even satisfied hand, and a mind calmer than it has been for a long time. For I shall be far away, before these lines are read, in a place where no one will dream of coming to look for me. And then Youdi will take care of me, he will not let me be punished for a fault committed in the execution of my duty. And they can do nothing to my son, rather they will commiserate with him on having had such a father, and offers of help and expressions of esteem will pour in upon him from every side.

So this third day wore away. And about five o'clock I ate my last tin of sardines and a few biscuits, with a good appetite. This left me with only a few apples and a few biscuits. But about seven o'clock my son arrived. The sun was low in the west. I must have dozed a moment, for I did not see him coming, a speck on the horizon, then rapidly bigger and bigger, as I had foreseen. But he was already between me and the camp, making for the latter, when I saw him. A wave of irritation broke over me, I jumped to my feet and began to vociferate, brandishing my umbrella. He turned and I beckoned him to join me, waving the umbrella as if I wanted to hook something with the handle. I thought for a moment he was going to defy me and continue on his way to the camp, to where the camp had been rather, for it was there no more. But finally he came towards me. He was pushing a bicycle which, when he had joined me, he let fall with a gesture signifying he could bear no more. Pick it up, I said, till I look at it. I had to admit it must once have been quite a good bicycle. I would gladly describe it, I would gladly write four thousand words on it alone. And you call that a bicycle? I said. Only half expecting him to answer me I continued to inspect it. But there was something so strange in his silence that I looked up at him. His eyes were starting out of his head. What's the matter, I said, is my fly open? He let go the bicycle again. Pick it up, I said. He picked it up. What happened to you? he said. I had a fall, I said. A fall? he said. Yes, a fall, I cried, did you never have a fall? I tried to remember the name of the plant that springs from the ejaculations of the hanged and shrieks when plucked. How much did you give for it? I said. Four pounds, he said. Four pounds! I cried. If he had said two pounds or even thirty shillings I should have cried, Two pounds! or, Thirty shillings! the same. They asked four pounds five, he said. Have you the receipt? I said. He did not know what a receipt was. I described one. The money I spent on my son's education and he did not know what a simple receipt was. But I think he knew as well as I. For when I said to him, Now tell me what a receipt is, he told me very prettily. I really did not care in the least whether he had been fooled into paying for the bicycle three or four times what it was worth or whether on the other hand he had appropriated the best part of the purchase money for his own use. The loss would not be mine. Give me the ten shillings, I said. I spent them, he said. Enough, enough. He began explaining that the first day the shops had been closed, that the second—. I said, Enough, enough. I looked at the carrier. It was the best thing about that bicycle. It and the pump. Does it go by any chance? I said. I had a puncture two miles from Hole, he said, I walked the rest of the way. I looked at his shoes. Pump it up, I said. I held the bicycle. I forget which wheel it was. As soon as two things are nearly identical I am lost. The dirty little twister was letting the air escape between the valve and the connection which he had purposely not screwed tight. Hold the bicycle, I said, and give me the pump. The tyre was soon hard. I looked at my son. He began to protest. I soon put a stop to that. Five minutes later I felt the tyre. It was as hard as ever. I cursed him. He took a bar of chocolate from his pocket and offered it to me. I took it. But instead of eating it, as I longed to, and although I have a horror of waste, I cast it from me, after a moment's hesitation, which I trust my son did not notice. Enough. We went down to the road. It was more like a path. I tried to sit down on the carrier. The foot of my stiff leg tried to sink into the ground, into the grave. I propped myself up on one of the bags. Keep her steady, I said. I was still too low. I added the other. Its bulges dug into my buttocks. The more things resist me the more rabid I get. With time, and nothing but my teeth and nails, I would rage up from the bowels of the earth to its crust, knowing full well I had nothing to gain. And when I had no more teeth, no more nails, I would dig through the rock with my bones. Here then in a few words is the solution I arrived at. First the bags, then my son's raincoat folded in four, all lashed to the carrier and the saddle with my son's bits of string. As for the umbrella, I hooked it round my neck, so as to have both hands free to hold on to my son by the waist, under the armpits rather, for by this time my seat was higher than his. Pedal, I said. He made a despairing effort, I can well believe it. We fell. I felt a sharp pain in my shin. I was all tangled up in the back wheel. Help! I cried. My son helped me up. My stocking was torn and my leg bleeding. Happily it was the sick leg. What would I have done, with both legs out of action? I would have found a way. It was even perhaps a blessing in disguise. I was thinking of phlebotomy of course. Are you all right? I said. Yes, he said. He would be. With my umbrella I caught him a smart blow on the hamstrings, gleaming between the leg of his shorts and his stocking. He cried out. Do you want to kill us? I said. I'm not strong enough, he said, I'm not strong enough. The bicycle was all right apparently, the back wheel slightly buckled perhaps. I at once saw the error I had made. It was to have settled down in my seat, with my feet clear of the ground, before we moved off. I reflected. We'll try again, I said. I can't, he said. Don't try me too far, I said. He straddled the frame. Start off gently when I tell you, I said. I got up again behind and settled down in my seat, with my feet clear of the ground. Good. Wait till I tell you, I said. I let myself slide to one side till the foot of my good leg touched the ground. The only weight now on the back wheel was that of my sick leg, cocked up rigid at an excruciating angle. I dug my fingers into my son's jacket. Go easy, I said. The wheels began to turn. I followed, half dragged, half hopping. I trembled for my testicles which swing a little low. Faster! I cried. He bore down on the pedals. I bounded up to my place. The bicycle swayed, righted itself, gained speed. Bravo! I cried, beside myself with joy. Hurrah! cried my son. How I loathe that exclamation! I can hardly set it down. He was as pleased as I, I do believe. His heart was beating under my hand and yet my hand was far from his heart. Happily it was downhill. Happily I had mended my hat, or the wind would have blown it away. Happily the weather was fine and I no longer alone. Happily, happily.

In this way we came to Ballyba. I shall not tell of the obstacles we had to surmount, the fiends we had to circumvent, the misdemeanours of the son, the disintegrations of the father. It was my intention, almost my desire, to tell of all these things, I rejoiced at the thought that the moment would come when I might do so. Now the intention is dead, the moment is come and the desire is gone. My leg was no better. It was no worse either. The skin had healed. I would never have got there alone. It was thanks to my son. What? That I got there. He often complained of his health, his stomach, his teeth. I gave him some morphine. He looked worse and worse. When I asked him what was wrong he could not tell me. We had trouble with the bicycle. But I patched it up. I would not have got there without my son. We were a long time getting there. Weeks. We kept losing our way, taking our time. I still did not know what I was to do with Molloy, when I found him. I thought no more about it. I thought about myself, much, as we went along, sitting behind my son, looking over his head, and in the evening, when we camped, while he made himself useful, and when he went away, leaving me alone. For he often went away, to spy out the lie of the land and to buy provisions. I did practically nothing any more. He took good care of me, I must say. He was clumsy, stupid, slow, dirty, untruthful, deceitful, prodigal, unfilial, but he did not abandon me. I thought much about myself. That is to say I often took a quick look at myself, closed my eyes, forgot, began again. We took a long time getting to Ballyba, we even got there without knowing it. Stop, I said to my son one day. I had just caught sight of a shepherd I liked the look of. He was sitting on the ground stroking his dog. A flock of black shorn sheep strayed about them, unafraid. What a pastoral land, my God. Leaving my son on the side of the road I went towards them, across the grass. I often stopped and rested, leaning on my umbrella. The shepherd watched me as I came, without getting up. The dog too, without barking. The sheep too. Yes, little by little, one by one, they turned and faced me, watching me as I came. Here and there faint movements of recoil, a tiny foot stamping the ground, betrayed their uneasiness. They did not seem timid, as sheep go. And my son of course watched me as I went, I felt his eyes in my back. The silence was absolute. Profound in any case. All things considered it was a solemn moment. The weather was divine. It was the close of day. Each time I stopped I looked about me. I looked at the shepherd, the sheep, the dog and even at the sky. But when I moved I saw nothing but the ground and the play of my feet, the good one springing forward, holding back, setting itself down, waiting for the other to come up. I came finally to a halt about ten paces from the shepherd. There was no use going any further. How I would love to dwell upon him. His dog loved him, his sheep did not fear him. Soon he would rise, feeling the falling dew. The fold was far, far, he would see from afar the light in his cot. Now I was in the midst of the sheep, they made a circle round me, their eyes converged on me. Perhaps I was the butcher come to make his choice. I took off my hat. I saw the dog's eyes following the movement of my hand. I looked about me again incapable of speech. I did not know how I would ever be able to break this silence. I was on the point of turning away without having spoken. Finally I said, Ballyba, hoping it sounded like a question. The shepherd drew the pipe from his mouth and pointed the stem at the ground. I longed to say, Take me with you, I will serve you faithfully, just for a place to lie and a little food. I had understood, but without seeming to I suppose, for he repeated his gesture, pointing the stem of his pipe at the ground, several times. Bally, I said. He raised one hand, it wavered an instant as if over a map, then stiffened. The pipe still smoked faintly, the smoke hung blue in the air an instant, then vanished. I looked in the direction indicated. The dog too. We were all three turned to the north. The sheep were losing interest in me. Perhaps they had understood. I heard them straying about again and grazing. I distinguished at last, at the limit of the plain, a dim glow, the sum of countless points of light blurred by the distance, I thought of Juno's milk. It lay like a faint splash on the sharp dark sweep of the horizon. I gave thanks for evening that brings out the lights, the stars in the sky and on earth the brave little lights of men. By day the shepherd would have raised his pipe in vain, towards the long clear-cut commissure of earth and sky. But now I felt the man turning towards me again, and the dog, and the man drawing on his pipe again, in the hope it had not gone out. And I knew I was all alone gazing at that distant glow that would get brighter and brighter, I knew that too, then suddenly go out. And I did not like the feeling of being alone, with my son perhaps, no, alone, spellbound. And I was wondering how to depart without self-loathing or sadness, or with as little as possible, when a kind of immense sigh all round me announced it was not I who was departing, but the flock. I watched them move away, the man in front, then the sheep, huddled together, their heads sunk, jostling one another, breaking now and then into a little trot, snatching blindly without stopping a last mouthful from the earth, and last of all the dog, jauntily, waving his long black plumy tail, though there was no one to witness his contentment, if that is what it was. And so in perfect order, the shepherd silent and the dog unneeded, the little flock departed. And so no doubt they would plod on, until they came to the stable or the fold. And there the shepherd stands aside to let them pass and he counts them as they go by, though he knows not one is missing. Then he turns towards his cottage, the kitchen door is open, the lamp is burning, he goes in and sits down at the table, without taking off his hat. But the dog stops at the threshold, not knowing whether he may go in or whether he must stay out, all night.

That night I had a violent scene with my son. I do not remember about what. Wait, it may be important.

No, I don't know. I have had so many scenes with my son. At the time it must have seemed a scene like any other, that's all I know.

MOLLOY

I must have got the better of it as I always did, thanks to my infallible technique, and brought him unerringly to a proper sense of his iniquities. But the next day I realized my mistake. For waking early I found myself alone, in the shelter, I who was always the first to wake. And what is more my instinct told me I had been alone for some considerable time, my breath no longer mingling with the breath of my son, in the narrow shelter he had erected, under my supervision. Not that the fact of his having disappeared with the bicycle, during the night or with the first guilty flush of dawn, was in itself a matter for grave anxiety. And I would have found excellent and honourable reasons for this, if this had been all. Unfortunately he had taken his knapsack and his raincoat. And there remained nothing in the shelter, nor outside the shelter, belonging to him, absolutely nothing. And this was not yet all, for he had left with a considerable sum of money, he who was only entitled to a few pence from time to time, for his savings-box. For since he had been in charge of everything, under my supervision of course, and notably of the shopping, I was obliged to place a certain reliance on him in the matter of money. And he always had a far greater sum in his pocket than was strictly necessary. And in order to make all this sound more likely I shall add what follows.

1. I desired him to learn double-entry book-keeping and had instructed him in its rudiments.

2. I could no longer be bothered with these wretched trifles which had once been my delight.

3. I had told him to keep an eye out, on his expeditions, for a second bicycle, light and inexpensive. For I was weary of the carrier and I also saw the day approaching when my son would no longer have the strength to pedal for the two of us. And I believed I was capable, more than that, I knew I was capable, with a little practice, of learning to pedal with one leg. And then I would resume my rightful place, I mean in the van. And my son would follow me. And then the scandal would cease of my son's defying me, and going left when I told him right, or right

when I told him left, or straight on when I told him right or left, as he had been doing of late, more and more frequently.

That is all I wished to add.

But on examining my pocket-book I found it contained no more than fifteen shillings, which led me to the conclusion that my son had not been content with the sum already in his possession, but had gone through my pockets, before he left, while I slept. And the human breast is so bizarre that my first feeling was of gratitude for his leaving me this little sum, enough to keep me going until help arrived, and I saw in this a kind of delicacy!

I was therefore alone, with my bag, my umbrella (which he might easily have taken too) and fifteen shillings, knowing myself coldly abandoned, with deliberation and no doubt premeditation, in Ballyba it is true, if indeed I was in Ballyba, but still far from Bally. And I remained for several days, I do not know how many, in the place where my son had abandoned me, eating my last provisions (which he might easily have taken too), seeing no living soul, powerless to act, or perhaps strong enough at last to act no more. For I had no illusions, I knew that all was about to end, or to begin again, it little mattered which, and it little mattered how, I had only to wait. And on and off, for fun, and the better to scatter them to the winds, I dallied with the hopes that spring eternal, childish hopes, as for example that my son, his anger spent, would have pity on me and come back to me! Or that Molloy, whose country this was, would come to me, who had not been able to go to him, and grow to be a friend, and like a father to me, and help me do what I had to do, so that Youdi would not be angry with me and would not punish me! Yes, I let them spring within me and grow in strength, brighten and charm me with a thousand fancies, and then I swept them away, with a great disgusted sweep of all my being, I swept myself clean of them and surveyed with satisfaction the void they had polluted. And in the evening I turned to the lights of Bally, I watched them shine brighter and brighter, then all go out together, or nearly all, foul little flickering lights of terrified men. And I said, To think I might be there now, but for my misfortune! And with regard to the Obidil, of whom I have refrained from speaking, until now, and whom I so longed to see face to face, all I can say with regard to him is this, that I never saw him, either face to face or darkly, perhaps there is no such person, that would not greatly surprise me. And at the thought of the punishments Youdi might inflict upon me I was seized by such a mighty fit of laughter that I shook, with mighty silent laughter and my features composed in their wonted sadness and calm. But my whole body shook, and even my legs, so that I had to lean against a tree, or against a bush, when the fit came on me standing, my umbrella being no longer sufficient to keep me from falling. Strange laughter truly, and no doubt misnamed, through indolence perhaps, or ignorance. And as for myself, that unfailing pastime, I must say it was far now from my thoughts. But there were moments when it did not seem so far from me, when I seemed to be drawing towards it as the sands towards the wave, when it crests and whitens, though I must say this image hardly fitted my situation, which was rather that of the turd waiting for the flush. And I note here the little beat my heart once missed, in my home, when a fly, flying low above my ash-tray, raised a little ash, with the breath of its wings. And I grew gradually weaker and weaker and more and more content. For several days I had eaten nothing. I could probably have found blackberries and mushrooms, but I had no wish for them. I remained all day stretched out in the shelter, vaguely regretting my son's raincoat, and I crawled out in the evening to have a good laugh at the lights of Bally. And though suffering a little from wind and cramps in the stomach I felt extraordinarily content, content with myself, almost elated, enchanted with my performance. And I said, I shall soon lose consciousness altogether, it is merely a question of time. But Gaber's arrival put a stop to these frolics.

It was evening. I had just crawled out of the shelter for my evening guffaw and the better to savour my exhaustion. He had already been there for some time. He was sitting on a tree-stump, half asleep. Well Moran, he said. You recognize me? I said. He took out and opened his notebook, licked his finger, turned over the pages till he came to the right page, raised it towards his eyes which at the same time he lowered towards it. I can see nothing, he said. He was dressed as when I had last seen him. My strictures on his Sunday clothes had therefore been unjustified. Unless it was Sunday again. But had I not always seen him dressed in this way? Would you have a match? he said. I did not recognize this far-off voice. Or a torch, he said. He must have seen from my face that I possessed nothing of a luminous nature. He took a small electric torch from his pocket and shone it on his page. He read, Moran, Jacques, home, instanter. He put out his torch, closed his notebook on his finger and looked at me. I can't walk, I said. What? he said. I'm sick, I can't move, I said. I can't hear a word you say, he said. I cried to him that I could not move, that I was sick, that I should have to be carried, that my son had abandoned me, that I could bear no more. He examined me laboriously from head to foot. I executed a few steps leaning on my umbrella to prove to him I could not walk. He opened his notebook again, shone the torch on his page, studied it at length and said, Moran, home, instanter. He closed his notebook, put it back in his pocket, put his lamp back in his pocket, stood up, drew his hands over his chest and announced he was dying of thirst. Not a word on how I was looking. And yet I had not shaved since the day my son brought back the bicycle from Hole, nor combed my hair, nor washed, not to mention all the privations I had suffered and the great inward metamorphoses. Do you recognize me? I cried. Do I recognize you? he said. He reflected. I knew what he was doing, he was searching for the phrase most apt to wound me. Ah Moran, he said, what a man! I was staggering with weakness. If I had dropped dead at his feet he would have said, Ah poor old Moran, that's him all over. It was getting darker and darker. I wondered if it was really Gaber. Is he angry? I said. You wouldn't have a sup of beer by any chance? he said. I'm asking you if he is angry, I cried. Angry, said Gaber, don't make me laugh, he keeps rubbing his hands from morning to night, I can hear them in the outer room. That means nothing, I said. And chuckling to himself, said Gaber. He must be angry with me, I said. Do you know what he told me the other day? said Gaber. Has he changed? I cried. Changed, said Gaber, no he hasn't changed, why would he have changed, he's getting old, that's all, like the world. You have a queer voice this evening, I said. I do not think he heard me. Well, he said, drawing his hands once more over his chest, downwards, I'll be going, if that's all you have to say to me. He went, without saying goodbye. But I overtook him, in spite of my loathing for him, in spite of my weakness and my sick leg, and held him back by the sleeve. What did he tell you? I said. He stopped. Moran, he said, you are beginning to give me a serious pain in the arse. For pity's sake, I said, tell me what he told you. He gave me a shove. I fell. He had not intended to make me fall, he did not realize the state I was in, he had only wanted to push me away. I did not try to get up. I let a roar. He came and bent over me. He had a walrus moustache, chestnut in colour. I saw it lift, the lips open, and almost at the same time I heard words of solicitude, at a great distance. He was not brutal, Gaber, I knew him well. Gaber, I said, it's not much I'm asking you. I remember this scene well. He wanted to help me up. I pushed him away. I was all right where I was. What did he tell you? I said. I don't understand, said Gaber. You were saying a minute ago that he had told you something, I said, then I cut you short. Short? said Gaber. Do you know what he told me the other day, I said, those were your very words. His face lit up. The clod was just about as quick as my son. He said to me, said Gaber, Gaber, he said—. Louder! I cried. He said to me, said Gaber, Gaber, he said, life is a thing of beauty, Gaber, and a joy for ever. He brought his face nearer mine. A joy for ever, he said, a thing of beauty, Moran, and a joy for ever. He smiled. I closed my eyes. Smiles are all very nice in their own way, very heartening, but at a reasonable distance. I said, Do you think he meant human life? I listened. Perhaps he didn't mean human life, I said. I opened my eyes. I was alone. My hands were full of grass and earth I had torn up unwittingly, was still tearing up. I was literally uprooting. I desisted, yes, the second I realized what I had done, what I was doing, such a nasty thing, I desisted from it, I opened my hands, they were soon empty.

That night I set out for home. I did not get far. But it was a start. It is the first step that counts. The second counts less. Each day saw me advance a little further. That last sentence is not clear, it does not say what I hoped it would. I counted at first by tens of steps. I stopped when I could go no further and I said, Bravo, that makes so many tens, so many more than yesterday. Then I counted by fifteens, by twenties and finally by fifties. Yes, in the end I could go fifty steps before having to stop, for rest, leaning on my faithful umbrella. In the beginning I must have strayed a little in Ballyba, if I really was in Ballyba. Then I followed more or less the same paths we had taken on the way out. But paths look different, when you go back along them. I ate, in obedience to the voice of reason, all that nature, the woods, the fields, the waters had to offer me in the way of edibles. I finished the morphine.

It was in August, in September at the latest, that I was ordered home. It was spring when I got there, I will not be more precise. I had therefore been all winter on the way.

Anyone else would have lain down in the snow, firmly resolved never to rise again. Not I. I used to think that men would never get the better of me. I still think I am cleverer than things. There are men and there are things, to hell with animals. And with God. When a thing resists me, even if it is for my own good, it does not resist me long. This snow, for example. Though to tell the truth it lured me more than it resisted me. But in a sense it resisted me. That was enough. I vanquished it, grinding my teeth with joy, it is quite possible to grind one's incisors. I forged my way through it, towards what I would have called my ruin if I could have conceived what I had left to be ruined. Perhaps I have conceived it since, perhaps I have not done conceiving it, it takes time, one is bound to in time, I am bound to. But on the way home, a prey to the malignancy of man and nature and my own failing flesh, I could not conceive it. My knee, allowance made for the dulling effects of habit, was neither more nor less painful than the first day. The disease, whatever it was, was dormant! How can such things be? But to return to the flies, I like to think of those that hatch out at the beginning of winter, within doors, and die shortly after. You see them crawling and fluttering in the warm corners, puny, sluggish, torpid, mute. That is you see an odd one now and then. They must die very young, without having been able to lay. You sweep them away, you push them into the dust-pan with the brush, without knowing. That is a strange race of flies. But I was succumbing to other affections, that is not the word, intestinal for the most part. I would have described them once, not now, I am sorry, it would have been worth reading. I shall merely say that no one else would have surmounted them, without help. But I! Bent double, my free hand pressed to my belly, I advanced, and every now and then I let a roar, of triumph and distress. Certain mosses I consumed must have disagreed with me. I, if I once made up my mind not to keep the hangman waiting, the bloody flux itself would not stop me, I would get there on all fours shitting out my entrails and chanting maledictions. Didn't I tell you it's my brethren that have done for me.

But I shall not dwell upon this journey home, its furies and treacheries. And I shall pass over in silence the fiends in human shape and the phantoms of the dead that tried to prevent me from getting home, in obedience to Youdi's command. But one or two words nevertheless, for my own edification and to prepare my soul to make an end. To begin with my rare thoughts.

Certain questions of a theological nature preoccupied me strangely. As for example.

1. What value is to be attached to the theory that Eve sprang, not from Adam's rib, but from a tumour in the fat of his leg (arse?)?

2. Did the serpent crawl or, as Comestor affirms, walk upright?

3. Did Mary conceive through the ear, as Augustine and Adobard assert?

4. How much longer are we to hang about waiting for the Antichrist?

5. Does it really matter which hand is employed to absterge the podex?

6. What is one to think of the Irish oath sworn by the natives with the right hand on the relics of the saints and the left on the virile member?

7. Does nature observe the sabbath?

8. Is it true that the devils do not feel the pains of hell?

9. The algebraic theology of Craig. What is one to think of this?

10. Is it true that the infant Saint-Roch refused suck on Wednesdays and Fridays?

11. What is one to think of the excommunication of vermin in the sixteenth century?

12. Is one to approve of the Italian cobbler Lovat who, having cut off his testicles, crucified himself?

13. What was God doing with himself before the creation?

14. Might not the beatific vision become a source of boredom, in the long run?

15. Is it true that Judas' torments are suspended on Saturdays?

16. What if the mass for the dead were read over the living?

And I recited the pretty quietist Pater, Our Father who art no more in heaven than on earth or in hell, I neither want nor desire that thy name be hallowed, thou knowest best what suits thee. Etc. The middle and the end are very pretty.

It was in this frivolous and charming world that I took refuge, when my cup ran over.

But I asked myself other questions concerning me perhaps more closely. As for example.

1. Why had I not borrowed a few shillings from Gaber?

2. Why had I obeyed the order to go home?

3. What had become of Molloy?

4. Same question for me.

5. What would become of me?

6. Same questions for my son.

7. Was his mother in heaven?

8. Same question for my mother.

9. Would I go to heaven?

10. Would we all meet again in heaven one day, I, my mother, my son, his mother, Youdi, Gaber, Molloy, his mother, Yerk, Murphy, Watt, Camier and the rest?

11. What had become of my hens, my bees? Was my grey hen still living?

12. Zulu, the Elsner sisters, were they still living?

13. Was Youdi's business address still 8, Acacia Square? What if I wrote to him? What if I went to see him? I would explain to him. What would I explain to him? I would crave his forgiveness. Forgiveness for what?

14. Was not the winter exceptionally severe?

15. How long had I gone now without either confession or communion?

16. What was the name of the martyr who, being in prison, loaded with chains, covered with wounds and vermin, unable to stir, celebrated the consecration on his stomach and gave himself absolution?

17. What would I do until my death? Was there no means of hastening this, without falling into a state of sin?

But before I launch my body properly so-called across these icy, then, with the thaw, muddy solitudes, I wish to say that I often thought of my bees, more often than of my hens, and God knows I thought often of my hens. And I thought above all of their dance, for my bees danced, oh not as men dance, to amuse themselves, but in a different way. I alone of all mankind knew this, to the best of my belief. I had investigated this phenomenon very fully. The dance was best to be observed among the bees returning to the hive, laden more or less with nectar, and it involved a great variety of figures and rhythms. These evolutions I finally interpreted as a system of signals by means of which the incoming bees, satisfied or dissatisfied with their plunder, informed the outgoing bees in what direction to go, and in what not to go. But the outgoing bees danced too. It was no doubt their way of saying, I understand, or, Don't worry about me. But away from the hive, and busily at work, the bees did not dance. Here their watchword seemed to be, Every man for himself, assuming bees to be capable of such notions. The most striking feature of the dance was its very complicated figures, traced in flight, and I had classified a great number of these, with their probable meanings. But there was also the question of the hum, so various in tone in the vicinity of the hive that this could hardly be an effect of chance. I first concluded that each figure was reinforced by means of a hum peculiar to it. But I was forced to abandon this agreeable hypothesis. For I saw the same figure (at least what I called the same figure) accompanied by very different hums. So that I said, The purpose of the hum is not to emphasize the dance, but on the contrary to vary it. And the same figure exactly differs in meaning according to the hum that goes with it. And I had collected and classified a great number of observations on this subject, with gratifying results. But there was to be considered not only the figure and the hum, but also the height at which the figure was executed. And I acquired the conviction that the self-same figure, accompanied by the selfsame hum, did not mean at all the same thing at twelve feet from the ground as it did at six. For the bees did not dance at any level, haphazard, but there were three or four levels, always the same, at which they danced. And if I were to tell you what these levels were, and what the relations between them, for I had measured them with care, you would not believe me. And this is not the moment to jeopardize my credit. Sometimes you would think I was writing for the public. And in spite of all the pains I had lavished on these problems, I was more than ever stupefied by the complexity of this innumerable dance, involving doubtless other determinants of which I had not the slightest idea. And I said, with rapture, Here is something I can study all my life, and never understand. And all during this long journey home, when I racked my mind for a little joy in store, the thought of my bees and their dance was the nearest thing to comfort. For I was still eager for my little joy, from time to time! And I admitted with good grace the possibility that this dance was after all no better than the dances of the people of the West, frivolous and meaningless. But for me, sitting near my sun-drenched hives, it would always be a noble thing to contemplate, too noble ever to be sullied by the cogitations of a man like me, exiled in his manhood. And I would never do my bees the wrong I had done my God, to whom I had been taught to ascribe my angers, fears, desires, and even my body.

I have spoken of a voice giving me orders, or rather advice. It was on the way home I heard it for the first time. I paid no attention to it.

Physically speaking it seemed to me I was now becoming rapidly unrecognizable. And when I passed my hands over my face, in a characteristic and now more than ever pardonable gesture, the face my hands felt was not my face any more, and the hands my face felt were my hands no longer. And yet the gist of the sensation was the same as in the far-off days when I was well-shaven and perfumed and proud of my intellectual's soft white hands. And this belly I did not know remained my belly, my old belly, thanks to I know not what intuition. And to tell the truth I not only knew who I was, but I had a sharper and clearer sense of my identity than ever before, in spite of its deep lesions and the wounds with which it was covered. And from this point of view I was less fortunate than my other acquaintances. I am sorry if this last phrase is not so happy as it might be. It deserved, who knows, to be without ambiguity.

Then there are the clothes that cleave so close to the body and are so to speak inseparable from it, in time of peace. Yes, I have always been very sensitive to clothing, though not in the least a dandy. I had not to complain of mine, tough and of good cut. I was of course inadequately covered, but whose fault was that? And I had to part with my straw, not made to resist the rigours of winter, and with my stockings (two pairs) which the cold and damp, the trudging and the lack of laundering facilities had literally annihilated. But I let out my braces to their

fullest extent and my knickerbockers, very baggy as the fashion
is, came down to my calves. And at the sight of the blue flesh,
between the knickerbockers and the tops of my boots, I sometimes thought of my son and the blow I had fetched him, so
avid is the mind of the flimsiest analogy. My boots became
rigid, from lack of proper care. So skin defends itself, when
dead and tanned. The air coursed through them freely, preserv-
ing perhaps my feet from freezing. And I had likewise sadly
to part with my drawers (two pairs). They had rotted, from
constant contact with my incontinences. Then the seat of my
breeches, before it too decomposed, sawed my crack from Dan
to Beersheba. What else did I have to discard? My shirt? Never!
But I often wore it inside out and back to front. Let me see. I
had four ways of wearing my shirt. Front to front right side out,
front to front inside out, back to front right side out, back to
front inside out. And the fifth day I began again. It was in the
hope of making it last. Did this make it last? I do not know. It
lasted. To major things the surest road is on the minor pains
bestowed, if you don't happen to be in a hurry. But what else
did I have to discard? My hard collars, yes, I discarded them all,
and even before they were quite worn and torn. But I kept my
tie, I even wore it, knotted round my bare neck, out of sheer
bravado I suppose. It was a spotted tie, but I forget the colour.

When it rained, when it snowed, when it hailed, then I found
myself faced with the following dilemma. Was I to go on leaning
on my umbrella and get drenched or was I to stop and take
shelter under my open umbrella? It was a false dilemma, as so
many dilemmas are. For on the one hand all that remained of the
canopy of my umbrella was a few flitters of silk fluttering from
the stays and on the other I could have gone on, very slowly,
using the umbrella no longer as a support, but as a shelter. But
I was so accustomed, on the one hand to the perfect watertight-
ness of my expensive umbrella, and on the other hand to being
unable to walk without its support, that the dilemma remained
entire, for me. I could of course have made myself a stick, out of
a branch, and gone on, in spite of the rain, the snow, the hail,

leaning on the stick and the umbrella open above me. But I did not, I do not know why. But when the rain descended, and the other things that descend upon us from above, sometimes I pushed on, leaning on the umbrella, getting drenched, but most often I stopped dead, opened the umbrella above me and waited for it to be over. Then I got equally drenched. But that was not the point. And if it had suddenly begun to rain manna I would have waited, stock still, under my umbrella, for it to be over, before taking advantage of it. And when my arm was weary of holding up the umbrella, then I gave it to the other hand. And with my free hand I slapped and rubbed every part of my body within its reach, in order to keep the blood trickling freely, or I drew it over my face, in a gesture that was characteristic, of me. And the long spike of my umbrella was like a finger. My best thoughts came to me during these halts. But when it was clear that the rain, etc., would not stop all day, or all night, then I did the sensible thing and built myself a proper shelter. But I did not like proper shelters, made of boughs, any more. For soon there were no more leaves, but only the needles of certain conifers. But this was not the real reason why I did not like proper shelters any more, no. But when I was inside them I could think of nothing but my son's raincoat, I literally saw it, I saw nothing else, it filled all space. It was in reality what our English friends call a trench-coat, and I could smell the rubber, though trench-coats are not rubberized as a rule. So I avoided as far as possible having recourse to proper shelters, made of boughs, preferring the shelter of my faithful umbrella, or of a tree, or of a hedge, or of a bush, or of a ruin.

The thought of taking to the road, to try and get a lift, never crossed my mind.

The thought of turning for help to the villages, to the peasants, would have displeased me, if it had occurred to me.

I reached home with my fifteen shillings intact. No, I spent two. This is how.

I had to suffer other molestations than this, other offences, but I shall not record them. Let us be content with paradigms.

I may have to suffer others in the future. This is not certain. But they will never be known. This is certain.

It was evening. I was waiting quietly, under my umbrella, for the weather to clear, when I was brutally accosted from behind. I had heard nothing. I had been in a place where I was all alone. A hand turned me about. It was a big ruddy farmer. He was wearing an oilskin, a bowler hat and wellingtons. His chubby cheeks were streaming, the water was dripping from his bushy moustache. But why describe him? We glared at each other with hatred. Perhaps he was the same who had so politely offered to drive us home in his car. I think not. And yet his face was familiar. Not only his face. He held a lantern in his hand. It was not lit. But he might light it at any moment. In the other he held a spade. To bury me with if necessary. He seized me by the jacket, by the lapel. He had not yet begun to shake me exactly, he would shake me in his own good time, not before. He merely cursed me. I wondered what I could have done, to put him in such a state. I must have raised my eyebrows. But I always raise my eyebrows, they are almost in my hair, my brow is nothing but wales and furrows. I understood finally that I did not own the land. It was his land. What was I doing on his land? If there is one question I dread, to which I have never been able to invent a satisfactory reply, it is the question what am I doing. And on someone else's land to make things worse! And at night! And in weather not fit for a dog! But I did not lose my presence of mind. It is a vow, I said. I have a fairly distinguished voice, when I choose. It must have impressed him. He unhanded me. A pilgrimage, I said, following up my advantage. He asked me where to. He was lost. To the Turdy Madonna, I said. The Turdy Madonna? he said, as if he knew Turdy like the back of his hand and there were no Madonna in the length and breadth of it. But where is the place in which there is no Madonna? Herself, I said. The black one? he said, to try me. She is not black that I know of, I said. Another would have lost countenance. Not I. I knew my yokels and their weak points. You'll never get there, he said. It's thanks to her I lost my infant boy, I said, and kept his mamma. Such sentiments could not fail to please a cattle breeder. Had he but known! I told him more fully what alas had never happened. Not that I miss Ninette. But she, at least, who knows, in any case, yes, a pity, no matter. She is the Madonna of pregnant women, I said, of pregnant married women, and I have vowed to drag myself miserably to her niche, and thank her. This incident gives but a feeble idea of my ability, even at this late period. But I had gone a little too far, for the vicious look came back into his eye. May I ask you a favour, I said, God will reward you. I added, God sent you to me, this evening. Humbly to ask a favour of people who are on the point of knocking your brains out sometimes produces good results. A little hot tea, I implored, without sugar or milk, to revive me. To grant such a small favour to a pilgrim on the rocks was frankly a temptation difficult to resist. Oh all right, he said, come back to the house, you can dry yourself, before the fire. But I cannot, I cannot, I cried, I have sworn to make a bee-line to her! And to efface the bad impression created by these words I took a florin from my pocket and gave it to him. For your poor-box, I said. And I added, because of the dark, A florin for your poor-box. It's a long way, he said. God will go with you, I said. He thought it over. Well he might. Above all nothing to eat, I said, no really, I must not eat. Ah Moran, wily as a serpent, there was never the like of old Moran. Of course I would have preferred violence, but I dared not take the risk. Finally he took himself off telling me to stay where I was. I do not know what was in his mind. When I judged him at a safe remove I closed the umbrella and set off in the opposite direction, at right angles to the way I was going, in the driving rain. That was how I spent a florin.

Now I may make an end.

I skirted the graveyard. It was night. Midnight perhaps. The lane is steep, I laboured. A little wind was chasing the clouds over the faint sky. It is a great thing to own a plot in perpetuity, a very great thing indeed. If only that were the only perpetuity. I came to the wicket. It was locked. Very properly. But I could not open it. The key went into the hole, but would not turn.

Long disuse? A new lock? I burst it open. I drew back to the other side of the lane and hurled myself at it. I had come home, as Youdi had commanded me. In the end I got to my feet. What smelt so sweet? The lilacs? The primroses perhaps. I went towards my hives. They were there, as I feared. I lifted the top off one and laid it on the ground. It was a little roof, with a sharp ridge, and steep overhanging slopes. I put my hand in the hive, moved it among the empty trays, felt along the bottom. It encountered, in a corner, a dry light ball. It crumbled under my fingers. They had clustered together for a little warmth, to try and sleep. I took out a handful. It was too dark to see, I put it in my pocket. It weighed nothing. They had been left out all winter, their honey taken away, without sugar. Yes, now I may make an end. I did not go to the hen-house. My hens were dead too, I knew they were dead. They had not been killed in the same way, except the grey one perhaps, that was the only difference. My bees, my hens, I had deserted them. I went towards the house. It was in darkness. The door was locked. I burst it open. Perhaps I could have opened it, with one of my keys. I turned the switch. No light. I went to the kitchen, to Martha's room. No one. There is nothing more to tell. The house was empty. The company had cut off the light. They have offered to let me have it back. But I told them they could keep it. That is the kind of man I have become. I went back to the garden. The next day I looked at my handful of bees. A little dust of annulets and wings. I found some letters, at the foot of the stairs, in the box. A letter from Savory. My son was well. He would be. Let us hear no more about him. He has come back. He is sleeping. A letter from Youdi, in the third person, asking for a report. He will get his report. It is summer again. This time a year ago I was setting out. I am clearing out. One day I received a visit from Gaber. He wanted the report. That's funny, I thought I was done with people and talk. Call back, I said. One day I received a visit from Father Ambrose. Is it possible! he said when he saw me. I think he really liked me, in his own way. I told him not to count on me any more. He began to talk. He was right. Who is not right? I left him. I am clearing out. Perhaps I shall meet Molloy. My knee is no better. It is no worse either. I have crutches now. I shall go faster, all will go faster. They will be happy days. I shall learn. All there was to sell I have sold. But I had heavy debts. I have been a man long enough, I shall not put up with it any more, I shall not try any more. I shall never light this lamp again. I am going to blow it out and go into the garden. I think of the long May days, June days, when I lived in the garden. One day I talked to Hannah. She gave me news of Zulu, of the Elsner sisters. She knew who I was, she was not afraid of me. She never went out, she disliked going out. She talked to me from her window. The news was bad, but might have been worse. There was a bright side. They were lovely days. The winter had been exceptionally rigorous, everybody said so. We had therefore a right to this superb summer. I do not know if we had a right to it. My birds had not been killed. They were wild birds. And yet quite trusting. I recognized them and they seemed to recognize me. But one never knows. Some were missing and some were new. I tried to understand their language better. Without having recourse to mine. They were the longest, loveliest days of all the year. I lived in the garden. I have spoken of a voice telling me things. I was getting to know it better now, to understand what it wanted. It did not use the words that Moran had been taught when he was little and that he in his turn had taught to his little one. So that at first I did not know what it wanted. But in the end I understood this language. I understood it, I understand it, all wrong perhaps. That is not what matters. It told me to write the report. Does this mean I am freer now than I was? I do not know. I shall learn. Then I went back into the house and wrote, It is midnight. The rain is beating on the windows. It was not midnight. It was not raining.

Appendix

The following three English translations of passages from the original French version of *Molloy* were all published prior to the first English-language edition of the novel (Paris: The Olympia Press, 1955). A fourth text, published under the title 'Molloy' in *New World Writing*, vol. 5 (New York: New American Library, [April] 1954), pp. 316–23, is not reproduced here, since, aside from being considerably shorter (running from 'I am in my mother's room' to 'all that between two suns abides and passes away'; pp. 3–12 in the present edition), it is almost identical to the one published in *Merlin*. Strictly speaking, the three texts are not 'extracts' from the English translation of the novel; rather, they are earlier versions of that translation as finally published in book form. A brief analysis of some of the significant differences between these texts and the corresponding passages in the Olympia Press edition is offered in the preface to the present edition, and the texts are reprinted here to give the reader an opportunity to consider these variations in full. Square brackets indicate editorial interventions, which have been kept to a minimum.

This text is the first of 'Two Fragments' (the second being the opening of Malone Dies*) published in* Transition Fifty, *no. 6 (Paris: Transition Press, 1950), pp. 103–5. It appeared before the original French edition of the novel and was translated by Beckett alone. It corresponds to pp. 64–6 in the present edition.*

I left the shelter of the doorway and began to lever myself forward, slowly swinging through the sullen air. There is rapture, or there should be, in the motion that crutches give, in the succession of little flights, in the taking off and landing among the thronging sound in wind and limb who have to fasten one foot to the ground before they dare lift the other. But these are reasonings, based on analysis. And though my mind was still taken up with the question of my mother and with the desire to know if I was in her vicinity, it was gradually less so, perhaps because of the silver in my pocket, but I think not, and also because these were ancient cares, and the mind cannot brood on the same cares for ever, but needs fresh cares from time to time, so as to revert with renewed vigour, when the moment comes, to ancient cares. But is it legitimate to speak here of fresh and ancient cares? I think not, but it would be difficult to prove. What I may venture to assert, without fear of covering myself with ridicule, is that I gradually lost interest in knowing among other things what town I was in and if I should soon find my mother and settle the matter that concerned us. And even the nature of that matter grew dim, without however disappearing completely, for it was no small matter and I was bent on it. All my life, I think, I had been bent on it. Yes, in so far as I was capable of being bent on something all a lifetime long, I had been bent on settling this matter between my mother and me, but I had never succeeded in doing so. And while I said to myself that time was running out and that it would be soon too late, if it were not so already, to arrive at the settlement in question, yet at the same time I felt myself carried away towards other cares, other spectres. And far more than to know what town I was in, my haste was now to leave it, even though it were the right one, where my mother had waited so long and perhaps was waiting still. And it seemed to me that if I kept going forward in a straight line I should necessarily leave it, sooner or later. So I applied myself to this, to the best of my ability, making allowance for the drift towards the right hand of the feeble light that was my guide. And my pertinacity was such that I did in fact arrive at the ramparts, at nightfall, having no doubt described a quarter of a circle at least, through bad navigation. It is true I stopped many times, to rest, but not for long, for I felt harried, wrongly perhaps. But in the country there is another justice, and other judges, at first. And having passed the ramparts I was obliged to admit that the sky was clearing, prior to its winding in the other shroud, that of night. Yes, the great cloud was ravelling, discovering here and there a pale and dying sky, and the sun, while its actual disk remained hidden, was manifest in the livid tongues of fire darting towards the zenith, falling and darting again, ever more pale and languid, and doomed no sooner lit to be extinguished. This phenomenon, if I may trust the memory of my observations, was characteristic of my region. Things are perhaps different now. Though I fail to see, having never left my region, what right I have to speak of its characteristics. No, I never escaped, and even the limits of my region were unknown to me. But I believed them to be far away. But this belief was based on nothing serious, it was a simple belief. For if my region had come to an end at a reasonable remove, surely a sort of gradation would have marked the fact. For regions do not come suddenly to an end, as far as I know, but gradually merge into one another. And I never came across anything of this nature, but however far I went, and in no matter what direction, it was always the same sky, and the same earth, precisely, day after day and night after night. On the other hand, if it is true that regions gradually merge into one another, and this remains to be proved, then I may well have left mine many times, without knowing it. But I preferred to abide by my simple belief and its voice that said, Molloy, your region is vast, you have never left it and you never shall. And wheresoever you wander, within its distant limits, things will always be the same, precisely. It would thus appear, if this is so, that my movements owed nothing to the places they caused to vanish, but were due to something else, to the buckled wheel that carried me, in unforeseeable jerks, from fatigue to rest, and inversely, for example. But now I do not wander any more, anywhere any more, and indeed I scarcely stir hand or foot, and yet nothing is changed. And the confines of my room, of my bed, of my body, are as remote from me as were those of my region, in the days of my splendour. And the cycle continues, joltingly, of flight and bivouac, in an Egypt without bounds, without infant, without mother.

2

This translation of the opening of the novel was published under the title 'Extract from Molloy*' in* Merlin, *vol. 2, no. 2 (Autumn 1953), pp. 88–103. It is identified in* Merlin *as having been 'translated from the french by p. w. bowles', and corresponds to pp. 3–24 in the present edition.*

I am in my mother's room. It's I who live there now. I don't know how I got there. Perhaps in an ambulance, certainly a vehicle of some kind. I was helped. I'd never have got there alone. There's this man who comes every week. Perhaps I got here thanks to him. He says not. He gives me money and takes away the pages. So many pages, so much money. Yes, I work now, a little like I used to, except that I don't know how to work any more. That doesn't matter, apparently. What I'd like now is to speak of the things that are left, say my good-byes, finish dying. They don't want that. Yes, they're more than one, apparently. But it's always the same one that comes. You'll do that later, he says. Good. The truth is I haven't much will left. When he comes for the fresh pages he brings back the previous week's. They are marked with signs I don't understand. Anyway I don't read them. When I've done nothing he gives me nothing, he scolds me. Yet I don't work for money. For what then? I don't know. The truth is I don't know much. For example my mother's death. Was she already dead when I came? Or did she only die later? I mean enough to bury. I don't know. Perhaps they haven't buried her yet. In any case I have her room. I sleep in her bed. I piss and shit in her pot. I have taken her place. I must resemble her more and more. All I need now is a son. Perhaps I have one somewhere. But I think not. He would be old now, nearly as old as me. It was a little chambermaid. It wasn't real love. The real love was in another. We'll come to that.

Her name? I've forgotten it again. It seems to me sometimes that I even knew my son, that I helped him. Then I tell myself it is impossible. It is impossible I could ever have helped anyone. I've forgotten how to spell too, and half the words. That doesn't matter apparently. Good. He's a queer card who comes to see me. He comes every Sunday apparently. The other days he isn't free. He's always thirsty. It was he told me I'd begun all wrong, that I should have begun differently. He must be right. I began at the beginning, like an old fool, can you imagine that. Here's my beginning. Because they're keeping it apparently. I took a lot of trouble with it. Here it is. It gave me a lot of trouble. It was the beginning, you see. Whereas now it's nearly the end. Is what I do now any better? I don't know. That's beside the point. Here's my beginning. It must mean something, since they're keeping it. Here it is.

This time, then once more I think, then perhaps a last time, then I think it'll be over, with that world too. Premonition of the last but one but one. All grows dim. A little more, and you'll go blind. It's in the head. It doesn't work any more, it says, I don't work any more. You go dumb as well and sounds fade. The threshold scarcely crossed that's how it is. It's the head. It must have had enough. So that you say, I'll manage this time, then perhaps once more, then perhaps a last time, then nothing more. You are hard set to formulate this thought, for it is one, in a sense. Then you try to pay attention, to consider with attention all those dim things, saying to yourself, laboriously, It's my fault. Fault? That was the word. But what fault? It's not goodbye, and what magic in those dim things to which it will be time enough, when next they pass, to say goodbye. For you must say goodbye, it would be folly not to say goodbye, when the time comes. If you think of the forms and light of other days it is without regret. But you seldom think of them, with what would you think of them? I don't know. People pass too, hard to distinguish from yourself. That is discouraging. That's how I saw A and C going slowly towards each other, unconscious of what they were doing. It was on a road remarkably bare, I mean without hedges or ditches or any kind of border, in the country, for cows were chewing in enormous fields, lying and standing, in the evening silence. Perhaps I'm inventing a little, perhaps embellishing, but on the whole that's how it was. They chew, swallow, then after a short pause effortlessly bring up the next mouthful. A neck muscle stirs and the jaws begin to grind again. But perhaps I'm remembering things. The road, hard and white, seared the tender pastures, rose and fell at the whim of hills and hollows. The town wasn't far. It was two men, unmistakably, one short and one tall. They had left the town, first one, then the other, and the first, weary or remembering a duty, had retraced his steps. The air was sharp, for they wore greatcoats. They looked alike, but no more than others do. At first a wide space lay between them. They couldn't have seen each other, even had they raised their heads and looked about, because of this wide space, and then because of the undulating land, which caused the road to be in waves, not deep, but deep enough, deep enough. But the moment came when together they went down into the same trough and in this trough finally met. To say they were acquainted, no, nothing warrants it. But perhaps at the sound of their steps, or warned by some obscure instinct, they raised their heads and observed each other, for a good fifteen paces, before they stopped, breast to breast. Yes, they did not pass each other by, but halted, face to face, as in the country, of an evening, on a deserted road, two wayfaring strangers often do, without there being anything extraordinary about it. But they knew each other perhaps. Now in any case they do, now I think they will know each other, greet each other, even in the depths of the town. They turned towards the sea which, far in the east, beyond the fields, climbed high in the waning sky, and exchanged a few words. Then each went on his way. Each went on his way, A towards the town, C by ways he seemed hardly to know, or not at all, for he went with uncertain steps and often stopped to look about him, like someone trying to fix landmarks in his mind, for one day, perhaps, he may have to retrace his steps, you never know. The treacherous hills where fearfully he ventured were no doubt only known to him from afar, seen perhaps from his bedroom window or, one black day, from the summit of a monument which, having nothing in particular to do and turning to height for solace he had paid his few coppers to climb, up the winding stones. From there he must have seen it all, the plain, the sea, and then these very hills that some call mountains, indigo in places in the evening light, their serried ranges crowding to the sky-line, cloven with hidden valleys that the eye divines from sudden shifts of colour and then from other signs for which there are no words, nor even thoughts. But all are not divined, even from that height, and often where only one escarpment is supposed, and one crest, in reality there are two, two escarpments, two crests, riven by a valley. But now he knows these hills, that is he knows them better, and if ever again he sees them from afar it will be I think with other eyes, and not only that but the within, all that inner space one never sees, the brain and heart and other caverns where thought and feeling hold their sabbath, all that too quite differently disposed. He looks old and it is a sorry sight to see him solitary after so many years, so many days and nights unthinkingly given to that rumour rising at birth and even earlier, *What shall I do? What shall I do?* now low, a murmur, now precise as the headwaiter's *And to follow?* and often rising to a scream. And in the end, or almost, to be abroad alone, by unknown ways, in the gathering night, with a stick. It was a stout stick, he used it to thrust himself onward, or as a defence, when the time came, against dogs and marauders. Yes, night was gathering, but the man was innocent, greatly innocent, he had nothing to fear, though he went in fear, he had nothing to fear, there was nothing they could do to him, or very little. But he can't have known it. I wouldn't know it myself, if I thought about it. Yes, he saw himself threatened, his body threatened, his reason threatened, and perhaps he was, perhaps they were, in spite of his innocence. What business has innocence here? What relation to the innumerable spirits of darkness? It's not clear. It seemed to me he wore a cocked hat. I remember being struck by it, as I wouldn't have been for example by a cap or by a bowler. I watched him recede, overtaken by his anxiety, at least by an anxiety which was not necessarily his, but of which as it were he partook. Who knows if it wasn't my own anxiety overtaking him. He hadn't seen me. I was perched higher than the road's highest point and flattened what is more against a rock the same colour as myself, that is grey. The rock he probably saw. He gazed around as if to engrave the landmarks on his memory, and must have seen the rock in the shadow of which I crouched like Belacqua, or Sordello, I forget. But a man, a fortiori myself, isn't exactly a landmark, because. I mean if by some strange chance he were to pass that way again, after a long lapse of time, vanquished, or to look for some forgotten thing, or to destroy something, his eyes would search out the rock, not the haphazard in its shadow of that unstable fugitive thing, still living flesh. No, he certainly didn't see me, for the reasons I've given and then because he was in no humour for that, that evening, no humour for the living, but rather for what doesn't stir, or stirs so slowly that a child would scorn it, let alone an old man. However that may be, I mean whether he saw me or whether he didn't, I repeat I watched him recede, at grips (myself) with the temptation to get up and follow him, perhaps even to catch up on him one day, so as to know him better, be myself less lonely. But in spite of my soul's leap out to him, at the end of its elastic, I saw him only darkly, because of the dark and then because of the terrain, in the folds of which he disappeared from time to time, to re-emerge farther on, but most of all I think because of other things calling me and towards which too one after the other my soul was straining, unmethodical, distracted. I mean of course the fields, whitening under the dew, and the animals, ceasing from wandering and settling for the night, and the sea, of which nothing, and the sharpening line of crests, and the sky where without seeing them I felt the first stars tremble, and my hand on my knee and above all the other wayfarer, A or C, I don't remember, going resignedly home. Yes, towards my hand also, which my knee felt tremble and of which my eyes saw the wrist only, the heavily veined back, the pallid rows of knuckles. But that is not, I mean my hand, what I wish to speak of now, everything in due course, but A or C returning to the town he had just left. But after all what was there particularly urban in his aspect? He was bare-headed, wore sand-shoes, smoked a cigar. He moved with a kind of loitering indolence which rightly or wrongly seemed to me expressive. But all that proved nothing, refuted nothing. Perhaps he had come from afar, from the other end of the island even, and was approaching the town for the first time or returning to it after a long absence. A little dog followed him, a pomeranian I think, but I don't think so. I wasn't sure at the time and I'm still not sure, though I've hardly thought about it. The little dog followed wretchedly, after the fashion of pomeranians, stopping, describing long girations, giving up and then, a little farther on, beginning all over again. Constipation is a sign of good health in pomeranians. At a given moment, pre-established if you like, I don't mind, the gentleman turned back, took the little creature in his arms, drew the cigar from his lips and buried his face in the orange fleece, for it was a gentleman, that was obvious. Yes, it was an orange pomeranian, the less I think of it the more certain I am. And yet. But would he have come from afar, bare-headed, in sand-shoes, smoking a cigar, followed by a pomeranian? Did he not seem rather to have issued from the ramparts, after a good dinner, to take his dog and himself for a walk, like so many citizens, dreaming and farting, when the weather is fine? But was not perhaps in reality the cigar a cutty, and were not the sand-shoes boots, hobnailed, dust-whitened, and what prevented the dog from being one of those stray dogs that you pick up and take in your arms, from compassion or because you have long been straying with no other company than the endless roads, sands, shingle, bogs and heather, than this nature answerable to another court, than at long intervals the fellow convict you long to stop, embrace, suck, suckle and whom you pass by, with hostile eyes, for fear of his familiarities. Until the day when, your endurance gone, in this world for you without arms, you catch up in yours the first mangy cur you meet, carry it the time needed for it to love you and you it, then throw it away. Perhaps he had come to that, in spite of appearances. He disappeared, his head on his chest, the smoking object in his hand. Let me try and explain. From things about to disappear I turn away in time. To watch them out of sight, no, I can't do it. It was in this sense he disappeared. Looking away I thought of him, saying, He dwindles, dwindles. I knew what I meant. I knew I could catch him, lame as I was. I had only to want to. And yet no, for I did want to. To get up, to get to the road, to set hobbling off in pursuit of him, to hail him, what could be easier. He hears my cries, turns, waits for me. I am up against him, up against the dog, gasping, between my crutches. He is a little frightened of me, a little sorry for me, I disgust him not a little. I am not a pretty sight, I don't smell good. What is it I want? Ah that tone I know, compounded of pity, of fear, of disgust. I want to see the dog, see the man, at close quarters, know what smokes, inspect the shoes, find out other things. He is kind, tells me of this and of that and of other things, whence he comes, whither he goes. I believe him, I know it's my only chance to—my only chance, I believe all I'm told, I've disbelieved only too much in my long life, now I swallow everything, avidly. What I need now is stories, it took me a long time to know that, and I'm not sure of it. There I am then, informed as to certain things, knowing certain things about him, things I didn't know, things that troubled me, even things that never troubled me. What language. I am even capable of having learnt what his profession is, I who am so interested in professions. And to think I try my best not to talk about myself. In a moment I shall talk about the cows, about the sky, if I can. There I am then, he leaves me, he's in a hurry. He didn't seem to be in a hurry, he was loitering, I've already said so, but after three minutes talking with me he is in a hurry, he has to hurry. I believe him. And once again I am I will not say alone, no, that's not like me, but, how shall I say, I don't know, restored to myself, no, I never left myself, free, yes, I don't know what that means but it's the word I intend to use, free to do what, to do nothing, to know, but what, the laws of the mind perhaps, of my mind, that for example water rises in proportion as it drowns you and that you would do better, at least no worse, to obliterate texts than to blacken margins, to fill in the holes of words till all is blank and flat and the whole ghastly business looks like what it is, senseless, speechless, issueless misery. So I doubtless did better, at least no worse, not to disturb myself from my observation post. But instead of observing I had the weakness to return in spirit to the other, the man with the stick. Then the murmurs began again. To restore silence is the role of objects. I said, Who knows if he hasn't simply come out to take the air, relax, stretch his legs, disinflame his brain by stamping the blood down to his feet, so as to ensure himself a good night, a joyous awakening, an enchanted morrow. Was he carrying as much as a scrip? But this gait, the anxious looks, the club, could these be reconciled with one's conception of what is called a little turn. But the hat, a town hat, an old-fashioned town hat, which the least wind would carry far away. Unless it was attached under the chin, by means of a string or an elastic. I took off my hat and looked at it. It is fastened, it has always been fastened, to my buttonhole, always the same buttonhole, at all seasons, by a long lace. I am still alive then. That may come in useful. The hand that had seized the hat and held it still I thrust as far as possible from me and caused to come and go in an arc. So doing, I watched the lapel of my greatcoat, and saw it open and close. I understand now why I never wore a flower in my buttonhole, though it was large enough to hold a whole bunch. My buttonhole was set aside for my hat. It was my hat that I beflowered. But it is neither of my hat nor of my greatcoat that I hope to speak at present, it would be premature. Doubtless I shall speak of them later, when the time comes to draw up the inventory of my goods and possessions. Unless I lose them between now and then. But even lost they will have their place, in the inventory of my possessions. But I am easy in my mind, I shall not lose them. Nor my crutches, I shall not lose my crutches either. But I shall perhaps one day throw them away, I must have been on the top, or on the slopes, of some considerable eminence, for otherwise how could I have seen, so far away, so near at hand, so far beneath, so many things, fixed and moving. But what was an eminence doing in this land with hardly a ripple? And I, what was I doing there, and why come? These are things that we shall try and discover. But these are things we must not take seriously. There is a little of everything, apparently, in nature and freaks are common. And I am perhaps confusing several different occasions, and different times, deep down, and deep down is my dwelling, oh not deepest down, somewhere between the mud and the scum. And perhaps it was A one day at one place, then C another at another, then a third the rock and I, and so on for the other components, the cows, the sky, the sea, the mountains. I can't believe it. No, I will not lie, I can easily conceive it. No matter, no matter, let us go on, as if all arose from one and the same weariness, on and on hoarding, until there is no room, no light, for any more. What is certain is that the man with the stick did not pass by again that night, because I would have heard him, if he had, I don't say I would have seen him, I say I would have heard him, I sleep little and that little in the daytime. Oh not systematically, in my life without end I have dabbled with every kind of sleep, but at the time now coming back to me I took my doze in the daytime and, what is more, in the morning. Let me hear nothing of the moon, in my night there is no moon, and if it happens that I speak of the stars it's inadvertently. Now of all the noises that night not one was of those heavy uncertain steps, or of that club with which he sometimes smote the earth until it quaked. How agreeable it is to be confirmed, after a more or less long period of vacillation, in one's first impressions. Perhaps that is what tempers the pangs of death. Not that I was so conclusively, I mean confirmed, in my first impressions with regard to—wait—C. For the wagons and carts which a little before dawn went thundering by, on their way to market with fruit, eggs, butter and perhaps cheese, in one of these perhaps he would have been found, overcome by fatigue or by discouragement, perhaps even dead. Or he might have gone back to the town by another way too far away for me to hear its sounds, or by little paths through the fields, crushing the silent grass, pounding the silent ground. And so at last I came out of that distant night, divided between the murmurs of my little world, its dutiful confusions, and those so different (so different?) of all that between two suns abides and passes away. Never once a human voice. But the cows, when the peasants passed, crying in vain to be milked. A and C I never saw again. But perhaps I shall see them again. But shall I be able to recognize them? And am I sure I never saw them again? And what do I mean by seeing and seeing again? An instant of silence, as when the conductor taps on his stand, raises his arms, before the unanswerable clamour. Smoke, sticks, flesh, hair, at evening, afar, flung about the craving for a fellow. I know how to summon these rags to cover my shame. I wonder what that means. But I shall not always be in need. But talking of the craving for a fellow let me observe that having waked between eleven o'clock and midday (I heard the angelus, recalling the incarnation, shortly after) I resolved to go and see my mother. I needed, before I could resolve to go and see that woman, reasons of an urgent nature, and with such reasons, since I did not know what to do, or where to go, it was child's play for me, the play of an only child, to fill my mind until it was rid of all other preoccupation and I seized with a trembling at the mere idea of being hindered from going there, I mean to my mother, there and then. So I got up, adjusted my crutches and went down to the road, where I found my bicycle (I didn't know I had one) in the same place I must have left it. Which enables me to remark that, crippled though I was, I was no mean cyclist, at that period. This is how I went about it. I fastened my crutches to the cross-bar, one on either side, I propped the foot of my stiff leg (I forget which, now they're both stiff) on the projecting front axle, and I pedalled with the other. It was a chainless bicycle, with a free-wheel, if such a bicycle exists. Dear bicycle, I shall not call you bike, you were green, like so many of your generation, I don't know why. It is a pleasure to meet it again. To describe it in detail would be a pleasure. It had a little red horn instead of the bell fashionable in your days. To blow this horn was for me a real pleasure, almost a vice. I will go further and declare that if I were obliged to record, in a roll of honour, those activities which in the course of my interminable existence have given me only a mild pain in the balls, the act of blowing a rubber horn would figure among the first. And when I had to part from my bicycle I took off the horn and kept it about me. I believe I have it, still, somewhere, and if I use it no more, it is because it has gone dumb. Even motor-cars have no horns today, as I understand the thing, or rarely. When I see one, through the lowered window of a stationary car, I often stop and blow it. This should all be re-written in the pluperfect. What a rest to speak of bicycles and horns. Unfortunately it is not of them I have to speak, but of her who brought me into the world, through the hole in her arse if my memory is correct. First taste of the shit. So I shall only add that every hundred yards or so I stopped to rest my legs, the good one as well as the bad, and not only my legs, not only my legs. I didn't properly speaking get down off the bicycle. I remained astride it, my feet on the ground, my arms on the handle-bars, my head on my arms, and I waited until I felt better. But before I leave this earthly paradise, suspended between the mountains and the sea, sheltered from certain winds and exposed to all that Auster vents, in the way of scents and langours [*sic*], on this accursed country, it would ill become me not to mention the awful cries of the corncrakes that run in the corn, in the meadows, all the short summer night long dinning their rattles. And this enables me, what is more, to know when that unreal journey began, the second last but one of a form fading among fading forms, and which I here declare without further ado to have begun in the second or third week of June, at the moment that is to say most painful of all when over what is called our hemisphere the sun is at its pitilessmost and the arctic radiance comes pissing on our midnights. It is then the corncrakes are heard. My mother never refused to see me, that is she never refused to receive me, for it was many a long day since she had seen anything at all. I shall try and speak calmly. We were so old, she and I, she had had me so young, that we were like a couple of old cronies, sexless, unrelated, with the same memories, the same rancours, the same expectations. She never called me son, fortunately, I couldn't have borne it, but Dan. I don't know why, my name is not Dan. Dan was my father's name perhaps, yes, perhaps she took me for my father. I took her for my mother and she took me for my father. Dan, you remember the day I saved the swallow. Dan, you remember the day you buried the ring. I remembered, I remembered. I mean I knew more or less what she was talking about, and if I hadn't always taken part personally in the scenes she evoked, it was just as if I had. I called her Mag, when I had to call her something. And I called her Mag because for me, without my knowing why, the letter g abolished the syllable Ma, and as it were spat on it, better than any other letter would have done. And at the same time I satisfied a deep and doubtless unacknowledged need, the need to have a Ma, that is a mother, and to proclaim it, audibly. For before you say mag you say ma, inevitably. And da, in my part of the world, means father. Besides for me the question did not arise, at the period I'm worming into now, I mean the question of whether to call her Ma, Mag or the Countess Caca, she having for countless years been as deaf as a post. I think she was quite incontinent, both of faeces and water, but a kind of prudishness made us avoid the subject when we met, and I could never be certain of it. In any case it can't have amounted to much, a few niggardly wetted goat-droppings every two or three days. The room smelt of ammonia, oh not merely of ammonia, but of ammonia, ammonia. She knew it was me, by my smell. Her shrunken hairy old face lit up, she was happy to smell me. She jabbered away with a rattle of dentures, and most of the time didn't realize what she was saying. Anyone but myself would have been lost in this clattering gabble, which can only have stopped during her brief instants of unconsciousness. In any case I didn't come to listen to her. I got into communication with her by knocking on her skull. One knock meant yes, two no, three I don't know, four money, five goodbye. I was hard put to ram this code into her ruined and frantic understanding, but I did it, in the end. That she should confuse yes, no, I don't know and goodbye, was all the same to me, I confused them myself. But that she should associate the four knocks with anything but money was something to be avoided at all costs. During the period of training therefore, at the same time as I administered the four knocks on her skull, I stuck a bank-note under her nose or in her mouth. In the innocence of my heart! For she seemed to have lost, if not absolutely all notion of mensuration, at least the faculty of counting beyond two. It was too far for her, yes, the distance was too great, from one to four. By the time she came to the fourth knock she imagined she was only at the second, the first two having been erased from her memory as completely as if they had never been felt, though I don't quite see how something never felt can be erased from the memory, and yet it is a common occurrence. She must have thought I was saying no to her all the time, whereas nothing was further from my purpose. Enlightened by these considerations I looked for and finally found a more effective means of putting the idea of money into her head. This consisted in replacing the four knocks of my index-knuckle by one or more (according to my needs) thumps of the fist, on her skull. That she understood. In any case I didn't come for money. I took her money, but I didn't come for that. My mother. I don't think too harshly of her. I know she did all she could not to have me, except of course the one thing, and if she never succeeded in getting me unstuck, it was that fate had earmarked me for less compassion-ate sewers. But it was well-meant and that's enough for me. No it is not enough for me, but I give her credit, though she is my mother, for what she tried to do for me. And I forgive her for having jostled me a little in the first months and spoiled the only endurable, just endurable, period of my enormous history. And I also give her credit for not having done it again, thanks to me, or for having stopped in time, when she did. And if ever I'm reduced to looking for a meaning to my life, you never can tell, it's in that old mess I'll stick my nose to begin with, the mess of that poor old uniparous whore and myself the last of my foul brood, neither man nor beast. I should add, before I get down to the facts, you'd swear they were facts, of that distant summer afternoon, that with this deaf blind impotent mad old woman, who called me Dan and whom I called Mag, and with her alone, I—no, I can't say it. That is to say I could say it but I won't say it, yes, I could say it easily, because it wouldn't be true. What did I see of her? A head always, the hands sometimes, the arms rarely. A head always. Veiled with hair, wrinkles, filth, slobber. A head that darkened the air. Not that seeing matters, but it's something to go on with. It's I who took the key from under the pillow, who took the money out of the drawer, who put the key back under the pillow. But I didn't come for money. I think there was a woman who came each week. Once I touched with my lips, vaguely, hastily, that little grey wizened pear. Pah. Did that please her? I don't know. Her babble stopped for a second, then began again. Perhaps she said to herself, Pah. I smelt a terrible smell. It must have come from the guts. Odour of antiquity. Oh I'm not criticizing her, I don't diffuse the perfumes of Araby myself. Shall I describe the room? No. I shall have occasion to do so later perhaps. When I seek refuge there, bet, all shame drunk, my prick in my rectum, who knows. Good. Now that we know where we're going, let's go there. It's so nice to know where you're going, in the early stages. It almost rids you of the wish to go there. I was distraught, who am so seldom distraught, from what should I be distraught, and as to my motions even more uncertain than usual. The night must have tired me, at least weakened me, and the sun, hoisting itself higher and higher in the east, had poisoned me, while I slept. I ought to have put the bulk of the rock between it and me before closing my eyes. I confuse east and west, the poles too, I invert them readily. I was out of sorts. They are deep, my sorts, a deep ditch, and I am not often out of them. That's why I mention it.

Nevertheless I covered several miles and found myself under the ramparts. There I dismounted in compliance with the regulations. Yes, on entering and leaving town the police compel cyclists to dismount, cars to go into bottom gear and horse-drawn vehicles to slow down to a walk. The reason for this regulation is I think this, that the ways into and of course the ways out of this town are narrow and darkened by enormous vaults, without exception. It is a good rule and I observe it meticulously, in spite of the difficulty I have in advancing on my crutches pushing my bicycle at the same time. I managed somehow. Being ingenious. Thus we cleared these difficult straits, my bicycle and I, together. But a little further on I heard myself hailed. I raised my head and saw a policeman. Elliptically speaking, for it was only later, by way of induction, or of deduction, I forget which, that I knew what it was. What are you doing there? he said. I'm used to that question. I understood it immediately. Resting, I said. Resting, he said. Resting, I said. Will you answer my question? he cried. So it always is when I'm reduced to confabulation, I honestly believe I have answered the questions I am asked and in reality I do nothing of the kind. I won't reconstruct the conversation in all its meanderings. It ended in my understanding that my way of resting, my attitude when at rest, astride my bicycle, my arms on the handlebars, my head on my arms, was a violation of I don't know what, public order, public decency. Modestly I pointed to my crutches and ventured one or two noises regarding my infirmity, which obliged me to rest as I could, rather than as I should. But there are not two laws, that was the next thing I thought I understood, not two laws, one for the healthy, another for the sick, but one only to which all must bow, rich and poor, young and old, happy and sad. He was eloquent. I pointed out that I was not sad. That was a mistake. Your papers, he said, I knew it after a moment. Not at all, I said, not at all. Your papers! he cried. Ah my papers. Now the only papers I carry with me are bits of newspaper, to wipe myself, you understand, when I have a stool, oh I don't say I wipe myself every time I have a stool, no, but I like to be in a position to do so, if I have to. Nothing strange about that, it seems to me. In a panic I took this paper from my pocket and thrust it under his nose. The weather was fine. We took the little side streets, quiet, sunlit, I springing along between my crutches, he pushing my bicycle, with the tips of his white-gloved fingers. I wasn't—I didn't feel unhappy. I stopped a moment, I made so bold, to lift my hand and touch the crown of my hat. It was scorching. I felt the faces turning to look after us, calm faces and joyful faces, faces of men, of women and of children. I seemed to hear, at a certain moment, a distant music. I stopped, the better to listen. Go on, he said. Listen, I said. Get on, he said. I wasn't allowed to listen to the music. It might have drawn a crowd. He gave me a shove. I had been touched, oh not my skin, but none the less my skin had felt it, it had felt a man's hard fist, through its coverings. While still putting my best foot foremost I gave myself up to that golden moment, as if I had been someone else. It was the hour of rest, the forenoon's toil ended, the afternoon's to come. The wisest perhaps, lying in the squares or sitting on their doorsteps, were savouring its languid ending, forgetful of recent cares, indifferent to those at hand. Others on the contrary were using it to make their plans, their heads in their hands. Was there one among them to put himself in my place, to feel how removed I was then from him I seemed to be, and in that remove what strain, as of hawsers about to snap. It's possible. Yes, I was straining towards those spurious deeps, their lying promise of gravity and peace, from all my old poisons I struggled towards it, safely bound. Under the blue sky, under the watchful gaze. Forgetful of my mother, set free from the act, merged in this alien hour, saying, respite, respite. At the police station I was [haled before] a very strange official. Dressed in plain-clothes, in his shirt-sleeves, he was sprawling in an arm chair, his feet on his desk, a straw hat on his head and protruding from his mouth a thin flexible object I could not identify. I had time to become aware of these details before he dismissed me. He listened to his subordinate's report and then began to interrogate me in a tone which, from the point of view of civility, left increasingly to be desired, in my opinion. Between his questions and my answers, I mean those deserving of consideration, the intervals were more or less long and turbulent. I am so little used to being asked anything that when I am asked something I take some time to know what. And the mistake I make then is this, that instead of quietly reflecting on what I have just heard, and heard distinctly, not being hard of hearing, in spite of all I have heard, I hasten to answer blindly, fearing perhaps lest my silence raise their anger to fury. I am full of fear, I have gone in fear all my life, in fear of blows. Insults, abuse, these I can easily bear, but I could never get used to blows. It's strange. Even spits still pain me. But they have only to be a little gentle, I mean refrain from hitting me, and I seldom fail to give satisfaction, in the long run. Now the sergeant was content to threaten me with a cylindrical ruler, and was repaid, little by little, by the discovery that I had no papers in the sense this word had a sense for him, nor any occupation, nor any domicile, that my surname escaped me for the moment and that I was on my way to my mother, whose charity kept me dying. As to her address, I was in the dark, but knew how to get there, even in the dark. The district? By the slaughterhouse your lordship, for from my mother's room, through the closed windows, I had heard, stilling her chatter, the bellowing of the cattle, that violent raucous tremulous bellowing not of the pastures but of the towns, their slaughter-[h]ouses and cattle-markets. Yes, after all, I had perhaps gone too far in saying that my mother lived near the slaughterhouse, it could equally well have been the cattle-market, near which she lived. Don't worry, said the sergeant, it's the same district. I took advantage of the silence which followed these kind words to turn towards the window, blindly or nearly, for I had closed my eyes, proffering to that blandness of blue and gold my face and neck alone, and my mind empty too, or nearly, for I must have been wondering if I did not feel like sitting down, after such a long time standing, and remembering what I had learnt in that connection, namely that the sitting posture was not for me any more, because of my short stiff leg, and that there were only two postures for me, the vertical, drooping between my crutches, sleeping on my feet, and the horizontal, down on the ground. And yet the desire to sit down came upon me from time to time, came back upon me from a vanished world. And I did not always resist it, forewarned though I was. Yes, my mind felt it surely, this tiny sediment, incomprehensibly stirring like grit at the bottom of a puddle, while on my face and great big Adam's apple the air of summer weighed and the splendid summer sky. And suddenly I remembered my name, Molloy. My name is Molloy, I cried, all of a sudden, now I remember. Nothing compelled me to give this information, but I gave it, hoping to please I suppose. They let me keep my hat on, I don't know why. Is it your mother's name, said the sergeant, it must have been a sergeant. Molloy, I cried, my name is Molloy. Is that your mother's name, said the sergeant. What? I said. Your name is Molloy, said the sergeant. Yes, I said, now I remember. And your mother? said the sergeant. I didn't follow. Is your mother's name Molloy too? said the sergeant. I thought it over. Your mother, said the sergeant, is your mother's—Let me think! I cried. At least I imagine that's how it was. Take your time, said the sergeant. Was mother's name Molloy. Very likely. Her name must be Molloy too, I said. They took me away, to the guard-room I suppose, and there I was told to sit down. I must have tried to explain. I won't go into it. I obtained permission, if not to lie down on a bench, at least to remain standing, propped against the wall. The room was dark and full of people hastening to and fro, malefactors, policeman [sic], lawyers, priests and journalists I suppose. All that made a dark, dark forms crowding in a dark place. They paid no attention to me and I repaid the compliment. Then how could I know that they were paying no attention to me and how could I repay the compliment, since they were paying no attention to me? I don't know. I knew it and I did it, that's all I know. But suddenly a woman materialized before me, a big fat woman dressed in black, or rather in mauve. I still wonder today if it wasn't the social worker. She was holding out to me, on an odd saucer, a mug full of a greyish concoction which must have been green tea with saccharine and powdered milk. Nor was that all, for between mug and saucer a thick slab of dry bread was precariously lodged, so that I began to say, in a kind of anguish, It's going to fall, it's going to fall, as if it mattered whether it fell or not. A moment later I myself was holding, in my trembling hands, this little pile of tottering disparates, in which the hard, the liquid and the soft were joined, without understanding how the transfer had been effected. Let me tell you this, when social workers offer you, free[,] gratis and for nothing, something to hinder you from losing consciousness, which with them is an obsession, it is useless to recoil, they will pursue you to the end of the earth, the vomitory in their hand. The Salvation Army is no better. Against the charitable gesture there is no defence, that I know of. You sink your head, you put out your hands all trembling and twined together and you say, Thankyou, thankyou lady, thankyou kind lady. To him who has nothing it is forbidden not to relish filth. The liquid overflowed, the mug rocked with a noise of chattering teeth, not my teeth. I had no teeth, and the sodden bread sagged more and more. Until, panic-stricken, I flung it all far from me. I did not let it fall, no, but with a convulsive thrust of both my hands I threw it on the floor, where it smashed to smithereens, or against the wall, far from me, with all my strength. I will not tell what followed, for I am weary of this place, I want to leave this place. It was late afternoon when they told me I could go. I was advised to behave better in future. Conscious of my wrongs, knowing now the reasons for my arrest, alive to my irregular situation as exposed by the enquiry, I was surprised to find myself so soon at freedom once again, if that was what it was, unpenalized. Had I, without my knowledge, a protector in high places? Had I, without knowing it, favourably impressed the sergeant? Had they succeeded in reaching my mother and obtaining from her, or from the neighbours, partial confirmation of my statements? Were they of the opinion that it was useless to prosecute me[?] To apply the letter of the law to a creature like me is not an easy matter. It can be done, but reason is against it. It is better to leave things to the police. I dont [sic] know. If it is unlawful to be without papers, why did they not insist on my getting them. Because that costs money and I had none? But in that case could they not have appropriated my bicycle? Probably not, without a court order. All that is incomprehensible. What is certain is this, that I never rested in that way again, my feet obscenely resting on the earth, my arms on the handlebars and on my arms my head, rocking and abandoned. It is indeed a deplorable sight, a deplorable example, for the people, who so need to be encouraged, in their bitter toil, and to have before their eyes manifestations of strength only, of courage and of joy, without which they might collapse, at the end of the day, and roll on the ground. I have only to be told what good behaviour is, and I am well behaved, within the limits of my physical possibilities. And so I have never ceased to improve, from this point of view, for I—I used to be intelligent and quick. And as far as good-will is concerned, I had it to overflowing, the exasperated good-will of the over-anxious. So that my repertory of permitted attitudes has never ceased to grow, from my first steps until my last, executed last year. And if I have always behaved like a pig, the fault lies not with me but with my superiors, who corrected me only on points of detail instead of showing me the essence of the system, after the manner of the great English schools, and the guiding principles of good manners and how to proceed, without going wrong, from the latter to the former, and how to trace back to its ultimate source a given comportment. For that would have allowed me, before parading in public certain habits such as the finger in the nose, the scratching of the balls, digital emunction and the peripatetic piss, to refer them to the first rules of a reasoned theory. On this subject I had only negative and empirical notions, which means that I was in the dark, most of the time, and all the more completely as a lifetime of observations had left me doubting the possibility of systematic decorum, even within a limited area. But it is only since I have ceased to live that I

think of these things and the other things. It is in the tranquillity of decomposition that I remember the long confused
emotion which was my life, and that I judge it, as it is said that
God will judge us, and with no less impertinence. To decompose is to live too, I know, I know, don't torment me, but one
sometimes forgets. And of that life too I shall tell you perhaps
one day, the day when I know that when I thought I knew I was
merely existing, and that passion without form or stations will
have devoured me down to the rotting flesh itself, and that when
I know that I know nothing, I am only crying out as I have
always cried out, more or less piercingly, more or less openly.
Let me cry out then, it's said to be good for you. Yes, let me cry
out, this time, then another time perhaps, then perhaps a last
time. Cry out that the declining sun fell full on the white wall of
the barracks. It was like being in China. A confused shadow was
cast. It was I and my bicycle. I began to play, gesticulating,
waving my hat, moving my bicycle to and fro before me,
blowing the horn, watching the wall. They were watching me
through the bars. I felt their eyes upon me. The policeman on
guard at the door told me to go away. He needn't have, I was
calm again. The shadow in the end is no better than the
substance. I asked the man to help me, to have pity on me. He
didn't understand. I thought of the food I had refused. I took a
pebble from my pocket and sucked it. It was smooth, from
having been sucked so long, by me, and beaten by the storm. A
little pebble in your mouth, round and smooth, appeases,
soothes, makes your [sic] forget your hunger, forget your thirst.
The man came towards me, displeased by my slowness. Him
too they were watching, through the windows. Somewhere
someone laughed. Inside me too someone was laughing. I took
my sick leg in my hands and passed it over the frame. I went. I
had forgotten where I was going. I stopped to think. It is
difficult to think riding, for me. When I try and think riding I
lose my balance and fall. I speak in the present tense, it is so
easy to speak in the present tense, when speaking of the past. It
is the mythological present, don't pay any heed to it. I was

already settling in my raglimp stasis when I remembered that it wasn't done. I went on my way, that way of which I knew nothing, qua way, which was nothing more than a surface, bright or dark, smooth or rough, and always dear to me, in spite of all, and the dear sound of that which goes and is gone, with a brief dust, when the weather is dry. There I am then, before I knew I had left the town, on the canal-bank. The canal goes through the town. I know I know [sic], there are even two. But then these hedges, these fields? Don't torment yourself Molloy. Suddenly I see, it was my right leg, the stiff one, then. Toiling towards me along the tow-path I saw a team of little grey donkeys, on the other bank, and I heard angry cries and dull blows. I got down. I put my foot to the ground the better to see the approaching barge, so gently approaching that the water was unruffled. It was a cargo of nails and timber, on its way to some carpenter I suppose. My eyes caught a donkey's eyes, they fell to his little feet, their brave fastidious tread. The boatman rested his elbow on his knee, his head on his hand. Every three or four puffs, without taking his pipe from his mouth, he spat into the water. The horizon was burning with sulphur and phosphorous [sic], it was there I was bound.

3

Published under the title 'Extract from Molloy' *in the* Paris Review, *5 (Spring 1954), pp. 124–35, this text is identified therein as having been 'Translated by Patrick Bowles in collaboration with the author'. It corresponds to pp. 68–79 in the present edition.*

There are people the sea doesn't suit, they prefer the mountains or the plain. Personally, I feel no worse there than anywhere else. Much of my life has ebbed away before this shivering expanse, to the sound of waves in storm and calm, and the claws of the surf. Before, no, more than before, one with, spread on the sand, or in a cave. In the sand I was in my element, letting it trickle between my fingers, scooping holes that a moment later filled in or that filled themselves in, casting it in the air by handfuls, rolling in it. And in the cave, lit by the beacons at night, I knew what to do to be no worse than anywhere else. And that my land went no further, in one direction at least, did not displease me. And to feel there was one direction at least in which I could go no further, without first wetting myself, then drowning myself, was a blessing. For I have always said, First learn to walk, then you can take swimming lessons. But don't imagine my region ended at the coast, that would be a grave mistake. For it was this sea too, its reefs and distant islands, and its hidden depths. And I too once went forth on it, in a sort of oarless skiff, but I paddled with an old bit of driftwood. And I sometimes wonder if I ever came back, from that voyage. For I see myself putting to sea, and the long hours without landfall, I do not see the return, the tossing on the breakers, and I do not hear the frail keel grating on the shore. I took advantage of being at the seaside to lay in a store of sucking stones. Yes, on this occasion I laid in a considerable store. I distributed them equally among my four pockets and sucked them turn and turn about. This raised a problem which I first solved in the following way. I had say sixteen stones, four in each of my four pockets, these being the two pockets of my trousers and the two pockets of my greatcoat. Taking a stone from the right pocket of my greatcoat, and putting it in my mouth, I replaced it in the right pocket of my greatcoat by a stone from the right pocket of my trousers, which I replaced by a stone from the left pocket of my trousers, which I replaced by a stone from the left pocket of my greatcoat, which I replaced by the stone which was in my mouth, as soon as I had finished sucking it. In this way there were always four stones in each of my four pockets, but not quite the same stones. And when the desire to suck took hold of me again, I drew again on the right pocket of my greatcoat, certain of not taking the same stone as the last time. And while I sucked it I rearranged the other stones in the way I have just described. And so on. But this solution did not satisfy me fully. For it did not escape me that, by an extraordinary hazard, the four stones circulating thus might always be the same four. In which case, far from sucking the sixteen stones turn and turn about, I was really only sucking four, always the same, turn and turn about. But I shook them well in my pockets, before I began to suck, and again, while I sucked, before transferring them, in the hope of obtaining a more general circulation of the stones from pocket to pocket. But this was only a makeshift that could not content a man like me. So I began to look for something else. And the first thing I hit upon was that I might do better to transfer the stones four by four, instead of one by one, that is to say, during the sucking, to take the three stones remaining in the right pocket of my greatcoat and replace them by the four in the right pocket of my trousers, and these by the four in the left pocket of my trousers, and these by the four in the left pocket of my greatcoat, and finally these by the three from the right pocket of my greatcoat, plus the one, as soon as I had finished sucking it, which was in my mouth. Yes, it seemed to me at first that by so doing I would arrive at a better result. But on further reflection I had to change my mind, and confess that the circulation of the stones four by four came to exactly the same thing as their circulation one by one. For if I was certain of finding each time, in the right pocket of my greatcoat, four stones totally different from their immediate predecessors, the possibility nevertheless remained of my always chancing on the same stone, within each group of four, and consequently of my sucking, not the sixteen turn and turn about as I wished, but in fact four only, always the same, turn and turn about. So I had to seek elsewhere than in the mode of circulation. For no matter how I caused the stones to circulate, I always ran the same risk. It was obvious that by increasing the number of my pockets I was bound to increase my chances of enjoying my stones in the way I planned, that is to say one after the other until their number was exhausted. Had I had eight pockets, for example, instead of the four I did have, then even the most diabolical hazard could not have prevented me from sucking at least eight of my sixteen stones, turn and turn about. The fact of the matter is I should have needed sixteen pockets for all my anxiety to be dispelled. And for a long time I could see no other conclusion but this, that short of having sixteen pockets, each with its stone, I could never reach the goal I had set myself, short of an extraordinary hazard. And if at a pinch I could double the number of my pockets, were it only by dividing each pocket in two, with the help of a few safety-pins let us say, to quadruple them seemed to be more than I could manage. And I didn't feel inclined to take all that trouble for a half-measure. For I was beginning to lose all sense of measure, after all this wrestling and wrangling, and to say, It's either all or nothing. And if I was tempted for an instant to establish a more equitable proportion between my stones and my pockets, by reducing the former to the number of the latter, it was only for an instant. For it would have been an admission of defeat. And sitting on the shore, before the sea, the sixteen stones spread out before my eyes, I gazed at them in anger and perplexity. For just as I had difficulty in sitting on a chair, or in an arm-chair, because of my stiff leg you understand, so I had none in sitting on the ground, because of my stiff leg and my stiffening leg, for it was about this time that my good leg, good in the sense that it was not stiff, began to stiffen. [I] needed a prop under the ham you understand, and even under the whole length of the leg, the prop of the earth. And while I gazed thus at my stones, brooding on endless martingales all equally defective, and crushing handfuls of sand, so that the sand ran through my fingers, and fell back on the strand, yes, while I held thus in suspense my mind and a part of my body, one day suddenly it dawned on the former, dimly, that I might perhaps achieve my purpose without increasing the number of my pockets, or reducing the number of stones, but simply by sacrificing the principle of trim. The meaning of this illumination, which suddenly began to sing within me, like a verse of Isaiah, or of Jeremiah, I did not penetrate at once, and notably the word trim, which I had never met with, long remained obscure. Finally I seemed to grasp that this word trim could not mean anything else, anything better, than the distribution of the sixteen stones in four groups of four, one group in each pocket, and that it was my refusal to consider any distribution other than this that had vitiated my calculations until then and rendered the problem literally insoluble. And it was on the basis of this interpretation, whether right or wrong, that I finally reached a solution, inelegant assuredly, but sound, sound. Now I am willing to believe, indeed I firmly believe, that other solutions to this problem might have been found, and indeed may still be found, no less sound, but much more elegant, than the one I shall now describe, if I can. And I believe too that had I been a little more insistent, a little more resistent [sic], I could have found them myself. But I was tired, tired and I contented myself ingloriously with the first solution that was a solution, to this problem. But not to go over the heartbreaking stages through which I passed before I came to it, here it is, in all its hideousness. It was merely (merely!) a matter of putting for example, to begin with, six stones in the right pocket of my greatcoat, or supply-pocket, five in the right pocket of my trousers, and five in the left pocket of my trousers, that makes the lot, twice five ten plus six, and none, for none remained, in the left pocket of my greatcoat, which for the time being remained empty, empty of stones that is, for its usual contents remained, as well as occasional objects. For where do you think I hid my vegetable knife, my silver, my horn and the other things, that I have not yet named, perhaps shall never name. Good. Now I can begin sucking. Watch me closely. I take a stone from the right pocket of my greatcoat, suck it, stop sucking it, put it in the left pocket of my greatcoat, the one empty (of stones). I take a second stone from the right pocket of my greatcoat, suck it, put it in the left pocket of my greatcoat. And so on until the right pocket of my greatcoat is empty (apart from its usual and occasional contents) and the six stones I have just sucked, one after the other, are all in the left pocket of my greatcoat. Pausing then, and concentrating, so as not to make a balls of it, I transfer to the right pocket of my greatcoat, in which there are no stones left, the five stones in the right pocket of my trousers, which I replace by the five stones in the left pocket of my trousers, which I replace by the six stones in the left pocket of my greatcoat. At this stage then the left pocket of my greatcoat is again empty of stones, while the right pocket of my greatcoat is again supplied, and in the right way, that is to say with other stones than those I have just sucked. These other stones I then begin to suck, one after the other, and to transfer as I go along to the left pocket of my greatcoat, being absolutely certain, as far as one can be in an affair of this kind, that I do not suck the same stones as a moment before, but others. And when the right pocket of my greatcoat is again empty (of stones), and the five I have just sucked are all in the left pocket of my greatcoat, then I proceed to the same redistribution as a moment before, or a similar redistribution, that is to say I transfer to the right pocket of my greatcoat, now again available, the five stones in the right pocket of my trousers, which I replace by the six stones in the left pocket of my trousers, which I replace by the five stones in the left pocket of my greatcoat. And there I am ready to begin again. Do I have to go on? No, for it is clear that after the next series, of sucks and transfers, I shall be back where I started, that is to say with the first six stones back in the supply pocket, the next five in the right pocket of my stinking old trousers and finally the last five in left pocket of same, and my sixteen stones will have been sucked once at least in impeccable succession, not one sucked twice, not one left unsucked. It is true that the next time I could scarcely hope to suck my stones in the same order as the first time and that the first, seventh and twelfth for example of the first cycle might very well be the sixth, eleventh and sixteenth respectively of the second, assuming the worst came to the worst. But that was a drawback I could not avoid. And if in the cycles taken together utter confusion was bound to reign, at least within each cycle taken separately I could be easy in my mind, at least as easy as one can be, in a proceeding of this kind. For for each cycle to be identical, as to the succession of stones in my mouth, and God knows I had set my heart on it, the only means were numbered stones or sixteen pockets. And rather than make twelve more pockets or number my stones, I preferred to make the best of the comparative peace of mind I enjoyed within each cycle taken separately. For it was not enough to number the stones, but I would have had to remember, every time I put a stone in my mouth, the number I needed and look for it in my pocket. Which would have spoilt the taste of stones for me, in a very short time. For I would never have been sure of not making a mistake, unless of course I had kept a kind of register, in which to tick off the stones one by one, as I sucked them. And of this I believed myself incapable. No, the only perfect solution would have been the sixteen pockets, symmetrically disposed, each one with its stone. Then I would have needed neither to number nor to think, but merely, as I sucked a given stone, to move on the fifteen others, each to the next pocket, a delicate business admittedly, but within my power, and to call always on the same pocket when I felt like sucking. This would have freed me from all anxiety, not only within each cycle taken separately, but also for the sum of all cycles, though they went on forever. But however imperfect my own solution was, I was pleased at having found it all alone, yes, quite pleased. And if it was perhaps less sound than I had thought in the first flush of discovery, its inelegance never diminished. And it was above all inelegant in this, to my mind, that the uneven distribution was painful to me, bodily. It is true that a kind of equilibrium was reached, at a given moment, in the early stages of each cycle, namely after the third suck and before the fourth, but it did not last long, and the rest of the time I felt the weight of the stones dragging me now to one side, now to the other. So it was something more than a principle I abandoned, when I abandoned the equal distribution, it was a bodily need. But to suck the stones in the way I have described, not haphazard, but with method, was also I think a bodily need. Here then were two incompatible bodily needs, at loggerheads. Such things happen. But deep down I didn't give a tinker's curse about being off balance, dragged to the right hand and the left, backwards and forwards. And deep down it was all the same to me whether I sucked a different stone each time or always the same stone, until the end of time. For they all tasted exactly the same. And if I had collected sixteen, it was not in order to ballast myself in such and such a way, or to suck them turn about, but simply to have a little store so as never to be without. But deep down I didn't give a fiddler's curse about being without, when they were all gone they would be all gone, I wouldn't be any the worse off, or hardly any. And the solution to which I rallied in the end was to throw them all away but one, which I kept now in one pocket, now in another, and which of course I soon lost, or threw away, or gave away, or swallowed. It was a wild part of the coast. I don't remember having been seriously molested. The black speck I was, in the great pale stretch of sand, who could wish it harm? Some came near, to see what it was, whether it wasn't something of value from a wreck, washed up by the storm. But when they saw the jetsam was alive, decently if wretchedly clothed, they turned away. Old women and young ones, yes, too, come to gather wood, came and stared, in the early days. But they were always the same and it was in vain I moved from one place to another, in the end they all knew what I was and kept their distance. I think one of them one day, detaching herself from her companions, came and offered me something to eat and that I looked at her in silence, until she went away. Yes, it seems to me some such incident occurred about this time. But perhaps I am thinking of another stay, at an earlier time, for this will be my last, my last but one, there is never a last, by the sea. However that may be I see a woman coming towards me and stopping from time to time to look back at her companions. Huddled together like sheep they watch her recede, urging her on, and laughing no doubt, I seem to hear laughter, far away. Then it is her back I see, as she goes back, now it is towards me she looks back, but without stopping. But perhaps I am merging two times in one, and two women, one coming towards me, shyly, urged on by the cries and laughter of her companions, and the other going away from me, unhesitatingly. For those who came towards me I saw coming from afar, most of the time, that is one of the advantages of the seaside. Black specks in the distance I saw them coming, I could follow all their antics, saying, It's getting smaller, or, It's getting bigger and bigger. Yes, to be taken unawares was so to speak impossible, for I turned often towards the land too. Let me tell you something, my sight was better at the seaside! Yes, raking far and wide over these vast flats, where nothing lay, nothing stood, my good eye saw more clearly and there were even days when the bad one too had to look away. And not only did I see more clearly, but I had less difficulty in saddling with a name the rare things I saw. These are some of the advantages and disadvantages of the seaside. Or perhaps it was I who was changing, why not? And in the morning, in my cave, and even sometimes at night, when the storm rages, I felt reasonably immune from the elements and mankind. But there too there is a price to pay. In your box, in your caves, there too there is a price to pay. And which you pay willingly, for a time, but which you cannot go on paying forever. For you cannot go on buying the same thing forever, with your little pittance. And unfortunately there are other needs than that of rotting in peace, it's not the word, I mean of course my mother whose image, blunted for some time past, was beginning now to harrow me. So I went back inland, for my town was not strictly speaking on the sea, whatever may have been said to the contrary. And to get to it you had to go inland, I at least knew of no other road. For between my town and the sea there was a kind of swamp which, as far back as I can remember, and some of my memories have their roots deep in the immediate past, there was always talk of draining, by means of canals I suppose, or of transforming into a vast port and docks, or into a city on piles for the workers, in a word of redeeming somehow or other. And with the same stone they would have killed the scandal, at the gates of their metropolis, of a stinking steaming swamp in which an incalculable number of human lives were yearly engulfed, the statistics escape me for the moment and doubtless always will, so complete is my lack of interest in this aspect of the question. It is true they actually began work and that work is still going on in certain areas in the teeth of adversity, setbacks, epidemics and the apathy of the Public Works Department, far from me to deny it. But from this to proclaiming that the sea came lapping at the ramparts of my town, there was a far cry. And I for my part will never lend myself to such a perversion (of the truth), until such time as I am forced to or find it convenient. And I knew this swamp a little, having risked my life in it, cautiously, on several occasions, at a period of my life richer in illusions than the one I am trying to patch together here, I mean richer in certain illusions, in others poorer. So there was no way of coming at my town directly, by sea, but you had to disembark well to the north or the south and take to the highways, just imagine that, for they had never heard of Watt, just imagine that too. And now my progress, slow and painful at all times, was more so than ever, because of my short stiff leg, the same which I thought had long been as stiff as a leg could be, but damn the bit of it, for it was growing stiffer than ever, a thing I would not have thought possible, and at the same time shorter every day, but above all because of the other leg, supple hitherto and now growing rapidly stiff in its turn but not yet shortening, unhappily. For when the two legs shorten at the same time, and at the same speed, then all is not lost, no. But when one shortens, and the other not, then you begin to be worried. Oh not that I was exactly worried, but it was a nuisance, yes, a nuisance. For I didn't know which foot to land on, when I came down. Let us try and get this dilemma clear. Follow me carefully. The stiff leg hurt me, admittedly, I mean the old stiff leg, and it was the other which I normally used as a pivot, or prop. But now this latter, as a result of its stiffening I suppose, and the ensuing shock to nerves and sinews, was beginning to hurt me even more than the other. What a story, God send I don't make a balls of it. For the old pain, do you follow me, I had got used to it, in a way, yes, in a kind of way. Whereas to the new pain, though of the same family exactly, I had not yet had time to adjust myself. Nor should it be forgotten that having one bad leg plus another more or less good, I was able to nurse the former, and reduce its sufferings to the minimum, to the maximum by using the former exclusively, with the help of my crutches. But I no longer had this resource! For I no longer had one bad leg plus another more or less good, but now both were equally bad. And the worse, to my mind, was that which till now had been good, at least relatively good, and whose change for the worse I had not yet schooled myself to endure. So in a way, if you like, I still had one bad leg and one good, or rather less bad, with this difference however, that the less bad now was the less good of heretofore. It was therefore on the old bad leg that I often longed to lean, between one crutch-stroke and the next. For while still extremely sensitive, yet it was less so than the other, or it was equally so, if you like, but it did not seem so to me, because of its seniority. But I couldn't! What? Lean on it. For it was shortening, don't forget, whereas the other, though stiffening, was not yet shortening, or so far behind its fellow, that to all intents and purposes, intents and purposes I'm lost, who cares. If I could even have bent it, at the knee, or even at the hip, I could have made it seem as short as the other, long enough to land on the true short one, before taking off again. But I couldn't. What? Bend it. For how could I bend it, when it was stiff? I was therefore compelled to work the same old leg as heretofore, in spite of its having become, on the sensory level at least, the worse of the two and the more in need of nursing. Sometimes to be sure, when I was lucky enough to chance on a road conveniently cambered, or by taking advantage of a not too deep ditch or any other breach of surface, I managed to lengthen my short leg, for a short time. But it had done no work for so long that it did not know how to go about it. And I think a pile of dishes would have better supported me than it, which had so well supported me, when I was a tiny tot. And another factor of disequilibrium was here involved, I mean when I thus made the best of the lie of the land, I mean my crutches, which I would have needed one short and one long if I was to remain vertical. No? I don't know. In any case the ways I went were for the most part little forest paths, that's understandable, where differences of level, though abounding, were too confused and too erratic to be of any help to me. But did it make such a difference after all, as far as the pain was concerned, whether my leg was free to rest or whether it had to work? I think not. For the suffering of the leg at rest was constant and monotonous. Whereas the leg condemned to the increase of pain inflicted by work knew the decrease of pain bestowed by work suspended, the space of an instant. But I am human, I think, and my progress suffered, from this state of affairs, and from the slow and painful progress it had always been, whatever may have been said to the contrary, was changed, saving your presence, to a veritable calvary, without limit to its stations or hope of crucifixion, though I say it myself, and no Simon, and reduced me to frequent halts. Yes, my progress reduced me to stopping more and more often, it was the only way to progress, to stop. And though it is no part of my tottering intentions to treat here in full, as they deserve, these brief moments of the immemorial expiation, I shall nevertheless deal with them briefly, out of the goodness of my heart, so that my story, so clear till now, may not end in darkness, the darkness of these towering forests, these giant leaves where I hobble, listen, fall, rise, listen and hobble on, wondering sometimes, need I say, if I shall ever see again the hated light, at least unloved, stretched palely between the last boles, and my mother, to settle matters, and if I would not do better, at least just as well, to hang myself from a bough, with a liane.